REBEL *heart*

BRIGHTON WALSH

COPYRIGHT

Coming home to find out my ex is my new roommate is a nightmare...especially when I've been pretending to hate her for years.

Harper Davidson has been ingrained on my heart since we were kids, and now she's tattooed on my skin. But she'll never know about either. Not when she's better off thinking we're enemies.

Having her in my space every day and sharing a wall with her every night is a challenge I never saw coming. A challenge I'm not sure I'm up to.

Especially when our daytime games turn into nighttime dares, pushing each other to the breaking point until our neighbors know exactly who's making her scream.

As lines blur and feelings deepen, we begin teetering on the edge of something more. And it's becoming harder to pretend that this is nothing—that she is nothing.

Because this second chance is starting to feel like a last chance.

It's always been her for me, but I'm broken beyond repair and don't know how to be the man she needs. These demons in my closet are never silent, and I'll do anything to keep them from dragging her down with me.

Even if that means letting her go again.

CONTENT NOTES

Please be advised that this book contains content that may be upsetting for some readers. Should you prefer detailed information in order to have the best reading experience, please visit the author's website or scan the QR code below to view a full list of content notes.

For the brave ones fighting to live another day.
The world needs you.

CHAPTER ONE

LEVI

SOME DAYS, I would've preferred to throw my phone into the ocean than be on the receiving end of another fucking alert from the family text thread. It was a continuous stream of trivial bullshit, generally instigated by my little sister, so I rarely responded. And yet, the thread moved on just fine without me.

It made me wonder what else would move on fine without me.

Made me wonder what it'd be like if I just...didn't exist anymore. If my family were preparing to commemorate the eleventh anniversary of *my* death instead of our mom's. If I'd been the one who'd died on the boat that day instead of her. Or if my death had happened in the hundreds of other ways I'd willed it to over the years through reckless behavior alone.

But I knew why it hadn't. Why I was still here, going through the motions. Left to suffocate under the weight of my regrets.

I didn't deserve anything less.

I deserved to witness the wreckage I'd caused. To see the pain reflected on my siblings' faces. Feel the heavy loss, not only of my mom, but of theirs, too, every day of my miserable life.

ADDISON:

Seriously

It's in just a few weeks

I need to know

Stop ignoring these texts, Levi!

Since our mom's death, I'd broken one of her only rules more times than I could count. *Never sail alone.* I'd gone out on the ocean on my own dozens—*hundreds*—of times, and nothing had happened, despite all my spoken and unspoken wishes otherwise.

I was still fucking here.

Yet she went out *once* by herself in a storm, and it was all over. A beautiful life snuffed out, taken away far too soon.

And it was all my fault.

ADDISON:

@Levi

@Levi

@Levi

BECK:

Jesus, will you stop? Go to his workshop if you need an immediate answer FFS.

AIDEN:

It doesn't matter how often you tag Levi. You know he's not responding.

ADDISON:

BRADY

Do a drive by

BRADY:

I'm on duty, Addison.

ADDISON:

Perfect!

FORD:

Pretty sure that wasn't a yes, little D.

I glanced over at my phone, the preview screen showing more than a dozen texts, all from my siblings and that fucking group text. Beck was on my shit list for suggesting our little sister pop over to my den of solitude, and Aiden was right. I had no intention of responding. Ford was, too, for that matter. As town sheriff, Brady definitely wasn't going to use Starlight Cove resources to satisfy Addison's demands.

The familiar hum of the belt sander filled my workshop, the sound soothing me in the same way the ocean's waves did. Wood shavings rained down as I guided the machine along the hull of my current project. This ancient boat had seen better days, but it wasn't a lost cause. Not yet anyway. In my fifteen years in this industry, I'd only encountered a handful of vessels that were. With grueling effort on my part—and a shit-ton of money on my clients'—most boats could be transformed back to their former glory, assuming I was the one restoring them.

My clients didn't get a sparkling personality or excellent customer service when they worked with me, but they did get the best boatbuilder and craftsperson on the East Coast. And I got to make a living with minimal human interaction. Win-win all around.

Out here in my workshop, it was just me and whatever boat I'd been commissioned to build or fix. Exactly how I liked it— everyone leaving me the fuck alone.

Shutting off the sander, I swiped a forearm across my brow

just as my phone buzzed with another text. My jaw ticked as I glanced over, prepared for more family bullshit, but it was my best friend's—now brother-in-law's—name on the screen.

CHASE:

Don't forget you have somewhere to be tonight.

Dropping my head back, I groaned toward the high ceiling. I hadn't forgotten. It would've been impossible to since Chase had reminded me half a dozen times. But that didn't mean I hadn't tried.

Visiting his parents' home was the last thing I wanted to do today—or ever, really. I loved the Lockharts like family, but going to the place that had been such a staple in my adolescence meant excavating memories I'd rather leave buried.

Without responding, I focused back on my work, running my hand along the hull of the 1930s Hacker-Craft. When she'd arrived at my workshop, a little worse for wear, I'd already been able to envision how this beauty would look once she was fully restored to her former glory. I wouldn't stop until I made it happen. I reached for the sander, ready to dive back in, just as my phone buzzed again.

CHASE:

I'm serious, dickhead. Stop ignoring everyone's texts. Somehow my wife's mad at ME for YOUR bullshit.

I had half a mind to text back and tell him I wasn't ignoring anything—how could I when a text came in every thirty fucking seconds and constantly pulled me away from what I was paid to do?—but that I was simply choosing not to respond.

CHASE:

> No excuses about tonight. I already told Mom
> you'd be there, so she's making your favorite.
> Don't make her come find you because you
> know she will.

"Fuck." Resting my elbows on my knees, I brushed the sawdust from my hands and blew out a heavy sigh.

Chase's mom, Marianne, was the closest thing my siblings and I'd had to a mother in more than a decade. Being our mom's best friend, she'd stepped up during our darkest days, when our own worthless father couldn't be bothered to. Even when she didn't have to. Even when we'd made it difficult. Even though I *still* made it difficult.

Which was why skipping out on one of her dinners made me an asshole.

I grabbed my phone and typed out a quick response.

LEVI:

> What time?

CHASE:

> 5. Dad's out of town for work, so she wants
> help with some shit before dinner. And bring
> wine.

It was already after four, which meant I needed to haul ass if I didn't want to be late. After putting away my tools and locking up the warehouse, I headed the couple blocks to my apartment, doing my best to dodge all the wanderers. People were every-fucking-where—far more than usual—and that only soured my mood further.

Once at my apartment building, I took the stairs two at a time and let myself inside. The space was small, but it was quiet and away from my family's resort. Most importantly, it was *mine*. That was all I needed.

After a quick shower, I pulled on a pair of jeans and a black T-shirt, ran a hand through my hair, and called it good enough. I made a quick detour to the kitchen to grab a bottle of Marianne's favorite wine before heading out.

With the carnival beginning tomorrow and running through next week, tourists had already started flooding Starlight Cove, making Main Street a fucking nightmare. Navigating my bike through this clusterfuck would take too long, so I strode straight for the marina. The familiar scents and sounds of the ocean washed over me, solace and pain mingling together as always.

And, as always, I shoved the solace aside, undeserving of it, and focused on the pain instead.

CHAPTER TWO

LEVI

THE MOTORS on my fully restored trawler hummed as I eased up to Chase's parents' dock. After tying off and shutting down the engines, I stepped onto the weathered planks and made my way up the hill toward the place that had been my second home since childhood.

The Lockharts' beachside house had been theirs for decades, but Chase had recently talked his parents into finally allowing him to pay for renovations. Like he always said, what good was all that pro-hockey-player money if he couldn't use it on the people he loved?

I knocked twice on the slider before opening the door and stepping inside, just like I'd done a hundred times before. Voices boomed from the back of the house, so I headed in that direction.

"Chase," Marianne said, exasperation heavy in her tone. "You have to be gentle with my babies. They aren't one of your hockey pucks that you can slam around wherever you want."

"I don't *slam* them wherever I want, Mom. I artfully and skillfully slap them into the net."

"Well, I don't want you to slap these anywhere, either. This is an African violet, and Bonnie—"

"Who the hell is Bonnie?" Chase grumbled.

"—doesn't do well with your giant man hands. Where's Levi? He knows exactly how the plants—Bonnie included—need to be handled."

"Oh, because Levi has such *delicate* hands? We're the same size, Mom."

"All I know is not a single one of my babies fell ill—"

"*Fell ill?*" Chase snorted.

"—when Levi helped me set up your old room as my plant nursery. And I just think—oh!" She spotted me in the doorway and shot a warm smile in my direction. She was petite, dwarfed even more standing next to Chase's 6'3" stature, her gray-streaked blond hair pulled back into a ponytail. "There you are, honey. Just the man I wanted to see."

Chase glanced over his shoulder at me. "Oh good, there's delicate Levi with his tiny man hands, ready to save the day."

I shoved the bottle of wine I'd brought into his stomach, causing him to let out an oomph. "I can't help that your mom loves my hands and all they can do."

Chase gripped the neck of the wine bottle and pointed it in my direction like a weapon. "Don't you ever fucking say that again."

I shrugged. "You're banging my sister."

"I *married* your sister, you ass clown."

"Doesn't matter. I still get a permanent free pass to say whatever I want to your mom."

Marianne clapped her hands once, the sound as sharp as a coach's whistle. "Boys! I swear, you're worse now than you were when you were twelve. At least back then, we had Harper to temper things a bit."

A brick to the face would've been less jarring than that mere mention of her name. Just hearing it was a sledgehammer to my chest, same as it'd been for more than a decade. Memories of what we'd once been tried to surface before I shoved them down, locking them up tight where they belonged.

"Now, if you want to eat at a reasonable time, we need to get choppin'." Marianne pinned both of us with her patented Mom Stare. Then, to me, she asked, "You remember what I told you last time?"

I dipped my chin in a nod, grateful for the distraction. "Gentle hands make for happy plants."

"That's right." With her brows raised, Marianne gestured to me while shooting a pointed glance at her son. "You see? Levi understands."

"Did you want me to contact my lawyer about drawing up some adoption papers?" Chase asked. "You're already making his favorite meal instead of mine, so we might as well make this official."

Marianne swatted her hand through the air before settling it on my back, her touch warm and gentle as she rubbed soft circles against me. "We don't need a piece of paper to tell us what we already know. Levi's been like another son since day one."

That was true. Chase's parents had treated me like a part of their family my entire life. Even when I'd tried to push them away—something I'd done a whole fucking lot, with everyone in my life, some more successfully than others. And even when I didn't deserve it.

"Why are we moving all these out of here anyway?" Chase asked, carefully cradling the plants Marianne handed to him. "Didn't you just set this up because your kids weren't giving you grandchildren fast enough?"

"Yes, well." She sniffed. "Since my eldest child and only son decided to go off and elope without me, his father, or any of his sisters in attendance—or even word that it was happening—I thought maybe things were progressing quickly. And I want to be ready for those grandbabies! The least you could do after shutting us out of the most important day of your life is to give me my dying wish—to have grandkids to spoil before I leave this earth."

My heart stopped...just froze in my fucking chest. I snapped my gaze to Marianne, eyeing her from head to toe and looking for any obvious signs of illness or distress. Panic gripped me by the throat at the thought of losing her after everyone else. A million thoughts raced through my mind, all focused on what was wrong, what I could do to help, how I could stop it. *Actually* stop it this time.

But when I slid my gaze to Chase, I realized he wasn't concerned at all.

With a scoff, he rolled his eyes. "You're not dying, Mom. Don't say shit like that. Jesus Christ, I swear you're as dramatic as my wife."

As subtly as I could, I released the pent-up breath I'd been holding and willed my heart to settle back into a steady rhythm. All while keeping up the facade that everything was fine. That my heart hadn't plummeted to my feet, that I hadn't gone straight to worst-case scenarios.

It'd been ten years—eleven in just a few weeks—since my mom had died, and shit like this still had me in a choke hold.

Marianne grinned at her son. "Is it any wonder you love us both beyond measure?"

"Never been a wonder for me," he said.

"Oh, you." Marianne walked up to Chase and pinched his cheek before patting it lightly. "Always my sweet boy. But I still don't forgive you for making me find out you got married on one of Mabel's Lives."

"I knew I should've slipped that woman more money," Chase grumbled.

"I'm not sure what you expected when you asked the town gossip to officiate. She even mentioned the gift basket she was sending your way—full of a variety of toys designed to give a woman plea—"

"*All right, Mom,*" Chase cut in, loud enough to drown out the rest of Marianne's words. "Jesus. I never want to hear you utter *toys* and *give a woman pleasure* in the same sentence again."

Without missing a beat, Marianne turned to me, settling an oversized hanging basket in my arms. "And what about you, Levi? It's about time for you to settle down, isn't it? You're not getting any younger, you know. Thirty-one is knocking on your door, and you're the last single one left of your whole family."

And it was going to stay that way. I hadn't allowed myself to be interested in anyone in a very long time, and I had no plans to change that anytime soon.

"Perhaps you'll find a special someone at the carnival this weekend or next," she said. "You never know who you might run into."

"But that means he'd have to *go* to the carnival," Chase said. "And that ain't happening."

Marianne shot me a frown. "Not going? But you used to love them when you were little! You three would *beg* to spend whole days there, you remember?"

Remembering was all I seemed to do anymore. Remembering and regretting and wishing it all could've been different.

"When was the last time you went to one?" she asked.

Twelve years, but who was counting?

I shrugged. "Can't remember, but it's not really my scene anymore."

She tsked and shook her head, eyeing me with a scrutinizing expression. "Funnel cakes and Ferris wheels are *everyone's* scene, Levi."

Fortunately, she let the subject drop without another word as Chase and I did her bidding. After we'd successfully relocated all seven thousand plants from his room-turned-literal-nursery-turned-prospective-baby-nursery to be scattered all over the house, the three of us sat down for dinner.

Marianne dished heaping portions of pot roast and mashed potatoes onto each of our plates before settling into her chair. "Since we can't turn a corner without hearing the exciting things Chase has coming up this week with the new hockey camp, why don't you tell me how things are going with you, Levi? Work is going well? I worry about you, you know. In that apartment all by yourself. Away from your family. And running your own business on top of it all." She tutted and shook her head. "I imagine that's stressful, making sure you can stay afloat."

I didn't exactly advertise my two-year wait list so it wasn't a surprise she had no idea, but I hated the thought of her concerning herself with me. "You don't have to worry about me or the business," I said, tucking into my meal. "Things are going good."

She hummed skeptically as if she didn't believe me, and I had half a mind to pull up my bank account just to show her how *good* things were. It was the one part of my life where I wasn't a complete and total fuckup. "Maybe you can do some more boat tours for the resort. Branch out, perhaps expand your offerings a bit, just to bring in some more income."

I made an incremental fraction running boat tours for my family's beachside resort compared to what I did designing, building, customizing, and repairing boats. But I didn't do the tours for the money. I did them for my family. For our mom's legacy. And to keep alive the few memories I had left of her.

I hummed noncommittally. "Maybe. I'm sure your daughter-in-law is already on it."

"Speaking of... Where is my little angel?" Marianne asked, and neither Chase nor I could hold in our snorts.

Addison was a lot of things, but an angel wasn't one of them. I loved the little shit more than almost anyone and would do anything for her. But she grated on my nerves on a good day and drove me out of my mind the rest of the time.

"She's at the inn, bossing the contractors around," Chase said around a mouthful of mashed potatoes. "Between the hockey complex and the main inn renovations, she's been in heaven, ordering all those people around."

"You make sure to tell her to stop by this week. I've been missing my daughter-in-law."

While it had taken a while to come to terms with the fact that my best friend had been hooking up with my baby sister in secret—for ten fucking years, no less—I'd done so. Reluctantly. But I couldn't deny how good he was for her. Other than my brothers, Chase was the best man I knew, and I couldn't think of a better fit for Addison.

Though it'd been comforting to watch all my siblings move on, move forward, and overcome the demons of our past, I couldn't help but drown in them. Chained to a history I didn't deserve to escape.

After more coercing from Marianne where she encouraged me to attend the carnival because *you just never know*, she wrapped up the remaining leftovers for me, and I said my good-byes. I made my way down the steps toward the dock, glancing down at the beach. The sun was beginning to set, casting an orange glow across the water, and the warm breeze carried the salty tang of the ocean.

While the sea itself reminded me of my mom and all I'd lost —all *we'd* lost—the gleaming letters on the hull of my trawler reminded me of someone else entirely. Reminded me that despite years of fuckups, I'd done one good thing in my life.

But it was also a steadfast reminder of exactly why I was here.

Alone.

CHAPTER THREE

HARPER

IT WAS easy to forget the quirks of small-town living until you were thrown back into the trenches to experience them for yourself.

I'd traveled all over the world, had been transported in buses, trains, subways... Hell, I'd even ridden on a donkey once. But there was nothing quite like the ride in the back of an old man's car, the taped piece of paper in the windshield declaring it Starlight Cove's non-Uber, and the lack of working air conditioning to remind me just how far out of city life I was.

From the age of ten until I was almost eighteen, I'd spent every summer in Starlight Cove. My family had made the trip from Connecticut to our summer home on the beach, and I'd been in heaven for three months. This place had held a sort of ethereal quality to me back then—it'd been a fairy-tale getaway. Where, for a few months a year, I'd pretended I had a different life.

I'd adored it here...adored everything Starlight Cove had to offer. Until I hadn't.

Until a certain dark-haired, blue-eyed, mysterious bad boy had done exactly what everyone had warned me he would.

I'd come a long way since running from this town with a broken heart and without a backward glance. At least until last year, when a freelance assignment had sent me back to the one place I'd never intended to return. And now I was here for six weeks.

Six. Fucking. Weeks.

No matter how much I didn't want to be back in this tiny town along the Maine coast, and no matter how much I absolutely knew *he* didn't want me here, it seemed fate had other plans.

When the editor in chief of *Weekend Wanderlust* had reached out and offered me this assignment, all while dangling the carrot of a permanent position at my dream company if she liked what I delivered, I wasn't going to turn it down. I'd be stupid to do anything but show up with a smile and pretend like being back here didn't reopen old wounds I'd rather not revisit.

For the past twelve years, I'd done exactly what I wanted. Had given myself the freedom I'd never had as a child. As soon as my eighteenth birthday had rolled around, I'd turned my back on the carefully crafted plans my senate-hopeful father and Stepford mother had made for me. Without my input. Without my consent.

Up until that point, my entire life had been prepped, planned, and designed by other people. Each detail meticulously laid out for me without a care of what I wanted. Of what my dreams had been.

And while I'd spent the past decade-plus building the life *I* wanted, I'd grown restless. Unsettled.

The trouble was, I didn't know what I was still looking for.

"Here you are, dear." Arthur pulled up in front of the café on

Main Street, the sidewalks on either side of the road bustling with people.

As luck would have it, the café was directly across from my temporary home while I was in town, an apartment just above *Starlight Cove Gazette*'s corner shop. Mabel—owner of the newspaper, the town's surrogate feisty grandmother, and my landlord for the next six weeks—had promised I could use the newspaper's resources whenever I needed. Just another example of small-town living...

"Thanks, Arthur. I'm sure I'll be seeing a lot more of you while I'm here." Especially since I wasn't renting a car. No need when everything but Starlight Cove Resort was within walking distance.

After passing him some cash—Venmo might as well have been in another language to him—I climbed out of the car and grabbed my suitcase from the trunk.

Before my afternoon appointment, I was meeting Mabel to get the keys and a tour. After that, I'd be heading over to the high school to interview Chase Lockhart—former pro hockey player to the rest of the world, former best friend to me.

When we'd been younger, he'd been the third person in our little summertime trio. Somehow, despite that trio shattering, Chase had managed to rekindle our friendship years later. I'd tried like hell to sever all ties to this town, him included, but he hadn't let me. That was Chase in a nutshell, though—determined beyond reason. Hell, he'd been chasing after his now-wife for ten years, apparently. And if that wasn't dedication, I didn't know what was.

Since I had some time to kill, I hitched my purse over my shoulder and rolled my suitcase straight into the café. I'd had two delayed flights on my way here, which meant I'd been up since ass o'clock this morning. If I wanted to obtain anything usable this afternoon for my article, I needed to get some caffeine in me, stat.

The café was cute, with its weathered tables and mismatched chairs, black-and-white photos of Starlight Cove through the years covering the walls. I much preferred the diner at Starlight Cove Resort, though. But since the resort was run by the McKenzie family, and Levi McKenzie was the one and only person I planned to avoid like my life depended on it, I was going to have to make do with the café instead.

It was late morning, too late for the breakfast crowd but too early for lunch, so only a handful of people were inside. My gaze snagged on one just as she noticed me.

"Harper, hey!" Addison McKenzie—now Lockhart—stood at the counter, exuding the kind of presence someone a foot taller than her would give off. Her confident demeanor wasn't really a surprise since she'd grown up with five older, overbearing, protective brothers and had to learn how to hold her own against them.

"Hi, Addison." I offered her a warm smile and strode toward her, pulling my suitcase behind me.

"I take it you just got into town?" she asked, eyeing my luggage.

"After the travel day from hell, yes. I'm dead to the world, and it's not even noon."

"I know what you mean." She sagged against the counter, her eyes looking more tired than I could ever remember seeing. "I've been *exhausted* lately. We better get you a coffee. My treat."

After placing our orders with the barista, coffee for me and chamomile tea for her, we stood off to the side and waited for our drinks.

"I hear congratulations are in order." I tipped my chin toward the delicate band on Addison's left ring finger—not exactly the sizable rock I was used to seeing the WAGs of professional athletes wear, but it fit her.

She jerked her hand away from her stomach, her entire body jolting as she stared at me with wide eyes. "What? Congratulations about what?"

I tipped my head to the side, brow furrowed. "Your... marriage?"

"Oh! Right. My *marriage*. Of course. Thanks!" She flashed me a smile, her previous weirdness gone, before glancing down at her adorned finger. "Still feels surreal. Ten years of practically nothing, and now suddenly I'm *married* and we're renovating the main inn to make it our forever home."

"Chase never was one to let an opportunity pass him by."

"He's a persistent pain in my ass, that's for sure."

My lips twitched at her frank appraisal of my once-best friend. "He is. But you love it."

She blew out a long-suffering sigh and shook her head. "God help me, but I do."

With a shared laugh, we grabbed our drinks from the barista before scooting over to the condiment stand to fix up our orders.

She dumped an obscene amount of sugar into her tea and shot me a glance. "I'm so sorry we didn't have any cottages open for you while you're staying in town."

I waved her off as I added a splash of creamer and three sugars to my coffee. "Don't worry about it."

"I would've loved to have you stay with us, but the main inn is in shambles with the renovation. Aiden and Avery are staying with us at Chase's cabin. Which is a fucking nightmare, by the way. Even if the walls were five feet thick, I still don't think it'd be enough to drown out the sounds of my brother banging my best friend." She snapped a lid on her tea and shuddered. "And ever since that viral video last year, the resort cottages have been booking out for months."

"Seriously, don't apologize. I love that the resort is finally seeing the success it deserves." Their family-run business was a Starlight Cove staple—had been for decades—but it'd always been on its last legs. Now, it was thriving in a way I wasn't sure it ever had. "Besides, Mabel hooked me up with a short-term rental in town. It'll be a lot easier staying on Main Street since I don't have a car."

She hummed and took a sip of her tea. "Mabel, huh? Don't let that sneaky old woman corner you, or she'll be pitching you this month's special."

"That doesn't sound so bad."

Addison raised a brow. "Not until she explains, in great detail, the benefits of the most powerful clit suction toy she's ever offered."

I sharply inhaled the sip of coffee I'd just taken and spiraled into a coughing fit.

"Oh shit! Sorry, sorry." Addison shoved a wad of napkins my way before patting me on the back. "But I have to prepare you for it, you know? Don't want you walking into the lion's den unaware. Mabel's always been...colorful, but the field in which she grows her fucks has been barren for a while. The woman's not afraid of anything or anyone. I didn't want you to be caught off guard."

"Yeah, no," I said through a tight throat, my eyes watering. "Being caught off guard in the middle of a public café while drinking hot liquid is definitely better."

A loud, unrestrained laugh burst from her, the sound infectious. "Happy to help." She grabbed her tea, hooking a thumb over her shoulder as she gestured toward the door. "I gotta run and grab Chase, but I'll see you later today at the school, right?"

It might've been my first day in town, but there was no time like the present to start gathering content for this article. I ignored the whisper in the back of my mind that wondered if Levi would be there. He and Chase were still extremely close, as far as I knew. And with as big of a deal as opening day on this hockey camp was for Chase, it made sense that Levi would be around.

But I didn't care. And I certainly wasn't going to concern myself with it. If he was there, I'd ignore him. Just like I'd been doing for twelve years. He wasn't worth my worries.

He wasn't worth anything to me.

I pasted on a smile and dipped my chin in a nod. "I'll be there."

CHAPTER FOUR

LEVI

I LOVED MY FAMILY. I really did. But I couldn't deny how hard it was to be around them. Being in their presence only served to remind me of how much we'd lost. Of what I'd taken from them. And the painful memories my being around at all must've brought up for them. It would've been easier for everyone if I weren't here.

I'd spent years holing myself up, hiding away, but that had only worked while Addison had been at college. During that time, my brothers had been lost in their own grief, and we'd all been trying to keep the resort afloat in our mom's absence. My brothers all had each other, though. The Irish twins, Brady and Aiden. And the actual twins, Beck and Ford.

I'd been alone. Addison, my partner in crime growing up, had been off at school. Chase had already embarked on his hockey career and was clear across the continent in Vancouver. And anyone else who'd once cared about me was long gone or actively avoiding all contact.

But after Addison had graduated and returned home, every-thing changed.

She'd whipped the resort—and us—into shape like the little dictator she was, earning every bit of her little D nickname. Without taking no for an answer, she'd dragged me from my solitude, whether I'd wanted her to or not. And now, barely a day went by when I didn't see the little demon.

The past year notwithstanding, get-togethers with her and my brothers had been few and far between. But recently, they'd become more and more frequent as my siblings had started pairing off, one by one, until I was the only single one left.

Something sure as fuck was in the water around here, and I had no intention of catching whatever the hell it was.

Thanks to the new part-time help Chase had coerced Addison and Aiden into hiring for the resort, the family had been given some breathing room, allowing for a quick lunch at the café on Main Street. Since Brady and Ford were both on duty tonight, this was the only time that worked for everyone to celebrate the soft launch of the Lockhart Hockey Camp for Kids.

Since the actual complex Chase was building on the resort property wasn't yet complete, he'd been given permission to use the high school rink as a temporary stand-in for the trial run. He'd been working around the clock the past couple months to make this a reality, and there was no way I'd miss being there to support him. Especially when he'd given me that same support tenfold over the years.

"How much longer till those fucking construction trucks are gone, Lockhart?" Aiden grumbled as all eleven of us strode out of the café. Avery elbowed him in the gut, and he glanced down at her with a raised brow. "What? It's getting mud and shit all over the resort grounds."

"You can handle a mess once in a while." There was no missing the sexual undertone in her voice or the smirk she sent his way.

"Goddammit, Avery!" Addison glared at her best friend. "It's bad enough that you're staying so close I can *hear* you at night, but this, too? It's going to be like this for the rest of our lives, isn't it? You saying completely inappropriate things about my brother's and your sex life, and me just having to deal with it."

Avery grinned, completely unrepentant, and shrugged. "Yeah, probably. On the plus side, you get to do that to Levi now."

I snapped my head in Avery's direction. "The fuck she does."

I didn't care if Addison was married. I didn't care about the fact that I'd witnessed her and Chase climbing out of the back seat of his truck, no question as to what they'd been doing. I didn't care that I'd walked in on them going at it more times than should have been possible in the four goddamn months since they'd gone public. In my mind, those two were sleeping in separate beds and always would be.

"I don't want to hear it, either," Brady said, wrapping an arm around Luna as they led the group. "As far as I'm concerned, you're still a virgin."

"Ditto," the rest of my brothers chimed in.

Addison huffed, turning an indignant expression our way. "Well, if I have to hear about all the freaky shit you guys are doing, it's only fair that you have to hear about me!"

"I will duct-tape your mouth shut and lock you in a closet if you even think about it," I said.

Beck nodded, glancing back at us with Everly tucked into his side. "I'll help."

"I'll be on lookout." Ford shot a wink at his wife. "And make sure my beautiful, *do no harm* doctor wife doesn't know anything about it."

Quinn snorted and rolled her eyes but didn't argue.

"Brady and I will occupy Chase while it's taken care of," Aiden said.

Brady didn't agree with Aiden's statement, but he also didn't rebuff it. Plausible deniability for the sheriff and all that.

"You could try," Chase said, his tone daring my older brothers to give it a go.

"She's twenty-eight, not sixteen." Luna shot a glance at my brothers and me over her shoulder. "And she's married to *that*." She tipped her chin toward Chase with a smirk. "She's definitely getting fu—"

"Lawbreaker," Brady cut in, his low tone ringing with warning. "Don't even think about finishing that sentence, or you're gonna be in trouble when we get home."

She shot him a mischievous smile. "In that case, she's definitely getting fu—"

"That's our cue." With that, Brady offered a two-fingered wave over his shoulder and tugged a laughing Luna along behind him.

The rest of my brothers and their significant others followed suit, saying their goodbyes as they dispersed until it was just Chase, Addison, and me.

"Can I catch a ride with you guys over to the high school?" I asked.

"Yep." Chase twirled his keys around his finger. "We're parked around the corner."

"Let me run up and grab my gear, in case we do a pickup game."

He nodded as the three of us crossed the street, heading toward my apartment. Chase never let Addison get out of arm's reach, always having to touch her in some way. Including the undeniable sound of his hand smacking her ass as they walked into the building behind me.

I climbed the stairs and shot them a glare over my shoulder. "Seriously, I think I liked it better when you were hiding shit from me. I can't look at you two without seeing your hands on some part of her body, and it's fucking weird."

Chase just shrugged, a satisfied grin on his face like he was the luckiest man on earth. As long as he made Addison happy, I'd figure out a way to deal with all the PDA they seemed to be intent on subjecting me to. He rested his left hand on her stomach, his fingers spread wide, their wedding date inked on his ring finger for all to see.

I unlocked and opened my apartment door without taking my gaze off the two of them, the placement of his hand drawing my eye. It was possessive. Protective. As if she were— Without even finishing my thought, I shot my gaze to Addison's face before snapping it to Chase's. "Wait, are you preg—"

"Oh, honey," Mabel's voice called from somewhere inside my apartment. "I wasn't expecting you home until tonight!"

My thoughts derailed in an instant, and I hung my head, blowing out an exasperated breath. The older woman was always around, stopping by more days than not. And she didn't understand the meaning of privacy, instead just letting herself into my apartment whenever she saw fit. I'd learned a long time ago that it was easier to go along with her whims than fight them. Especially because she brought cookies half the time.

"Are you...reorganizing my brother's kitchen cabinets?" Addison asked, her brows raised as she stared at Mabel in disbelief. My sister turned toward me, hooking a thumb over her shoulder to Mabel. "Seriously...is she reorganizing your cabinets?"

"Not the first time," I mumbled.

"When he puts the spices in the same cabinet as his cups, what am I supposed to do?" Mabel asked. Her gray hair was in curlers, and she wore a shirt that read, *Prone to shenanigans and malarkey.* "It just doesn't make any sense."

I ran a hand through my hair and blew out a heavy sigh. "She's taken it upon herself to be my surrogate mother."

"Well, with no one else here to help, who's going to do it for you? I, for one, am happy to provide my assistance. And, actually, that's why I'm here."

"To reorganize his kitchen?" Addison asked.

"No, to let you know you won't be lonely living here all by yourself anymore." She shot us a smile I'd learned a long time ago meant nothing but trouble. "At least, not for a few weeks."

"Uh, what?" I asked, not bothering to hide the suspicion in my tone.

"A roommate," Mabel said, speaking slowly as if that would clear up everything.

"I don't have a roommate, Mabel," I said. "I live alone. I *like* to live alone. And you might be my landlord, but you can't just rent out a room in my apartment without my consent."

"Oh, but I can. Because, *technically*, it's still my apartment."

I raised a brow in her direction and crossed my arms over my chest. "The lease I signed says otherwise."

"Did you *read* the lease, honey?"

I didn't appreciate the condescension in her tone. Or the way she whipped a large packet of papers from her purse and offered them to me with a flourish, as if she'd just been waiting for me to challenge her.

She pointed to a section in the middle of the page. "It says right there that you're renting *one bedroom* in this apartment. Not the whole apartment. So, the living room, kitchen, and bathroom are all technically shared spaces. And the extra bedroom is free for me to rent! I had a friend in need, and who was I to say no to the sweet girl?"

I scanned over the document, realizing that the fucking rental agreement I'd signed was, in fact, for a single, solitary bedroom, not the whole apartment. And the sad part was I wasn't surprised in the least this conniving woman had pulled that over on me. What *was* a surprise was that she'd waited years to spring it on me.

"Jesus Christ, Mabel, are you serious?" I closed my eyes and pinched the bridge of my nose. "I don't want a stranger living in my apartment."

She shot me a huge smile and snatched the papers from me before stuffing them back in her oversized purse. "That's the best part! She's not a stranger. In fact, you all go way back, so I knew it wouldn't be a problem."

I could only manage to stare at her, no clue who she could possibly be referring to. I didn't go way back with anyone. Only my family, Chase, and—

Before her name even entered my mind, Harper Davidson stepped out of the extra bedroom and froze at the sight of us. Her attention pinged between the four of us before landing on me, and a jolt of awareness shot through me.

Just like fucking always when it came to her.

And just like fucking always, I immediately dropped my gaze to her left hand, equal parts relieved and angry there wasn't a ring on her finger.

She was still as gorgeous as ever—a blonde bombshell with lips I'd pictured wrapped around my cock more times than I would ever admit and curves that could make a grown man weep. Since I'd pushed her away all those years ago, I'd seen her in passing a handful of times, but I'd never really allowed myself to *look*, to soak in every inch of her, knowing just how dangerous it would be. Knowing exactly how easily she'd pull me right back into her orbit.

But she'd disarmed me enough by showing up in what was supposed to be my sacred space that there was no stopping it now.

Her hair was long and wavy, falling to the middle of her back, her blue eyes sparking with a fire that was brand-new. Her body was made for sin—something that was new, too, and so different from the wisp of a girl I'd once known—with full tits, a small waist, and a pair of thick hips I couldn't help but imagine gripping as I—

Jesus fucking Christ, what the hell was wrong with me?

She was going to be my undoing. She was *still* my undoing.

When we'd known each other more than a decade ago, she'd had an innocence about her. She'd been soft and sweet. Willing to conform to any expectation someone had of her. But it seemed life or circumstances or both had beaten that out of her, leaving behind a woman who dared you to cross her.

Except I already had. I'd crossed her. Before bailing entirely, I'd said the words I knew would hurt her. I'd broken her heart and left her to pick up the pieces on her own.

Worse, I'd known exactly what I was doing. Had known my unexpected words would cut her deep. It was why I'd said them—my assurance she'd leave me alone. That she'd never want anything to do with me again.

And it'd worked. She'd stayed away from me and from Starlight Cove for more than a decade.

Until now.

CHAPTER FIVE

HARPER

THIS COULD NOT BE HAPPENING. This seriously could *Not. Be. Happening.*

I should've known better than to trust Mabel when she'd said she had a place for me to stay. If there was one thing I'd learned in my life, it was that if something seemed too good to be true, it absolutely was. And this was the very embodiment of that adage.

I stared openmouthed at my new roommate. Levi fucking McKenzie.

My childhood best friend. The boy who'd shared his peanut butter and jelly sandwiches with me. Who'd held my hand as I jumped off the cliffs for the first time. Who'd chased me along the sandy shores for hours until we were both breathless and sunburned.

My first crush. My first kiss. My first time.

My first everything. Heartbreak, included.

I'd grown a lot in the twelve years since I'd left Starlight Cove behind. I'd changed as a person, both inside and out. I'd had struggles and celebrations. I'd rejected my parents' strict rules and the tiny box they'd shoved me into my whole life and gone off on my own. Broken away from their bindings without looking back and forged my own way, following my own rules.

But in all that time—across continents, through dozens of countries, over tens of thousands of miles—I'd never forgotten Levi.

And I'd never forgotten what he'd done to me.

He stood there, looking as stunned as I felt and more gorgeous than any man had a right to be. Especially one as cruel and thoughtless as him.

He'd grown from the boy I'd known, now standing several inches taller than my 5'10 frame... Had filled out, too, his body a carved masterpiece I didn't want to acknowledge but also couldn't deny. His dark-brown hair was overdue for a cut, wayward wavy strands hanging over his forehead as if even they couldn't be bothered to be tamed. His close-cropped beard did nothing to hide the sharpness of his jaw or those full lips I recalled in great detail how they felt against mine. But his eyes were what held me frozen.

Blue. Icy. Contemptuous.

Being on the other end of that hardened stare snapped me out of whatever attraction-induced coma I was currently battling. He didn't want me here; that much was clear. At least we agreed on something.

"There has to be a mistake," I finally said, breaking the silence. I turned toward Mabel, my eyes narrowed. "You told me you had the perfect place."

She shot me a smile and held her hands out as if to encompass the apartment. "I do! Isn't it perfect?"

Levi groaned and scrubbed a hand down his face. "Jesus Christ, Mabel. No, it's not fucking perfect. Why the hell would you think this was a good idea?"

"Harper needed somewhere to stay for six weeks—"

"*Six weeks*?" Levi snapped.

"—and the poor girl needs something cozy for that long. This little apartment is *very* cozy."

Levi's jaw ticked as he glared at Mabel, his feelings on the topic broadcast loudly without his saying a word. Though I couldn't say I was feeling much differently. Because just what the hell was I supposed to do now?

Chase cleared his throat into the heavy, awkward silence. "Well, this seems like something the three of you need to work out. So, we'll just—"

"Are you kidding?" Addison said, darting her gaze between Mabel, Levi, and me. "I'm not leaving now! It's just getting good."

Chase laughed and picked up his wife, scooping her right off her feet. "Nice try, you little chaos monster. You're in for it when we get home tonight." Then, as they were walking out of the apartment, he tossed over his shoulder, "We'll wait in the truck, man."

"There has to be something else," I said, unable to tamp down the pleading edge in my tone. I pulled out my phone and navigated to the search engine, refusing to listen to the whisper in the back of my mind that said it would be futile. Especially in mid-July in a tourist town along the coast.

Mabel made a sound of commiseration. "Oh honey, I'm afraid not. Besides the normal surges this time of year, the carnival is quite a draw for tourists. And the resort's been booked for months. Now that they're renovating the main inn, even those rooms aren't available. I'd let you use our spare room that Quinn rented for a while before she and Ford got hitched, but I'm not at all sorry to say we've turned that into a playroom."

"For your grandkids?" I asked.

"Heavens no! George might've installed a swing, but it's definitely for grown-up time." Mabel elbowed me and waggled her eyebrows.

"Oh Jesus Christ," Levi grumbled.

I couldn't even bring myself to look his way, too focused on getting myself out of this mess to be ensnared by him. "What about Starlight Shores? I know it's small, but maybe they have something."

Mabel tsked and shook her head. "They're fumigating. Nasty mice infestation. Tammy figures they'll be closed for at least a month."

"There has to be *something*." Even I could hear the panic seeping into my tone, but I couldn't help it. This was my worst nightmare. There was no way I'd be able to get the work done that I needed to while sleeping on the other side of a wall from Levi. Hearing his every movement. Running into him coming from the bathroom wearing nothing but a towel. Imagining him—

Well. Imagining shit I no longer had any business imagining.

"I'm sorry, sugar." Mabel patted my arm. "I checked all over when I knew you were looking for a place to stay, and this is the only available location in town. Plus, with the newspaper office right downstairs, it'll be nice while you're working on your article."

"Seems pretty fucking convenient," Levi mumbled under his breath, his narrowed gaze focused on Mabel.

Ignoring him completely, she said, "Besides, you're both grown-ups. I didn't throw you into an only-one-bed situation like that romance we read for book club last month. You each have your own room, plus plenty of space to share. I don't see what the problem is."

The problem was, I could've been sharing an eighty-thousand-square-foot mansion with Levi, and it still would've felt too small. But here, in an eight-hundred-square-foot apartment where we'd be sharing more than half the space? Where we'd have to run into each other, day in and day out, for six weeks? It was going to feel downright claustrophobic.

I darted my gaze over to Levi, only to find his eyes already locked on me. That brief connection, however tenuous it was, sent shivers racing down my spine. Long-forgotten memories of a time when it'd felt like he'd *seen* me surfaced all over again. And I absolutely could not entertain any of that bullshit.

"Well, I'll let you two get settled." Mabel hooked her purse on her arm and shuffled toward the door. "Wouldn't want to overstay my welcome."

Levi snorted as the door shut behind her, and then it was just the two of us in this too-small space.

A too-small space I was supposed to share for six weeks with the one man I'd never wanted to see again.

After several awkward moments in which we did nothing but glare at each other, he finally broke the silence. "What the hell are you doing here for six weeks?"

I narrowed my gaze on him, my arms crossed as if that would be an effective shield. The wall I'd built around my heart after he'd decimated it would protect me a hell of a lot better. "Excuse me?"

"Why are you here?" he enunciated slowly.

I raised a brow at him. "Too busy brooding to listen when Mabel mentioned the article I'm working on?"

His brows dipped, that glower firmly in place. It was something I'd grown accustomed to seeing during my brief stints back in Starlight Cove. Especially when it was usually directed at me. "That's not what I meant."

"Well, I'm not a mind reader, Levi, so you'll have to come out with it."

He stared at me for long moments, his jaw clenched, gaze hard, and I felt the intensity of it straight to my bones. It was truly unfair how gorgeous this man was. Also unfair how my body still responded to him, even when my mind knew better.

Finally, he said, "What happened to becoming a lawyer?"

I froze for half a second before huffing out an incredulous laugh. The absolute gall of this asshole. He'd shoved me out of his life without a backward glance. Cut off all ties to me. *Blocked* me everywhere he could. And he had the balls to ask me about my life and why I'd chosen the path I had? I didn't fucking think so.

"I don't owe you an explanation about my life. You want to know things about me? Do what every other shitty ex-boyfriend in the world does and use Google."

He kept his hard stare locked on me, his ticking jaw broadcasting his irritation. That, at least, was something we had in common. Just like he'd always done, Levi sucked up all the oxygen in a room, leaving me gasping for air, while he was unfazed. He was a robot. An uncaring, inconsiderate, gorgeous-as-fuck robot, and nothing good would come from cohabitating with him. Nothing but old memories—*bad* memories—would be unearthed during our time together.

But I didn't exactly have a choice.

This was the only place in town, and I'd already planned to avoid him while I was here. Since I'd be out and about anyway, gathering information, researching, and conducting interviews for this massive lifestyle write-up, I'd barely be in the apartment.

Surely I could steer clear of him during that time. I'd been doing it for twelve years.

What was six measly weeks?

CHAPTER SIX

HARPER

LEVI HADN'T BEEN able to get out of the apartment fast enough, which was fine with me. I definitely needed the breathing room. Not to mention, I had forty-five minutes before I was scheduled to head over to the high school, so I planned to take full advantage of my solitude to poke around. There was no way I was staying in enemy territory without getting the lay of the land.

I hit up the kitchen first, figuring it was the place least likely to have anything telling in it. It was basic—white cabinets and black appliances. Definitely not state-of-the-art, but it got the job done. The sink was empty, and the counters were spotless, free from clutter or fancy small appliances.

Next, I made my way into the living room. Facing a wall-mounted TV was a worn brown leather couch with a dark wood coffee table in front of it. It held only a stack of coasters...and Aiden's latest novel, *The Realm of Storm and Shadow*. I grabbed the hardcover, my brows shooting up.

Levi had always been a reader, as far back as I could remember. He'd carried a book with him wherever he went. Had shared them with me, actually. We'd swapped them back and forth, each reading a passage aloud. So, the fact that he had a book on his coffee table wasn't a surprise. It was that he had *this* particular book. Erotic romantasy wasn't exactly something I pictured him reading. The young adult romance novels I'd shared with him had been pushing it back then.

Sitting down on the couch, I flipped through the book, stopping on the page he'd bookmarked with an old receipt, and began reading.

Caelum clasped Aurelia's hand and led her to a secluded corner of the room, too desperate for her to wait. They weren't alone, but his cock didn't care. And from the way Aurelia was gripping his hand, her eyes brimming with mischief and desire, she couldn't wait, either.

The masquerade ball was full to bursting, guests dancing and laughing, some mere feet from where he and Aurelia were tucked away. But he couldn't be bothered with them. Couldn't think about dozens of people being near when he slid inside his sweet Aurelia. All that consumed his thoughts was the remembered sound of her soft moan that always accompanied that first thrust and how hot her cunt would be when he sank—

I snapped the book shut and dropped it onto the table as if it were on fire. But nope, that was just my entire body alight in flames. My breaths grew stuttered and my cheeks felt hot, but my body's reaction didn't stop there. My nipples also jumped in on the action, tightening while my pussy clenched around nothing.

This was ridiculous. I *read* these kinds of books—had read this very one, in fact, so none of what I read was shocking. This was just an overreaction because it'd been a long while for me, that was all. It had absolutely nothing to do with the unexpected intimacy of it—reading that particular book at that particular spot, right where Levi had left off...so similar to what we'd done as teens—and everything to do with it having been far too long since I'd been served orgasms by someone other than myself.

Shaking off those unwanted and unwelcome feelings, I continued on my quest, unabashedly nosing through the rest of his apartment. Looking for a glimpse of that teenage boy I'd been in love with all those years ago. It seemed to be a lost cause, though.

No matter where I snooped, I didn't find a single photo or knickknack. Nothing personal that would give me a glimpse into the man Levi had become and nothing to remind me of the boy I'd once loved. Other than that book on the coffee table, he had no personal touches anywhere.

It was barren, as if Levi had erased himself from his own home.

Once I'd made my way through the rest of the apartment, I hesitated on the threshold to Levi's bedroom, debating whether I should go inside. While he'd left his door unlatched, it was still mostly closed. And there was no doubt this would be crossing a line. In the end, though, I didn't care. Curiosity won out.

Slowly, I pushed open the door, unable to turn my back on this chance to get a glimpse of the man I'd once known. Salt air and cedar swept over me as soon as I stepped into his room. The scent was so familiar, it stopped me dead in my tracks. Made my heart ache and transported me straight back in time, filling my head with memories I'd spent years trying to forget.

I shook them from my thoughts, forcing myself to focus on the present. Gathering information was what I did for a living, and this was no different. It was just research.

Levi's bed was haphazardly made—the only sign in this whole apartment that someone lived here. The dark-gray duvet was rumpled on one side, the other half smooth and untouched. I shoved away the flicker of relief that raced through me at that sight because it didn't belong. I absolutely did *not* care if Levi had overnight guests in his home. It was none of my business whom he spent his evenings with and hadn't been in decades. Hell, maybe I'd be able to warn the poor girls the next time he brought one around.

My gaze swept across the rest of the room, taking in everything. Two nightstands bracketed his bed, a dresser sat along the opposite wall, and a bookcase filled with odds and ends stood in the corner. Jackpot.

Like a moth to a flame, I headed straight for it, my gaze pinging over the contents. Two framed photographs sat on the highest shelf, and I picked up the older one. It had been taken before my time in Starlight Cove, but there was no mistaking it was Levi's family.

His mom stood in front of *Endless Summer*, their large sailboat, all five boys gathered around her as a very young Addison sat propped on her hip. All of them were grinning at the camera, some with missing teeth, their happiness radiating from the image.

I replaced the frame and picked up the other. This one was steeped in melancholy that had been absent in the first, though I could guess why. Their mom was missing from this photo. Levi looked familiar, so much like the boy who'd broken my heart, I'd place it as being taken about ten years ago. He and his siblings stood in front of Starlight Cove Resort's sign, and though they smiled, it didn't reach their eyes. Sadness cloaked each and every one of them. And despite my less-than-positive thoughts of Levi, my heart broke for him and his whole family...for what they'd gone through.

When tragedy had struck the McKenzie family, I hadn't been

back to Starlight Cove for a couple years, but I'd been devastated, nonetheless. Grace McKenzie had always been so welcoming to me, so open in her affections—something my own mother had been severely lacking in. It was something I'd envied Levi for. Something I'd always appreciated. It had reassured me not all moms were as cold and distant as mine.

While I hadn't been able to attend the funeral, I *had* grieved the fact that Grace had been taken from this world far too soon.

I replaced the photo where I'd found it and scanned the rest of the shelves. Dozens of books in varying genres filled the bookcase. Thriller, nonfiction, fantasy, but the vast majority were romance novels—both spicy and tame—including one of my favorites from years ago. The last one we'd read together.

Unable to resist, I slid it from its place and flipped through the pages, recalling just how much I'd loved it as a teen. And recalling just how many times Levi had stopped to kiss me as we'd swapped the book back and forth, trading off passages to read.

As I fanned the pages, lost in memories from years ago, something fell out and fluttered to the floor. I closed the book and bent to retrieve it, my fingers stilling, my heart jumping into my throat when I realized what it was.

With shaky hands, I picked up the identical photo strip to one I'd ripped up years ago. I ran my gaze over the four black-and-white images of Levi and me smiling, laughing...kissing. We looked so happy.

We looked like we were in love.

It'd been taken the last night we'd been together. Before everything had imploded. Before he'd ripped out my heart with some well-aimed words designed to hurt.

A pit opened in my stomach, throwing me right back to that time and place. When I'd been the stupid girl who'd allowed herself to be blinded by his charms, thinking she was different. Thinking the two of us had something special.

It had all been nothing but a lie.

I shoved the photo strip back into the book before replacing it on the shelf. Then I turned and strode straight out of his room, kicking myself for entering in the first place. But that was what I got for snooping. More questions than answers. Questions I had no intention of delving into.

I was here to do a job and do it well, not reopen old wounds. Levi was no longer the boy I'd once known...once loved...no matter what kinds of mementos he'd hung on to.

And considering how long I was stuck under this roof with him, I needed to remember that.

———

LATER THAT AFTERNOON, Addison and I sat at the high school hockey rink. *Weekend Wanderlust*'s editor in chief wanted this article to have a lifestyle edge, including all the images that would accompany it. It was what was splashed all over social media anyway—those imperfect, slice-of-life moments that had made influencers a thing. Naomi was nothing if not strategic, so she wanted to capitalize on the trend. Because of that, I was the sole person in charge of all the media content while I was in town, navigating this entirely on my own.

Though, truth be told, I preferred it that way.

I worked better solo, knowing I was the only person I had to count on. When I put expectations on someone else's shoulders, I was inevitably let down. Life had proven that time and again. It was easier to handle everything on my own.

In the hours I'd been here, I'd managed to get some amazing shots of Chase out on the ice, running drills with the kids, giving them pep talks...being the kind of supportive, encouraging person I'd always known him to be. I had plenty of content, but I didn't want to leave early and miss anything, so I hung out in the stands.

Addison and I were the only ones left in the building besides Chase, the kids in the program...and Levi. I'd done my best to ignore him all afternoon, but it had been like trying to ignore a raging inferno.

While I'd been interviewing Chase's old coach, some of the kids and parents, as well as Chase himself, I swore I'd felt Levi's gaze on me, the hot brand of it warming me from the outside in, despite the freezing temps inside the rink. But every time I slid an inconspicuous glance in his direction, his focus had been on the boys or his phone or a spot on the wall. Literally anywhere but on me.

And I refused to admit, even to myself, how much that rankled.

I glanced over at Addison. She was living up to every ounce of her boss persona, an iPad propped on her lap as she conducted business from the bleachers.

"You'd probably be a lot warmer if you did this back at the resort instead of here," I said. "Maybe with a nice, sunny view of the ocean while you're at it."

She shot me a smile, wiggling her fingers encased in fingerless gloves. "But then I wouldn't get to be here when my hot beast of a husband is done and full of all those endorphins coursing through him. We never got to experience that post-hockey-game sex coma, so I'm *definitely* going to be fucking that man in the locker room as soon as he's done. Fair warning."

I huffed out a surprised laugh and raised my hands. "I won't stand in your way. And speaking of getting busy... You were right."

"I usually am, but about what, specifically?"

"Mabel. Somehow while I was trying to figure out a different place to stay besides your brother's apartment, she let me know she and George had a playroom in their home, complete with a sex swing."

Addison snorted and shook her head. "Not even a little bit surprised. She hosts her spicy book club in the parlor at the resort, and some of the things those women talk about would make a sex worker blush."

"Sounds like fun." And something I wouldn't mind getting in on. God knew it'd be the only action I'd be seeing in the near—or distant—future. "I'll have to find out when the next one is. I want to interview them while I'm there to talk to Aiden about his blockbuster romantasy career. Gotta say, I never saw that one coming."

"You aren't the only one. Shocked the hell out of me, too. But it makes sense. He's so bottled-up, I figure it's gotta go somewhere other than my best friend—and, by the way, she lets me know how well my brother's accomplishing that, despite my pleas for her to shut her damn mouth."

I grinned over at her. Though her words said she was sick of what her best friend was putting her through, there was no denying the affection in her tone. "Don't be too hard on her. I'm sure she's happy to have that kind of relationship with you."

"Oh, don't get me wrong. I love the girl. And I love telling her all the crazy, depraved things Chase and I get up to. It just really, *really* freaks me out to know that my brother has made her come more times in a single night than I can imagine and not broken a sweat."

Jesus. More times than she could imagine? I was lucky to get *one*, and Aiden was apparently handing them out like candy? Was this what I'd been missing by avoiding the dating pool? For the first time ever, I was second-guessing the focus I'd put on my career instead of on men, because my battery-operated boyfriends were growing tiresome.

My expression must have betrayed my interest and the natural questions that popped into my mind because she held up a hand and shook her head. "Nope. I'm not talking about it anymore. If you want to hear that story, you go right to the source and leave me out of it."

I was about to respond when a deep, throaty chuckle caught my ear, and I glanced out to the rink. Since I'd been talking with Addison, the kids had cleared the area. Now, it was just Chase and Levi on the ice.

While I was used to Chase's easygoing nature and his free-flowing smiles and laughter, that was something I hadn't seen from Levi in more than a decade. Even so, there was no reason the sound should have melted over me like honey, making me feel warm and gooey all over. Old memories I'd tried hard to forget shuttled to the forefront of my mind, sending me back to a time when his laugh had been as familiar as my own.

And there was no reason for my stomach to flip when Levi's gaze lifted to mine for the briefest moment, a flicker of something I couldn't quite name in his eyes, before it was gone in a blink. And then the smile dropped from his face, a cold frostiness replacing his once-warm expression.

It didn't matter that he'd kept some memento from when we were kids—one he probably didn't even remember he had. It also didn't matter that we were going to be roommates, stuck living together for the next six weeks. With a single look, he reminded me exactly what we were to each other.

Absolutely nothing.

CHAPTER SEVEN

LEVI

HARPER HAD BEEN HERE for a handful of hours, and already my apartment looked like the inside of a goddamn Sephora. Various bottles, hair ties and clips, glass jars full of who the hell knew what, and two different-sized curling irons were scattered across my bathroom counter. But that wasn't the worst part.

Clutter, I could handle. What I couldn't was the scent that now hung like a lingering mist in my previously safe space. It wasn't a secret that women smelled better than men. That was just a fact—one Addison had reminded my brothers and me of hundreds of times. But even knowing that, I hadn't been prepared for my apartment to smell like *Harper*.

I also hadn't been prepared for my cock to harden because of it.

From the second I'd walked in here to brush my teeth, the fucker had perked up at that very first inhalation and hadn't yet deflated. Which was really fucking inconvenient since I had to leave this room at some point and walk through my—now shared—hallway to get to my bedroom. All while wearing a flimsy pair of sweatpants as my cock tried valiantly to bust through its cotton prison.

I braced my hands on the counter and hung my head, my gaze pinging over the evidence that proved Harper was *living* here. With me. That the fiasco this afternoon hadn't all been just some awful dream. That Mabel *had* conned me when I'd signed this lease years ago, and I was now stuck with my ex in close quarters for weeks.

Stuck with the one woman I'd been trying to get over for more than a decade.

But that was a problem I could face tomorrow. It was late, and I was fucking exhausted after spending all day at the rink. I just wanted to go to sleep and forget this day ever happened. The trek from the bathroom to my bedroom was six steps, and the chances of running into Harper during those five seconds were slim to none.

Mind set, I opened the door and stepped into the hallway, just as a soft, lush body crashed into mine. Harper yelped, her hand flying to her chest as our bodies collided. Without even registering what I was doing, I reached out to steady her, gripping her waist before I could think better of it.

And I really fucking should have thought better of it.

Because if *smelling* her caused my cock to harden, it had nothing on the feel of her under my hands. It didn't matter that it wasn't skin on skin. It also didn't matter that she appeared to be using clothing as armor, wearing a T-shirt and too-long sweatpants, plus a hoodie, despite the fact that it was July. Even through those layers, I could still feel the softness of her body beneath, the dip of her waist and the tantalizing curve of those generous hips...

I dropped my hands like her skin was on fire. I should've turned around immediately and kept walking. Headed straight into my bedroom without looking back and definitely without saying a word. Instead, I glanced at what she was wearing and asked, "You go to bed like that?"

Her shock at the literal run-in was gone in an instant as she narrowed her eyes at me. Then slowly, deliberately, she allowed her gaze to skate down me from head to toe. Tracing over my bare chest, briefly cataloging the tattoos I'd had inked on me in the years we'd been apart, before slipping over my abs and lower still. Her attention stuttered on the one thing I'd been trying to keep under wraps, for all the good it had done me. Especially when the fucker was all too excited at her attention.

Her brow twitched when her gaze landed on my cock. Slowly, she lifted her eyes to mine, her head canted to the side. "You go to bed like *that*?"

Her words hung in the air between us, her meaning clear as day. Then, without another word, she stepped around me and headed for her bedroom. After opening her door, she glanced at me over her shoulder. The corner of her lips twitched as she allowed herself another glimpse at the very obvious bulge in my pants. "Hope you have the night you deserve."

DEPRIVATION WASN'T new to me. It was something I'd excelled at for years. For a hundred different reasons, my needs had been something I'd largely ignored. And I'd been able to with little difficulty.

But in all the years I'd been depriving myself of pleasure, I'd never had to lie in bed and listen to the sounds of the one woman who'd starred in all my fantasies shifting a wall away. I'd never particularly considered the walls within my apartment to be thin, but then again, I'd never had a reason to.

Now, though, as I lay in my bed, staring up at the ceiling cloaked in darkness, I could *hear* Harper. Every tiny sound stoked my imagination, the embers smoldering, and if I weren't careful, they'd spark into an inferno.

The soft shuffle of her footsteps across the hardwood floor. The slide of a drawer opening. The rustle of material—her bed or her clothes, I wasn't sure, but both fucked with my mind in equal measures.

Then came the squeak of her bed frame, and all my restraint was a lost cause.

I could picture her there, shedding all her layers until she was left in just a T-shirt. Or maybe she'd strip down to a tank top and panties. Maybe she slept completely naked, the sheets pooled around her, her gorgeous body on full display.

"*Fuck me,*" I muttered.

Swallowing hard, I forced myself to shove those thoughts aside and ignore the dozens of possibilities my mind was all too happy to conjure up. It didn't matter. I couldn't *let* it. I'd spent more than a decade reminding myself Harper was better off without me, and that hadn't changed.

Lying on the other side of a wall from her was pure torture, made worse by the fact that this was only the beginning. We had weeks in front of us, and every night would be more of the same.

Sleep felt like an impossibility, because how the hell was I supposed to relax when my thoughts were consumed by the one woman I'd never been able to forget?

Shoving off the covers, I sat up and scrubbed a hand down my face. I needed a distraction, something to take my mind off the fantasies currently playing on a loop in my mind, because I was seconds from doing something stupid. Like knocking on her door and begging her to put me out of my misery.

I tugged on my sweatpants and a T-shirt before slipping out

of my room. My workshop, at least, would be free from her—her sounds and her scent and her presence.

I headed for the front door as my phone buzzed with an incoming text. I pulled it out of my pocket and glanced at the screen.

CHASE:

How's the first night in cohabitation going?

LEVI:

Well, she still hates me, so I have that going for me.

CHASE:

Did you ever think that you could just come clean to her? Tell her the real reason you broke up with her? I mean, she's an adult now. I think it's probably safe.

I nearly laughed out loud at that. Safe for who? It wouldn't be safe for her, and it sure as hell wouldn't be safe for me. The truth was, I couldn't go down that path with her again, couldn't have her soften toward me at all. Walking away from her once had been one of the hardest things I'd ever done in my life.

I wasn't strong enough to do it again.

I pocketed my phone and glanced down the hallway toward her closed bedroom door. Then, without second-guessing it, I walked out of the apartment, escaping to the only place I had left.

CHAPTER EIGHT

HARPER

TURNED out living with Levi was exactly like living alone. It'd only been a couple days, but so far, I'd had the apartment all to myself. He was gone when I woke up in the morning and didn't return until well after I'd retreated to my room for the night. For all I knew, he never returned at all.

Maybe he'd decided to live in the construction zone at the resort. Maybe he roamed the streets of Starlight Cove all night long.

Maybe he had a girlfriend and was spending his nights in her bed.

Before I could stop it, a knot twisted up my stomach for no good reason. It certainly wasn't because I *cared* who Levi spent his time with. That was ridiculous and so far out of the realm of reality, it was laughable. It was obviously just old wounds brought back to life. The reminder that I hadn't been good enough for that role but someone else was. Nothing more.

Lightning flashed in the distance, the wind picking up as rain started to fall, and I hustled into the building, that hum under my skin urging me faster. I'd been terrified of storms since

I was a little girl. It didn't matter how old I got or how illogical it was. That fear had never left me.

I slipped my key into the lock and pushed open the door, readying myself for another night alone. I hated being by myself during storms—a reminder of all those years ago—but I'd gotten good at it. Especially living the life I did.

I had a system now—distractions in whatever form I could find. I'd grab something quick to eat and slip into my room, put on my noise-canceling headphones, and disappear into the book I was reading. Nothing like the escapism of a spicy romance to get my mind off that night I'd been trying most of my life to forget.

Except when I stepped inside the apartment, a mouthwatering scent hit me, and I froze on the spot. Levi stood in the kitchen, stirring something on the stove, his icy blue eyes connecting with mine immediately.

Fuck. Shit. Fucking shit. We hadn't been in the same space since the first night I'd moved in, and it'd been working just fine. I didn't know if upsetting that was a good idea.

But before I could even think about turning around and slipping right back out the door, a deafening crack of thunder split the air, shaking the floor beneath me. I jumped with a yelp, my hand flying to my chest as I shot a glance out the window at the ever-darkening sky. I hated how much storms continued to affect me, like I was still that little girl. I was a thirty-year-old woman who'd traveled the world by myself, for God's sake. I'd lived on my own since I was eighteen, handled shit without anyone's help. And yet, I was scared of a damn storm.

Worse, I hated that I was basically rolling over and exposing my underbelly to the one man I swore I'd never be soft around again.

"Don't be stupid and go back out there just to spite me," he said, turning away from me and back to the stove. "Besides, I made plenty."

I hesitated as the rain began to pelt the windows and eyed him. He stood with his back to me as he stirred something in a pot, his back muscles bunching and flexing under the thin cotton T-shirt he wore. Had it been anyone other than Levi, the sight would've been hot. A huge, tattooed man with inked sleeves down both arms cooking something that smelled amazing? Yeah, sign me up, please and thank you.

Unfortunately, the huge, tattooed man cooking was the last person in the world I wanted to spend even five minutes with, let alone a meal. And definitely not an evening. What if the power went out? What if we were stuck together, in the dark, with nothing but candlelight to illuminate the space?

Yeah, no. I was not at all interested in suffering through that.

The lights flickered, and I shot my gaze around, praying to whatever God would listen that I didn't actually *want* that to happen. My worst-case scenario was not a goddamn invitation to the universe. Thankfully, the power only flickered but remained strong. But that was merely half my issue. The other half was my ex-boyfriend, standing there looking like God's gift to women, and I was stuck in a too-small space with him.

Just as I reached for the knob, deciding I was totally fine cutting off my nose to spite my face, another crack of thunder shook the apartment. At the same moment, lightning lit up the sky, and a deluge of rain battered the windows, proving the storm wasn't coming. It was already on top of us.

Levi blew out a long, aggrieved sigh, as if I were getting on his last nerve. "Stop being so fucking stubborn and sit down. It's spaghetti, not a life sentence."

I couldn't say whether I stood frozen because of the storm or him, just that I was. My feet felt like they were encased in cement blocks, my fight, flight, or freeze instinct choosing my least favorite option. And then, as if the universe wanted to dump a bit more on top of me, a strong gust of wind rattled the windows, and the lights flickered once more before going out entirely.

"Fuck," I whispered, the word barely leaving me. My body flushed, my breaths coming quicker. Panic clawed its way up my chest as memories flooded me faster than I could stop them.

Being outside, pitch black except for when lightning lit up the sky. Lost in the dark as rain pelted my skin. Having no idea where I was or how to get back home. And knowing, without a doubt, no one even realized I was gone.

"Looks like your decision's made for you. You're not wandering around in a thunderstorm while the power's out," Levi said, his tone brooking no argument. As if he were the boss of me. It was something I normally would've snapped back at, but I couldn't find my voice at all, trapped in that time more than twenty years ago when I'd screamed myself hoarse. "Now, sit the fuck down while I get some candles."

It was dark in the apartment, not even a sliver of moonlight shining through the windows. I stood at the front door, gripping the knob in an effort to ground myself. Reminding myself I was here, in the present, with the one man I couldn't stand. I wasn't lost outside again. I was safe. Or as safe as I could be with Levi near.

I could hear him shuffling around, picked up his scent as he breezed past me, but I couldn't even see my hand in front of my face. Until suddenly, a metallic rasp sounded, followed by a soft click, and a flicker of light brightened the space.

Levi stood at the breakfast bar, a lighter in his hand as he lit a small candle. The flame illuminated his face, accentuating his sharp cheekbones and his full lips, and I was reminded once again how gorgeous my ex-boyfriend was. Because of course he was. Some things were just patently unfair.

He glanced at me then, his gaze flicking over me from head to toe, pausing briefly on the death grip I had on the doorknob. I could've sworn his eyes softened for the briefest moment before that hard expression was back on his face.

With a sigh, he walked straight toward me, removed the bag from my shoulder, and hung it on the hook by the door. Then he grabbed me by the elbow and guided me to the stool on the other side of the breakfast bar. "Sit."

He didn't wait for me to comply, just pushed me onto the stool before making his way around the counter and back into the kitchen. There was no doubt this was dangerous territory—sharing a meal, just the two of us, with nothing but candlelight to brighten the space—but I didn't move. And even if I had, I wasn't sure Levi wouldn't have dragged me right back.

As if my body knew I was still contemplating bailing, my stomach rumbled loud enough to be heard even over the raging storm outside. I'd been so busy today, I hadn't eaten anything since the breakfast sandwich I'd grabbed on my way to interview the mayor that morning, and I was paying for that now.

"Here." Levi set a plate in front of me, piled high with enough spaghetti to feed a small country, before turning his back to me to dish up his own.

Rather than take the stool directly next to mine, Levi remained in the kitchen, setting his plate down on the other side of the counter. Then he grabbed a couple glasses and a bottle of wine, expertly uncorking it, and poured me a healthy glass.

"Didn't take you for a wine guy." But I also wasn't going to complain because my nerves could use a little soothing.

He shrugged, lifting his eyes to mine for a brief moment as he poured himself a glass. "I'm not. I keep a couple bottles of

Marianne's favorite on hand. And I'm guessing you still hate beer."

I froze, startled that he remembered... Just like he seemed to remember I was scared of storms, if his bossing and efforts at distracting were any indication. I hated how much he seemed to recall about me, though I couldn't deny the tiny part inside that actually...enjoyed it.

This man was nothing but contradictions. Gruff, stern, off-putting on the outside. A prickly cactus to anyone looking. But that same prickly cactus kept his best friend's mom's favorite wine on hand and knew just what to say to get my stubborn ass to sit down, even when I wanted to do anything but.

I had to ignore every instinct in me that was drawn to the allure of that. The allure of *him*.

"You gonna eat, or are you waiting for me to feed you?"

I snapped my gaze to his, only to find him already staring at me. "Just trying to figure out if I was distracted long enough for you to poison my meal."

With his eyes still locked on mine, he took a long drink from his wineglass. Then he grabbed his fork and stabbed it onto my plate, gathering a large amount of noodles before slipping it into his mouth. He raised a brow at me as he chewed and swallowed, then tucked back into his own meal.

"Fine. Not poisoned." I blew out a heavy sigh, trying in vain to ignore the storm raging behind me...not to mention the storm that always seemed to rage between the two of us. I picked up my fork and twirled some pasta onto it, inhaling deeply at how good it smelled. I took a bite and forced myself not to moan at how delicious it was. Jesus, the asshole could cook, too?

After several long moments of silence between us, making the turbulent storm all that much louder and more distracting, I finally said, "So...how do you build a boat?"

Levi snorted, a sound that was so out of place for him, I did a double take. He shook his head as he stared down at his plate, any hint of amusement wiped clear from his face. Meeting my eyes again, he said, "You don't have to fake interest because you're keeping a scorecard. Just eat the fucking food, Harper."

"Maybe I *want* to have a conversation."

"You and I both know that's not true."

I narrowed my eyes at him, annoyed by the fact that he still knew me so well. "Fine. Maybe you're right. But this still needs to be a fair exchange."

"Why's that?"

"I don't like owing you something. This needs to be tit for tat."

"And you think me talking about myself is what I want out of this interaction?"

Before I could answer, a crack of thunder boomed as lightning flashed through the sky. I jumped, my fork clattering to my plate, though I'd thankfully swallowed back the scream lodged in my throat.

I picked up my utensil again, hoping like hell Levi hadn't noticed the tremors in my hand as I brought a bite to my mouth. Though, of course, that was wishful thinking. His eyes were like laser beams, focused on any weakness of mine he could find.

But instead of saying anything about it...instead of making fun of me or calling me out, he just sighed, a heavy, frustrated sound. Then, much to my shock, he started talking about boats. How he designed them, how he restored them, how he built them from scratch.

And somehow, through it all, he held my attention. The storm faded into the background as Levi spoke, his low, rumbling voice settling over me as his passion for his job bled into every word. While he explained his craft, I saw a tiny glimpse of the boy I'd loved all those years ago. The one who'd been rough around the edges but so sweet to me. So kind and giving.

At another loud crack, I jumped again, but this time, I noticed I wasn't the only one reacting to the storm. It was apparent in the tightening of Levi's muscles. The bunch of his shoulders. The rigidness of his jaw. And I felt like an idiot. An inconsiderate idiot at that. Because *of course* he'd hate storms. After everything he'd gone through...

"Why didn't you tell me you're scared of storms, too?"

"I'm not," he said immediately. Then, when I just stared at him in response, he blew out a long breath and leaned back against the counter at the opposite side of the kitchen, crossing his arms over his chest. His biceps bunched and flexed, the inked designs drawing my eye, making me long to discover them all. "I just don't particularly like them."

"For good reason." I cleared my throat, having no idea how to broach this but needing to, so I just went for it. "I wanted to tell you how sorry I am. About your mom."

A flurry of emotions passed over his face—anger and sadness and grief...so much grief, followed by...guilt?—before he wiped his expression clear and lifted his chin in acknowledgment. I thought he might open up about it. Talk about her a bit since I'd known her, too. But instead, he said, "Sounds like you owe me a story."

I blinked at him, unable to follow his abrupt change in topic. "About?"

"You never did tell me why you're scared of storms. And since you know my why, it's only fair. Tit for tat, right?"

Right. It was clear Levi's mom was off-limits, at least to me. And that was fine. It was understandable. And certainly shouldn't sting like it did.

I took a sip of wine and cleared my throat, averting my gaze. "When I was little, I got lost outside during a severe thunderstorm while my parents were throwing a party. It took them a while to realize I was missing."

Levi's jaw ticked, and I could almost make myself believe it was concern for me. In actuality, it was probably frustration over being stuck in this conversation for this much time. "How long?"

I shrugged, taking another drink to buy myself time. The truth was, eternity wouldn't have been long enough. "A while."

"How long, sparrow?"

His old nickname for me slammed into my chest, throwing me off-balance and leaving me grappling for purchase. I hadn't heard that in more than a decade, and I'd had no idea how much I would miss it once it was gone. I'd hated it when he'd first given it to me, a reminder that our time together was always fleeting because we'd only had the summers. That, in the end, I always had to leave, fly away for another year.

I stared at him, a thousand questions running through my mind, but he gazed back, not-so-patiently waiting for my response. As if he hadn't even noticed the word had slipped from his lips.

That was probably better for everyone anyway. Nothing good would come from going down memory lane with the man who'd broken my heart beyond repair.

I cleared my throat. "A few hours."

"Jesus Christ," he muttered.

"Everything turned out fine." If you didn't count the hours I'd spent screaming myself hoarse or the years of therapy I'd worked through as an adult or this neat little lifelong phobia.

He stared at me for a long moment, his eyes pinning me in place, searching in a way that felt like he could see straight into my soul. I wasn't so sure he couldn't.

Finally, he said, "I wouldn't expect anything less for the perfect Davidsons."

"Right." I huffed out a laugh and nodded.

My family was the furthest thing from perfect, though my parents had definitely pushed that narrative to anyone who'd listen. And though I'd walked the line they had guided me to, I'd veered off it with Levi. With him, I'd let my guard down as much as I could. Shown him parts of me I'd never shown anyone. And still, he hadn't seen.

After this long of being on my own, I should've been used to this feeling of loneliness, but it still packed a punch. More so with this man who'd had the power to wreck me once. I certainly wasn't going to give him the opportunity to do it again.

"Thanks for dinner." I pushed away my nearly empty plate as I drained my wineglass. I set it on the counter harder than I intended, but everything was bubbling up inside me, and I had no hope of containing it. "But don't think this changes anything between us."

He was silent long enough that I finally glanced up at him, only to find his attention already on me. Those ice-blue eyes probing in a way that made me shift in my seat. "Wouldn't dream of it."

CHAPTER NINE

LEVI

I'D SPENT a lot of my life thinking I deserved the worst. That I wasn't worthy of forgiveness after what I'd done...and certainly not worthy of happiness. And that hadn't changed.

Well, I was finally getting what I deserved, because having Harper in my apartment was turning into my worst fucking nightmare.

It was no secret that I liked my space. And I fucking loved my solitude. Which was why I'd never had or wanted a roommate. The closest I'd gotten was sharing a conjoined bathroom with Addison when we were growing up. I didn't like having to tiptoe around someone else or have someone silently judging my choices. And if my home was a mess, it was *my* mess.

Except now there was another person living in my space. One I'd been trying my damnedest to avoid. But I couldn't avoid the tells of her now residing in my apartment. The explosion of all her junk in the bathroom, an extra coffee mug in the sink, her shoes by the front door. And her scent I just couldn't seem to escape.

It shoved me back to a time I rarely allowed myself to travel to—back when everything was better. Before I'd realized what a disappointment I was, before I'd almost dragged Harper down with me, before my mom had died.

Before I'd fucked up everything good in my life.

Barring the night of the storm, I'd managed to avoid Harper for the most part by staying out of my apartment as much as humanly possible. It was a necessity at this point. Having a conversation with her only proved that not only did we still have insane chemistry, but I *liked* talking with her. I even liked her smart mouth and sassy replies. But I needed to shut that down immediately, because the truth was, I didn't trust myself around her.

The Starlight Cove carnival hadn't been in my plans this weekend...or ever. In fact, I generally tried to avoid any and all public events like the plague, unless I was literally dragged there by Addison. Too many people and way too fucking much conversation. I wasn't interested in any of it. But it was better than suffering through hours in what had once been my safe space, wondering when—or if—Harper would be coming home.

And if she'd be alone when she arrived.

I might've broken up with her all those years ago, but in no realm of reality could I handle seeing her bring another man into my apartment. And no fucking way could I handle *hearing* it. Since our bedrooms shared a paper-thin wall, that meant I was utterly fucked.

So instead of waiting for the inevitable, I took my ass to the carnival. I suffered through small talk from roughly a dozen people and made a couple consultation appointments for this week before coming across what made this entire night worth it.

The lobster corn dog stand.

They had been a staple in my youth, something I could only

get here at the carnival once a year. And they held a hell of a lot of memories I'd be better off forgetting.

I didn't know if it was because my defenses were already down or because I was just fucking hungry, but I didn't say no. Didn't walk away and go order something else instead, something that held no emotional attachment.

Instead, I gave in.

After waiting in the obscenely long line, sandwiched between a family with small children and a couple making out, I placed my order and now stood off to the side to wait. I stuffed my hands in my jeans pockets, trying to get lost in the chaos around me in an effort to keep my mind carefully blank. Here, of all places, I needed to be on my game, keeping the past firmly where it belonged.

But, just like always, Harper slipped through a crack in the walls I'd erected long ago, taking me back to the last time we'd been to this carnival. The last night we'd been together, period.

Her laughter had been infectious as she'd snuck bites of my order, teasing that she'd break up with me if I didn't share. She hadn't realized it then, but I would've given her anything she asked for—and even what she didn't. Case in point, my hoodie I'd slipped over her head when she'd been shivering in nothing but a sky-blue sundress that had perfectly matched her eyes. It looked so goddamn good on her, I hadn't been able to keep my hands to myself.

Without my permission, my thoughts shifted to later that evening. The Ferris wheel...and then after. When she'd been breathless and beautiful, eyes locked on mine as she'd ridden me in the back seat of her father's car.

The memories hollowed me out, just like always. I shoved them forcefully away, gritting my teeth against the ache in my chest. An ache I damn well deserved because *I'd* been the one to put it there.

"Lobster corn dog, extra spicy, side of mango salsa," Darnell called out.

Grateful for the distraction, I strode up to the counter. I reached for my order, gripping the basket just as another hand brushed against mine. A jolt of awareness shot down my arm at the same moment I registered who it was.

Harper. Because of fucking course.

Her hair was pulled back in a high ponytail, flyaway wisps curling around her face, and she wore an off-the-shoulder shirt. I hated how much the sight of all that skin drew my attention, like a fucking siren's call I couldn't ignore. I wanted to run my nose along her skin, inhaling deeply. Then I wanted to sink my teeth into the juncture where her shoulder met her neck, a little payback for getting my dick hard without even fucking trying. All while we were in a crowded place. And while I was supposed to be hating her.

The night of the storm might have felt like something shifted, but it hadn't changed anything between us. She'd said so herself.

"Whoa, a little quick on the draw there, Levi." Darnell grinned and slid another basket toward me. "Yours is up right here. That one's for Harper."

I tore my gaze from Harper's and snatched my food. Muttering a curt thanks to Darnell, I stepped back, putting a safe distance between Harper and me. Though, truth be told, no amount of distance between us would ever be safe.

"Quick on the draw, huh?" She raised a brow in my direction and gave me a slow once-over. "That's...enlightening."

Her appraisal might've been fueled by hate—or disgust at the very least—but my dick didn't know the difference. It twitched behind the fly of my jeans, ready and eager as fucking ever for her attention when it'd been subsisting on a poor substitute for far too long.

Instead of giving in to it, I needed to do what I did best and push her away by whatever means necessary. I leaned toward her, and it was like being transported back in time. The scent of her, combined with the salty air of the ocean and the smell of fried dough from the carnival vendors shoved me straight back in time. To a place I didn't deserve to remember.

Shaking myself from my thoughts, I didn't stop until my lips were a breath from her ear. Close enough to feel the heat radiating off her, watch the increased rise and fall of her chest. Against her ear, I murmured, "If you wanted to know how well I fuck now, sparrow, you could've just asked."

Her shoulders stiffened, her entire body going rigid, but not before I saw a shiver skate down her spine. And if I had any hope of keeping up this fucking facade, I shouldn't have been as satisfied as I was that I could still get a reaction out of her.

She jerked away, eyeing me with every ounce of disdain I damn well deserved. "Don't flatter yourself. I don't give a single shit what you do in the bedroom." Venom dripped from her tone, but the way her gaze flicked down to my lips betrayed every word coming out of her mouth.

"Who said anything about a bedroom?"

Harper's eyes flashed with irritation, but there was something else there, too. Something she definitely didn't want me to see. And, if I had to guess, something she definitely didn't want to feel. It made my cock hard just the same. She could fight it all she wanted, but there was no denying how much her body responded to mine, even when she was fueled by hate.

"I see you still enjoy acting like an ass," she said, that snooty tone reminding me exactly who her family was, exactly what her life was like away from Starlight Cove.

I clenched my teeth, jaw ticking, though I shouldn't have been irritated at her frank assessment. Her dismissal...her contempt was exactly what I wanted her feeling toward me. It was better for everyone that way.

"And I see your tastes haven't changed." I gestured with my chin toward her basket that was identical to mine—the way I'd taught her to order it when we were kids.

She grabbed a couple of napkins and glanced at me, giving me another once-over. Except this time, I saw nothing but contempt in her gaze, the flash of heat I'd seen long gone. "Oh, believe me. They have."

Then, without another word, she grabbed her basket and walked away, getting swallowed up by the crowd within seconds.

There was no denying our chemistry was still as strong as ever. No denying exactly how dangerous that was, either. I'd managed to hold on to my control for years, and now, within a matter of days of her being near, it felt like I was one tenuous thread away from it snapping.

CHAPTER TEN

LEVI

I HAD no idea why I was still at the carnival. Logically, I knew I'd have the apartment to myself if I went home. But logic didn't come into play when it came to Harper.

It never had.

So there I was, forty-five minutes later, wandering around as if I didn't have anything better to do with my time. All the while pretending like I didn't know exactly why I'd stayed.

"Well, holy shit. Has hell actually frozen over?" Chase called from in front of the duck hunt game, Addison glued to his side. "That has to be it because the Levi McKenzie I know would never *willingly* be at a town event his sister didn't drag him to."

I changed course, dodging passersby as I strode toward Chase and Addison. "Since this is apparently where boring married couples hang out on Friday nights, my stance stands."

"You take that back right now!" Addison swatted me with a giant teddy bear and glared up at me. "We're not *boring*. And didn't you just tell me you'd rather stab toothpicks under your fingernails than attend the carnival?"

I definitely had said that when she and I had been catching

up on *Vampire Diaries* last week. But that had been *before*. Before Mabel had screwed up my entire life. Before Harper had shown up in my apartment. Before I'd had her sweet-smelling shampoo in my shower and her scent invading every square inch of my space. Before I'd been close enough to feel a shiver skate down her spine and remember exactly what it had felt like to be inside her.

I flicked a glance to Chase, who wore a smirk that said he knew exactly why I was here and exactly why I needed to avoid my own damn apartment. But I'd be taking that shit to my grave. No way was I letting my sister in on any of it. The less she knew about my relationship—or lack thereof—with Harper, the better. Chase was the only one on earth who knew the whole story. Knew why I'd shoved her away all those years ago, with force and without mercy. And even that was one more person than I would have liked.

"I came to get a lobster corn dog. And I can't seem to make it ten feet without somebody stopping me to talk. Case in point." I lifted my chin at them. "So I've been stuck here ever since."

Not entirely a lie, just not the whole truth.

Chase clapped a hand on my shoulder. "Well, you came to the perfect spot at the perfect time. I just got the high score. Twenty-seven of those little fuckers."

"And?" I asked, brows raised.

"*And* how about a wager? I'll make it worth your while."

I crossed my arms over my chest, interest piqued. "I'm listening."

"You beat me, and I'll take care of unclogging the outdoor shower drains."

Now that was damn tempting. Chase knew exactly how much I hated doing that. Addison did, too, for that matter, which was exactly why the little demon shoved it onto my plate every chance she got.

"Oh my God, you're such a baby, Levi." Addison rolled her eyes. "It's not *that* bad."

"No? Then why don't you ever do it?"

Addison ignored me, suddenly pretending to be very interested in her phone.

Turning my attention back to Chase, I raised a brow. "And if you win?"

"Bragging rights are all I need."

Fuck me. It would have been better if he'd wanted something specific, because bragging rights with Chase went on for eternity. He'd been lording a one-on-one game of basketball he'd won over me for fifteen fucking years.

Worse, with those stipulations, I had no choice but to take the bet—especially since he didn't want anything from me—and he knew it.

His grin widened, and he slapped me on the back, shoving me toward the now-open stool. "You're up. Let me know when I can start shouting my win to the masses."

I settled on the seat and glanced back at them over my shoulder. "Don't want to stick around and watch me beat your ass?"

"Nah, Isaac will keep you honest." He lifted a chin toward the guy working the game. "Besides, I need to get my wife home, so I can—"

"Shut your fucking mouth right now."

He and Addison just laughed, the sound fading as they strode away, and I focused on the game. This was a safer version of the one we used to play as kids—using water instead of actual pellets—but the rules were the same. Hit as many of the targets on top of the moving ducks as possible. High score won your choice of prize.

"Just a second, folks," Isaac called. "We've got a faulty gun over here."

I glanced down the line to see where the holdup was and froze when my eyes landed on the last person I should have wanted to see and the one I couldn't seem to get out of my head. Harper sat on a stool all the way at the other end, unaware I was here. At least until Isaac said something and gestured in my direction to the only open seat on the line. The one directly next to me.

Fuck my fucking life.

I stared straight ahead, refusing to look at her as she slid onto the stool next to mine. But it didn't seem to matter. Every cell in my body sensed her proximity, pinging with an awareness I wished like hell I didn't possess when it came to her.

"I should probably make sure this one works." Though she said the words more to herself than anyone else, I heard them all the same. Right before she aimed the water gun at my chest and pulled the trigger.

I jolted back as the icy stream of water doused the front of my white shirt, soaking it in seconds. "Are you fucking kidding me?"

"What?" she asked, all faux innocence. "I didn't want to risk getting stuck with another faulty gun."

I pulled my soaked shirt away from my chest. "And you couldn't have tested it against the back wall?"

"Guess my aim's a little off."

I met her amused stare and clenched my jaw. "Yet you had no problem hitting the center of my chest."

She bit the corner of her lip as she allowed her gaze to track where I gestured to my chest, now visible through the shirt.

Except she wasn't just staring...she was *glaring*. As if my chest had personally affronted her.

"Beginner's luck," she finally said. And before I could call her out, a high-pitched bell signaled the start of the game.

Gripping my water gun tighter, I turned and concentrated on the moving targets in front of me. I needed to focus, but it was damn near impossible to block out Harper's presence. She'd always had that effect on me. Like every goddamn one of my senses was dialed to eleven whenever she was around. Had been since that very first summer when she'd shown up in Starlight Cove, and it'd only amplified over the years.

I managed to hit a few of the targets, despite the distraction. But I had nothing on Harper. She was on fire, nailing duck after duck. Beginner's luck, my ass. Though I should've remembered that. We'd spent hours playing these games when we were teenagers, running around like feral kids.

Back then, our time at the carnival had been spent laughing and stealing kisses wherever we could. Her smiles had been frequent and contagious. Something I'd taken for granted until they were gone.

Now, the smiles she shot my way held only contempt.

"What's wrong, Levi?" she asked without taking her eyes off her targets. "Distracted by something?"

I focused back on the game, cursing under my breath when I realized just how badly she was beating me. "Yeah, you running your mouth."

She hummed and shot me a look out of the corner of her eye. "You never used to complain about my mouth."

A strangled noise escaped me before I could bite it back. Thoughts of her mouth and everything she'd done to me with it slammed into me, an onslaught of memories I couldn't hope to block out. Memories I absolutely should not be thinking about. Memories I'd spent years trying to suppress.

She wasn't playing fair, and from the smirk curving the corner of her lips, she knew it.

The bell sounded again, signaling the end of the game. I'd missed nearly half the targets, too wrapped up in Harper's taunts and her presence to keep my focus. I swore under my breath as the final tally flashed.

"Would you look at that? New high score." Harper pointed to a white teddy bear hanging on display. "And I think I'll take that as my prize."

"You got it," Isaac said, plucking the bear from the hook before handing it to Harper.

I eyed her and the oversized teddy bear she'd chosen. "You're really going to carry that around all night?"

"Nah." She stood, slapping the bear against my still-wet chest, and offered a saccharine smile. "It's all yours. Figured you could use some company to ease the pain of your loss."

I glanced down at the bear that looked eerily similar to the stuffed animal I'd won for her at our last carnival together. The carnival we'd escaped from to fuck right there in the parking lot, frantic and frenzied. Like it would be our last time.

Little had we known, it was.

CHAPTER ELEVEN

HARPER

AN HOUR after my run-in with Levi, I stood in line for the Ferris wheel. This was my worst idea of the night, considering the last time I'd ridden it had been with the very person I wasn't supposed to be thinking about.

Back then, Levi had bribed the operator to let us have one final ride before they closed for the night. The guy had finally relented and allowed us on, just Levi and me alone under the stars. I could still remember how he'd looked at me that night. Like I was everything to him—the only thing in his world. And I'd been naive enough to think we had forever ahead of us. Joke was on me because he'd broken my heart the very next day.

It'd taken me years to get over him. And I'd done it while I'd been working my way through college, all alone in a strange city with no support system. But I'd learned a lot about myself during that time. The most important of all being I was the only person I could count on when things got tough.

Levi might be a different man than he'd been back then, but it didn't matter. It didn't matter that we were stuck together for six weeks. Or that he'd remembered my fear of storms and distracted me the other night while it passed. It didn't matter that our chemistry still crackled like lightning, my attraction to him burning hotter than the sun. *None* of it mattered because I had no intention of ever putting myself into a position like that again. And certainly not with a man like Levi.

"Single rider!" Mabel called from the front of the line, a white teddy bear clutched in her grip. "Come on, honey, you're up."

I shook myself from the memories and made my way toward her. She stood in front of the gondola, holding her arm out in a way that obscured the other rider from me. And then, because apparently I wasn't moving fast enough for her, she gave me a little push toward the bench.

I stumbled into the seat, breathing out a shocked huff over the fact that she'd basically shoved me in here before latching the bar without a moment's hesitation. It was only then that I glanced to my right and realized who sat next to me.

"Seriously?" Levi jerked on the bar, but it didn't move. "What the fuck, Mabel?"

Panic gripped my throat when I realized I was stuck in here with him with nowhere to escape. Even sharing an apartment, we could keep some distance between us. Being trapped this close to him was only asking for trouble. Especially considering what had happened between us the last time we'd ridden one of these in the pitch black of night. When he'd kissed me until I was breathless. Then he'd made me come on his fingers right there before dragging me to my dad's car and fucking me in the back seat.

"Mabel," I said, a warning in my tone. "Unlatch this. Now."

"What's that?" Mabel called, cupping her hand around her ear. "I can't hear you, but you kids have fun! I'll take care of Teddy."

With that, she pulled the lever for the ride, sending our cabin lurching upward. I gripped the bar across my front until my knuckles turned white, refusing to glance over at Levi. Refusing to even acknowledge his presence. But I could still feel him there, the energy rolling off him in waves.

I didn't know if it was the memory of what had happened the last time we'd been on this ride or the proximity of him being so close with nowhere for either of us to run, but my mind spun back to that night. How he'd kissed me as he slid his hand up the inside of my thigh. How he'd moved his fingers inside me, having learned over the summer exactly how I liked to be touched. How he'd brought me to the edge just as we'd crested the top of the ride. I'd fallen along with the gondola, Levi's name on my lips. But my hunger for him hadn't been nearly satisfied. It never had been back then.

I shook the thoughts from my mind and shifted in my seat, desperate to hide my reaction to the memory. It wasn't *Levi* causing this. It'd just been too long since I'd had good sex—hell, it'd been too long since I'd had a good orgasm, period—and I needed some relief. That was all.

The gondola reached the top of the Ferris wheel, the sparkling lights of the carnival spread out below us, glittering stars spread out above. It was a beautiful night, but I couldn't enjoy it. Not with him so close I could feel the heat of his body seeping into mine. Not with the memories of that night still breathing down my neck, despite my trying to shove them away.

"Something on your mind, sparrow?"

I slid him a glance out of the corner of my eye. "Just wondering how easy it would be to push you out of this ride."

A mocking grin swept across his mouth as he settled more comfortably in the seat, spreading his legs wide, the move pushing his thigh directly against mine. He rested his arm along the top of the seat, just a soft caress against the bare skin of my back. "That's too bad. I was thinking about the last time we were on this ride."

I swallowed thickly, pressing my thighs together as much for some crucially needed distance from him as to alleviate the incessant throbbing of my clit.

"You remember, don't you?" he murmured, his voice low and rough, as if he were just as lost to the memory as he wanted me to be. He leaned closer, his breath ghosting across my bare shoulder and sending goose bumps scattering across my skin. "When I slid my hand inside your panties and found you soaking wet? You wanted me to get you off right here. Wanted me to slip my fingers deep inside you and make you come. Begged for it, didn't you?"

I glared at him, my arms crossed over my chest to hide the no doubt very obvious points of my nipples. "Why are you doing this?"

"Tit for tat—that's your rule, right? You soaked me at the game. Figured I needed to repay the favor. Is it working?"

"Fuck you," I bit out, though the words lacked heat, especially when I could recall exactly how much he'd wanted it that night, too. Could still hear his soft groan muffled against my neck when he'd found me ready for him. And his eyes, full of need and hunger and a bit of awe, as if he couldn't believe he had the privilege of being with me. As if he couldn't believe I was his.

"I did. Right in the back of your dad's car, if I remember right." His words stirred up the memories I'd been valiantly avoiding, and I could practically feel the worn leather seat against my knees, Levi's hands gripping my hips as he guided me over him. His lips against mine, open but not kissing. Just breathing in our shared oxygen and looking at each other like we were everything. *Everything.*

In the end, we were nothing.

I lifted a shoulder in a shrug, feigning disinterest. "Wasn't all that memorable, to be honest."

"You sure? So you don't remember when you told me to shove down the front of your dress? To suck on your tits while you rode me? Don't remember how I had to press my hand over your mouth to muffle your screams? I worried the whole town was going to hear you coming apart on my cock. Turned out, I'd been right."

I stiffened at the roundabout mention of what had happened that night. When Levi had pulled out of me just as red and blue flashing lights illuminated the car's interior. I'd fumbled with my dress while Levi had hastily done up his jeans. And then there'd been the sharp rap of knuckles against the steamed-up window, leaving no question as to what we'd been doing.

We'd known we were screwed even before my dad arrived at the station. But what I hadn't known was that it was the beginning of the end for us.

I offered him a sympathetic look. "Sorry to burst your bubble, but I was faking it."

He chuckled lowly, swiping his thumb across his lower lip, bringing my attention to his mouth. "Keep telling yourself that, but we both know the truth." He leaned close until his lips brushed my ear. "You loved coming apart on my cock and screaming my name while you did."

"You're *such* a—"

"What? What am I?" he asked, a taunting lilt to his voice as he leaned closer. So close I could see the flecks of gold in his ice-blue eyes. Could count each one of his ridiculously long eyelashes. Could feel the ghost of his breath against my mouth.

I didn't know who moved first, but before I even realized what was happening, my hands were in his hair and he was cupping my nape, tugging me to him as he crushed his lips to mine. The kiss was frantic, all bottled-up passion and aggression exploding from both of us. There was nothing soft or sweet about this. It wasn't comforting like the kisses we'd once shared a lifetime ago.

I gasped into his mouth, the familiar taste and feel of him momentarily short-circuiting my brain. Which was the only explanation for why I kissed him back just as fiercely, giving as good as I got, a decade's worth of rage and heartbreak pouring out of me. Our mouths met over and over, the kiss full of anger and desire. Of frustration and buried pain and everything left unsaid between us.

I tugged hard on his hair, pulling a groan from his throat that shot straight to my pussy, making me throb with need. And God help me, but I wanted more. With Levi, I'd *always* wanted more.

Before I could make an awful mistake—like climb into his lap and beg him to fuck me right then and there—the ride jerked to a stop. We broke apart, chests heaving and eyes wide as we stared at each other.

Mabel was talking a mile a minute, but I couldn't pay attention to anything she was saying. Not when Levi's eyes bored into mine like he was trying to see into my fucking soul. Not when I was still trying to catch my breath after that kiss.

Not when it felt like we'd just taken a step we could never go back from.

Then, without a word, Levi tore his gaze from mine, shoved the bar off our laps, and stalked off. I sat there stunned, my lips still tingling from his kiss, a riot of emotions churning inside me. And through it all, I could only stare at his retreating form, wondering what the hell I'd just done.

CHAPTER TWELVE

HARPER

I'D MADE plenty of mistakes in my life. That tended to happen when you ventured into adulthood without any guidance. But the mistake I'd just made, losing my head and kissing Levi? The man who'd broken my heart—not just broken it, but demolished it? Well, I couldn't think of anything dumber.

Especially considering I had to *live* with the man for the next five weeks. I was stuck there with nowhere else to go, which meant I was at his mercy.

But worse than all of that was how fucking *good* the kiss had been.

I'd had a lot of years to build up our chemistry in my mind. Inflate it to something far beyond actuality. After a decade of lackluster dating experience, I'd begun to think everything I had felt with Levi had been in my head. That there was no way at fifteen, sixteen, seventeen years old, we'd had the kind of chemistry I hadn't been able to replicate. The kind I'd only read about in romance novels.

But from the second Levi's lips had touched mine again, that assumption was blown out of the water. And I had no idea what the hell to do with that information.

The last thing I wanted to do right now was head back to the apartment, because from Levi's quick, determined strides as he wove ahead of me through the few people remaining at the carnival, that was exactly where he was going. Unfortunately, I didn't have any other options. The carnival was closing, and every business in Starlight Cove had shut its doors for the evening hours ago.

Despite Levi's head start, he strode only a few paces in front of me, both of us heading straight for the exit. Neither of us acknowledging the other. That was fine with me. I needed time and space to process the kiss that never should've happened.

Once we made it to the parking lot, Levi headed to the right and toward a gleaming black-and-chrome motorcycle. Because of course the brooding asshole ex-boyfriend would have a motorcycle. I nearly rolled my eyes at the cliché of it all, but instead, I turned my attention toward the parking lot exit and the walk I had ahead of me. No way was Arthur still up and taking passengers.

"Where the hell are you going?" Levi called after me, drawing the attention of a few passersby.

I glanced back at him, finding his scowl pointed directly at me. "The apartment. Obviously."

"Where's your car?"

"Don't have one."

"So, what? You're just going to walk?" he asked incredulously.

The parking lot was mostly empty, a few scattered cars here and there. It was nearing midnight, but I didn't have any apprehensions of walking the streets of Starlight Cove this late. Mayberry had more crime than this little pocket of Maine.

I shrugged. "That's the plan."

"The fuck you are," he said, voice hard. "Get on. I'll give you a ride."

"I'm good."

He was silent for a moment, but it was the loudest quiet I'd ever heard. "I wasn't asking, Harper."

"Then it's a good thing I don't have to follow your orders."

The rev of his engine cut through the air. And I was absolutely not going to examine the feelings warring inside me, equal parts relief and disappointment that he'd relented. That he hadn't pushed harder. That he'd decided I *did* have it handled...just like always...and didn't need anyone else's assistance.

It was quite the mindfuck because while I definitely took care of my own shit, sometimes I wondered what it'd be like if I didn't have to. If someone else had my back. If I could count on another person to take care of me for no other reason than I deserved it and not because they got something out of it.

I hadn't even made it halfway through the parking lot before Levi's motorcycle rumbled up in front of me, blocking my path, and I stopped dead in my tracks.

He was hot under normal circumstances, to an annoying degree. But him straddling a motorcycle, jaw set, eyes hard as he pinned me with his intense gaze? He should've been a registered crime against humankind. I hated that I remembered exactly what his lips felt like under mine...exactly what his tongue tasted like...the exact tenor of his throaty groan the second I'd opened my mouth to him...

"Get on the bike, Harper," he said, voice low and firm. "We're going to the same place."

I crossed my arms over my chest and met his gaze with an unimpressed expression. "I can walk."

"I never said you couldn't. But it's midnight and you're alone. And I don't give a shit if we live in the most boring town in the country, I'm not just going to drive off and let you walk home by yourself. Now, get on the fucking bike."

I knew by his harsh tone and the steely, determined glint in his eyes that he wasn't going to relent, just like the night of the thunderstorm. Would probably, in fact, ride alongside me the entire way home and throw out taunting jabs just because he could.

So, with a sigh, I relented and strode toward him before gingerly climbing onto the back of his bike, sitting as far back as possible.

Levi passed a helmet to me over his shoulder. "Put this on."

"What about you?"

"Just put on the fucking helmet, sparrow."

With a sigh, I did as he told me before gripping the handle behind my seat, preparing myself to hold on tight so I didn't shift forward. It was bad enough that my legs bracketed his, especially considering the fact that I could feel the heat from his body seeping into mine. And especially considering the state of my pussy after that kiss. I needed to hold myself as far away from him as I possibly could.

He revved the engine and glanced back at me over his shoulder. "Hang on."

"I am."

I felt more than heard his sigh before he reached back and grabbed my arm, tugging it free from the handle and wrapping it around himself. I didn't give myself even a second to register what his body felt like beneath my fingers before I snatched my hand away, placing it back on the bar. "I'm good like this."

He glanced at me over his shoulder, his mouth set in a firm line, the tic of his jaw letting me know exactly what he thought of me and this line I'd drawn in the sand. Probably futile since he'd had his tongue in my mouth ten minutes ago, but I knew my limits. Wrapping my arms around him and holding tight was well past them.

This time when he revved the engine, we shot forward before he braked hard, effectively shoving me against his back. I let out a small squeak and wrapped my arms around him reflexively. And then before I even realized what he'd done, he took off like a bat out of hell. Tearing out of the parking lot and pointing us toward the main road that led here, his little tap on the outside of my thigh the punctuation to his silent *then I'll make you.*

Because of the space needed for the carnival, it was set up on the outskirts of town. Still, Starlight Cove wasn't exactly a metropolis and wasn't super spread out. We should've been back to the apartment in five minutes, but from my not-at-all-accurate calculations, it had been more than double that as Levi took the road along the coast rather than cutting straight into town.

And through it all, I held on tight, Levi's body warm and firm against me.

The full moon glittered on the surface of the ocean, the sound of crashing waves drowned out by the purr of the engine. The smell of the salty air combined with the scent of Levi made it easy to revert back in time. To the summers when it had felt as if we had nothing but forever stretched out in front of us. Nothing but possibilities.

I closed my eyes and allowed myself this moment when no one else was watching. I melted into his back, wrapping my arms more tightly around him, and imagined what life would be like if everything had been different.

There was no denying how good he felt against me, every

inch of my body pressed against every inch of his. The solid warmth of him reassuring in a way that had no place here.

Because I already knew what was on the other side of anything when it came to Levi. Pure and absolute heartbreak.

And there was no fucking way I was venturing down that path again.

CHAPTER THIRTEEN

LEVI

AS I SLID my key into the lock and gingerly opened the apartment door, I held my breath and listened for sounds of life inside. I exhaled in relief when nothing but silence greeted me, thankful for the reprieve, however brief it was. I knew it wouldn't last forever. It'd been a couple days, but eventually, I'd have to come face-to-face with Harper after that kiss on the Ferris wheel and the ride on my motorcycle.

I knew when I did, I'd have to fight the overwhelming urge to do it all over again. To feel her lips under mine, the soft glide of her tongue against my own... Listen to those breathy little moans and the tiny gasps that said she was loving every second of it. How, when we'd been riding, her arms had tightened around me, her hand pressed flat against my chest, right over my heart. As if she was commanding it to beat solely for her.

And that was exactly the kind of shit I couldn't be thinking about. Not when it came to Harper.

I tossed my keys on the counter and flicked the door closed behind me. Except instead of shutting, the door bounced back and smacked me in the arm. "What the fuck?"

Mabel poked her head through the open doorway. "Oh good, honey, you're home!"

"Would it have mattered if I wasn't?" I asked dryly. "We both know you would've just let yourself in."

She shot me an unrepentant smile and shrugged, as if to say *Yeah, probably.* "You forgot your teddy bear the other night when you ran off like your pants were on fire."

On reflex, I grabbed the stuffed animal Mabel pressed into my chest before tossing it on the counter. "You could've given it to one of the kids there. What the hell am I going to do with it?"

"I don't know, but I wasn't about to give your bear away. Especially when Harper won it for you."

"How do you know that?"

"Please, I heard about it three minutes after it happened. Don't underestimate the whisper network."

"You mean the gossips who have nothing better to do than talk about me and Harper?"

"Speaking of Harper..." Mabel said, shifting the conversation without remorse. She not so subtly glanced around at the space, as if hoping my temptation also known as my roommate was going to pop up from behind the counter. "I come bearing gifts to apologize for the little...*misunderstanding*...last week."

"Misunderstanding?" I leaned back against the counter, crossing my arms as I leveled her with a stare. "You mean when you invited someone to move in to my apartment without talking to me about it?"

"Yes, well, I'm sorry about that."

"So, you'll make her leave, then?" A boulder landed heavily in my gut as soon as the words left my lips. Like most everything else when it came to Harper, I ignored it.

Mabel scoffed and swatted a hand through the air. "Heavens no. But I did bring you cookies to wipe that grouchy look off your face." She held out a plastic container between us, as if she were presenting me with bars of gold.

Truth be told, she wasn't far off. Her cookies were fucking amazing, and she knew it. Knew she could get away with murder if she baked up a batch of these in apology. She pulled off the lid and wafted the container under my nose with a flourish. The cookies smelled delicious like always, but I froze when I got a good look at them.

"Mabel." I split my gaze between her serene face and the phallic-shaped cookies, overemphasized in their lewdness. "You didn't bring me cookies. You brought me dicks."

I couldn't even say I was surprised. When it came to this woman, *nothing* surprised me. For years, she'd been peddling her sex toys at the town festivals and markets, in her smut shack, and in the resort's parlor when she hosted book club, so I was used to her brand of eccentricity. What did surprise me, however, was the glittering silver cross on the head of the cock cookies.

I lifted my chin toward the treats. "What's that on the end of them?"

"Oh, that." Mabel cleared her throat and averted her gaze. "It's for your, ah, *accessory*."

And of course, because God or the universe or whoever was in charge of my fucked-up, useless life hated me, Harper chose that moment to walk out of her bedroom. "What accessory?"

As if she'd been invited to the conversation in the first place, she strolled right up to us, reached into the container, and plucked out one of the dicks. Her brows lifted as she got a better look at it.

I ignored her as best I could and narrowed my eyes on Mabel and her angelic face, which was the biggest facade I'd ever seen in my life. "How the hell do you even know about that?"

The older woman sniffed and straightened her shoulders. "Never underestimate the dedication of a journalist. Especially when it comes to penises. I'm sure Harper can regale you with stories while you snack on these." She grinned and shoved the plastic container into my hands.

"Are there walnuts in these?" I asked.

Harper shot me a surprised glance before wiping the expression clear from her face, looking to Mabel for a response.

"The cookies are clear of walnuts," Mabel confirmed. "Well, I'll leave you kids to it. Have fun!"

Before I could say anything in return, she scurried out of the apartment, the door shutting behind her with finality. And then it was just Harper and me in this too-small space, a dozen dicks between us, and the memory of our kiss haunting me. My body had no qualms about reminding me of that fact. It hummed with awareness, just like it always did when she was near.

Harper shook her head as she studied the cookie in her hand. "I don't get it. Why is there a cross on the—" Her words cut off abruptly as she snapped her eyes to mine. Then she let her gaze drop down my body until it rested on the front of my jeans.

I didn't know whether the lift of her brows was shock or interest, and I sure as hell had no intention of finding out. Except the traitorous bastard she was currently focused on twitched behind my fly, eager and fucking aching for any crumb of attention she gave it. Especially after the brief taste I'd had the other night.

But those feelings didn't belong here, and they definitely didn't belong between the two of us. Harper and I were nothing. By design.

By *my* design.

And I intended to keep it that way.

That meant I needed to squash whatever flicker of interest I still held for her before it sparked into an inferno. The night at the carnival had proven it wouldn't take much. She'd kissed me back with just as much urgency as I had. She'd held me just as tightly as I'd ached for her to.

And that was exactly the problem.

If she wasn't going to push me away, firmly, forcefully, and without hesitation, I had to do it for her. Or everything I'd done all those years ago would be for nothing.

I stepped into her space and leaned close. So close, her scent invaded my nose and my dick got even harder. She straightened, feigning aloofness, but I could tell she wasn't as immune to our proximity as she'd like me to believe. After the carnival, there was no misjudging her tells. No misunderstanding that this attraction wasn't one-sided.

Dipping my head, I inhaled deeply and traced my nose along the curve of her shoulder and up her neck without ever touching her skin. Her breaths came out in soft pants against my cheek, a rosy flush spreading down her neck and across her chest.

With my lips brushing her ear, I murmured, "If I tell you the secret, will you get on your knees and pray to it, sparrow?"

If I hadn't been so close to her, I would've missed the hitch in her breath. How, for a split second, she stopped breathing entirely, her body reacting to my words or my nearness or *me* before she could squash it.

Same as mine did.

But just as quickly as that reaction came, she shoved it down and stepped back. Away from me. That cool, aloof mask slipped back into place as she regarded me with disinterest.

"I'm not much for praying." With her eyes locked on mine,

she lifted the cookie to her mouth. "And I'll never get on my knees for you."

Then, without another word, she bit the head of the dick clean off before spinning on her heel and stalking back to her bedroom.

CHAPTER FOURTEEN

HARPER

Text thread with Mabel, Harper, and Levi:

5:57 p.m.

MABEL:

Don't eat the cookies! I REPEAT: DO NOT EAT
THE COOKIES!!! I mixed up my containers and
gave you the ones that were supposed to be for
book club!

MABEL:

Hello?

MABEL:

HELLO??

MY BODY FELT relaxed and heavy, like my mattress was a
cloud I could sink straight into and never leave. Except for one
thing—I was starving. But that wasn't remotely adequate to

describe what I was feeling. This uncontrollable need to inhale anything. *Everything.* Immediately.

As soon as I'd bitten off the bejeweled head of one of Mabel's peen cookies, I'd gone straight to my room and sequestered myself away. It was safer that way. I didn't want to chance being in a small space alone with Levi. Not after the other night. And definitely not after earlier in the kitchen when he'd once again proven he didn't need to kiss me to make me lose my mind. Apparently, he could do that with a whisper of a touch and a handful of words, perfectly illustrating just how potent our chemistry still was. He'd easily had me conjuring up exactly what he'd suggested—me on my knees before him, worshipping his cock with my hands and my mouth.

My nipples tightened, my pussy thrumming with a need that had, frustratingly, never been present with anyone but Levi. Whether I wanted it to or not, my body responded to his soft, seductive tone and those weighted stares that made me feel like he saw straight through me. Made me feel like he *knew* me, though that was impossible. He didn't know me. Not anymore. Maybe not ever.

After our little encounter, I'd locked myself away with no intention of leaving, despite the fact that I hadn't eaten anything all night but a dick cookie. My stomach was reminding me of that now, loudly and uncontrollably.

Usually I kept a couple protein bars in my bag for instances like this. I'd traveled enough that I'd learned I didn't want to be stuck somewhere without sustenance. But I'd eaten them on my travel day from hell and hadn't replenished yet, which meant my room was barren.

But the kitchen wasn't.

I tiptoed my way across my room before cracking open my door and poking my head out, glancing both ways to make sure the coast was clear. When I didn't hear or see anything, certain Levi was tucked away in his bedroom, I crept out into the hall before beelining straight for the kitchen, my stomach rumbling the entire time.

I started at one end and worked my way around the space, opening and closing cupboards and drawers without much care or delicacy, but I was ravenous now. Too starved to think of anything but finding some snacks. Brownies or pretzels or crackers or chips. *God*, I really wanted some chips. If I didn't find a bag in the next fifteen seconds, I was going to—

"Need something, sparrow?" Levi's low, controlled voice startled a scream out of me, and I whirled around, launching a potholder at his head.

It smacked him in the chest before sliding down and presumably landing on the floor. But I couldn't drag my gaze away from the devil himself to verify.

He stood in the entryway to the kitchen, one shoulder propped against the wall, his massive arms crossed over his bare chest. And holy shit, had I ever seen anything so mouthwatering? His chest, dusted with dark hair, was thick and broad, his arms sculpted with the same ridiculous muscles and covered in ink that sure as hell hadn't been there twelve years ago.

Back then, he'd been a bit lanky. Still cute in the mysterious bad boy kind of way, but nothing like the imposing man standing before me now.

Full sleeves covered both his arms up to his shoulders, other tattoos scattered up his sides and on his chest, an amalgamation of objects so perfectly blended together, it was hard to pull apart any single image. Part of me wanted to stroll right up to him and inspect each design. Study their shapes and dissect their meanings, demand he tell me what each one signified. Trace each delicate line with my fingers before using my tongue to see if he tasted as good as I remembered.

And the other part of me wanted to run away screaming, yearning for any amount of separation I could force between us. But that wasn't going to work forever. Especially when I was stuck here, living with him for the time being, and we both needed to figure out how to deal with it. How to be in the same space without screaming at each other or shoving our tongues down each other's throats.

So instead of doing either of those things, I planted my feet and stood my ground, pretending I wasn't standing before him in my far-too-skimpy pajamas and attempting to give off an air of confidence I certainly didn't feel. Never mind that my gaze continued its perusal of his body, sweeping over every carved inch of him before snagging on the indecently low waistband of his gray sweatpants. A shadow of hair at the bottom of his happy trail peeked out, catching my attention—he was *definitely* going commando—before my eyes dipped lower still.

It was then that I recalled exactly what had shut me into my room in the first place. My gaze caught on the nearly obscene outline of his cock, and I squinted one eye, wishing for my X-ray vision to finally manifest. Over the years, I'd had more than enough dreams featuring his dick to remember it. That had been twelve long years ago, though, and I wondered what it looked like now with a piercing through the tip. And God help me, but I wondered what it would *feel* like, too.

My breath grew shallow, thinking of what he was hiding beneath his sweatpants—good God, did it *move*? And somehow, despite all my reservations, despite knowing what a monumentally bad idea it would be...desperately wanting it. Wanting *him*.

"Well?" Levi's voice was low and rough, the single syllable

sounding like it was scraped straight from his throat. "You want to tell me what you need?"

His words sent awareness rocketing through my body, my nipples tightening into stiff peaks, and I was absolutely *not* going to give him the satisfaction of seeing that. Of knowing how much he affected me. How much he *still* affected me.

And definitely not after I'd made a fool out of myself during that kiss on the Ferris wheel, practically throwing myself at him.

I cleared my throat, the sound far too loud in the otherwise silent space, and crossed my arms over my chest. Lifting my chin, I regarded him with what I hoped passed for a bored expression. "Chips. I need chips."

He studied me for a moment. Long enough that I started to shift on my feet, my body tingling at his undivided attention. And then he pushed off from the wall, dropping his arms to his sides as he stalked toward me. His eyes were dark and hungry, focused on me in a way that made it difficult to look away. He was all confidence and swagger, his presence taking up far more of the space than his body did. And I couldn't deny how attractive I found it. How attractive I found *him*.

Not trusting myself, I twisted away from his approaching form, as much to hide my reaction as to force myself to stop ogling him. I faced the cabinets, rummaging through them once more to no avail. And then he stepped up behind me, the heat of his body seeping into mine and his crisp, clean scent surrounding me. His warm skin brushed against mine where I was bare, and I cursed myself for thinking it was a good idea to come strolling out here in nothing more than a tank top and a pair of lounge shorts. Like I was in my own apartment or hotel room where I didn't have to worry about anyone else.

But I *did* have to worry.

I had to worry about Levi and this damn pull between us

that wouldn't fucking go away. This incessant hum beneath my skin that just wouldn't quiet. The undeniable reactions my body still had to him.

He braced one hand on the counter next to my hip. With his other arm, he reached into the cabinet in front of me, effectively caging me in. His scent surrounded me, the warmth of him seeping into my bones. I didn't move...didn't dare even breathe. Afraid that the slightest shift would press more of my body against his when it already felt like I was on fire.

It didn't matter, though, because *he* moved. Even with my eyes closed, I could sense him there, his face dipping closer to mine. His breaths swept over the exposed skin of my shoulder and across my collarbone, and my entire body broke out in goose bumps, my breathing growing ragged. I curled my fingers over the edge of the counter, hoping my grip would ground me when it felt like my entire body was at risk of floating away.

I couldn't make sense of what he was doing, unsure where I ended and he began or why he was standing so close, his breath against the back of my neck, the fine wisps of hair at my nape fluttering with each one of his exhales.

"I've got exactly what you need, sparrow." His voice was low in my ear, sinful like melted dark chocolate, and I had to bite my lip to stifle a moan, unwilling to let it escape.

My clit throbbed, my pussy clenching around nothing as he revved me up with little more than a handful of words and only the tease of his touch. God, what would it feel like to be with him like that again? To get lost in his body. See if my memories had overinflated everything or if it really was as good as I remembered.

A loud crinkling jerked me out of my daze, and I snapped my eyes open to find him holding a bright-yellow bag of chips in front of me. It was a bucket of ice water dumped over my head, a harsh shove back into reality. I exhaled sharply, feeling so fucking stupid for allowing myself to get lost in the pull that was Levi.

I knew better. And I needed to act like it.

Without thinking twice, I snatched the bag from his grasp and shoved my ass back against him, the move pulling a sharp grunt from him. And while that would've been satisfying under normal circumstances, I was distracted by the feel of him against my ass. Thick and hard and ready for me.

This was a bad idea. *Such* a fucking bad idea. To be this close to him when I was feeling so loose and languid, my body warm and soft for some reason I couldn't explain.

Without a word, I strode out of the kitchen, needing some room to breathe. The old Harper would have retreated into her room, tucked herself away, and hidden. Been quiet. Docile.

But I wasn't the old Harper anymore.

I'd lived that life for eighteen years. Had compressed myself to fit every narrow expectation my parents had of me. Had contorted myself to be who they saw fit for public consumption.

A glimpse of the Harper I was today had shone through during my years of friendship with Chase and Levi, back when we'd been kids. But it had been only small peeks, tiny sparks of who I would eventually become.

It was time Levi learned I wasn't the old me anymore.

So, I didn't slink away. I didn't tiptoe down the hall and retreat into my bedroom. I took up space.

I sauntered into the living room, turned on the television, and sat right in the middle of the couch, uncaring as he watched me from the kitchen. *Wanting* him to. I needed him to see I wasn't going to hide away like he probably assumed.

I needed him to see exactly who he was playing with now.

CHAPTER FIFTEEN

LEVI

I STOOD stock-still in the kitchen, gripping the edge of the counter so hard my knuckles turned white. Harper sat in my living room, making herself at home as she scrolled through the options on TV, ignoring me as best she could. Eventually, she settled on a teen drama Addison had been begging me to watch for months and curled up with the open chip bag in her lap, looking more at ease than I'd seen her since she arrived.

Half of me was tempted to follow after her, push her buttons a little bit more, because witnessing that fire in her eyes got my dick hard. The other half knew it was a bad idea all around, and it would be best if I retreated to my room. Reinforced those walls I'd gotten really fucking good at using as a shield, especially when it came to her.

So, of course, because I was a fucking idiot, I pretended to get lost in the show.

But really, I was lost in her.

I couldn't tear my eyes away, finally allowing myself to study her without restraint. Her hair was piled on top of her head in a messy knot, and that only accentuated the long line of her neck and her mostly bare shoulders, save for tiny straps I could bite straight through if given the chance.

I watched, transfixed, as she popped a chip into her mouth while absent-mindedly pushing a wayward strand of hair behind her ear. It was a familiar gesture I'd seen her do a thousand times before, and it made me ache for what we used to have. For what we'd never have again.

Though more than a decade had passed since we'd been together and she'd changed by leaps and bounds, she was still the most beautiful woman I'd ever laid eyes on. And my gut twisted at the realization that she'd never truly be mine again.

Against my better judgment, I abandoned my spot in the kitchen and wandered toward her, hovering on the other side of the breakfast bar before shifting to stand behind the couch. Still, she didn't look my way, her attention focused on the show playing on-screen. Before I could stop myself or second-guess what I was doing, I sank down next to her on the couch, having no choice since she'd taken the middle cushion.

She didn't say a word, though, from the tiny furrow between her brows, I knew she was aware of my presence. I relaxed back against the cushions, our bare shoulders brushing as I did so, and I could've sworn I heard her breath hitch.

This was a bad fucking idea. Especially when, thanks to this languid feeling spreading through my body, I was about ninety-nine percent sure we were high. Mabel had laced our cookies and then run off to let us deal with the fallout like the conniving old bat she was.

I hadn't been high in ten years—for the same reason I didn't allow myself to get well and truly drunk anymore. I didn't deserve the reprieve. Didn't deserve to escape my thoughts...to not be weighed down by the grief that was like an anchor around my neck. But I couldn't go back in time and not eat those cookies, so there was nothing to be done about this than to ride it out.

Halfway through the first episode of this show that wasn't half bad, I reached over and grabbed a handful of chips. Then I shot her a look out of the corner of my eye, wondering how she was going to take the news. "You know we're high, right?"

She snapped her head in my direction, all pretense of her ignoring me long gone. Her eyes were wide as she stared at me openmouthed. "We're *what*?"

"High as fuck," I confirmed with a nod. "The cookies were laced."

"Oh my God." She exhaled sharply, sinking even farther into the couch. "Oh my *God*."

"Yep."

"I've never been high before." She glanced over at me, her brows raised. "What do we do now?"

I could think of a hundred things I *wanted* to do. Lean over and kiss her again, for one. Brush my fingers along all that bare skin, see if it was as soft as it looked. As soft as I remembered. I wanted to drop to my knees, spread her legs wide, and feast on her cunt until she screamed my name. Wanted to sink so deep inside her there was no longer her and me. There was only *us*.

Instead, I shoved those thoughts aside and shrugged. "Watch some mindless TV and eat whatever shit we can find until the high wears off."

———

SOMEHOW, when we hadn't been rummaging through the kitchen for whatever else we could find to eat, we'd shifted positions. Sinking deeper and deeper into the couch, and subsequently melting closer and closer together. As if no time at all had passed since we'd been together. As if doing so was as natural as breathing.

And now, my head was in Harper's lap, her fingers tangled in my hair, and my hand was curled around her bare thigh. Like that was exactly how we were supposed to be.

We were on episode three of *One Tree Hill*, and we hadn't yet killed each other. Hadn't succumbed to an explosive make-out session, either, which I wasn't sure if I was relieved or frustrated about.

Every once in a while, she'd giggle at something on the show, letting out a little snort as she did so. And the sound was so familiar, an ache set up residence in my chest, a painful reminder of what we'd once had.

"So, have you always been addicted to teen dramedies, or is this a new affliction?"

I snorted and shook my head. "If I tell you that, you're sworn to secrecy."

She leaned forward, bringing her face closer to mine, her features upside down from where I was lying. Her scent enveloped me, and I wanted to stay here forever. Wanted to be with her for whatever bit of this life I had left.

"Who am I going to tell?" she asked, brow raised.

"That's not a promise."

"Fine." She rolled her eyes. "I promise."

I breathed out a heavy sigh and grumbled, "It's all Addison's fault. The little demon got me hooked on *Vampire Diaries*."

Harper let out a bark of laughter before falling into a fit of giggles, tipping sideways until she was draped over me. Her giggles were a sound I hadn't heard from her in more than a decade. I couldn't stop the answering smile from sweeping across my mouth as she laughed until she was gasping, tears streaming down her face.

After long moments, she let out a few soft chuckles and settled back into the couch. Then she ran her fingers through my hair, admitting softly, "I missed hanging out with you like this."

I knew it was just the high talking. Never in a million years would she have said that otherwise. But I wanted to pretend that wasn't it. Pretend everything was fine and this was normal. This was just our life.

This could have been our life.

"Do you remember the night we snuck into Old Man Davey's orchard?" she asked.

A lazy grin swept over my mouth as I recalled the memory. "I think you probably ate half a dozen peaches before he came storming out of his house. He was so pissed, waving his cane around and shouting about calling the sheriff if we didn't get the hell off his property."

"I've never run so fast in my life," Harper said on a laugh. "I would've been caught for sure if you hadn't been there to drag me out behind you."

"If I hadn't been there, you wouldn't have done it in the first place."

"True. You always did have a knack for getting me into trouble. But I still owe you thanks for saving my ass that time."

"You paid it. When I helped you sneak up the trellis outside your bedroom window, you leaned out and kissed me." I remembered it perfectly, as if it had happened last week instead of nearly fifteen years ago. "I swear, you tasted like peaches. I still can't eat one without my dick getting hard."

Harper tightened her fingers in my hair, her lips parting as she stared down at me. Happiness and what looked an awful lot like longing passed in her eyes, but both were gone in a blink. Then, as if the moment had never happened, she cleared her throat and averted her attention back to the TV. "I'm not the same person I was back then. I want you to know that. You had a hold over me when we were younger, and you crushed me when you broke things off. But I haven't given anyone that kind of power since. And I have no intention of starting now."

As another episode started, Harper's words settled over me, a stark reminder of exactly what I'd done to her. Exactly how my choices had shaped her into the person she was today—a person I didn't even know. A person I didn't *deserve* to know. Not after the things I'd done.

CHAPTER SIXTEEN

LEVI

Text thread with Mabel, Harper, and Levi:

5:57 p.m.

MABEL:

Don't eat the cookies! I REPEAT: DO NOT EAT THE COOKIES!!! I mixed up my containers and gave you the ones that were supposed to be for book club!

MABEL:

Hello?

MABEL:

HELLO??

Text thread with Mabel, Harper, Levi:

8:18 a.m.

LEVI:

Do you always make pot-laced replicas of my junk for your book club?

MABEL:

Oh no! You ate them?? How bad was it?

HARPER:

It wasn't great, Mabel.

MABEL:

Oh dear. You, too?? This was an honest to God accident. I swear!

HARPER:

You better hope I don't have to take a drug test for my job.

MABEL:

What is it the kids say? My bad? At least you two are agreeing on something!

I HADN'T SEEN Mabel's warning texts until this morning, but I wasn't sure they would've mattered. Even knowing how dangerous it was, I hadn't been able to stay away from Harper last night. Not after inhaling two of those cookies and stumbling upon her in the kitchen wearing a tiny tank top and even tinier shorts, her ass and those thick hips and thighs making my mouth water.

Like, *literally* made my mouth water.

She'd always had that pull on me, though. Not just her body, but *her*. From day fucking one, and that hadn't changed. Not with time and not with distance. Not even with a whole pile of lies between us.

But that was exactly why I'd forced myself to retreat last night before more damage could be done. I'd made an excuse and bailed in the middle of episode four. She might've only opened up to me like that because she'd been high, but I damn well knew she was telling the truth.

The walls I'd erected years ago were crumbling after only a few short *days*, and we still had five weeks together. I needed to get my head on straight, and I needed to do it immediately so I didn't revert to the idiot I'd been back then.

Thank God I had my workshop to escape to because I wasn't in any position to be around other people right now. This space was my sanctuary and always had been since Chase and I had started coming here as teens, apprenticing for my mentor before he'd hung up his hat for good. No matter what bullshit was going on in my life, I knew I'd be able to escape here.

I ran my sander along the hull of the thirty-foot Bayliner, smoothing out the rough edges left from shaping the wood. The rhythmic back-and-forth motion allowed my mind to blank as I lost myself in this work I loved so much. The one steady thing I'd had over the past decade-plus.

The warehouse door opened, and someone came strolling in like they owned the fucking place. From where I was working, I couldn't see them, but I didn't have to to know it was my best friend. No one else besides his wife dared to enter my workshop unannounced or without an appointment. And Addison's toddler-sized legs had no hope of sounding like the long, casual strides Chase was currently taking.

My back was to him as I continued sanding the hull of the boat, and I didn't bother turning around or greeting him. I knew he was here for something, so I just waited for him to speak.

Though, when he did, I wished I'd steered the conversation in a different direction entirely, cutting this off at the pass before it could even begin.

"*So.*" He dragged out the word, a note of amusement in his tone. "I hear you ate some uniquely shaped cookies last night that may or may not but definitely were laced with some good old Mary Jane."

Hanging my head, I blew out a long, weary sigh and closed my eyes. Was it too fucking much to ask for some goddamn privacy in this town? "Who else knows?"

"If I had to guess?" Chase pulled over a chair and flipped it around, sitting in it backward. "The entirety of Starlight Cove and probably those in a twenty-five-mile radius. Thankfully, Mabel didn't do a Live about it because she knew she'd have Brady up her ass if she did."

"Silver linings," I said dryly. "That why you're here?"

"I'm here for two reasons, actually."

"And I bet I'm not going to like either of them."

Chase continued as if I hadn't spoken. "First of all, *two* piercings? Jesus, man. You lost a bet to Ford and still decided not to quit at just one? You had to go and be extra and pierce a fucking cross into the head of your dick?"

I slid him a look out of the corner of my eye. "You really came over here to talk about my dick?"

Chase barked out a laugh and shook his head. "Just curious, is all. Maybe I should get one. Wonder if Addi—"

"Nope." I stabbed a finger in his direction and shot him a glare. "We're not doing *that.* As long as it doesn't have to do with you getting dick jewelry to satisfy my sister, tell me why you're here."

His grin widened before he cleared his throat, the tiny furrow between his brows belying his concern. "I came to find out how you and Harper fared spending a night in the same place while stoned out of your minds."

"It was fine," I answered too quickly.

He studied me long enough that I had no doubt he knew I

was lying. That was what three decades of friendship did for a person. "So nothing happened, then?" he asked, unconvinced.

Not exactly. But between the cuddle fest last night and the make-out session on the Ferris wheel over the weekend, absolutely nothing *good* happened. It was all trouble with a capital T.

The smile slowly melted off Chase's face as he stared at me. "Oh shit. That bad?"

"It wasn't good."

"What happened?"

"Which time?"

"*Which time*?" he asked incredulously. "What the fuck do you mean, which time?"

"There was an...incident. At the carnival." I cleared my throat. "On the Ferris wheel."

Chase snapped his gaze to mine, his brows raised in a silent question.

With a sigh, I admitted, "We just made out a little."

"Oh, is that all?"

"And last night..." Well, last night was far, far worse. It was one thing to still be attracted to each other. To have chemistry that arced between us, fueled by hate on her end and a never-ending gravitation on mine. It was another thing altogether to fall right back into that comfort and familiarity we used to have. That was downright dangerous. "Look, it doesn't matter. But both instances are enough to know I can't have her in my home for five more weeks." I sighed and scrubbed a hand over my face. "I need to figure out how to get her the fuck out. And I need your help to do it."

"Whoa." He held up his hands and leaned back. "Don't pull me into this. I love you both. You know that. But the shit between you two is between *you two*."

I glared at him. "You're *my* best fucking friend. Now, quit bullshitting me and *help*. I need her gone, Chase. Or all we're going to do is hurt each other, over and over."

He must have noticed the desperation I tried valiantly to hide because he stared at me for long moments before blowing out a sigh. "Fine. You want to make her leave? Just do something that makes her uncomfortable. So much so that staying is no longer an option."

That made sense, but it seemed too tame for what I needed to happen immediately. Especially when it felt like she and I were one bad decision away from implosion. I didn't have time to dance around this. To wait for her to come to her senses and get the hell out. I needed her gone. Immediately. Fucking yesterday.

Which meant I was going to have to play to win.

CHAPTER SEVENTEEN

HARPER

A FEW DAYS following the events I refused to think about—if only I could get my dreams to cooperate—I was downstairs in *Starlight Cove Gazette*'s office. Being in this space was like stepping back in time. The office was a fairly good size, with exposed brick walls and a tin ceiling. It held two large desks, one of which still contained an old typewriter, and a row of black metal filing cabinets along the far wall. An abandoned fax machine sat in the corner next to an outdated, oversized copy machine.

It wasn't the fanciest office I'd ever worked in by far, but it was quiet and quaint. Mabel also always had a fresh pot of coffee brewed and waiting for me, even when she wasn't here to greet me. And you couldn't put a price on that.

But most importantly, Levi was nowhere in the vicinity. And apparently, that was exactly what my traitorous body needed. Especially after our first week of living together. We'd experienced more in that short time than I'd intended to in the entirety of my stay in Starlight Cove. It was time to reinforce my walls, because they were a little too close to crumbling for my comfort.

While I could work from anywhere, doing so at the public spaces in town opened me up to the possibility that I'd inadvertently run into him while I was there. Worse was attempting to work in the apartment. Especially after the kiss on the Ferris wheel. And really fucking especially after whatever the hell that was when we'd been high. Laughing? *Cuddling*? I'd never been high before, but surely that wasn't normal. I had clearly lost my damn mind, and he wasn't far behind.

The constant anticipation of his possible arrival at home was enough to derail my creative flow. Not to mention, my mind kept drifting to the other night anytime I caught sight of the couch. My focus was shit, and that made it incredibly difficult to get any work done. And my work was the entire reason I was here in Starlight Cove in the first place. The whole reason I was stuck with Levi as a roommate. I couldn't allow myself to forget that.

The front door to the *Gazette* opened, the bells on the doorknob jingling and dragging me out of my thoughts.

"Oh good!" Mabel shot me a grin and strode toward me. She wore a bright-purple T-shirt that read *Blow me* with a picture of a dandelion and carried a plastic container in her hand. "Just the person I wanted to see."

I minimized the search engine window and turned in my chair to face her. "Morning, Mabel. What can I do for you?"

"I wanted to apologize for the little...*mix-up* the other night."

I raised a brow at her. "And what mix-up would that be?"

She glanced over both shoulders as if checking for witnesses, then turned back to me. Leaning forward, she dropped her voice into a low whisper as if we weren't the only two people in the building. "The *marijuana* cookies. I swear to high heaven, it was a mistake! But I hope everything worked out okay between you and Levi. You weren't too uncomfortable, were you?"

While it had been happening? No, I hadn't been uncomfortable. The scary part was I didn't know if it had been the effects of the weed or if it was just that easy to fall back into that comfort, that familiarity with Levi again. But there was no denying it had been.

And I couldn't—wouldn't—take the chance on it happening again. Not while I was here. Not ever.

He'd put me through the wringer once in my life, and that was more than enough. I'd lost my family, my boyfriend, and my two best friends in a single swoop. In the blink of an eye, I'd lost *everything*. Chase and I hadn't reconnected until a couple years later. Which meant I'd been well and truly alone during the hardest time of my life.

Whether through self-preservation or intention, I'd continued on the same way in the years since. I'd never experienced another friendship like I'd had with those two. Even Chase's and my friendship hadn't recovered completely.

But more importantly, I'd never opened myself up to another *relationship* like I'd had with Levi. I had no intention of subjecting myself to that kind of pain ever again. Even a single night was rare. It was just easier to take care of my needs myself than it was to welcome someone into my life so intimately. Especially when I'd learned the hard way that a partner as unselfish...as hungry for me as Levi had once been wasn't the norm.

"It was fine, Mabel," I said. "No big deal. But I'd appreciate it if the next time you brought me cookies, they weren't laced *or* replicas of Levi's penis."

Because God knew I didn't need any reminders. My dreams were already off the rails with little hope of being reined in.

"Of course, dear! What are your thoughts on vulvas? I'm

trying out a new cookie cutter for book club and wanted to bring a batch by as an apology."

"For your apology?" I asked dryly.

"You could say that." She placed the container on the desk and lifted the lid, showcasing pink-frosted vulva cookies, in a dozen different shades, shapes, and sizes. "I figure if I pass these around enough, it'll be subliminal messaging for the men in town to go *downtown* a bit more, if you catch my drift. Would you believe most of the women who come to my pleasure parties say their fellas don't ever do that particular deed? Hogwash, I tell you."

What I did *not* need to be thinking about was someone going down on me. Especially when the last person to do it with any kind of hunger, finesse, or skill had been Levi. No doubt thanks to the years before we'd finally had sex, when we'd practiced by doing *everything but.*

"That's...altruistic of you."

"Look, honey, *everyone* should be having good sex. It makes for happier people, and the world could do with as much of that as possible, don't you think?" She lifted the container toward me. "Well, go on. You need sustenance since you've been working so hard down here this week."

"No walnuts?"

"No, ma'am. The only nuts I used were on Levi's cookies." Mabel cackled at her own joke, and I couldn't help but smile along as she gestured for me to take a cookie. "How are things coming? Any chance you want to spill what you're working on? You know, one journalist to another."

I grabbed a treat from the container, a smirk playing on my lips. While I absolutely held journalistic confidentiality to the utmost regard, what I was here for wasn't exactly a secret, especially at this point in my process. "I'm obviously planning to showcase Starlight Cove, but I think the slant I'm going to take is focusing on the *secret* of Starlight Cove. Why this tiny little town attracts so many famous people, both as permanent and seasonal residents."

"That's a wonderful idea! When Chase moved back, I mentioned how amazing it was that we had two famous people residing in town, both him and Aiden." Mabel leaned toward me conspiratorially. "But it didn't start with them, you know."

I perked up, sitting a little straighter in my seat. While I'd found a few others so far in my research—a Nobel Prize winner, an astronaut, and an Olympic gold medalist—I was interested in whatever details Mabel could give me. She'd lived here her whole life and was a wealth of information on the town, not to mention the people who resided in it. I held up my phone between us. "You mind if I record this?"

"Of course not, honey. Let's see, there's old Gil Jacobson. His blueberry pie won 'Best Pie in New England' five years running back in the '90s. Best I've ever had, and that's the God's honest truth. And Kelly Kramer has the largest collection of ceramic cats in the whole state! Where she's found room for 517 of those, I'll never know." Mabel shook her head and chuckled. "Oh! Can't forget about Vincent Prattle. He grows the biggest zucchini you've ever seen, damn near the size of a small dog. He used to win first prize at the state fair every year. But they finally had to ban him from entering a couple years ago just to give someone else a chance."

With every objectively non-famous person Mabel ticked off, I sank back into my chair as disappointment crept in. While my editor hadn't explicitly laid out what the focus of this article should be—had, in fact, told me to run with it however I saw fit —I wanted this piece to be something special. Something different from a run-of-the-mill article about a beautiful town on the coast. There were already hundreds, maybe even thousands, of those same stories that could be told at any number of locations across the country. I wanted this to be uniquely Starlight Cove.

Besides that, I knew if I gave the article a spin that kept people reading, my chances at that permanent position increased exponentially.

I tried not to let the disappointment show on my face, knowing I still had several weeks to do my own research, but I couldn't help but be let down. Mabel's testimony could have given me a jump-start on my findings or, at least, pointed me in the right direction.

"—and those goats...I tell you what, they deserved every single one of those ribbons!"

I offered her a forced smile. "I have no doubt they did. Thanks for this information, Mabel. I'm not sure I'll need to use much"—*or any*—"of it, but I appreciate your insight."

"No problem at all, honey." Mabel's eyes brightened as she shot me a wide smile. "Oh! I almost forgot to mention Stan."

"Who's Stan?"

"You know, *Stan*." She jerked a thumb over her shoulder, gesturing toward the front windows. "As in One Night *Stan*'s, the bar?"

"Wait, that's named after someone?"

Mabel hummed in affirmation. "Oh yes. He was a very popular musician a few decades ago. 'Course, he went by a stage name back then. Now, what was it..." She trailed off, tapping a finger on her lips, then shook her head. "Can't recall, but I'm pretty sure his band won some of those fancy gold records."

Now, that was something I hadn't known. Though I had a tiny flicker of a memory from my first summer here—a concert in the park, maybe? But it was buried too far under decades of other things that it wasn't coming to me immediately.

"That's great. Thanks, Mabel. I'll swing by later this week and chat with Stan."

"Gonna need a lot of luck with that, honey. Nobody's really sure what happened with him. And his boys are pretty tight-lipped, all four of 'em. Let me tell you, they give the McKenzie boys a run for their money in grumpiness. But I know the power of a good journalist. I have all the faith that you can get some good info out of them."

CHAPTER EIGHTEEN

HARPER

AFTER MABEL LEFT, I did some preemptive digging on the owner of One Night Stan's. While I found plenty of info about Stan's time in the limelight with his band, there was next to nothing on his life here in Starlight Cove, bar a few mentions and a couple photos of his family—his beautiful wife and their four sons, all of whom were well into their thirties by now. In fact, all information seemed to stop completely a few years back. And there was nothing I loved more than a mystery to solve.

I'd been so sidetracked with this new path, it was almost seven by the time I headed up to the apartment. Except for the night of the thunderstorm, I usually got home around six every evening and didn't hear Levi come in until well after I'd retreated to my room. I could only hope tonight would be no different.

I wasn't ready to see him yet after what had happened earlier in the week. When we'd melted into each other on the couch. His hand had been cupped protectively, possessively, around my bare thigh, and though the touch hadn't been indecent, it had felt more intimate than anything I'd experienced in a long damn time.

What shook my foundation more than anything, though, was that it had happened with Levi. And that I'd *allowed* it to.

Tentatively, I stepped into the apartment and closed the door softly behind me. At first, nothing was out of the ordinary. It felt still and silent in the space as I locked the door and set down my laptop bag.

At least until that first moan hit my ears.

It was soft. Feminine. And I'd deny until my last dying breath what the thought of Levi here with another woman did to me. All without my awareness or permission. Because cognitively, I didn't care what—or who—he did. We weren't together and hadn't been for what felt like a lifetime. We weren't even friends. Whom he chose to spend his time with—in or out of the bedroom—was of no consequence to me.

So then, why the hell was my stomach seizing, my heart leaping into my throat before bottoming out straight to my feet? Worse was the fact that the moans were too loud to be coming from his bedroom. Which meant he was fucking some random woman in our shared space. And I had no choice but to walk straight past him and his not-so-quiet friend.

Well, fuck him. I wasn't going to scurry away, escape out the front door and come back hours later when he was done. For the next month, this was my home, too, and I wasn't going to let him run me out of it. No matter what the thought of him with someone else did to my insides.

Rolling my shoulders back and straightening my spine, I took a couple deep breaths, steeling myself for what I'd find. And then I strolled into the living room with the sole focus of making it to my bedroom without catching a glimpse of the live porno that was happening in the apartment.

That was until an overexaggerated moan drew my attention as I passed through the living room. It took a moment for my brain to register what I was seeing since it was so incongruent from what my imagination had previously conjured.

Instead of being met with a random woman bent over the couch, head tossed back in pleasure as Levi fucked her from behind, I found him sitting there. Alone. His sweat-pants were pushed down in the front, and his hand was wrapped around his cock. All while porn played on the TV.

My breath caught in my throat at the sight of him stroking himself. I couldn't stop myself from taking in every inch of him. The hair falling carelessly over his heavy-lidded eyes, lips parted with his labored breaths. The tattoos scattered over the carved muscles of his arms, chest, and abdomen, just begging for my touch.

What drew my eye the most, though, was his straining erection as he gripped it in his fist. His cock was thick, long, hard, and so fucking intimidating. Especially with the piercings—yes, plural—through the head.

But what shocked me more than anything wasn't how much bigger he seemed than what I remembered or how different it looked with the new accessory. It was the very unmistakable pair of hot-pink panties clenched in his fist as he stroked up and down the length of his cock. *My* hot-pink panties. I must have dropped them that morning when I'd brought my laundry back to my bedroom.

I'd spent years of my life hating this man. Hating what he'd done to me. And though I still held on to that with a tenuous grip, I couldn't deny my body's reaction to seeing him like this. Knowing he was using some part of me to get off.

I also couldn't deny how much I seemed to like having that

power over him, when it had always felt like he'd been the one in control.

My nipples tightened, and a flush worked its way through my body as I studied each rise and fall of his chest. Each measured stroke of his fist. Each swipe of his thumb over the head of his cock and his answering groans. Then there was the pure hunger written all over his face as he watched me, his gaze never once straying to the porno playing on the TV.

He didn't take his eyes off me, and there was no mistaking the ravenous glint in his gaze as he regarded me. As if he'd been edging himself for an hour, maybe more. As if he'd just been waiting for me to arrive.

It took a moment, but the pieces finally started clicking into place... Him sitting out here in our shared space, watching porn on the TV instead of on his phone, locked away in his room like any self-respecting adult. The panties clutched in his fist. The intense way he was staring at me.

That little fucker. He *wanted* me to find him like this. I just didn't know why.

I crossed my arms, as much to give off an air of indifference as to hide my body's reaction to him. "So this is what we're doing now?"

He shuddered out a breath as he swiped his thumb wrapped in my silk panties over the head of his cock. "I'm not sure what you're doing. I'm just trying to get off."

"With my panties," I said flatly. "In the middle of the living room."

"Looks like. It's my apartment. If you don't like it, you can leave."

There it was. This whole thing was nothing more than a ruse. Just a game of chicken, one in which a win meant pushing me out of this space. But I had no intention of losing, and I was absolutely not leaving.

His gaze traveled over me from head to toe, and I felt it along every single one of those inches. It was just a ghost of a caress, but my body lit up as if it felt his touch. Finally, when he met my eyes again, his were full of so much heat, I had to force my body not to outwardly react. Not when this was obviously just a joke to him.

"Or you can come join me." His voice was low and rough, threaded with a need I would've bet money had been real had I not known what was behind this whole act.

Oh, he was good. Really fucking good. He knew exactly what he was doing, and he was, no doubt, counting on it working.

Except Levi was playing by an old set of rules.

The Harper he'd known back then didn't exist anymore. The one who was naive, sheltered, and subservient. The one who'd back down without question and leave without a fuss, not wanting to make waves. The one who'd only begun to explore her sexuality and the power of it.

But I wasn't her anymore, and I hadn't been in a long time. He underestimated me. And he underestimated exactly how much I wanted to stay. Not here with him, obviously, but in Starlight Cove.

I wanted that promotion, that permanence I hadn't ever had in my life. And no way was I allowing Levi to push that out of my grasp. No way I was going to allow him to scare me away.

"Fine." Without another word, I turned on my heel and strode to my bedroom, leaving the door partially open.

I rummaged through my things, making as much noise as possible. Only partly because I wasn't exactly sure where the item I was looking for was located. But mostly because I wanted him to think I was in here packing in a rush. Because that was what he'd hoped. I could see it in the taunting glimmer in his eyes. In that stubborn set of his chin. He expected me to cave.

But it would be much more satisfying to bring Levi to his knees—literally or figuratively—instead.

CHAPTER NINETEEN

LEVI

IF I'D KNOWN Harper would fold after ninety seconds of a little bit of porn on the TV and a glimpse of my cock, I would've stopped fucking around and done this two days ago instead of dragging my feet like I had been.

I'd arrived back at the apartment early tonight instead of waiting until after she was tucked away in her room like I'd been doing, save for the night of the thunderstorm. Except, she'd come home later than she usually did, which meant I'd been sitting here for more than an hour, dick in hand, as mindless porn played in the background. But that hadn't been what held my attention...what had me so fucking hard I was ready to blow.

It was the smooth glide of Harper's silk and lace panties as I used them to stroke my cock. Picturing her here beside me. Replaying her throaty moans as I'd swept my tongue into her mouth. Recalling exactly how hot her pussy had been against me as she'd straddled my bike. I'd worked myself up so many times to the thought of her, only to stop, panting and holding myself back, so I was strung tighter than I'd been in years.

I wanted to come. Desperately.

Actually, what I really wanted was her kneeling between my spread thighs, mouth open and ready for me to blow against her tongue. Or better yet, begging for it deep inside her perfect cunt.

It would be so easy to finish myself off—the tiniest brush of this material against the head of my dick—but now wasn't the time. Not when I could hear her packing in a rush, the distinct sound of drawers opening and closing as she no doubt threw her shit together to leave.

It was supposed to be music to my fucking ears.

This was exactly what I wanted. More importantly, it was what I needed. Her gone. Out of my apartment...out of my *life*... once and for all. Unable to turn me inside out without even trying. I'd get my shitty life back, get my head on straight. I'd finally be able to fucking *breathe* again.

So then, why was there a pit in my stomach at the thought of her gone for good?

Much sooner than I would have thought possible, the riffling noises coming from her room stopped, and silence descended on the apartment. I shut off the cringey porn and tucked myself back into my sweatpants, still hard and aching for her, like that was anything new.

Dropping my head back onto the cushions and closing my eyes, I willed my dick to soften. To calm the fuck down already. But it was no use. Not when I saw Harper every time I closed my eyes. How she'd looked when she'd walked in here, completely fucking ravenous as she'd taken me in. And how fervently she'd tried to appear unaffected by me.

She'd forgotten how well I knew her. How I'd spent multiple summers studying her reactions. How accurately I could read every inch of her. And from her flushed cheeks to her hard nipples and her hungry gaze, there was no denying I'd gotten to her.

No denying how fucking much my dick liked that, either.

It didn't matter that my brain was yelling at me to knock it the fuck off. That we weren't doing that with her again, despite the memory of her tongue against mine less than a week ago. My cock had a mind of its own when it came to Harper, and it was wholly focused on her.

I just about had myself under control, my dick finally listening to reason and beginning to calm down. And then the unmistakable hum of a vibrator pierced the air.

My eyes shot open as I jerked my head up, and I glanced toward Harper's bedroom. She'd left her door open a bit, and I had a direct line of sight to her bed from where I sat on the couch. While I couldn't see anything explicit, I could make out the curve of her bare shoulder, her mass of blond waves falling over it. The flush of her neck and the slope of her chin. Her parted lips, deep pink and fucking gorgeous. And her eyes, heavy lidded and intense. Focused directly on me.

There was a challenging glint in them I'd never seen before but couldn't deny how much I loved. I swallowed harshly, curling my hands into fists as if that would be enough to hold me back from what always drew me closer to her. That invisible string that had connected us our entire lives.

But it was no use, and I was a fool for even trying.

I moved without thought, equal parts eager to see her spread out how I was imagining and to block out even the thought of it. In the end, the former won out.

Before I even registered what I was doing, I was standing outside her bedroom. Looking in on the one and only woman who'd starred in my fantasies for half my life.

She lay on her bed, sheets pooled around her. A fucking work of art. Her body had changed since we'd been together, filling out in ways that nearly tore a groan straight from my chest. Her tits were full and lush, peaked with tight, rosy nipples that I wanted in my mouth. Her hips were wide and full, flaring from her waist, her legs shapely and strong. And I'd give nearly anything to have them wrapped around my head while I feasted on her sweet little cunt.

But what held my attention most was her pussy, pink and wet, and the small toy resting on her clit.

"What are you doing?" I asked, my voice low and rough.

"I thought this was what we did now. Tit for tat, right?" A shudder stole over her, and her words came out breathless, husky. "Aren't you going to ask to come in?"

I swallowed harshly, unwilling to move forward, but equally unwilling to leave. I curled my fingers around the doorframe, as much to hold myself back as to hold myself up.

"Well?" she asked.

"No," I managed through a tight throat.

She dragged her hand over her soft belly, up to cup one of her full tits, her thumb and forefinger tugging at her nipple. "You sure?"

Rather than answer her—because I couldn't...too worried about what would come out if I opened my mouth—I just stood in silence, my eyes never leaving her.

She pressed a button on her toy, kicking the speed up a notch, and she jolted at the sensation. Her eyes were hooded as she stared at me, hunger and challenge written in their depths. "You just want to stand there and watch?"

No, I didn't want to fucking *watch*. I wanted to join her. Wanted to press that toy on her clit until she'd come so many times, she was begging me to stop. And only then, when she was dripping onto the sheets and swollen with need, would I fuck her. Hard and fast and rough, taking out all this frustration I felt on her siren body. Working myself up over and fucking over by pushing her to her breaking point before finally, *finally* giving in and allowing myself to come.

I wanted to tell her how pretty her pussy was. How many times I'd dreamed of her mouth and her hands and her gorgeous tits. How fucking badly I wanted to sink deep inside her. How desperately I wanted to taste her. Remind myself exactly how sweet she was. Hear her moan my name as she came, all while her cunt clenched around me.

But in the end, I did nothing.

I stood there, unable to tear my eyes away, but also unwilling to give in to my desire to wrap my hand around my cock and jerk off to the sight of her. I didn't deserve it. Not when we were here because of my stupid fucking idea. Because I was an idiot who'd fucked up yet again.

Instead, I watched as she worked herself higher, her eyes locked on mine the entire time. Her breaths grew faster, her tits rising and falling with each harsh inhale and exhale. Her pussy grew wetter, now glistening and flushed a deep pink.

And then, finally, after driving me to the brink, she broke.

The softest gasp left her lips as her back arched off the bed, her legs falling open even more while she shuddered through her release. I could've sworn my name left her lips as she came, but it had to be my fucked-up mind playing tricks on me.

The sight of her like that, spread open and vulnerable, her pussy aching and empty, her gaze stuck on mine like I was giving her exactly what she needed even from across the room, was what pushed me over the edge.

Without even touching my dick, I came in my fucking pants

like I was sixteen goddamn years old again. Like I didn't have years of deprivation under my belt. Hadn't learned to control my impulses without difficulty. Instead, I was tossed straight back to a time when Harper had me wrapped around her damn finger and didn't even know it.

CHAPTER TWENTY

HARPER

ONE NIGHT STAN'S was dark when I walked inside, despite it being late afternoon. A few patrons were scattered about, but the bar was mostly empty. Which was exactly what I'd hoped.

In an effort to distract myself from what had happened the other night between Levi and me, I'd spent the morning researching Stan—aka Duke Nova, lead singer of Bad Karma. Mabel had been correct; they'd won several Grammys and a few American Music Awards back in the '80s, '90s, and early aughts. They were the "it" band of their time.

But what I found incredibly interesting was that all content about Stan—or Duke, for that matter—faded into nothing several years ago. It was as if he had fallen off the face of the earth. And I intended to find out why.

I strolled up to the empty bar and took a seat on a stool, setting my purse on the one next to it. I glanced around at the space, taking it all in. It'd been years since it had been updated... if ever.

The bar itself was worn, with nicks and scratches marring the dark wood surface. Mismatched tables and booths were scattered throughout the space, and signed posters from several once-popular bands lined the walls, no doubt an homage to Stan's roots. A jukebox sat silent in the corner, and the small dance floor directly in front of it remained empty. At the far back, a doorway led to another room, filled with what looked like a couple pool tables.

After a couple minutes, a man who rivaled Brady in size—namely, it looked like he bench-pressed semitrucks for fun—strode out from behind a swinging door carrying a bin of glasses. With dark hair, piercing eyes, and stubble dusting his sharp jawline, he was undoubtedly attractive. Objectively speaking. But it seemed my radar for objectivity was off.

Because no matter how hot this man was, I couldn't help but compare him to Levi.

We hadn't spoken again since our mostly silent exchange the other night, when I'd shamelessly gotten myself off in front of him. Initially, I'd just wanted to push back. Give him a taste of his own medicine. I hadn't anticipated that he would stand there and watch. Hadn't anticipated the hungry scrape of his gaze over my body. Hadn't anticipated how much I would like it, either.

"What can I get you?" The bartender's deep voice snapped me out of my thoughts. From the sparse pictures I'd found online of Stan and his family, this guy looked like one of the sons, though I wasn't sure which one because of how much they all resembled one another. Still, it was game time.

"I'll take a glass of red, please."

"You got a preference?" he asked, his words just a low grumble.

"House favorite works," I said and shot him my warmest smile. The same smile that had been known to entice more than one stranger into spilling their deepest, darkest secrets.

Barely sparing me a glance, he nodded and grabbed the

bottle of wine before pulling down a glass. He poured me a healthy amount that would've cost me upward of twenty bucks in the city, then set it in front of me.

"Thanks," I said, taking a sip and glancing around at the mostly empty space. "Quiet in here today."

He didn't even glance in my direction, only offering a grunt in response. Jesus, it was like having a conversation with a brick wall.

"Do you get busier at night?" I pressed on, hoping to get him talking.

"Sometimes," was all he said as he started shelving the clean glasses.

Apparently, I'd started with the most difficult brother. But that was fine. I hadn't yet met a challenge I couldn't conquer.

I took another small sip of my wine and nodded. "This place is probably packed on the weekends. Especially with the history."

He froze and glanced at me with a raised brow that was more challenging than curious. "History?"

I cleared my throat. "Yeah, wasn't this place originally owned by the lead singer of...what was that band called again?"

With a heavy sigh, he unloaded the last of the clean glasses before tossing the rack under the counter. Then he braced his hands on the weathered bar top and stared me down, the move all the more intimidating, thanks to his size. The glower alone would've had a lesser woman shrinking back. Fortunately, that wasn't me. "Look, lady. I don't have time for small talk. So either order something else or let me work in peace."

I pressed my lips together and nodded, knowing when to surrender. In my excitement for details, I'd made a rookie mistake and rushed it. "Right, sorry."

He shook his head as if he couldn't believe the gall I had and strode through the swinging door without a backward glance, leaving me alone at the bar. This guy clearly wasn't the way in—like driving seventy miles an hour into the side of a building instead of using the front door. But luckily, I had three other brothers to interview, and I could only hope at least one of them would be a bit more talkative.

After I finished my glass of wine and dropped some cash on the counter, I grabbed my bag and slid off the stool just as the front door opened with the first patrons of the night. A group of women poured in, laughing loudly and immediately livening up the place.

"Harper!" Addison called, shooting a grin in my direction.

Luna, Everly, Quinn, and Avery followed her, the group of them looking as comfortable with one another as lifelong friends, though I knew none of them were. During my brief stints in Starlight Cove, I'd met them all at one time or another, but I knew Addison the best, based on my history in town. Luna had also become somewhat of a friend—as much as I had friends anyway—thanks to my first trip back to Starlight Cove more than a year ago when we'd connected at one of her yoga classes.

She strode up to me, enveloping me in a hug, the soft scent of lavender and jasmine wrapping around me. "Hey, Harper, I was wondering when I'd finally get to see you."

"Hi," I said, returning her hug. "How've you been?"

"I'm good." She pulled back, holding me at arm's length, her mouth turned down at the corners as she swept her gaze over me. "How about you? Everything okay? You look a little... unsettled."

I didn't know if it was thanks to my unfruitful interview with Brick Wall or the memories of the other night with Levi, but I didn't particularly want to talk about either. I waved her off with a smile I'd long since perfected, making sure no one else saw the cracks in my facade. "I've been making some questionable decisions lately."

"Questionable, huh?" Luna got a knowing glint in her eye. "Sometimes those are the best ones."

"I'm not so sure about that." I hiked my bag higher on my shoulder and lifted my chin toward the door. "I was just heading out."

"You should stay and have dinner with us!" She squeezed my arm, gesturing toward the table the rest of the girls had descended upon. "We've escaped the men, and I, for one, am ready for some girl time."

"Same," Quinn said. "Living with Ford is testosterone overload. If I have to pick up any more of my husband's dirty socks that never manage to find their way into the laundry basket, I'm going to scream."

"It's the beard trimmings for me," Everly added. "How does one man have so much hair?"

Avery nodded in agreement. "Thank God for the sex is all I can say."

"Amen to that." Addison lifted a water glass in cheers.

"Harper's got it the worst of all of us," Luna said, eyeing me speculatively. "She's got all the negatives of living with a man without the sex to balance things out."

My cheeks flushed as a memory of that night with Levi came to me unbidden. How he'd watched me from the door, his gaze boring into me as if he never wanted to look away. I hoped to God my thoughts didn't show on my face, because I had absolutely no intention of discussing that particular transgression with anyone, least of all this group of women, one of whom was Levi's *sister*.

"Oh, I definitely need to hear the details about that whole situation," Avery said.

I cleared my throat, tapping into the poker face I'd perfected over my years in journalism. "There's not much to tell." Definitely not the fact that he'd welcomed me home by jacking off in the living room, then watched me get myself off. "We mostly just ignore each other."

"Uh-huh," Luna said, disbelief heavy in her tone. "I am extremely well-versed in this, and tension like you two have always explodes one way or another—usually fighting or fucking."

I huffed out a forced laugh and shook my head. "I'm pretty sure the only thing that's going to explode is my sanity."

"Come on and sit already," Addison said, pushing out the empty chair next to her. "We'll have some drinks and good food to distract you from my annoying brother."

"That's why we're all here, to be honest. Her annoying brothers," Quinn said, and the rest of them laughed.

Everly shot me a warm smile, sunshine personified. "A night out with the girls sounds like exactly what you need."

I stood there, holding my bag and actually...hesitating. For the first time in my life, I was tempted by their offer. I didn't do girlfriends—or any friends at all, for that matter, Chase notwithstanding. But that was mostly due to his persistence than anything else.

After the fallout with Levi, I'd separated myself from others, closed myself off from friendships—from relationships of any kind—whether intentionally or not. It had taken me months to get over the loss of one of the most important people in my life, not to say anything about my second best friend or the only family I'd known, and I hadn't wanted to go through that again.

But I had no intention of staying in Starlight Cove. No plan to cultivate any sort of lasting relationships here. This place was just a small blip on my radar, like all the others that had come before it and all those that would come after. A moment in time I'd eventually forget. So what did this hurt?

Besides, my other option was going back to the apartment and hoping like hell Levi wasn't there. Because I had no idea what the fuck I was going to say when I came face-to-face with the man who'd watched me come mere days ago.

"All right. I'll stay for one drink." I settled into the seat Addison had pushed out for me, and cheers went up around the table.

"So, how's the article coming?" Luna asked, sitting down on my other side. "What's the scoop on our little town?"

I breathed out a laugh and shook my head. "I'm sure you guys know more than I do. At least right now."

"This is for *Weekend Wanderlust*, right?" Everly asked. "That must be fun, working for such a huge magazine."

"It definitely has its perks. I'm just freelancing for them now" —*though hopefully not for long*—"but they've sent me to parts of the world I probably wouldn't have seen otherwise."

"That sounds amazing." Avery propped her chin in her hand, eyes bright. "I love traveling. Do you have a team who goes with you?"

"Sometimes they'll send a photographer, but even if they do, we don't always work side by side. So it's just me a lot of the time."

Everly studied me, her brow pinched, lips turned down at the corners. "That sounds kind of lonely."

I pasted on a smile and shrugged. "You get used to it."

The truth was, she wasn't entirely wrong. While I'd traveled all over the world, had met some amazing people, been immersed in cultures I never would have if it weren't for my career, I couldn't deny that it was isolating sometimes. But I'd never regretted the choices I'd made years ago—choosing this career I loved over a family whose love came with rules and stipulations, if at all.

Snagging a permanent position with *Weekend Wanderlust*, embarking on unlimited journeys that would take me all over the world on my own, was exactly what I wanted.

Wasn't it?

CHAPTER TWENTY-ONE

HARPER

SOMEHOW, one drink turned into multiple pitchers of margaritas shared between everyone except Addison, who was DD for the rest of the group. I wasn't much of a drinker normally, so I was feeling the couple I'd had, a pleasant hum warming me from the inside out.

A couple hours in, after we'd demolished a platter of nachos and several other apps, Avery gasped, her eyes wide as she stared across the table. She snatched Luna's wrist as she reached for the pitcher of margaritas. "Whoa, whoa, *whoa*... What the hell is this?"

"What?" Addison asked, eyes pinging between them.

"And why the hell are you wearing a ring?" Avery continued.

"*What?*" This time, the single word was little more than a screech. Addison grabbed Luna's hand and yanked it toward her, her mouth dropping open when she got a good look. "Oh my God, is that an *engagement* ring? I thought you said you didn't want the 'government-sanctioned imprisonment' of marriage!"

Quinn pointed a finger in Luna's direction. "You totally did say that."

"It's Brady." Luna shrugged as if that explained it and grabbed the pitcher, pouring everyone but Addison another round. Then she added, "Besides, it turns out if you're hand-cuffed long enough and teased within an inch of your life, you agree to just about anything."

"And the thing you agreed to was marrying my brother?" Addison yelled, not giving a single shit about the rest of the patrons in the bar. Thankfully, no one even looked up at her outburst. Obviously, Starlight Cove was used to her dramatics.

With a smirk, Luna leaned back in her chair and tipped her head to the side. "He's very...persuasive."

Addison groaned and hung her head in her hands. "Oh God, that sounded like a sex thing. That was *totally* a sex thing, wasn't it? I thought we talked about this! No mentioning my brothers and sex in the same sentence when I'm around." Addison shot an accusatory glare at the rest of the women. "And that's supposed to go for every one of you."

Avery held her hands up in surrender. "I've been very good. I didn't tell you anything about the laundry room incident with Aiden on Tuesday."

"And I haven't said a word about the spicy scene Beck and I reenacted from the book we read last week." Everly mimed zipping her lips.

"I also didn't share the new toy Ford came home with or how many times he made me a very happy girl last night."

"You're all the absolute *worst*, I hope you know that."

Laughing, Luna reached over and patted Addison's hand. "Sorry, girl, but Brady has an *amazing* di—"

"Okay, all right!" Addison snapped, cutting off Luna and shooting a glare at everyone else, all of whom were quite clearly extremely tipsy.

The table erupted in laughter, and I couldn't stop a grin from sweeping across my mouth. I didn't have much to contribute to this conversation, but I'd be lying if I said I wasn't enjoying the hell out of it. Especially with the buzz of alcohol flowing through my veins. And especially because this was exactly the kind of relationship—the kind of found family—I'd always craved.

"But seriously, what is *up* with these men?" Quinn asked, shaking her head. "All Ford has to do is look at me a certain way, and I'm done for. I hate it."

With a grin, Everly leaned over, bumping Quinn's shoulder with her own. "No, you don't."

Quinn let out a heavy sigh, clearly aggrieved. "No, I don't."

"It's like they're magicians," Everly said, taking a sip of her margarita.

Avery waved a hand through the air. "Nah, they're not magicians. They just have magic peens."

Everyone but Addison laughed, and she glared at each of them in turn. "You bitches always have to ruin a good time, don't you? I'm changing the subject." She turned toward me. "So, Harper, catch me up. How are your asshole parents?"

Everly huffed out a surprised laugh. "Oh my God, Addison, I can't believe you said that."

"I can." Avery snorted and rolled her eyes, pouring herself another round. "Her filter's gone on a normal day, but add in all the pregnancy hormones, and it's been a *ride*."

Addison froze next to me as silence descended on the table, but Avery didn't seem to realize anything was amiss. She took a huge sip of her margarita and hummed, doing a little shimmy in her seat, oblivious to the silence that had fallen.

Luna placed a hand on the table and leaned forward, splitting her gaze between Addison and Avery. "Add in the what now?"

"Your parents, Harper?" Addison insisted loudly, pretending not to notice how everyone had frozen, their attention zeroing in on her. "How're they doing?"

"Um..." I shot a glance around the table, unsure what the hell was going on but too drunk to care. This wasn't something I usually shared with many—or anyone at all—but the words came tumbling out without thought. "I don't really talk to them anymore. Haven't for years."

"I'm sorry, that's obviously quite terrible, but I can't pay attention to anything else right now..." Everly shook her head, eyes wide. "Did Avery say *pregnancy hormones*?"

Finally realizing what she'd done, Avery gasped and slapped her hands over her mouth as she shot her panicked gaze around the table. "Oh shit. Oh *shit*." She waved her hands through the air. "No, I didn't! I definitely did not do that! Everyone pretend you didn't hear a thing! Just rewind time. What were we talking about before? Addison's brothers' magic dicks? Let's just go back to that!"

Everyone stared openmouthed at Addison, stunned silent, their reactions as dramatic as cartoon characters. I tried and failed to keep the laughter inside me, but it was no use. I fell into a fit of giggles, nearly toppling over. And before long, everyone but Addison joined in until we were leaning into one another with tears streaming down our faces.

"Okay, that's it," Addison said, pulling out her phone and shooting a grumpy Gus look in our direction that rivaled any of her brothers. Unfortunately for her, that only made us laugh harder. "You're all cut off. And I'm calling in reinforcements."

Group text with Brady, Aiden, Beck, Ford, Levi, and Addison
11:02 p.m.

ADDISON:

I know I said I'd be DD tonight

But you all need to come pick up your women

They're drunk off their asses

And annoying the fuck out of me

FORD:

You said the magic words. I will happily come collect my drunk wife because that means this guy's getting laid. On my way

Levi named the conversation "Trivial Bullshit"

ADDISON:

Hilarious, Levi

AND WAIT

I need to tell you guys something first

Before your drunk ass women do

Because I totally know they will

I wanted to do this at the morning meeting on Saturday

But my hand's been forced

I have no choice but to do it now

BECK:

Jesus, what is it already?

FORD:

I'm in my Jeep waiting, so hurry up.

ADDISON:

Okay, you might want to sit down for this

It's a pretty big deal

Are you ready?

LEVI:

For fuck's sake, Addison. Spit it out.

ADDISON:

Okay

You asked for it

Here it goes…

I'm pregnant

ADDISON:

Hello?

ADDISON:

HELLO?

ADDISON:

Why isn't anyone saying anything?

I said I'm PREGNANT

ADDISON:

DID YOU HEAR ME?

Group text with Brady, Aiden, Beck, Ford, and Levi
11:08 p.m.

AIDEN:

Everyone already knew that, right?

BRADY:

For a couple weeks, yeah

BECK:

Same here

LEVI:

Got suspicious about a week ago, but yeah

FORD:

Little D's gonna be piiiiiissed. Who's gonna
break it to her?

AIDEN:

I vote Brady

FORD:

Seconded

BECK:

Yep

LEVI:

Agreed

BRADY:

Fuckers

Group text titled: Trivial Bullshit
with Brady, Aiden, Beck, Ford, Levi, and Addison
11:11 p.m.

BRADY:

Were we not supposed to know that?

ADDISON:

BRADY, STOP BEING A DICK RIGHT NOW

You didn't know shit

BRADY:

You can't keep anything from us. Didn't you learn that with the whole sneaking around with Chase thing?

AIDEN:

You seriously need to work on your stealth if you're trying to keep shit like this a secret.

ADDISON:

Fine

So you two knew

But the others didn't

FORD:

Sorry, little D

BECK:

Whoops?

LEVI:

If you didn't want people to figure it out, tell Chase to stop palming your stomach like a basketball and standing over you like a fucking guard dog.

BRADY:

And he should maybe be a bit more covert when he's making a 2am run to Bayhaven for whatever your hungry ass is craving.

BECK:

Same with your weird AF requests at the diner. A BLT with grape jelly instead of mayo? I'm supposed to believe that's normal?

ADDISON:

I hate every single one of you fuckers

And I can't wait to share all the gross stuff that's happening to my body

LEVI:

I think I speak for all of us when I say we pass

ADDISON:

TOO FUCKING BAD

You ruined my announcement

So you're gonna hear about mucus membranes

And whatever the fuck else I wanna tell you

AIDEN:

Can't wait.

ADDISON:

Now I mean it…

Come get your women

Margaritas were had

You might need to carry a couple out of here

They ordered another pitcher while I've been texting you

AIDEN:

Leaving now

FORD:

Yep

BECK:

Right behind them

BRADY:

I'm already outside Stan's

LEVI:

I don't have a woman, so I'm good where I am.

ADDISON:

Nice try

Harper's drunk

Like super toasted

But there is a hot bartender here

One of Stan's sons

The big, mean one

He could probably help her if you can't be
bothered

CHAPTER TWENTY-TWO

LEVI

I HAD no idea why I dropped everything without thought and headed toward One Night Stan's after Addison's last text. Harper wasn't my responsibility, and she hadn't been in a long damn time.

But I wasn't about to leave her drunk ass in the hands of some fucking bartender, regardless if it was one of Stan's sons. Hell, *because* he was.

Brady's empty car was already parked out front, and the rest of my brothers pulled in as I strode across the street. The noise was deafening as soon as we walked through the front door. A quick glance around showed that everyone *but* Addison was drunk off their asses, just as she'd promised, which meant we had our hands full.

I couldn't be bothered to pay attention to anything going on around me, though. Not when Harper's eyes met mine as soon as I walked in, her entire face lighting up at the sight of me. Smile wide and eyes bright, she looked at me like she used to, before everything had shattered between us. Looked at me like I was the sun and the moon and every single star in the sky. Like I was her everything. And fuck if that wasn't a sledgehammer straight to my chest, forcing the old forgotten organ to beat again.

I shook the delusional thought from my mind and strode toward her, scanning her from head to toe. She wore a short dress the color of her eyes and sky-high sandals, her mile-long legs on full display. And the sight of her wearing that was only made worse by the fact that I'd seen everything she had underneath it just the other night. I knew how pink her pussy was and the exact shade of her nipples. I knew her belly was soft and round and my fingers would disappear into the lush swell of her hips if I held her tight while I fucked her.

Jesus Christ, this woman was going to kill me without even trying.

"All right, drunkie." I stood in front of her, doing my best to ignore the dopey smile on her face as she stared up at me. "Let's get you home."

"Home, huh?" she asked, a teasing glint in her eyes, and I kicked myself for the slip.

The word had no place between us. Even if it was exactly what we'd dreamed of when we were younger, the two of us sitting on the cliffs under a black sky filled with stars. Talking about shit we had no business discussing so young.

Dreaming of a life. *Together*.

Funny how things turned out. Sure, we were living under the same roof, like we'd always planned. Except, in our plans, I wasn't a complete waste of space, I hadn't fucked things up, and she'd never hated me.

And right now, with the way she was looking at me like she used to, I could pretend she didn't.

"You didn't have to come get me. I'm fine on my own." She moved to stand, wobbled on her shoes, and fell right back into her chair.

"Yeah, looks like," I said dryly, tugging her up and making sure she was steady on her feet this time.

"I don't know how you ladies manage to get this wasted every time you get together." Brady wrapped an arm around a stumbling Luna, glancing around at the rest of the women.

"We're very dedicated to the cause," Quinn said with a grin, leaning heavily into Ford.

"And we were drinking extra tonight"—Avery leaned forward, nearly toppling over the table until Aiden wrapped an arm around her waist to catch her—"because Addison's *pregnant*. But you didn't hear that from me." She mimed zipping her lips and tossing away the key, except she slapped Aiden in the face as she did so.

"Looks to me like you drank about *five* extra, bunny." Aiden tugged her upright and headed toward the door, glancing over his shoulder at our sister. "Why'd you let her drink so much, Addison?"

Harper was trying her best to appear unaffected at my side, but I had to reach out and steady her more than once.

"Seriously," Beck grumbled, leading a droopy-eyed Everly out of the bar. "You couldn't cut them off a couple pitchers ago?"

"Well, excuse the fuck out of me!" Addison huffed, planting her hands on her hips and shooting a glare at each of us, even those who didn't say a damn word. "I guess I was preoccupied, what with *growing your very first niece or nephew* and all. By the way, thanks for the congratulations, you assholes."

"Congratulations," all of us said as one, but she just continued giving us the stink eye.

"We'd love nothing more than to give you inescapable bear hugs, but we're a little preoccupied at the moment. I need to get my extremely drunk wife home." Ford guided Quinn through the bar. "But don't think this means you're getting out of the brother puppy pile, little D! Group congratulations at the next all-family meeting."

Addison scoffed and rolled her eyes as we all made our way outside into the crisp evening air, my hand hovering at the small of Harper's back. "Please, you'll all forget, and I'll continue on without any sweaty, stinky hugs."

"Nah." Aiden shook his head, holding the car door open for Avery. "I'm putting it on the calendar for Saturday."

"Great," Addison grumbled.

"Don't pretend like you don't love it," I said, keeping one eye on Harper. "You okay to drive home?"

"I'm *pregnant,* not drunk." Addison rolled her eyes before blowing out a long sigh. "Besides, word got back to Chase, and he's on his way to pick me up, despite my car being here *and* despite the fact that I'm perfectly capable of driving myself."

No sooner had she said the words than Chase's truck came rumbling down the street, faster than necessary, considering Addison wasn't going anywhere.

"You love that, too." I reached out and ruffled her hair. "I'm happy for you guys. Even if you are going to be an absolute fucking menace the next few months."

"Maybe I'll keep it up the rest of my life. How about that?"

"So, no different from usual?"

"Oh, fuck off." She flipped me off, but her words lacked heat.

I waved at Chase as he pulled into a parking spot. "Tell him I'll call him tomorrow."

"I will. I'll let him know you had your hands full." She

smirked, tipping her chin to my right. "Speaking of, she's escaping..."

I glanced over to find a wandering Harper roaming aimlessly down the street. With a muttered curse, I took off after her. "Hey." Once I was close enough, I hooked an arm around her waist and tugged her toward me. "Get back here."

Stumbling into me with a giggle, she rested her hand on my chest to brace herself as she stared up at me. Her expression was so open, so honest, so unguarded, it was like old times. "Whoa. Is the ground moving?"

"Nope, that's just you."

"I can fix that." She stopped in the middle of the damn street, attempting to balance on one foot and remove the neck-breaking, sexy-as-hell sandals she wore. Unfortunately for her, she was drunk, and even standing on solid ground was proving too difficult. She stumbled and let out a giggle, even though she nearly rolled her ankle in the process.

"Jesus Christ," I grumbled, shooting out my hands to grip her hips and steady her.

Knowing what I was going to have to do to get this woman into our apartment, I heaved out a sigh and tugged off my hoodie. Then I squatted down, brushing her fumbling hands away from the tiny buckles on her ankles, and removed her shoes for her, ignoring the soft satin of her skin against my fingertips.

She rested her hands on my shoulders and breathed out a hum of contentment when first one bare foot then the other met the ground. "This is pretty nice."

"What's that?"

"You doing this for me."

"I have ulterior motives." I wrapped my hoodie around her waist because she'd definitely be flashing her ass otherwise, and that wasn't happening. Hooking her shoes on my fingers, I stood, lifting her over my shoulder in the process.

She broke into a fit of laughter as I strode toward the apartment, and then, without warning, she slapped my ass.

I froze in the middle of the sidewalk, tightening my grip around her soft thighs. "Was that necessary?"

"Probably not."

"At least you admit it." I climbed the stairs inside our building, all while she was groping my ass and I was reminding myself she never would have done that if she weren't completely shit-faced.

"You've got a really great ass," she said and gave it another hard smack. "Has anyone ever told you that? Even upside down, it's spiracular. Um…spitacular. Err…*spectacular*."

"Jesus Christ, woman. Exactly how many margaritas did you have?"

"Don't know. Didn't count. Maybe twenty-seven?" She sighed, pinching my ass this time. "Better question—how many squats do you have to do to get an ass like this? Two…three thousand a day?"

"I thought you were exaggerating with the twenty-seven drinks, but now, I'm not so sure."

"Maybe Mabel can make a cookie of your ass because I seriously want to take a bite out of it." And then, as if she spoke her words into existence, she sank her teeth into my right ass cheek.

I froze with my key halfway toward the lock and glanced over my shoulder. "Did you just bite me?"

"Yes," she said with a hell of a lot of haughtiness for someone who was currently hanging over my shoulder upside down. "And I'm not sorry about it, either. Been dreaming about this ass for weeks."

I unlocked and opened the front door, attempting to ignore

the fact that she'd been dreaming about me. "Okay, you *definitely* had twenty-seven margaritas."

Sober Harper would've been mortified at spilling that bit of information, not to mention all the groping. As soon as I was over the threshold, I dropped her shoes by the door and set her down on her feet, reaching out to steady her when she wobbled a little.

"Whoa." She shot her arms out and gripped my wrists, eyes wide and smile bright. "That was fun. Can I have another ride?"

My mind immediately shot to an entirely different kind of ride she could give me, the sounds of her from the other night still fresh. That soft little whimper as she came. She wouldn't whimper with me, though. She'd scream.

And that line of thinking absolutely did not belong here, especially right now.

"Nope. Time for you to go to bed," I said. "And you probably want to take something before you crash, or you're going to wake up with one hell of a hangover."

"No, I won't. Never had a hangover a day in my life." She pursed her lips, her brow furrowed. "But that's probably more because I've never had friends to go out with. And it's kinda sad to get drunk by yourself."

At her admission, something uncomfortable lodged deep in my chest. I'd never allowed myself to think about Harper's life after I shut her out of mine. Intentionally. I'd been secure in the knowledge that she didn't have to give up her dreams to stick around for some kid who—as her dad succinctly put it—was a waste of space and who wouldn't amount to anything. Doing so was the coward's way out, but I knew if I got curious about her life, I'd go looking. And if I went looking, I wouldn't be able to stop myself from going to *her*.

That was the last thing she'd needed from me. In order for

her to get what she'd planned, the life she'd had set for years, I needed to not be in it. Her dad had made that perfectly clear.

"Well, I've been drunk plenty," I said. "And I'm telling you to take some ibuprofen and drink a lot of water or you're gonna regret it."

"Fine." She pursed her lips, one eye squinted shut as she regarded me. "But first, I gotta get out of these clothes. I'm so hot. Why's it so hot in here?"

Before I could even comprehend her words, she shucked my hoodie, reached for the hem of her dress, and tugged it up, revealing inch after delectable inch of her gorgeous body. I stood there frozen for way longer than I should have, but when Harper Davidson started shedding clothes in front of you, there was nothing you could do but watch.

At least until she got stuck with the garment halfway off. With the dress covering her face and her arms tangled over her head, she stumbled into a wall before letting out a giggle-snort.

"Jesus Christ," I muttered, blowing out a deep sigh and scrubbing a hand over my face. "You couldn't wait till you got into your room to strip?"

"Why?" She spun toward me. Her arms were still above her head, tangled in her dress, which gave me an unencumbered view of her wearing a pale-purple lace bra and white cotton panties. Objectively speaking, the bottoms were plain. Boring. But the tiny pink bow at the front of them was going to haunt my dreams for the next six months, easy. "You've already seen it all before. Just the other night, actually."

"A fact I am painfully aware of."

After a nonstop struggle—one in which I was absolutely not going to help—she finally extricated herself from the dress and tossed it on the floor, letting out a hoot of triumph.

"Feel better?" I asked, if for nothing more than to give myself something to do other than stare at every inch of skin she'd revealed.

"Almost." She turned her back to me, the view of her ass in those panties causing my dick to stir. And then she reached back, unhooked her bra, and tossed it over her shoulder.

I caught it before it smacked me in the face, and I tipped my head back, blowing out a heavy breath. "Fucking hell."

"You can stop staring at the ceiling," she said. "I don't mind if you watch."

As she'd proven damn well the other night. And there was no realm of reality where I wouldn't love it, too. I'd deprived myself of a hell of a lot over the years, women included, and I'd gotten really fucking good at it. But having *this* woman—this nearly *naked* woman—living in my apartment and enticing me day in and day out was the greatest temptation I'd ever faced.

"Can you handle getting in bed on your own?"

She made a sound of agreement, and I took that as my permission to step away, gather a couple things, and give myself some fucking room to breathe.

Thankfully, by the time I made it back into her bedroom with the supplies, she was in her bed, the sheet pulled up under her arms. I blew out a sigh, equal parts relieved and disappointed, and I fucking hated myself for the latter.

"Shit," she said.

"What's the matter?" I asked, standing at the side of her bed.

She stared up at me, her makeup smudged, hair wild, eyes half lidded. Looking like she'd had a hell of a good night. "I forgot something."

I tipped my chin toward her nightstand, where I'd set some ibuprofen and a bottle of water. "I already grabbed everything for you."

She shook her head, eyes bright with mischief as she

grinned up at me, and I knew I was in trouble. "It's not to help my hangover. It's to help my pussy."

"Jesus Christ, Harper." I groaned and scrubbed a hand over my face. "You can't say shit like that to me."

"Why not?"

"You know damn well why." *Because I'm not good enough for you—I've never been good enough for you—and going down this path with you again is a bad fucking idea.*

"Don't even pretend like this is tempting you. You've spent most of the time staring at the ceiling anyway."

I clenched my jaw, crossing my arms as I met her stare. "Don't mistake my chivalry for disinterest, sparrow."

Her lips kicked up at the corner. "Are you saying you like to look at me?"

"Of course I fucking like to look at you. Have you seen yourself?"

She squinted one eye at me, as if trying to read if I was being honest. All she had to do was glance at the front of my jeans to see the proof of exactly how fucking much I liked it.

"I need my toy," she finally said. "The one I used when you watched. Will you get it for me?"

Images of her using it immediately popped into my mind, and my cock grew hard as steel behind my fly. I cleared my throat, but it was no use. My voice still came out rough. "No, I'm not going to get your toy."

"C'mon, please? Don't you wanna play our game again?"

I swallowed harshly, forcing myself to shake my head, despite the fact that I wanted nothing more than what she was suggesting.

She blew out a long-suffering sigh before shimmying beneath the covers, obviously ridding herself of her panties. In all her adjustments, the sheet slipped farther down her body, exposing her tits to me, but she was completely unconcerned.

"Then I guess my fingers will have to do." She wiggled them at me before slipping her hand under the sheet and spreading her legs wide. "It'll take longer, but maybe not since you're here. You'll talk me through it, won't you?"

CHAPTER TWENTY-THREE

LEVI

I WAS OFFICIALLY IN HELL. Sitting on the edge of the bed with a naked Harper spread out next to me, telling me it was going to take longer to get herself off unless I talked her through it…pure purgatory. On the one hand, I wouldn't mind if it took a fucking eternity if she let me watch.

On the other hand, I might actually die.

"Exactly how drunk are you?" I managed through a tight throat. How I was able to form words at all was a fucking mystery.

"You know how many margaritas I had. Besides, we just did this, remember?" She bit her lip, her eyes hooded as she stared up at me. "I came harder than I have in forever because you were watching. I wanna know what happens if you do more than just watch."

"You're playing with fire, sparrow."

She shot me a lazy grin. "I'm counting on it."

The bed shifted with her movements. And though I kept my gaze on her face, I could tell by the sigh that left her softly parted lips and the flutter of her eyelashes that she had her hand on her pussy.

I swallowed down the fistful of gravel lodged in my throat. "You're going to regret this in the morning."

"I won't remember it in the morning." She kicked the sheet the rest of the way off, and I had to force myself not to track the movement. Not to turn around and see everything she'd uncovered. "Now, are you going to help me or not?"

I tried my hardest to keep my gaze on her face, but when I could *hear* how wet she was, my control snapped. I glanced down, wishing like hell those were my fingers playing in her dripping cunt. Wishing it was *me* pulling those noises from her throat.

"You used to be so sweet, didn't you? Never asking for what you wanted, just taking whatever I gave you. But it looks like you've turned into a dirty fucking girl." I licked my lips, dying for a taste of her but forcing myself not to touch. "Or is that just for me? Am I the only one who gets to see this side of you?"

"Yes," she said in a whisper, and the admission made my cock twitch in my jeans, loving that it was all for me. And I was fucking desperate to explore what she'd never given anyone else.

"Look at you. Your needy cunt is dripping, isn't it? I want to lick it all up. We both know you'd taste fucking delicious. You always were."

"Do it. *Please.*"

I breathed out a pained laugh. "As much as I love you begging me, this is all you tonight."

"But I need you," she said, her words more a whine than anything. "Need to be taken care of so bad."

I tried not to get hung up on her words since she was half out of her mind. And especially since she didn't mean them. She didn't need *me*. She just needed to get off.

"Well, go on, then. Sink those fingers deep. Let me hear how fucking much you need it."

With a whimper, she did as I directed, slipping two fingers into her cunt before dragging them out. She set a gentle pace, much slower than I would have. Much slower than she needed, if the way she was rolling her hips was any indication.

"That's not going to get you off, and you know it." I tipped my chin toward her hand. "Fuck yourself faster. And rub that pretty little clit while you're at it."

"God," she breathed, her nipples pebbling as she arched her back. "You didn't use to talk like this."

Because I had been just a teenager, too worried to voice all the filthy thoughts running through my head. Especially with a girl like Harper. Someone who was prim and posh, someone so polished, she shone. Someone who came from the kind of well-off family she did. I was terrified of scaring her away, terrified of losing her because I knew exactly what I had. That was something I never would've admitted to her in a million years.

But she was right—she wasn't going to remember any of this in the morning. I could say whatever I wanted to her, tell her all the secrets I kept just for myself, and it wouldn't matter. In the end, none of this would matter.

"That's because I was worried about keeping you." I braced my hands on either side of her shoulders and leaned down, careful not to touch her, despite how badly I wanted to. When our lips were so close, I could feel her breath on mine, I murmured, "Things change in twelve years. And you might be in my apartment, begging for my words to make that gorgeous pussy come, but you're not mine, are you? Not anymore. Haven't been for a long time."

"I remember what it was like to be yours," she whispered, her fingers moving in tight, fast circles around her clit, the fingers on her other hand fucking deeper into her cunt. "I think about it sometimes."

Fuck me. In more than a decade, *nothing* had tempted me like this woman. She was going to be my goddamn downfall, and she didn't even know it.

I sat back, allowing my gaze to skate over every inch of her. Soak in the flush of her neck and chest, all the way down to those luscious, pink-tipped tits. And lower still, to the dip of her waist and the accentuated flare of her generous hips. Then her fingers, working fast and frenzied against the prettiest pussy I'd ever seen. The only pussy I ever fantasized about when the deprivation got to be too much and I finally allowed myself the relief.

"I think about it every time," I admitted, allowing myself to because it was safe. "Seeing you laid out like this, your gorgeous fucking body on display..." I swiped a thumb over my lower lip and shook my head. "It's impossible to pretend I haven't been inside you. I remember *everything*."

"Like what?" she whispered, her breaths growing shallower.

"I remember exactly what it felt like to have your tight little cunt squeezing my cock. How sweet you tasted. How much you loved it when I played with your tits. And those throaty whimpers in my ear when I'd push too deep. We never quite worked up to the whole thing, did we?"

She moaned in response, her eyes glazed, lips parted, fingers working feverishly.

"But if I fucked you now, you'd take it. Wouldn't you, baby? We'd make it fit."

"*God.*"

Her pussy was obscene, spread tight around her fingers, flushed a deep pink, and so wet, she was dripping onto the sheets. My mouth watered, eager for a taste of her after way too fucking long. Desperate to feel her again.

My cock was painfully hard, and if I didn't get out of here in the next three minutes, I was going to have another problem on my hands like the other night.

"Time to be my dirty girl, sparrow." I glanced down at her fingers buried deep in her cunt, her other hand flying across her clit. "Come all over your fingers and pretend it's my cock."

"Levi," Harper breathed, her lips parted, chest rising faster and faster with each passing moment. "I wanna know something."

"What's that?"

She let out a soft moan, her legs shaking now, and whispered, "How many others have there been?"

I tore my gaze from her pussy and looked into her eyes, hazy and lust-drunk. Soft and vulnerable. My deprivation was something I usually kept to myself. My penance for all the shit I'd done wrong in my life and something no one else needed to be concerned with. I never wanted any of my baggage heaped onto those I loved.

But I could admit it to her now, when she was half out of her mind. When she'd never remember it anyway.

"None."

The word had barely left my mouth before Harper moaned and came, my name leaving her lips as she'd stared up at me with something I could delude myself into believing was love.

I knew it wasn't. It could never be. Not after what I'd done to her. And definitely not considering the man I was, someone with a thousand demons haunting me.

Someone impossible to love.

Case in point, I shouldn't even be sitting on her bed right now. I should have forced myself to walk away as soon as she'd started stripping. Should have shuttled her to her room and walked out without another word. Instead, I'd hung around too long, pushed myself too damn far.

I was fucked. And a fucking asshole for sitting here and watching her. Not just watching her, but guiding her. *Directing* her.

"Thank you," she murmured, the words barely more than a whisper, and then she was out. Dead to the world.

I pulled the sheet over her, covering her up. Then, after double-checking I'd brought in everything she would need, I slipped from her room and strode straight to the bathroom. If I was already going to hell for what I'd done, I might as well make it count.

I stripped out of my clothes and climbed beneath the hot shower spray, closing my eyes as the steam rose around me. And though deprivation was my default, I didn't even try to stop myself from reaching for Harper's body wash and pouring some of it into my palm.

The scent of her surrounded me as I wrapped my fist around my cock, my mind conjuring up images of her moments ago. Recalling the expression on her face when I'd breathed the single syllable of admission. The word that had seemed to send her over the edge more than any of my filth had. And that only got me harder. Though the constant thoughts of her flitting through my mind definitely weren't helping.

Memories of the single summer we'd had when everything had been perfect. When she'd been mine and she'd known I was hers and we hadn't been able to keep our hands off each other. When I'd snuck into her bedroom a dozen times to fuck her quietly while her dad was two doors down. Or when we'd bail on a group outing and escape to the cove or the beach or the back seat of a damn car.

I shoved those thoughts to the back of my mind because they only made me feel worse. For what we'd lost. For what I'd cost us.

Instead, I focused on her now. On the gorgeous-as-fuck woman she'd become. The one who didn't put up with any shit, who spoke her mind and didn't care if you liked it. The one who'd met my tongue stroke for stroke on the top of the Ferris wheel, who pulled out her toy and got off with me watching. The one who begged me to help her come with just my words.

Her body was a fucking masterpiece, tits high and full, hips lush and thick, and I wanted to watch that ass bounce as I fucked her from behind. Wanted her breathy little sighs in my ear and her nail marks down my back. Wanted her begging me to fuck her harder, faster. Wanted her begging for *more*.

Groaning, I squeezed my eyes shut, hanging my head as I braced my left hand on the tile wall. I swiped my thumb over the head of my cock, focusing on my piercings before stroking down the length, too far gone to stop now.

A thousand fantasies flitted through my mind as I pumped my shaft in long, quick strokes. And every single one of them featured Harper.

Her on her knees, her mouth open and ready and waiting for everything I could give her. Her sweet little tongue poking out to lick around my head, catching every drop of precome. The gentle scrape of her teeth before she tugged on my piercings, all while those fire-filled eyes peered up at me with more than contempt.

Then it switched to her riding my face, her hands braced on the headboard while she ground her cunt down against my mouth. Then she was on her back, her legs pressed up to her chest as I pounded into her with abandon.

I thought about how sweet she'd taste, how tight she'd be.

The soft little whimper she'd give me when I pushed just a little harder, just a little deeper. Watching her cunt stretch around my cock, stuffed so fucking full of me, there was no telling where I ended and she began.

But through it all, through every single fantasy reel, she looked at me with something other than hate shining in her baby blues. That, and the remembered whisper of my name on her lips as she came, was all it took.

"*Fuck*," I groaned, my orgasm tearing through me as I shot off against the wall, the scent of her filling up my lungs. And there was no hope of stopping her name from slipping past my lips.

Wishing, not for the first time, that she was mine.

CHAPTER TWENTY-FOUR

HARPER

ADDISON:

Double bacon cheeseburger

3 shots of pickle juice

Purple vitamin water

HARPER:

Are you trying to make me puke?

ADDISON:

I'm trying to make you NOT puke

Trust me

I'm a professional

IF I HADN'T ALREADY MADE this appointment with Chase for a proper interview, I wasn't sure I would have gotten out of bed at all today. Fortunately, the texts from Addison with her tried and true hangover cure had worked like a damn miracle.

Not to mention the ibuprofen, bottle of water, and a somehow perfectly hot cup of coffee that was exactly to my liking sitting on my nightstand.

I had no idea how any of it had gotten there. Fairies could've delivered it for all I knew. I was just grateful I'd had it, along with Addison's suggestions.

After downing a few ibuprofen with the entire bottle of water, I'd done as she'd told me. And while it hadn't been fun ingesting all of that, her little cure-alls actually worked. By late morning, I no longer felt like I was dying, and by midafternoon, I felt relatively normal, save for the lingering headache.

Mabel gave me a ride over to the resort since she had book club today, this time in a cabana on the beach. As soon as she shut off the car, she shot off, tittering on about making sure this week's boob cookies were set up and ready before everyone else got there.

The main inn was under construction, which meant the entire space was in chaos, with various workers milling about. Meticulous Aiden who thrived on order just had to be *loving* that.

With my laptop bag slung over my shoulder and a pink bakery box in hand, I strode through the entryway, glancing around for Addison. I found her just outside the parlor, bossing around a man who looked to be approximately twice her size. The guy regarded her with rapt attention, not of attraction but respect. Pretty impressive for a five-foot-nothing pregnant mama-to-be.

After finishing her conversation with the contractor, she headed over to me, eyeing me up and down. "Well, you don't *look* like death warmed over. How're you feeling?"

I breathed out a laugh and rubbed my fingers over my forehead. "Not gonna lie, it was touch and go there for a while. Thanks for dropping by with all that stuff."

"All what stuff?"

"The ibuprofen, bottle of water, and a perfect cup of coffee, made exactly how I like it..." I said, hesitancy seeping into my tone.

Addison froze and glanced at me with one brow raised. "You had all that waiting for you this morning?"

"Yeah..." I said, drawing out the word. "You didn't leave it?"

"Wasn't me. But I'm glad you had all that because it seems like things were probably a little rough for you this morning."

I blew out a breath and attempted to rub away the dull ache behind my right temple. "I wasn't sure I was going to make it."

Addison tossed her head back on a laugh. "I thought that might be the case after Levi had to carry you home."

I froze, my brain not quite comprehending her words. A brief, foggy memory came to mind—lying in bed, boneless and sated, soft lips against my forehead...and then nothing. "He...did what now?"

She nodded, shooting me a sly smile. "Yep. Took off your sandals, covered your ass with his hoodie to make sure you didn't flash anyone, and tossed you over his shoulder. Then he marched you straight home. When you went along without argument, I knew you were toasted," she said. "Especially when you slapped his ass."

I sputtered. "I *what*?"

She shrugged like this was a common occurrence. For all I knew, maybe it was. Maybe Levi frequently carried home drunk women who smacked his ass in thanks. It was a great ass, so they probably got in some light groping, too.

And just why the hell did that bother me so much?

Last night was little more than a blur. I remembered the not-at-all-productive talk with Brick Wall, joining the girls for dinner, talking about books and men and...probably other things, too, but I couldn't recall.

And now that Addison had mentioned it, a flicker of last night came to mind. Levi in my bedroom, making sure I had what I needed...

Wait...*he'd* been the one who'd set out all that stuff on my nightstand, not Addison. And definitely not a fairy. When I'd woken up in my bed this morning, I'd been alone and completely naked. Not unusual for me after drinking, but I'd felt a tiny niggle in the back of my mind about Levi.

Apparently, that niggle was him taking care of me. Or perhaps it was the whole him carrying me home and me playing a drum solo on his ass part.

"Oh my God." I groaned and rubbed my fingers over my brow. "That was the most I've drunk...maybe ever."

"No shit?" Addison shook her head. "Damn, girl, you really jumped in with both feet. Avery was down for the count this morning, and you matched her drink for drink."

"Did I? I don't remember much of anything after she ordered that last pitcher of margaritas. But your hangover miracle really *is* a miracle."

"Told you."

I handed her the box I'd brought with me, filled with a dozen donuts from the bakery in town. "A little thank-you-slash-congratulations for the mama-to-be."

Her eyes widened, and she snatched the box from me. "Oh my God, you know the way to a pregnant woman's heart, don't you?"

I laughed, waving her off when she offered me a donut before grabbing two for herself. "How've things been here? Your brothers take it okay since Avery spilled the beans?"

Addison shook her head, swiping away some chocolate frosting from the corner of her mouth. "Oh, she didn't spill. I texted them because I knew she—or one of the rest of those loudmouths—would. So at least the boys heard it from me first. I've been threatened with a puppy pile at the Saturday meeting. In the meantime, they've all just been walking around, high-fiving, and calling each other *Unc*." She rolled her eyes and mumbled, "Idiots," but there was no hiding the affection in her tone.

Her family had been through so much, all of it after I'd already been out of their lives, so I hadn't witnessed the fallout. But I knew it had to have been tremendous with how close they'd all been to their mom and how little their dad had always been involved.

It was good to see that even after they'd lost her, they'd managed to grow closer than I remembered their being when we were kids. They all deserved that peace. Every single one of them.

THIS WAS my favorite part of the job. Talking to people... listening to their stories. Asking the right questions to uncover details even they didn't realize were lost in their memories.

As Chase sat across from me at one of the tables down by the beach, I readied my equipment for the interview, setting out my notebook with the list of questions I'd jotted down and a pen. Then I placed my phone on the table between us and navigated to the recording app.

"Okay, we can get started if you're ready. Let me just turn on my recorder..." I pressed the button on my phone, the software starting up as I glanced at my notepad, deciding where to dive in first.

Chase barked out a laugh, then reached over and pressed the red circle on my phone, stopping the recording. "Seriously?"

I glanced at him, brows raised. "Oh, are you not okay if I record this interview?"

"Interview?" He scoffed, leaning back in his chair and linking his hands behind his head as he shot me a grin. "I was kind of hoping we could just talk. You know, as friends."

Friends. Right. The trouble with that was I wasn't in Starlight Cove to be someone's friend. I was here to complete an assignment. And hopefully to complete it well enough to be offered a permanent position with the magazine. Chase's and my history didn't change that, no matter how close we'd once been.

I cleared my throat, tapping my pen twice on my notebook. "Right now, we're not friends. You're Chase Lockhart, hockey superstar who's decided to settle back in Starlight Cove, and I'm here to interview you. As previously discussed." I raised a brow, reaching over to press the record button again. "So if we could just—"

Before I could even finish the sentence, Chase pressed the red button, stopping the recording once again.

I barely bit back a groan of frustration. "Seriously?"

"How about we chat first? We haven't really had a chance to since you've been back in Starlight Cove. Hell, I don't think we've really talked since we grabbed lunch last year in Chicago."

Clenching my jaw in an attempt to rein in my irritation, I folded my hands on top of the table. "Well, this isn't our usual once-a-year lunch. We're talking today specifically for the article I'm writing. And I'm not going to quote something you mention during a conversation with a friend. I didn't think I had to say this, but I take my job very seriously."

He lifted a single shoulder in a shrug. "And I take my friend-ships very seriously."

I huffed out a breath and barely stopped myself from rolling my eyes. "Do you really, now? The years I spent alone say otherwise."

There was a heavy pause, one in which I wished like hell I could turn back time. Rewind to twenty seconds ago and never allow those words to leave my mouth. Because what was the point after all this time? He'd moved on. I thought I had, too.

"Fuck," Chase said under his breath as he scrubbed a hand down his face. Then he leaned forward, resting his forearms on the table, and met my gaze head on. "I owe you an apology, Harper."

I pressed my lips together and shook my head, not in any kind of headspace to deal with this right now. Maybe not ever. It'd been more than a decade since all that had gone down, and I'd moved past it. At this point, I was fine going the rest of my life never discussing it. "Can we not do this now, please?"

"I think we're long overdue, actually. I was a shit friend to you."

I raised a brow, crossing my arms over my chest as I leaned back in my chair. "Can't argue with that. But it's fine. I'm sure you had other things going on in your life."

He dipped his chin in a nod of acknowledgment. "I did. But so did you. And you didn't have a support system to fall back on like I did."

I swallowed hard, averting my gaze as I tried shoving back the lump that had suddenly risen in my throat. I didn't cry. And I certainly didn't cry in front of other people. "Yeah, well. I handled it."

"Of course you did," he said, his tone full of admiration. "You're Harper fucking Davidson, and I don't think there's been anything in your life you haven't been able to handle. But just because you *can* doesn't mean you should have to."

If only life worked that way... I'd been handling shit on my own for years because the other option was crawling back to my parents after cutting them out of my life. And I had zero interest in doing that. No matter how lonely it got. They were like a cancer, and I wasn't going to allow them to spread their poison into my life any longer.

"I don't want to sit here and give you excuses, but Levi was a wreck after everything went down with you two. A total fucking disaster." Chase blew out a heavy breath as he glanced at the table between us. "He was doing everything he could to escape. Alcohol. Drugs. Whatever. I was worried he'd—" Chase cut himself off, clearing his throat as he averted his gaze.

Worried he'd...what? My stomach tied itself in knots, a thousand different possibilities flying through my mind, each one worse than the last. Had he really spiraled that far? And at what point had he stopped?

Needing to know, I voiced my thought. "Worried he'd what?"

Chase pressed his lips together and shook his head, tracing a mindless pattern on the tabletop with his fingertip. "Just know he's been stuck in a downward spiral of self-destructive behavior for a long time. Anything so he doesn't have to think about it."

"So *he* didn't have to think about it? He was the one who ended things, Chase. It was his choice."

"Maybe. But maybe there's more to it than you think."

"Well, I'd love to hear about it."

Chase ran a hand along his stubbled jaw as he regarded me. "I wish I could tell you, but this really isn't my story to share. Just know that not everything was—or is—as it seems. And you two need to sit down like grown-ass adults and have an actual conversation, rather than yelling and pissing matches or whatever the hell it is you two do when you're alone in that apartment."

Flashes of the night I'd walked in on Levi in the living room immediately came to mind. How hot he'd made me. How he'd looked at me as he'd stood there and watched. How he'd sounded...

"Time to be my dirty girl, sparrow."

I nearly shook the thought from my head because it didn't make any sense. Levi hadn't said a word that night.

So then, why could I hear him so perfectly in my mind?

"Time to be my dirty girl, sparrow. Come all over your fingers and pretend it's my cock."

My entire body flushed, heat creeping up to pool in my cheeks. I cleared my throat, pushing away the unwelcome memories. I couldn't think about that night right now. Not when Chase was sitting across from me, studying me carefully. The last thing I needed to do was fixate on whatever my mind had obviously conjured up as if it had come from Levi.

"Why are you telling me all this?" I finally asked.

Chase shrugged. "Because you need to know. And Levi's sure as hell not going to tell you. Not unless you push. He likes to pretend for the whole fucking world that he's fine. But he never pretends he's *happy*. That's because he hasn't been in a long damn time. Not since the last night you two spent together, if I had to guess."

I shook my head, staring at him openmouthed because none of that made sense. Not with how Levi's and my history played out in my mind. "*He* was the one who broke *my* heart, Chase. Or have you forgotten that part?"

"I haven't. And I can guarantee you, neither has he." He braced his forearms on the table and leaned toward me. "Talk to him. I mean it. Before you leave Starlight Cove for good, I want you to talk to him about this. So I don't have to keep any more fucking secrets. And so maybe I can finally have my two best friends again."

I ENDED my chat with Chase with more questions than answers, his words echoing in my mind, refusing to let up. But regardless of their persistence, I couldn't reconcile them with what I'd been telling myself for years. What I'd thought I'd known was true—that Levi had been cold, cruel, and calculating when he'd ended things and then disappeared off the face of the earth. Blocking me everywhere he could without remorse or regret.

How could I have possibly gotten that wrong?

I wandered along the beach, needing time alone to think before I headed back to the apartment. Before I saw Levi again.

It was so peaceful down here, the water lapping at the shore and the soft ocean breeze through my hair. As kids, Levi and I had spent hours on the beach, talking about our dreams for the future. A future we were supposed to share together.

Those memories felt like a lifetime ago now. So much had changed since I'd left Starlight Cove behind. *I'd* changed. The hopeful, naive girl I'd been back then was long gone, replaced by someone more guarded, more cynical. Someone who'd learned the hard way that dreams didn't always come true. And people didn't always stay.

Still, Chase's admission tugged at something inside me. Made me wonder if there was more to the story than I realized. More to the breakup than what met the eye.

I'd spent the past decade thinking that Levi had broken things off without a backward glance. That I meant nothing to him. His harsh words—words I'd spent years trying to forget—and the cold, detached way he'd said them flooded my mind.

I don't love you. I never really did. I was only interested in a good time, and I'm bored now. This was just a summer fling anyway. It never meant anything.

I swallowed down the hurt that always crept in when my memories overwhelmed me. But for the first time, I tried to look at what had happened objectively. See if I'd missed anything when I'd been blinded by my hurt.

I could still see him standing there, shoulders hunched, head down. His hands had been shoved into his pockets as the sunset illuminated him from behind. He hadn't even looked me in the eye. Not once. At the time, I'd thought he couldn't stand the sight of me, but now I wondered if maybe he just simply *couldn't.* Because if he did, maybe he wouldn't have been able to go through with it at all...

If even an ounce of what Chase said was true, this changed things.

This changed *everything.*

And though I wanted to cling to the anger and betrayal I'd been carrying since Levi had ended things, I had to admit, at least to myself, that it might be more complicated than that.

My feelings certainly were.

When he'd broken up with me, he'd taken a piece of my heart, leaving a gaping wound behind. That ever-present hurt was a constant ache that simmered under the surface, flaring up whenever he was around. Manifesting itself into pure anger. I wanted to cling to that like a security blanket, using it to keep him at a distance. Using it to protect myself because I'd been through too much...hurt by every single person who'd supposedly loved me.

But as much as I wanted to hate Levi, and as much as it

would make things easier if I did, I didn't. Not really. I hated what he'd done to me. To us.

I could admit that, more than anything, I was hurt by him. Confused and blindsided and now, years later, still a little heartbroken, if I was being completely honest. But I didn't hate him.

This whole situation would've been a hell of a lot easier if I did.

Still, I couldn't reconcile the details Chase had given me with what had actually happened. None of it made sense. Not why Levi would do it or why he'd stayed away.

True, the night before he'd broken things off, we'd been caught having sex in the back seat of my dad's car. But his parents hadn't been the ones to freak out—he'd been eighteen at the time anyway. But mine? Mine had lost their shit and spouted all kinds of threats.

Before we'd even left the police station, they'd yelled and screamed about how I was ruining my life with a boy like Levi. Someone who wouldn't amount to anything more than a worthless drunk like his father. How I was tarnishing their name and my dad's future in politics. How they'd cut me off if I didn't end things immediately.

That didn't exactly work out as they'd hoped, though the end result was the same.

I was no longer with Levi, thanks to his doing, but it had also been the night I'd decided to stop playing my parents' game. I was no longer allowing their rules to restrict me. I was ready to forge my own path. Move forward with my life how I saw fit, rather than forcing myself into the framework they'd crafted for me or following the plans they'd made for me.

And when I'd told them as much, they'd been the ones to give the ultimatum. Them and the life they'd created for me—or nothing.

So, I'd chosen nothing.

In reality, it had been *everything*. Just not them.

I didn't know what had truly happened the night Levi broke things off. I didn't know if he was just giving lip service, and if he had been, why? And why couldn't he tell me what had *actually* happened? Why couldn't he have reached out at some point over the past decade-plus and made things right?

But I did know one thing—Levi and I needed to talk. I could finally admit these feelings I had toward him weren't hate. I was angry, without a doubt. Pissed at everything that had happened. But I still felt lingering affection, tied up with hurt and heartbreak.

And the only reason that remained was because the connection between us was still going strong, the string tying us together thin and frayed but attached. Something neither time nor distance had been able to sever.

CHAPTER TWENTY-FIVE

LEVI

ADDISON:

I thought you were gonna stop by today

LEVI:

Something came up

ADDISON:

Bullshit

You found out Harper was going to be here

And you're avoiding

Like usual

LEVI:

Or maybe I just didn't want a lecture from you. Jesus, you've gotten self righteous in this pregnancy.

ADDISON:

That's a lie and you know it

I've ALWAYS been self righteous

LEVI:

Can't argue with that.

ADDISON:

I gave Harper my hangover cure this morning

LEVI:

And?

ADDISON:

Apparently I didn't need to

Because someone left all kinds of goodies on her nightstand

Including her exact coffee order

You know anything about that?

ADDISON:

Hello?

I said DO YOU KNOW ANYTHING ABOUT THAT?

LEVI:

And I ignored you. Was that not clear?

ADDISON:

You're a dick

Maybe I should ignore you instead of telling you what I know

LEVI:

Pretty sure I don't care.

ADDISON:

You're right

You definitely don't care that your favorite roommate has a full dance card today

LEVI:

Wtf does that even mean?

ADDISON:

It means Harper's got interviews all day

With one of Stan's boys

So maybe don't wait up

But you don't care

Right?

Harper

I WALKED TOWARD THE APARTMENT, determination in my stride. Clouds had moved in since my time at the resort, and a storm was on the horizon, a low rumble of thunder sounding in the distance. I jolted, my entire body tightening in the same way it had forever, and I quickened my pace to get home faster.

Home.

That thought had me tripping over absolutely nothing, the realization that I wasn't walking away from the storm but *toward* Levi hitting me like a wrecking ball.

And just when in the hell had that happened?

At some point between when I'd arrived in town—full of anger and hurt and hostility...all the things that had been masquerading as hate—and now, there'd been a shift.

Maybe it had happened when Levi had made dinner and talked me through that first thunderstorm in town, distracting me from my fears even while he battled his own.

Maybe it had happened when we'd been high, too inebriated to put our guards up, allowing us to be vulnerable and talk like we used to.

Maybe it had happened when we'd kissed on the Ferris

wheel. When he'd held my face as if I was precious, even while he ravished my mouth like he couldn't get enough.

Maybe it had happened when he'd come to pick me up from One Night Stan's, even though he didn't have to, just to make sure I got home okay.

Maybe it had happened when he'd given me everything I needed to recover from a hangover. Including my usual coffee order, despite the fact that I'd never drunk it when we were teens and hadn't done so around him as adults.

Or maybe it had happened when he'd put me to bed last night. The evening as a whole was a blur, but glimpses were seeping in...foggy memories finally beginning to surface. Like him bracing himself on either side of my shoulders and brushing a kiss on my forehead, the scent of him warm and comforting, making me feel safe and secure.

Making me feel like I was finally home.

I had no idea when things had shifted, just that the talk with Chase had shaken something loose inside me. And now, here I was, rushing toward Levi instead of away from him like I'd been doing for more than a decade.

I climbed the stairs to the apartment, another low rumble of thunder quickening my steps. I didn't even know if Levi was home. Didn't know if he'd be here to soothe my frayed nerves—both from the impending storm and from the talk I knew we needed to have. But I...actually hoped he was. A sentiment I was finally allowing myself to admit, even just to myself.

I slid my key into the lock and opened the door, listening for movement, but the apartment was still and silent. Trying to rein in my disappointment, I set down my bag before shutting and locking the door behind me, then turned back around just as Levi strode out of the bathroom.

Wearing nothing but a towel.

Water dripped from his nearly black hair onto his bare shoulders, the droplets rolling down along his chest and over every sculpted inch of him. Inches I wasn't too proud to admit I wanted to trace. With my tongue. I was eager to study this new Levi, the one he'd grown into during our time apart. Figure out what made him tick. Learn him in ways I'd never known before.

"Hi," I said. Brilliant. I was a journalist who made my living with words, and "hi" was the best I could come up with?

"Hey," he said, his voice just a low rasp. He held the towel closed with one hand, running his other hand through his hair, the muscles in his arm bunching and flexing with the movement. And my *God*, was there anything about this man's physique that was fair? He was a Greek god, carved from stone, and here for my viewing pleasure.

I couldn't tear my eyes away from him, sucking in a sharp breath as my gaze snagged on the tattoos covering his body. The ink stood out in stark contrast against his skin, especially the few scattered over his chest—an anchor above his heart and a compass rose on his rib cage, details of it I couldn't quite make out. And then there were his full sleeves, their designs flowing effortlessly into one another, as if they'd all been created to exist together. I ached to reach out and trace along each one with my fingertips, follow every line and curve and ask him to tell me what they meant.

Levi flexed his hand on the towel, drawing my attention there...then lower still. To the unmistakable bulge the flimsy fabric couldn't hope to hide. A not-so-tiny part of me hoped like hell he'd lose his grip and the towel would go falling to the floor. Pool in a puddle at his feet and give me an unobstructed glimpse of the man I'd been dreaming about since I'd arrived.

Not to mention the years before.

The silence hung heavily in the space between us as we

stared at each other, and I felt it like a hum beneath my skin. I swallowed thickly, attempting to ignore the tug low in my belly and the throb between my thighs.

He cleared his throat and lifted his chin toward a tray on the breakfast bar. "Mabel, uh, brought over some more cookies. No pot this time, but they'll still be fucking delicious. They always are."

I snapped my gaze to his, my breath catching as his words sank in, unlocking something inside me as a deluge of memories came to the forefront of my mind.

Levi sitting on the edge of my bed, his eyes dark with hunger as he watched me touch myself. As he talked me through it. But his hands had never once settled on my skin, his words the only thing he'd used on me last night.

Look at you. Your needy cunt is dripping, isn't it? I want to lick it all up. We both know you'd taste fucking delicious. You always were.

My breath caught as more came to me, one after another after another.

Sink those fingers deep. Let me hear how fucking much you need it.

It's impossible to pretend I haven't been inside you.

Fuck yourself faster. And rub that pretty little clit while you're at it.

If I fucked you now, you'd take it. We'd make it fit.

I took a step toward him, my breaths coming too fast, but I gave up trying to act like I had everything under control. I didn't. Not by a long shot.

I knew we needed to talk. I deserved to know what had really happened that night he'd walked away. Why he'd called things off. A million unsaid things hung in the space between us.

But what was one more night when thousands had already passed us by?

I didn't want to take the chance that a discussion would scare him off. Not now, when I could hear the rumbling thunder in the distance. And certainly not now that I'd finally allowed myself to admit I wanted him. Desperately. And after the memories I recalled from last night, I had no doubt he felt the same.

"Sparrow?" Levi walked toward me, his brows pinched. "You okay?"

"Fine," I said. Croaked, really. Because I was anything but fine.

I was strung tight, my body buzzing with awareness, my heart thrumming too loudly in my ears. I was tired of pretending. Tired of fighting this pull that was ever-present between us.

The one that had never actually gone away.

He studied me, sweeping his gaze over me from head to toe, lingering on the low dip of my blouse, the flare of my hips in this fitted skirt, and I felt it as surely as if it had been an actual caress. Finally, he glanced away, his jaw ticking. "I thought you were going to be gone all night for interviews."

That had been the plan, but I had no idea how he knew that because I never told him. After my interview with Chase, I'd intended to pop over to One Night Stan's and try my luck again. This time, hopefully with a different—*nicer*—brother.

Instead, all I'd wanted was to be home. With Levi.

I took another step toward him, settling between him and the breakfast bar, until we were mere inches apart. Close enough I could feel the heat pouring off him, could inhale his warm, fresh scent straight into my lungs, could count the drops of water dotting his skin. "I came to some realizations while I was out and decided I needed to be here instead."

He swallowed thickly, his gaze dipping to my lips before meeting my eyes again. "What realizations were those?"

"Well, for one thing, we're not even."

"What do you mean, we're not even?"

"Last night... You saw me get mine, but you left before I got to enjoy the show." I reached out, stopping just before touching his skin, and traced his anchor through the air. "Seems only fair that you return the favor."

He stiffened, his entire body going rigid. "What do you remember about last night?"

"Not a lot." It wasn't entirely a lie. While I'd been flooded with glimpses, I still didn't have the whole picture. But I had enough to know he'd said some filthy things to me, all while keeping his hands to himself. That impeccable restraint, hard at work.

"Harper," he said, his voice low and rough. He finally dropped the grip he had on his towel to clutch the edge of the counter on either side of my hips, his knuckles white from the effort of holding himself back.

"You want to know what I think?"

"I'm sure you're going to tell me either way."

I flashed him a smile. "I think you've spent all these years perfecting your restraint." It was written in every rigid line of his body. How he held himself back when he was around me. Not allowing himself to cross the threshold of my bedroom when I got off with the toy, and not allowing himself to touch me last night. "But I also think you've had twelve years to fantasize about everything you want to do to me."

He locked his eyes on mine. "And what makes you think you wouldn't be horrified by those fantasies?"

This time when I reached out, I allowed my fingertip to touch his skin as I traced the design inked over his heart, too preoccupied by his closeness to pay it much attention. "What makes you think I would be?"

He huffed out a breath and shook his head, dragging his

gaze down my body in a way that wasn't at all respectful. "Because you might be the one who hates me, but I'd fuck you like I did."

A shiver stole over me, skating down my spine, as my nipples tightened and my panties grew wet. Just from his fucking words. He had the power to turn me inside out, and he was clueless about that fact.

"You have no idea what I'd like." I ran my hand down the front of him, over the carved muscles of his chest and abdomen, finally stopping at his low-slung towel. "I know what I'm getting into. So what's it going to take for you to give in?"

He stared at me for long moments. We stood so close, I could feel his breath ghosting over my lips, the scent of him surrounding me and making me forget anything outside our little bubble existed.

"You don't know what you're asking," he finally said.

"No? Why don't you enlighten me, then? What would it be like between us?"

He huffed out a laugh and shook his head. "It wouldn't be soft and sweet like it used to be."

I thought back to every time we'd had sex as teens. Back then, we'd been on everyone else's timetable, sneaking around so no one would see, and we'd gotten very creative. I wouldn't say any of our times were particularly soft or sweet. They were fast and frantic, both of us too hungry for each other for anything else.

"I know exactly what you're thinking," he said and shook his head. "But even in the car or on the cliffs or behind the cove, I still fucked you nice and easy. Still made it sweet for you."

He slid his gaze down my body, a filthy caress, and my entire being perked up at the attention.

"But I wouldn't take you to bed, sparrow. I wouldn't lay you out on the sheets and whisper how beautiful you are. It wouldn't be lights out, missionary until you came once and I followed." Still gripping the countertop, he moved his hands closer to me until his wrists pressed against my hips, the heat of them sending a delicious zing through my body. Then he leaned forward, his lips brushing my ear. "It'd be rough and dirty. I'd make you show me how much you want it, make you fucking beg for it. And then I'd give it to you. Over and over again, until you couldn't take it anymore. Your body would be so wrung out, you'd cry with every release. But instead of stopping, I'd lick up your tears and make you come again, just because I could." He pulled back enough to meet my gaze. "And even when I made it hurt a little, you'd still want more."

His words swept through me, stoking that low, simmering fire already inside me. Instead of turning me off, he'd only ignited an inferno. One that burned solely for him.

I rested my hands on his shoulders, dragging my thumbs up the column of his neck. "What are you waiting for?"

That clearly wasn't the answer he'd been expecting. His brows rose the tiniest fraction as he stared at me, and I wondered if this had all been for nothing. If, despite everything I'd said, his restraint was strong enough to hold him back. If, maybe, he just wasn't as drawn to me as I'd assumed. Wasn't as drawn to me as I was to him.

And then, before I could step away, before I could slink off to my room and try to forget making an ass of myself, everything changed. The air in the room shifted as Levi's restraint finally snapped.

"Fuck it," he muttered before wrapping his hand around my nape and tugging my face down to his.

CHAPTER TWENTY-SIX

HARPER

I DIDN'T EVEN HAVE time to register what was happening before Levi's lips were on mine. This kiss was hard and aggressive. Full of every ounce of bottled-up tension I felt, reflected back at me tenfold. Levi wasn't hesitant or tentative. He just took. He licked into my mouth, his tongue sliding against mine as he held me to him like he was afraid I was going to disappear.

Like he couldn't bear to let me go a second time.

"This what you wanted? Is your pussy feeling needy tonight?" He pulled away long enough to lift me up onto the counter in front of him. Then he sat down on one of the stools and tipped his chin toward me. "Show me."

"What?" I asked, breathless and distracted.

"Show me," he enunciated, his words hard, eyes even harder. "Show me the greedy little cunt I need to take care of. Show me how much you want it."

I sat frozen for a few moments, stunned into silence. Though not from fear or hesitation. From pure need. I wanted this man more than I could remember ever wanting anyone else.

And I was tired of waiting.

I shifted my weight from side to side, sliding my skirt up my thighs and over my hips until it pooled at my waist. And then I rested my heels on his thighs and spread my legs wide, giving him a glimpse of my pussy and the wet scrap of lace covering it.

He tutted and shook his head. "Panties, too."

"If you want them off, do it yourself."

He raised a brow at me, a challenging glint in his eyes. "You sure that's what you want, sparrow?"

"That's what I said, isn't it?"

"Fine, but remember you asked for this." Before I could clarify what he meant, he gripped my panties in his fists and tugged hard, the material pulling taut across my skin before the flimsy lace sides snapped. He smacked the outside of my thigh and said, "Up."

I followed his demand without thought, too shocked to do anything else. Pressing my heels on his thighs, I lifted my ass off the counter so he could remove my underwear completely. When I was settled back on the countertop, he slid his hands up the insides of my thighs, spreading his legs wide and taking mine with them. Giving himself an unencumbered view of my pussy.

"Since you love it so much, how about a little tit for tat?" He brushed his thumbs along the creases where my legs met my body, so close to where I needed him but still a mile away. "I'm going to make you drip onto this counter without touching your pussy, and you're going to get on your knees for me tonight."

I huffed out a laugh. He thought a lot of himself—and I was inclined to believe it—but there was no way. I was aroused, for sure. But I'd never been that turned on in my life, even with him. I'd love to see him try, though. "Deal."

"Good. Now, take off that worthless top and show me your tits."

There was no use playing coy, not when this was exactly what I'd wanted from the moment I'd walked in. So I did as he asked, relishing the look of pure hunger written on his face as I removed my cami and bra, tossing both on the floor next to him.

"Fucking gorgeous," he muttered, so low I wasn't sure I was supposed to hear. He cupped my breasts and pushed them together, letting out a low groan of approval when my nipples beaded at his touch. "Gonna fuck these before the night's through."

I shifted on the counter, reveling in his appreciation of my body. Especially when it looked like he wanted to fall to his knees right here and worship my breasts for hours. He hummed low in his throat and brushed his lips over the stiff peak of my right breast. A shudder rolled through me at the rough scrape of his beard against my delicate skin, juxtaposed by the soft brush of his lips over my nipple. I arched my back at his touch, sliding my fingers into his hair to hold him close, needing more.

"You *are* a greedy little thing, aren't you?" he said, his words holding a taunting lilt.

"Not greedy enough, apparently. Thought you said I'd be dripping. There is an expiration on that tit-for-tat situation."

"Don't rush me, or I'll make it last twice as long." With his eyes locked on mine, he sucked my nipple into his mouth before catching it with his teeth and tugging hard enough to drag a gasp from me.

The sharp sting melted away as he circled the tight peak with his tongue, and I couldn't hope to hold back my moan. Not when there was a direct line between my clit and my breasts, his attention making me squirm. I wanted more—*needed* it—and he somehow knew, giving it to me without my saying a word.

He scraped his beard against my delicate skin, then kissed away the lingering burn. Over and over again, he gave me rough and gentle, pleasure mixed with pain, and I had no idea I'd like it so much. Had no idea he'd do exactly what he'd said he would— have me a panting, dripping mess without ever touching my pussy.

When he finally pulled back, his pupils were blown wide and his cheeks were flushed, the only signs of his own arousal. "How about we see how I did?"

Except I already knew. I could *feel* how wet I was. How wet he'd made me.

A petulant part of me didn't want to show him. Didn't want to prove him right. My knees pressed together of their own volition, intent on keeping the secret to myself. At least until Levi clamped a hand down on the inside of my thigh, slapping it hard enough to sting.

"Don't get shy on me now, sparrow. Spread your legs and show me what's mine tonight."

His eyes were what made me comply. Pure hunger and want reflected back at me...and he was pissed as hell about it. No doubt because I'd made that infamous restraint snap. I was watching him unravel, thread by thread, and I loved seeing this raw version of him.

With slow, measured movements, I spread my knees wide, unapologetically showing him everything he'd done to me. The noise he let out was guttural, a soft growl that seemed to be torn from inside him.

"Look at you," he murmured. "This pretty little pussy is just begging for it, isn't she? What's the matter, sparrow? Nobody's been taking care of this sweet little cunt?"

A shiver racked my body. I had no idea how his voice could cause such a visceral reaction in me, but there was no denying it did. But he wasn't immune to me, either, and I wanted to see that last thread holding him back unravel completely.

I reached down and ran my fingertips through my slit. Dipping two fingers inside, I groaned at how sensitive I was, how desperately I needed to come. How desperately I needed *him*. How desperately I wanted him to feel the same.

With a wicked grin, I slipped my fingers free and reached toward Levi, tracing his lips and coating them in my arousal. "It's not getting taken care of now, either. You gonna do something about that, or should I go get my toy?"

I was waving a red flag in front of a bull, and I knew it. But considering how my nipples tightened and my clit throbbed, I couldn't deny how much I liked it, either.

With his eyes locked on mine, Levi slowly, deliberately, licked my arousal from his lips, and a groan rumbled in his chest. He cupped the insides of my thighs, guiding his hands down until he swept his thumbs along the apex, brushing them closer and closer to exactly where I needed him.

Then, without warning, he pulled one of his hands back and brought it down on my clit.

The soft slap against my sensitive nerves startled a gasp out of me. "What the hell?"

"We already decided I get to do what I want tonight, didn't we?" He continued the torturous brushes against my skin, always working me up but never where I needed them to be. "I told you what you were in for, and you agreed. So that means I get to take care of this pussy however I see fit because it's mine tonight. Right now, I want to tease it. I want to make you so desperate to come, you can't concentrate. You can't think straight. Your sole obsession is what part of my body is touching you and what I'll do next. But first, I need you to give me a word."

I shook my head at the abrupt change in subject. "A what?"

"A word, sparrow. Give me a word. Something you'll remember."

In case I needed him to stop. *Jesus.* This was so far out of the realm of my experiences, I felt like I'd been dropped into the middle of the ocean without a life jacket. Still, I was all in.

I said the first word that came to mind. "Peaches."

"Good girl," he said, his voice low and rough, approval threaded through. And I couldn't deny how much my body lit up for it. "Now, you better speak up if you don't like something because I'm all out of nice. Got it?"

"You've never been nice." That was true. Levi wasn't *nice.* He didn't bend to the whim of others or roll over just because it was expected. But he was kind, more so than I'd given him credit for.

"I can be." This time when he brought his fingers to my pussy, his touch was soft. Just the barest caress over me. Not nearly what I needed in order to feel any sort of relief. I shifted, wanting to get closer, but he just made a gruff sound in the back of his throat and held his ground.

"Jesus, look at you. Lifting your hips, trying to get my fingers inside you. You're so fucking hungry for it, aren't you?" He pressed a kiss to the inside of my knee, and goose bumps erupted over my entire body. "You never used to be like this. You used to be soft and sweet. Is this what I've turned you into? Desperate and greedy...my dirty girl."

I moaned, not bothering to deny it, because he was right. I was rolling my hips, trying to get him closer. Trying to entice him to really touch me so I could finally get off.

"Let's see how much you want it." He finally slid two thick fingers inside me, pumping them slowly and watching me the entire time.

With a groan, I dropped onto my elbows, letting my head fall back as I focused on his hands, on where he was touching me.

Just like he'd said I would. It was all I could concentrate on. For what seemed like forever, he fingered me in slow, methodical strokes, curling those fingers deep inside me, all while brushing the lightest of touches over my clit. But he never quite gave me what I needed.

"Levi," I said, unable to stop his name from tumbling past my lips.

He glanced up at me, something sparking in his eyes. "What do you need, sparrow?"

"Please... Please just—" I had no idea what I was asking for. All I knew was my body was strung tight with need, and he was the answer.

He chuckled lowly and stood, allowing my legs to hang off the side of the counter. Bringing his body over mine, he sank his two middle fingers deeper inside me, all while pressing his palm hard on my clit, finally giving me some of the pressure I'd been craving. He brushed his lower lip along the shell of my ear, sending a shudder through me. "What did I tell you? We've only just gotten started, and you're already begging."

"I'm not—" Before I could get out whatever else I was planning to say, Levi's fingers were gone, and he stopped touching me entirely.

My nipples were hard peaks, aching and overly sensitive, my pussy clenching around nothing, while my clit throbbed for release. I dug my fingers into his biceps, holding him to me. "No! No, please..."

He continued withholding his touch, but I could feel the heat of him above my pussy, his fingers just out of reach. I had to force myself not to lift my hips toward him, just for that contact. I hated how much he'd made me crave him in such a short time, but I was too far gone to truly care. I wanted—*needed*—to come.

And I wanted *him* to make me.

I wrapped my hand around his nape and tugged him toward me until our lips brushed with every word. "Stop fucking around and make me come."

A slow smile swept across his mouth, a look that screamed trouble. "Just remember, you asked for this."

Without warning, he sank his fingers deep once again, thrusting them in a quick rhythm designed to make me fall fast. And I did. Within seconds, he pushed me over the edge. My body tightening...tightening until everything exploded all at once.

He was murmuring something in my ear, his fingers still moving skillfully inside me, but I couldn't hear him. Not with the blood rushing through my veins, the thrum-thrum-thrum of it drowning out everything else. My entire body was wrung out, yet still somehow strung tight.

Still needing more.

"*Fuck*," he groaned, the first tiny crack in his demeanor. He curled his fingers inside me, grinding his palm hard on my clit. "I've got you. Give me another one, just like that. I want this fucking counter soaked with you. And then I'm going to sit down and enjoy my meal."

CHAPTER TWENTY-SEVEN

LEVI

I HAD no idea how to make one night last a lifetime, but I was going to try my fucking hardest. Never in a million years had I thought I'd have another chance at being with Harper. I sure as hell didn't deserve one, yet here we were. And I wasn't going to waste it.

I'd been hard since she'd walked in, looking like a goddamn wet dream with a sheer black shirt over a camisole and a skirt that might as well have been painted on. The jealousy that had crept up at thinking she'd worn that while interviewing another man couldn't even quell my body's reaction. And now, after hearing my name on her lips while her pussy clamped down on my fingers...how her body shook and shuddered thanks to what I was doing to her? My cock was a fucking steel rod, aching for her.

And though I'd had plenty of experience ignoring my dick and depriving myself of release, this was something altogether different. My routine desires had nothing on the sight in front of me. A nearly naked Harper laid out on my counter, her black skirt rucked up around her waist, wearing those red fuck-me heels with her thighs spread wide. Flushed and panting, tits heaving, pussy soaking wet.

"How many is that, sparrow?"

She shook her head, and a full-body shudder rolled through her as I brushed my fingertips over her swollen clit. "I... I don't—"

"I haven't even fucked you with my tongue yet. And if you think I'm ending the night without tasting your come, you haven't been paying attention."

She whimpered even as she tilted her hips to get closer to my touch. "I don't know if I can."

"No? You know what you need to say to make me stop. But until you do, I'm going to do exactly what I want." I slid my palms down the insides of her thighs, brushing my thumbs over her pussy lips and spreading her wide for my gaze.

Her cunt was gorgeous and fucking obscene, flushed a deep pink, her clit so swollen it wouldn't take anything to make her go off. I could slide deep inside her, brush my thumb over her, and feel her come on my cock. But that would have to wait.

Right now, it was time for my feast.

I ran my nose along the crease of her thigh and inhaled deeply, groaning at the scent of her arousal. "You need it bad, don't you, baby?"

She reached for me, sliding her fingers through my hair, and tugged my face closer to her pussy. "Yes," she breathed. "God yes."

"How many more do you have for me?" Though her answer didn't really matter. I had no plans for stopping until she tapped out. There was nothing like the sweet torture of having her arousal on my tongue, on my fingers, and soaking my beard, all while denying myself any relief.

"I...I don't know." Her voice was threaded with a hint of awe, as if she couldn't believe what her body had already done. And I fucking loved that I'd been the one to coax it out of her. Just another first between us.

My towel had long since fallen off, and it now lay draped across the stool, doing nothing to hide my reaction to her. My dick, hard and fucking throbbing, was pointed directly at Harper, and I'd had to stop what I was doing more than once just to wrap a tight fist around my length and squeeze. Beat back this orgasm that was breathing down my neck.

Leaning forward, I blew a gust of air against her, teasing her just as much as I was teasing myself. My mouth watered, and I was desperate to taste her again after all this time. Desperate to make her come against my tongue over and over, making her pussy so swollen and sweet, she'd be begging to take every inch of me.

"*Levi.*"

I smirked at the pleading edge in her voice. "Tell me what you need, sparrow."

"Please, I just..." She shook her head, canting her hips closer to me. "Please, please, give it to me."

"Use your words and I might."

She huffed out a frustrated breath, her fingers tightening in my hair. She glared down at me, but the effect was ruined by her riotous hair, her flushed cheeks, the mascara smudged around her eyes. She looked fucking *ruined*, and I'd done that to her.

Finding her voice, she snapped, "I need you to lick my clit and make me come."

Fuck me. Unable to deny either of us any longer, I hooked my arms beneath her legs, leaned forward, and did as she asked. It was the barest hint of my tongue against her, just a light swirl around her clit, not even making direct contact. Still, she shot off immediately, her orgasm crashing through her without warning.

I groaned as her taste flooded my mouth, my cock throbbing like a fucking beast who was aching for her. I licked up her seam and tongued her entrance, tasting everything I'd done to her. Tasting how fucking much she wanted this. Wanted *me*.

"That's my girl. That orgasm was mine, wasn't it? I got you so worked up, your little pussy was aching for it. It's still aching for it, isn't it?"

She didn't answer, only moaned in response. Humming low in my throat, I dove in again, gripping her hips and holding her to my mouth, just as eager as she was. Needing to fucking devour her. I wanted my face covered in her, wanted her dripping down my chin by the time we were done.

I pulled back enough to slip two fingers inside her, curling them toward me. "Let's see how many more you've got in you."

"No, I—" Her words cut off on a moan when I finally made direct contact with her clit, fluttering my tongue over it in quick strokes before sucking it into my mouth. "Fuck. Oh *fuck*."

Her feet were propped on my thighs again, giving her the leverage she needed to roll her hips toward me with every flick of my tongue, every curl of my fingers inside her. Gripping my hair tighter, she held me to her pussy, grinding herself against my face. Every ounce of decorum gone, and I fucking loved it.

I groaned into her cunt, affixing my mouth to her and fucking her hard and fast with my fingers. Eager to taste another release.

She could shake her head all she wanted. Could say she didn't want to—or couldn't—come again. But when her body reacted like this, responding to every little touch, every tiny caress, there was no way I was tapping out before her. No matter how many times I had to reach down and grip the base of my cock to stave off my own orgasm. Not unless she uttered that one little word.

I was drunk on her taste, on the sounds of her moans and whimpers. Harper had always been an addiction, and that hadn't waned at all in our years apart. And if this was the only part I could have, I would take it. I'd cling on to it with both hands until I forced myself to finally let go.

In the meantime, I planned to make her come over and over, until she was begging for mercy. Wanted to ruin her for every other man. So that when, eventually, she left again, she'd never be able to forget me.

Or what we were together.

"Oh my God, you're gonna make me come again." Her words were breathless and disbelieving, her wide eyes locked on mine as she stared down at me. She held me tight against her until she crested again, her head dropping back on a moan as she rolled her hips toward me. "*Levi*."

Fuck *me*, but I loved the sound of my name on her lips like this. When she was riding that high, chasing that pleasure. When I was giving her everything she needed. I couldn't change the past—wouldn't want to when my choices had given her the life she currently had—but I could give her this.

I could give her tonight.

CHAPTER TWENTY-EIGHT

HARPER

I HAD NEVER COME SO MUCH in my life. Nearly naked, I lay on the counter, legs spread, tremors coursing through me as tears leaked from the corners of my eyes. My body felt like a live wire, every little touch sending shock waves through me.

And yet, even after all that, I still craved Levi.

There was no denying our history played a part in my body's response to him, but it was more than that. My Levi—the one I'd loved my entire adolescence—had been sweet. Rough around the edges, sure, but never mean. Especially not to me.

But *this* Levi—this angry man with the glowers and grunts, who held himself back as if in punishment for something, all while dishing out more pleasure than I'd ever known—was someone altogether new.

Someone I couldn't manage to get enough of.

He pulled back, his chest heaving, eyes dark with desire and his mouth still wet from me. He looked like a man teetering on the edge, and I wanted to push him over. Wanted to make him lose control entirely.

Just like he'd done to me.

"Are you finally going to fuck me now?" I asked, attempting to keep my voice even and pretending like I wasn't craving it with every breath.

"Not yet." He pushed the stool back from the counter and stood, his arms bracketing my hips. "You still owe me time on your knees."

I shuddered at his words, hating how much I loved when he talked to me like that, taking away a power I'd always held dear. One I'd fought for, had lost everything for. But here, as he took away every decision from me, my strength and pride warred with my desire.

In the end, the latter won.

I slid off the counter and braced my hands on his hips as I sank to the floor in front of him, allowing myself to soak in every inch of him. I wasn't sure I'd ever grow tired of looking at him, at the carved muscles of his chest and abdomen, the tattoos that decorated his body. I wanted to memorize each and every one he'd had inked into his skin, proof of a life lived without me.

That should've been a sledgehammer to the glass bubble surrounding us, halting every ounce of desire I felt for this man, but there was no stopping it. Not when I was this far gone.

His eyes were so full of want as he stared down at me, brushing his thumb along my cheek. "Such a good girl. My good, dirty girl."

I wanted to tell him I wasn't *his* anything, because he'd chosen that path. He'd made that choice for both of us, regardless of whatever reason he had. But I kept my mouth shut, dutifully ignoring the way my body lit up at his words, a part of me loving his claim.

I broke eye contact and glanced down, straight at his cock.

God, he was intimidating up close like this. I knew if I'd faced this beast head on as a teenager, there was no way I would've let him anywhere near me. Now, though, it was different...adorned with piercings I'd never seen. I stared at the four small silver balls around the head, and a thrill of anticipation shot through me, wondering what those would feel like inside me.

"Time to open up, sparrow." He wrapped his hand around his length and stroked once, his thumb playing with the piercings through his head before he brushed the tip against my lower lip. "Let's see how much that pretty little mouth can take."

My pussy clenched at his words, my clit still thrumming with the aftershocks of the too-many-to-count orgasms he'd given me. How the hell could I still be turned on? More importantly, how the hell could I still want *him*?

Needing to make him feel as out of control as I was, I wrapped my hand around his cock. Then, with my eyes locked on his, I swiped my tongue across the head, licking up the precome dripping down his length. He let out a soft groan, fisting my hair as I licked and sucked, playing with his piercings and taking my time. Teasing him like he'd done to me.

His hand tightened in my hair, but he never pushed. Never held me tight so he could shove his cock down my throat, satisfied with everything I gave him. I scraped my nails down his thighs before cupping his balls with one hand, his low groan sending a wave of pleasure through me.

When he was panting and cursing under his breath, I reached around to grip his ass and tug him forward, finally taking him deep. This time, his groan was loud and unrestrained as he tightened his fingers in my hair. His control was slipping, and I was eager to watch it. Couldn't deny how hot it was making me, knowing I had this kind of power over him.

Unable to stop myself, I dropped one hand from his ass and reached between my legs. I swiped my fingers through my pussy, moaning as I circled my clit.

Levi's eyes darkened, his fist tightening in my hair as he tugged my head back, guiding my eyes to his. "You really are my dirty girl, aren't you? Couldn't wait for me to fuck another orgasm out of you. You had to finger yourself while you choke on my cock."

I moaned around his length, my eyelids fluttering closed as a shudder worked its way through me. I sped up my movements, both with my mouth and my fingers. I was right on the edge, teetering on the brink of another orgasm and desperate for it. Desperate, too, to take him with me.

But before I could fall over the edge, Levi pulled back, tugged me to my feet, and crashed his lips down on mine. Moaning into his mouth, I didn't even have time to be pissed at the fact that he'd stolen my release from me. Not when he kissed me like that. Like I was the last woman on earth—the only one he wanted. It was frantic and hungry, and I groaned against him, loving the taste of myself on his tongue.

"You have a condom?" Levi muttered against my mouth, one hand gripping my ass, the other firm on my breast.

"You don't?" I asked, unable to keep the incredulity out of my voice. Because what single, thirty-year-old man with a healthy sex drive didn't have condoms at the ready?

He shook his head, not offering any other explanation.

I couldn't stop to think about the why of it. Not when my focus was solely on getting him inside me. Immediately. I needed him with a hunger I hadn't felt in far too long. Needed him filling me up. Needed to see if it was as good as I remembered.

Needed to prove to myself it *wasn't*.

Because no matter what happened with Levi and me...no matter if we finally had a discussion and things came to light...I wasn't staying. Not here in Starlight Cove, and not with him.

But I wasn't going to allow my mind to get tangled up in the unknown future. Because though we hadn't spoken it aloud, I held no delusions that this was more than a single night.

"I have an IUD. And haven't been with anyone in a while." A long damn while, but he didn't need to know that. "I'm clear. You?"

He studied me for a beat as if looking for something, then huffed out a breath and nodded. "Yeah. I'm clear."

"Then fuck me already."

Levi's eyes flared with heat, and he spun me around so I was bent over the counter. Leaning over me so his chest pressed along my back, he murmured, "Don't beg for something you're not ready for."

"Who said I'm not ready?" I glanced at him over my shoulder and shook my ass, feeling awfully cocky for someone who was literally dripping down her thighs. I should've been embarrassed at my body's reaction to him, but I couldn't find it in me to care.

"You're not ready because you're expecting something else. Even as much as I've told you otherwise, you're still thinking of how things used to be. But I'm not going to fuck you slow or sweet like back then." He brushed his hand down my spine, over the curve of my waist, and gripped my hip, digging his fingers into my flesh. He leaned over my back until his lips brushed my ear, his erection thick and hard against my ass. "I'm going to shove my cock so deep, it'll be all you can feel. So deep it takes your breath away. And then, just when you think you can't take any more, I'm going to give you the rest."

Levi did exactly as he'd warned. He swiped the head of his cock through my slit, gathering my wetness until it coated his length, his piercings teasing my clit with each pass. And then he thrust inside me, his cock stretching me to just this side of pain.

"Oh *shit*." I stared back at him with wide eyes, my breath caught in my throat as he filled me. And filled me some more.

He kept going, pushing deeper inside me until I gasped. "Told you, sparrow. Took your breath away. Now, are you ready for more?"

Without waiting for my answer, he thrust deep, giving me even more of him. So much I knew I wouldn't have been able to take him if he hadn't spent so much time working me up. Making me nearly delirious with need. He'd done it all just for this moment, so he could sink all the way inside.

I cried out, reaching back to dig my nails into his ass as he began to move. I met him thrust for thrust, arching my back and pushing against him. He gripped my hips, his fingers digging into my flesh as he filled me over and over again, fucking me like he was making up for lost time.

"Jesus Christ," he groaned. "You know how good you feel? How fucking hot this pussy is? Your greedy little cunt keeps sucking me deeper, desperate for me to fill her up."

"*God*." I knew he didn't just mean his cock, but his come, and the thought of it, the thought of him being the first man to empty himself inside me, made me ache for exactly that.

I couldn't help but wonder how many other women he'd been with like this.

How many others have there been?

None.

I gasped as the memory from last night slammed into me, my thoughts a jumbled mess even as my body responded to the realization that there'd only been me. If what he'd said was true, *there'd only been me.*

I sobbed out a breath—whether it was a moan or a cry, I wasn't sure. And through it all, Levi continued fucking me, alternating deep, driving thrusts with shallower ones, his piercings rubbing relentlessly against that spot inside me.

He wrapped his hand around the front of my throat, squeezing gently and tugging my head back until he brushed his cheek against mine. I could smell myself on him, and I loved that I'd marked him like he was about to mark me. "Is that what you want, dirty girl? You want my come so deep inside you, you'll still feel it tomorrow? Want a reminder of how good it felt when I was fucking you? How hard you came all over my cock?"

"Yes," I admitted on a whisper, too far gone to censor my thoughts. "Please...come inside me."

Levi swore under his breath and pulled out of me entirely. But before I could complain, he spun me around, lifted me onto the counter, and slammed his cock into me once again.

This was too intimate, being face-to-face—with his eyes boring into mine as he settled inside me. Especially with the realization I'd just come to.

I glanced away, unable to look him in the eye, but the reprieve didn't last long.

He gripped my face in one hand and tugged my attention back to him. "Eyes on me, sparrow." With his free hand, he slipped it between us, his thumb zeroing in on my clit.

Each brush of it against me sent a jolt through my body, my eyelids fluttering closed as sensations overwhelmed me—to say nothing at all about the steadiness of his gaze.

He squeezed my face tighter, and I snapped my eyes open, only to find him so close I could feel his breath on my lips.

"Eyes. On. Me," he said, his voice a low, firm demand. "Or I stop. And this sweet little pussy doesn't want that, does she?"

I whimpered and shook my head in the confines of his hold, already feeling the beginning of that delicious climb low in my belly.

And I finally stopped resisting. Stopped avoiding...stopped pushing him away and just gave in.

I wrapped one hand around the back of his neck and held him as tightly as he was holding me. Resting my other hand on his chest, I mindlessly traced the lines of the tattoo there—an anchor over his heart, a rope wrapped around it and carried away by a...sparrow? It was small, nestled among the block of script that stretched up to his shoulder, but there was no mistaking it now that I was actually looking.

My breath caught as I snapped my gaze to his, finding his eyes already on me, a thousand questions racing through my mind. Like, why would he permanently mark his body with a reminder of me if I meant nothing to him, as he'd claimed? And why would he stay away?

But before I could voice any of them, he pressed his forehead against mine, a low groan rumbling out of him. He pressed his thumb against my clit, and my entire body tightened, a moan leaving my lips. "There we go, sparrow. Now, be a good girl and give me one more. Soak my cock and show me how much you love it when I fuck you."

I locked my legs around his hips, pulling him deep, and that was all it took. "Oh my God. I'm—"

Before I could even get the words out, my orgasm tore through me, colors bursting behind my eyelids as wave after wave crashed into me. Levi dropped his face into my neck, groaning my name as he settled deep inside me, his cock pulsing with his own release.

Our past was messy and heartbreaking, a tangled ball of emotion I'd never been able to escape, regardless of how far I'd run. But in this moment, with his panting breaths in my ear and my heartbeat racing, I knew there was no more fighting this. No matter how much I tried to deny it, there was no escaping the truth.

Levi McKenzie still had a hold over me, and I wasn't sure that would ever change.

CHAPTER TWENTY-NINE

LEVI

I HAD no idea how long this dream was going to last, so I intended to take full advantage while I could. And whether I was lucid or not, a dream was exactly what this was. Harper, her body soft and pliant against me, looking at me like she never wanted it to end. Despite our history, despite our present circumstances.

And that was the danger here.

Right now, we were in this cocoon where nothing outside could reach us. Not real-life responsibilities, not the regrets from the past or the demons that never seemed to fully leave me, just recede once in a while, and certainly not the circumstances that proved Harper wasn't meant for this life.

She wasn't meant for me.

I'd known the moment she'd realized the tattoo on my chest had been for her. Knew she had questions about it, too. Fortunately, she hadn't voiced them. And I could only hope I'd be able to come up with a plausible lie by the time she did. Because there was no way I was telling her it was for her, that they *all* were for her. Every inch of me branded with her name, even if it didn't spell it out.

If she looked close enough, she'd notice the coordinates on the compass rose were the exact spot we'd met twenty years ago, and the script blending into the sparrow was a passage from her favorite book. She'd notice the Ferris wheel on my inner bicep and the sailboat nestled in the waves on my forearm and the peach tree on my shoulder blade.

Every one of them blended together, overlapping to be a coalescence that passed as being random. No one had ever questioned it, not even Chase. And that was where I'd gotten cocky, not doing more to hide the sparrow from her.

But I couldn't go back. And truthfully, I didn't know if I'd want to. If I did, it might shift everything. Maybe that little change would thrust us into an alternate reality where none of this had happened.

Fortunately, we were in *this* reality. One where I was curled around her, her body tucked up tight in front of mine. I'd lost count of how many times I'd been inside her in the short hours since this all began. While Harper had dozed on and off in between rounds, I hadn't wanted to, knowing with complete certainty that tonight was all I had.

So when she stirred awake and arched into me, a soft little hum in her throat as she pressed her ass against my dick, I wasn't going to say no.

I'd never say no when it came to her, and that was part of the problem.

I lowered my face into the crook of her neck and kissed along the column until my lips rested against her ear. "Does my greedy girl need it again?"

She reached back, digging her nails into my ass, her voice just a soft rasp. "I'm not the only one who's been greedy tonight."

That much was true, though she hadn't complained. Especially when my greed came in the form of making sure she got off as many times as possible. If my last count was to be trusted, she'd passed double digits a while ago.

"Don't even try to pretend you don't love how greedy I am." I reached down, hooking my hand under her knee and tugging her leg back over mine, opening her wide for me.

She hummed, arching as she reached up and slipped her hand around the back of my neck, a spark of satisfaction rolling through me as she sought me out. This wasn't—couldn't be— forever between us, but we had right now. And right now, Harper wanted me. Something I had no intention of denying her.

I ran my fingertips up and down her inner thigh but didn't give her what I knew she needed. Not yet. I'd spent years edging myself, never knowing how gratifying it could be to edge someone else.

"*Levi.*" The single word was nearly enough to coax a smile from me, her tone laced with frustration and irritation.

"Yeah?"

Rather than answer me with words, she reached down, threading our fingers together and guiding them straight to her pussy. As soon as we connected with her skin, we both let out groans.

"Jesus, sparrow. If I didn't know better, I'd say you got started without me." I ran my fingers through her slit before dipping one inside her. "Did you have a naughty dream about me?"

"Can't seem to stop dreaming about you, actually," she murmured.

My fingers stuttered against her skin, her admission shocking the hell out of me. I wanted to tell her that she and I were the same. That when my nights weren't plagued with nightmares of the day my mom died, Harper's was the only face I dreamed of.

But I couldn't admit that to her. Not now, not ever.

What I could do was be here, in this moment. Take everything she was willing to give me and stockpile my memory bank so I had something to recall the rest of my life.

"You feel that?" I asked, guiding both our fingers inside her. We pumped them together, side by side, as Harper let out a soft moan of pleasure. "You feel how fucking wet you are? How fucking much you need it?"

"Yes," she breathed, guiding our fingers faster inside her. "I do...I need it. Need you."

Even though I knew she meant me making her feel good, my heart still thumped painfully in my chest, aching for something I could never have.

"Look at you." I brought my face next to hers, running my beard along the curve of her jaw, my lips a whisper against her skin. "So fucking greedy for it. Tell me what you need."

Instead of answering, she gasped and arched harder against me, pressing her ass all over my cock while we fingered her together.

"That perfect ass and your little fuck-me sounds aren't enough, baby. I want you to tell me how bad you want it. How much you're dying to have me fuck you. I wanna hear you beg for it."

It was a sick game to play with her, considering it was something she'd never usually do. She'd never stoop so low...not unless she was desperate for it. I was just fortunate enough that right now she was desperate for *me*.

"Levi..."

I hummed into her neck, scraping my teeth along her delicate skin, and slipped my finger from inside her. She let out a soft whimper, one she probably didn't want me to hear, but she didn't stop fingering herself. Her hand moved faster as she rolled her hips in time with her fingers, each pass pushing her harder against my cock.

"That's how you want it?" I asked. "A mediocre orgasm by your own hand? Take it, then. If you're so greedy you can't wait for me, let's see how hard you can make yourself come."

I reached up and pinched her nipple, eliciting a gasp from her in response, her fingers moving even faster now. Her breathing grew stuttered as her entire body stiffened, then a shudder worked its way through her as she let out a low moan.

Jesus Christ, it was hot watching her make herself come. But it was even hotter when I was the one doing it.

"How was that, sparrow? Did that satisfy your needy little cunt?"

"No." She huffed out a frustrated breath and slipped her fingers from her pussy, reaching back for me. I caught her wrist and brought her fingers to my mouth, sucking them deep between my lips. I moaned as soon as her taste hit my tongue, my cock throbbing against her ass. Just as eager for her as she was for it.

"That tastes like you don't need another one since you already got yourself off. Was a lackluster orgasm better than the alternative?"

"Don't be an ass. I know you want it just as bad as I do."

That was true. The difference between us, though, was that I'd had more than a decade of practice at deprivation. And even though Harper writhing against me was one of the biggest temptations I'd ever experienced, there wasn't a doubt in my mind that I could hold out longer than she could.

"That doesn't sound like begging, sparrow."

Rather than say anything, she grabbed my hand and tugged it between her legs, guiding my fingers against her clit. I allowed her a moment of reprieve, letting her lead my movements until she melted into me, a satisfied hum leaving her throat. And just when that next whimper passed her lips, I pulled my hand away before bringing it down sharply against her clit.

She yelped and shot me a wide-eyed stare over her shoulder. "What the hell was that for?"

"I believe I told you to beg. And until you do, I'm not giving you anything." I brushed my lips against her neck and murmured, "Despite how badly I want to."

As those last words left my lips, her ire melted away, her gaze softening in a way that affirmed I'd said too much. That she was getting the wrong idea and that this could be more than what it was.

But she didn't ask about it, didn't confront me. Instead, she wrapped her fingers around my cock and stroked up the length. Unable to stop myself, I let out a groan into her neck, my fingers digging into the soft flesh of her inner thigh as I held her open for me.

"What do you want me to say?" She swiped her thumb over the head of my cock, driving me fucking wild. "You want me to tell you that my fingers aren't enough anymore? Not after I've had this"—she gave my cock a firm squeeze—"stuffing me so full, I can't breathe. That I already crave it? Or maybe I should just get straight to the point and tell you I want you inside me again. Please, Levi. Give me what I need."

I groaned, my cock jerking at her words. "That's my fucking girl. Go on, then. Fuck the cock you're so greedy for. Take every inch inside your needy cunt, and let's see how loud I can make you scream."

She hummed, slipping my dick through her slit before shifting it to her entrance and slowly sinking down. With every inch she took, she gasped. And even though her pussy was primed, so fucking wet and swollen from our night's activities, it still took effort for her to take all of me.

As she sank down on my length, I growled and dropped my forehead to her shoulder, getting lost in the feel of her. As incredible as her pussy felt wrapped around me, it was nothing compared to the deep ache that had settled in my chest. A constant reminder of everything I had to lose—of everything that wasn't mine to keep.

"Come on, sparrow," I said, interlocking our fingers and guiding them faster over her clit. "I know you can come harder than you did. And I want to feel it on every inch." I abandoned her fingers against her clit so I could press against her lower stomach, at the same time making my thrusts shallow as I dragged my piercings against her G-spot.

"Oh my God. Oh *fuck*." She strummed her fingers faster now, her soft whimpers rolling into low moans. Her entire body tightened as she arched into me, her cunt like a vise around my cock.

I groaned into her neck, clenching my teeth as I continued to fuck her, my restraint slipping away with every roll of her hips, every moan that left her mouth.

"*Levi*."

My name on her lips did it for me every fucking time, made me damn near lose my mind. My orgasm was too goddamn close, breathing down my neck, but I wasn't going to give in. Not until she got hers. "Time to fucking come. You had your little orgasm. Now this one is mine. Give me what I worked for and come all over my cock."

I pressed harder against her lower stomach, adding my fingers against her clit, and that was all it took. Harper's scream pierced the air, her cunt pulsing around me as she came, and I had no hope of holding anything back.

I sank deep, settling my cock as far inside her as I could. My orgasm tore through me, her name the only thing I allowed to pass my lips. Knowing, without a doubt, everything else had to remain unsaid.

CHAPTER THIRTY

LEVI

AFTER THAT LAST TIME, Harper had finally fallen into a deep sleep, her body heavy against mine. Meanwhile, I'd lain awake, the knowledge of just how badly I'd fucked up weighing heavily on my mind.

Last night had been a test, and I'd failed spectacularly. Had given in to the temptation I'd been fighting against for years—the one where I gave up, gave in, and went after exactly what I wanted.

Her.

Harper was curled into me, her leg thrown over mine, her head resting on my chest. When we were tangled together like this, it was easy to pretend everything was different. That this was what I woke up to every morning—the feel of her body against mine, her soft breaths sweeping over my chest.

But it wasn't. This wasn't our life...could never be.

Pressing my nose to her hair, I inhaled deeply and tightened my arm around her. Holding her close like I had a right to. Like I hadn't lost that privilege when I'd thrown it all away.

I glanced down at her, at the sleep lines on her face, the

shadow of makeup still smudged beneath her eyes. Her parents had always made sure she was poised and polished, their perfect little doll. Probably why I enjoyed seeing her like this, all sleep-rumpled and messy, especially knowing I'd been the one who'd done it to her.

I'd taken the prim and posh Harper Davidson, a distinguished woman, and I'd dirtied her up. I'd made her get on her knees for me...made her come so many times, she cried. Made her beg me to fuck her, to make her come. I'd made her so over-sensitive she recoiled from the lightest touch, all while craving it at the same time.

But dirtying her was what I was good at. It was what I'd always done...the entire reason I'd left her in the first place. From day fucking one, she'd deserved better than whatever the hell she'd get with me. And it was time I got back to reality.

I slipped out from under her, careful not to disturb her. She shifted slightly when I got out of bed before settling against the pillows and falling straight back to sleep. I watched her for longer than I should have, staring at the soft curve of her jaw, her pillowy lips parted in sleep, all the while wishing things could be different.

But they couldn't. That was a path I wasn't willing to consider. I needed to get out of here. Needed to figure out what the fuck I was supposed to do now.

She hadn't even been here for a month, and I hadn't been able to keep my dick in my pants. I'd gone twelve fucking years without it, and she had me snapping in mere weeks, with more still in front of us.

I threw on some clothes and slipped out of my room, not even wanting to shower before I left so I could smell her on me all day.

I was so completely and utterly fucked.

SINCE THE MORNING meetings had been temporarily relocated in deference to the construction happening at the main inn, I pulled into the diner parking lot and spotted Chase heading my way.

"What the fuck are you doing here?" He eyed me up and down as I climbed off my motorcycle. "Do I have my days mixed up? I thought it was Wednesday."

"It is Wednesday."

"Then my first question stands—what the fuck are you doing here?"

"Can I not go to the morning meeting?"

"You *can*. You just never do. And my wife has to threaten you with bodily harm to get you to show up."

"Yeah, well, I was in the neighborhood."

"In the neighborhood? What the—" Chase snapped his mouth shut and scanned me from head to toe, his brows inching up. "I take it leaving dirty dishes in the sink in an effort to push Harper out didn't work?"

"You never told me to leave dirty dishes in the sink."

"I told you to make her uncomfortable."

Yeah, and I'd taken it exactly as far as I'd needed to.

He must've read the guilt on my face because he narrowed his eyes. "What did you do?"

I shrugged like it was no big deal and glanced away. "I threw some porn on the TV and made sure she caught me in the middle of jerking off in the living room."

Chase let out a groan and scrubbed a hand down his face. "Jesus Christ, man. You are so fucking stupid. When I told you to make her uncomfortable, I meant doing shit like leaving the toilet seat up so she falls in at three a.m. or eating all her food.

Don't take out the garbage, use the bathroom floor as your personal hamper. I didn't mean rub one out in the fucking living room."

I crossed my arms over my chest. "Well, maybe you should have been a little bit more specific, then."

He studied me for long moments before finally shaking his head. "So, you slept together. Saw that one coming a mile away," he muttered. He raised a brow in my direction. "How was it?"

The look I shot him must have been answer enough.

"Right. Saw that coming a mile away, too." He reached up and ran a hand over the stubble covering his jaw. "Well, how did you leave things?"

With her none the wiser, looking like a goddamn angel spread out on my sheets. Except everyone knew an angel didn't belong with someone whose demons had been haunting him for years.

"I just left."

His brows hit his hairline as he stared at me. "Without saying anything."

"She was asleep."

He groaned and scrubbed a hand down his face. "You fucking idiot."

"Thanks, man."

"Did you stop to think for one second that leaving her alone after you fucked her might bring back some feelings from the last time you left her?"

I froze as his words sank in. *Fuck me.* He was right. I hadn't even considered how my leaving without a word might resurrect bad memories for her. I'd been too focused on keeping my walls intact and ultimately protecting her from whatever stain I'd bring to her doorstep.

But in doing so, I'd treated her like some random hookup I

could just fuck and flee. Worse, she had no idea she meant more to me than that because I'd made sure of it. Made sure to hide that she still—that she'd *always*—meant everything to me.

"I see by the look on your face that you're starting to get it. At least send her a text. Because now that your sister's seen you"—he gestured to the little shit peering at us through the diner's front window—"you're not going anywhere."

Cursing under my breath, I pulled out my phone and shot off a quick text to Harper before stepping inside the diner. I ignored everyone's questioning gazes as I took a seat in my usual booth.

"Hey, we can puppy pile early," Ford said, standing and immediately heading toward Addison, a giant grin splitting his face.

She held her arms out in front of her and shot a glare at each one of us. "I'm not going to be held liable for anything that happens if you shake or jostle me at *all*."

Ignoring her threats, Chase strode up to her and pulled out a sucker from his pocket. "How about a ginger lollipop?"

Addison's irritation melted away, and she exhaled deeply, relief written across her face as she glanced up at her husband. "How did you know?"

He tucked her into his side and pressed a kiss to her temple. "You're not exactly a delicate puker, Addie."

Shooting him a glare, she elbowed him in the stomach before sinking back into his side. Chase caught her without hesitation, the move so wholly natural, I had no idea how I'd never seen their connection during the years they'd been sneaking around. The ease between them reminded me of how Harper and I used to be. Before I'd thrown away the best thing I'd ever had in my life.

"You hear that?" Addison said, giving Ford the stink eye. "I'm not a delicate puker, so you can puppy pile me at your own risk."

Ford shrugged, enveloping both her and Chase in a hug. "I'm a firefighter, little D. It wouldn't be the first time I've been puked on."

"As the sheriff, I can definitively say same here." Brady stood from his chair with Aiden following.

"All I'm saying is, I better not have to clean up anybody's puke in my diner," Beck grumbled but joined in the group hug.

I was the last over, my brothers' arms welcoming me into the fold as we surrounded Chase and Addison, the two people who were expanding our little family of six. She grumbled the entire time, mumbling about making sure to shoot any vomit in our direction. But I didn't miss the way she wiped at the corner of her eye or the soft sniffle when we all finally pulled away.

After everyone was settled in their seats, Brady cleared his throat. "Before we dive into anything, we need to talk." He darted his gaze around at us, lingering longer on me. Finally, he cleared his throat. "Dad came by the station last week."

My body stiffened at the mention of our father, something that didn't slip past Brady's notice.

He went on. "I wasn't in, but Deputy Traeger passed along the message. Apparently, Dad wants to talk."

Aiden cleared his throat and shot a glance around the group. "He's been calling me, too, leaving messages and asking if I'll see him."

Addison perked up, her interest solely on them. She'd always felt differently about our dad than my brothers or I did. We'd protected her from the worst of it, not wanting her to experience what we'd had to. The broken promises and the abandonment, even while he was right there. But in doing so, that meant she had an unrealistic view of our father. She didn't know the extent of his selfishness. Had never truly witnessed how little he cared about anything or anyone but himself and his fucking gin.

"Is he…" Addison's gaze pinged between Brady and Aiden. "Do you think he's trying to make amends?"

"Maybe. I talked to Mabel," Brady said. "Apparently, he got out of rehab last month."

"Great, so we're one of his twelve steps. Again." I couldn't keep the derision out of my tone, having been here too many times to count.

Brady leaned forward, bracing his forearms on the table in front of him. "This is the longest stint in rehab he's ever had. By far."

"So what."

"So maybe we listen."

I huffed out an incredulous laugh, glancing around at my family who used to be on my side with this, even if they didn't know the full extent of his sins. Didn't know the full extent of mine, either.

Where they saw an alcoholic and an absentee father, I saw someone who was complicit in our mom's death. I'd been stupid enough to give him a message that night, thinking he'd pass it along to her. But instead, he'd done what he always did best. Drank himself stupid before passing out, the message for my mom never delivered.

If it had been, she wouldn't have gone out. Would have known exactly where Addison and I were that night. She wouldn't have been on that fucking boat in the raging storm if he'd done the one thing I'd asked him to.

She'd still be here with us today. We wouldn't have spent the past almost eleven years without the light that had always led this family. And Addison would be able to celebrate her pregnancy with her mother...and my niece or nephew would have a doting grandma to spoil them.

Instead, we had nothing but memories.

"If the rest of you want to let that piece of shit back into your lives, that's on you. I haven't been interested for the past decade, and I'm sure as hell not interested now." Without another word, I stormed out of the diner and settled on my bike. I gripped the handles tightly, frustration seeping into my bones.

I'd never particularly liked my father. It was hard to like someone who chose the bottle over you every single day. But after Mom had died, after his addiction aided in taking her away from us, robbed us of our mother...robbed Addison and Chase's kid of a grandmother?

I'd never hated someone more, and that was never going to change.

CHAPTER THIRTY-ONE

HARPER

I SHOULD HAVE KNOWN BETTER. I'd been down this path before, and now I was thirty fucking years old and here again.

I had no idea why I'd thought this time would be different. I'd gone into it with eyes wide open, knowing exactly what this was and exactly what this wasn't. But waking up in Levi's bed, alone, my pussy still aching from what he'd done to me last night, was a sharp reminder of a past I'd spent twelve years trying to forget.

Levi McKenzie was a mistake I just kept making.

But apparently, sex made me stupid. Despite my trying to keep control of the situation, he'd turned me inside out with his fingers and his mouth and his cock. With his filthy words that had, somehow, seemed almost reverent.

Apparently, I'd just been in a dick stupor because that assessment couldn't have been further from the truth. Not when the sheets were cold and the apartment beyond his bedroom door was still and silent.

But that was fine. This was exactly the reminder I needed. I was in Starlight Cove to do a job, nothing more. I wasn't here to reminisce or get my world rocked harder than it ever had been before. I was here to write the best article *Weekend Wanderlust* had ever seen and snag that permanent position.

Which meant I still had three weeks here, living with him. But I was going to have to find a way to deal, because there was no way I was backing down now.

I tossed the covers off and slipped out of bed, ignoring the ache between my thighs and the way my skin still smelled like him. Flashes from last night came to me unbidden. It had felt like he'd gone down on me for hours, unable to get enough. He'd held off every one of his orgasms longer than I'd thought possible, only relenting when I'd begged him to.

And I had. I'd begged.

Somehow he'd reduced me to a boneless pile of nerve endings, constantly awaiting his next touch. *Craving* it. In the short hours we'd spent together last night...in the kitchen, in the living room, in the shower, in this very bed...he'd made me want more. And then the sleepy middle-of-the-night fuck had left me more confused than ever.

Well, no more of that.

After getting dressed and grabbing my laptop bag, I headed downstairs to the *Gazette*, ready to get started on the day. I wanted to dive into the weekly column Mabel had asked me to write for the paper—a visitor's guide to Starlight Cove. Tackling a few of those was the least I could do to repay her for use of the office space. I also needed to gather my notes from my interviews I'd done thus far and start piecing together my article for *Weekend Wanderlust*.

The one thing that would get my mind off Levi was doing a little more digging on Stan. As soon as the bar opened, I planned to stop in and hopefully run into another one of his sons. Though I'd struck out with one, I had no intention of doing the same with any of the others.

I'd just sat down at my temporary desk when my phone pinged with an incoming text. Levi's name popped up on my screen, and the sight sent a flurry of butterflies swirling in my stomach before I could squash the reaction. I shook my head, pissed at myself that he'd managed to get under my skin so thoroughly in so little time.

LEVI:

Sorry I had to take off early. Resort meeting this AM.

I huffed out a disbelieving breath. Did he think I'd buy that? I'd been around here enough that I knew the resort schedule. Knew they had daily morning meetings. I also knew Levi rarely attended them, doing anything and everything in his power to skip. The only ones he showed up for were the ones Addison forced him to attend.

Which meant his text was complete bullshit. Which also meant he'd bailed, plain and simple.

Though, I wasn't sure why I was surprised. And it wasn't like I *cared*. It didn't bother me that he snuck out without a word, leaving me naked and alone in his bed. As earth-shattering as last night had been, I could classify it as nothing more than scratching an itch. Just a way to get him out of my system once and for all.

But even though I tried to tell myself that, I knew it was only lies. There was a hollow ache in my chest when I pictured him sneaking out this morning. And I couldn't deny how much I'd hoped to wake tangled up in him, his fingers trailing up and down my spine.

I knew now it was nothing more than a ridiculous fantasy, one I was silly for entertaining.

Leaving him on read, I set my phone facedown in an attempt to block it—and him—out, and I refocused on my work. This morning, I needed to transcribe my interview notes and start organizing the article. I'd pop over to One Night Stan's a little later and work my magic with another of Stan's sons.

But until then, the *Gazette* was blissfully Levi-free, and I intended to take full advantage of that reprieve.

I'D JUST FINISHED TRANSCRIBING my notes from my interview with Aiden when my phone rang, and I hated the tiny part of me that hoped it was Levi. But I flipped it over to find *Weekend Wanderlust*'s editor in chief's name flashing on the screen.

I sat up a little straighter in my chair and ran a hand down my blouse, as if she could see me, before answering. "Naomi, hi."

"Harper," she said, her voice crisp and cool as always. "I wanted to check in and see how the piece is coming. How're things going up in Maine? Have you nailed down an angle yet?"

I leaned back in my chair, glancing at my scattered notes. It didn't look like much yet, but it never did. This was all just part of my process. "I think so. I'm digging into the secret allure of Starlight Cove...whatever it is that draws so many high-profile people here, not just to vacation but as permanent residents."

She hummed thoughtfully, and I held my breath, waiting for her reaction. While she hadn't given me many—or any—parameters for this piece, at the end of the day, she had to approve it. Not just for it to be published, but for a good shot at that job offer I was chasing. "I like it," she said finally, and I breathed out a sigh of relief. "And I think our readers will, too. Anything standing out so far?"

"Maybe," I hedged, not wanting to divulge too much, especially if the Stan angle didn't pan out. "I've got a few paths I'm exploring, but I don't want to get into specifics in case they end up being dead ends."

"Fair enough. Just keep me updated on how things are going. And let me know if you need anything from me."

"Will do."

After ending the call, I was cautiously optimistic. *I like it* was practically a ringing endorsement from Naomi, who kept her emotions locked down tighter than Fort Knox. While the Stan angle was still up in the air, I wasn't giving up yet. I just needed one of his sons to open up, and the odds I could make that happen with four of them were pretty good.

I stuffed my phone into my laptop bag as I headed over to the bar. I'd tried the casual pop-in last time—something the son I'd spoken to may have assumed had been fake—so I was leaning into the whole journalist thing this time, making it a bit more official.

It was late afternoon, so the bar wasn't crowded, only a few scattered patrons around. A man stood behind the bar, talking to a customer who sat at one of the stools. This guy was leaner than the man I'd spoken to last time, but there was no missing the resemblance to Brick Wall. Fortunately, though, this one's wide grin and unrestrained laughter hinted at a better reception, something I was eternally grateful for.

The guy shot me a warm smile and sauntered over to me as I settled on a barstool. "What can I get you?"

"An iced tea would be great."

"You got it." He knocked twice on the bar top before fixing

my drink, his attention split between his task and me. "I don't think I've seen you around. You just visiting?"

"I'm here for a few weeks, working on an article. I'm Harper."

"Nice to meet you, Harper," he said, extending his hand to me. His grip was warm and firm, his hand encasing mine in a way that should've sent electricity coursing through me. Unfortunately, all I could think about was how a single brush of Levi's finger against my skin sent more heat crackling through me than this.

He set the iced tea in front of me and braced his hands on the bar. "So...an article? About Starlight Cove?"

"About the *secret* of Starlight Cove. Why it seems to be a magnet for the rich and famous."

He huffed out a laugh. "And let me guess...this is about my dad."

Well, this turned out to be easier than I thought.

"Not entirely, but he's definitely part of the overall story. Starlight Cove has seen its fair share of celebrities, in various capacities. A *New York Times* best-selling author, a former pro hockey player. An astronaut, a Nobel Prize winner...a rock star." I took a sip of my tea and shrugged. "I've already interviewed the first four, and now I was hoping to get some information on your dad. Starlight Cove's a far cry from a world tour. What brought him back here?"

"You'd have to ask him that." He braced his forearms on the bar top and leaned toward me, shooting me a lazy grin. "But enough about my old man. I've got a beautiful woman at my bar, and I don't intend to waste that opportunity."

After more than an hour of nonstop flirting on Charmer's part as he expertly avoided any and every question I lobbed his way, I finally admitted defeat and headed out. No further along with this article than I had been when I'd stepped through the door earlier. On top of that, I'd forgotten to get something for lunch, and my stomach wasn't happy about it.

I grabbed a salad from a food truck on the corner and headed back to the *Gazette*. So far, I was 0 for 2 on my Stan inquiries, and that was beginning to chip away at my confidence in getting some answers. I was reading over my notes, nearly done with my salad at this point, when I remembered I'd never responded to Levi's text that morning. I was in a better place mentally, having firmly shifted back into professional mode—a reminder of why I was here in the first place—so I pulled my phone from my bag and typed out a quick reply, not allowing myself to dwell on it.

HARPER:

Don't worry about it. I have other things to focus on today.

The dots from his end popped up immediately, and I kept one eye on the screen while I finished off my lunch.

LEVI:

More interviews?

HARPER:

Several, including Stan's sons

I couldn't stop myself from including that bit of information, a petty part of me wanting to prove to Levi I wasn't sitting around, hung up on him. Not like I'd been the last time he'd left me.

LEVI:

You better not be wearing what you wore last night.

Heat burned in my cheeks, irritation swamping me at his demand. The fucking audacity of this man. He couldn't have it both ways. *He'd* been the one to bail. Was it possible that I would've done the same thing if I'd woken up first? Well, I guess we'd never know.

HARPER:

Remind me why that's any of your business?

LEVI:

How about the fact that it was my cock you were coming all over just a few hours ago? Or maybe the fact that I made you come so hard on my tongue, I still tasted you this morning?

I stared at his message, irritation and arousal warring within me, my thoughts consumed by memories of last night and early this morning. His filthy words and the reactions he'd managed to coax from my body...making me feel things I'd never felt before.

Clearing my throat, I absent-mindedly scratched the column of my neck as flashes whipped through my mind. The harsh scrape of his beard against my jaw, between my breasts, on the insides of my thighs. Then, directly on my pussy, the roughness of it perfectly contrasting with the soft glide of his tongue against my clit.

Annnnnd that was enough of that. My body was already overheated, the flush on my cheeks spreading down my neck until I felt hot all over.

I shook my head to clear my thoughts, debating how to reply. I typed and deleted several responses, none of them quite right. I didn't want to give him the satisfaction of knowing he'd gotten to me. Not after this morning. Not after he'd left. Again.

My skin felt hot and itchy, no doubt in response to the pain in the ass who could rile me up without even trying. I took a sip of my water, hoping to clear the tickle from my throat, but it persisted. I scratched my neck again, trying to focus on my text to Levi, but the tingling sensation was spreading, now crawling up my neck and over my jaw. My lips felt swollen, my tongue too big for my mouth.

Realization slammed into me a second before I reached for my purse—somehow, I'd ingested walnuts. I'd been here before, so I knew, without a doubt, I was having an allergic reaction. The salad I'd grabbed from the food truck must've been cross-contaminated with them. I rummaged through my purse for my EpiPen, knowing I needed to stay calm. I was fine. Everything was *fine*. I knew from experience my seeming decrease in oxygen was from panic and not a closed airway.

Not yet anyway.

Frustration getting the better of me, I dumped the contents of my purse onto my desk and rummaged through everything, frantically searching for what I already knew in my gut wasn't there because it wasn't in the pocket it always was. Before hopping on the plane to Starlight Cove, I'd double-checked to make sure I had my pen with me—I never went anywhere without it. That meant it must've fallen out at some point in the few weeks I'd been here.

Knowing time was of the essence, I shoved everything back into my purse and took off outside and to the entrance to the apartment. I ran up the stairs, fumbling with my keys, my hands shaking as I attempted to unlock the door. Maybe it was stupid to come up here instead of flagging down someone on the street or just calling 9-1-1, but things weren't that bad just yet. And chances that my EpiPen was inside the apartment were exponentially higher than happening by someone who had one with them.

Once inside, I tossed my purse on the counter and hurried to my room, riffling through my items with urgency. All the while doing my best to ignore the increasing tightness in my throat, the overwhelming panic gripping my chest. And wondering how much time I had before I passed out.

CHAPTER THIRTY-TWO

LEVI

IF ANYONE ASKED, I would deny exactly how long I'd been staring at my fucking phone, watching Harper's text bubbles appear and disappear over and over again. Frustrated, I shoved a hand through my hair, willing a text to pop up. Had I gone too far? Maybe. Probably.

But fuck, it was like all my reason ceased to exist when it came to her. She turned me into an idiot where she was concerned, and I didn't know how to stop it.

Didn't know how to stop this pull demanding I find her, either.

I had no idea where she was right now, but she usually spent her days at the *Gazette*, so that was as good a guess as any. Tired of waiting on her reply, I was grateful my workshop was half a block from the building and that I could dip out of work whenever I wanted.

A few minutes later, I popped into the office, scanning the space but finding it empty. Harper's laptop was open on her desk, her screen still lit up, so she couldn't have gone too far.

Figuring she might've run up to the apartment for something, I headed that way, fully prepared to hunt her down if I had to.

When I got to the landing at the top of the stairs, I found our apartment door wide open. My brows pinched as I glanced around, looking for...what, I had no idea, but something felt off.

"Harper?" I called, stepping into the space and hoping for a clue to what was going on.

I heard her before I saw her, tearing through her room as if she were hunting for buried treasure. The sound was so reminiscent of the night that had started it all—that first domino crashing into the rest—that it gave me a moment's pause. At least until I stepped into her doorway and saw the panic on her face, the fear in her eyes.

"What's wrong?" I asked, darting my gaze around as if I'd be able to find the culprit for her fear.

"Walnuts," she managed to croak, her breaths little more than wheezes.

The single word shot a jolt of panic through me, recalling the one and only other time she'd had an allergic reaction around me. We'd been fifteen, wandering through the Fourth of July festival with a bag of caramel corn. Little had we known, a couple of the vendor's candied walnuts had snuck into the bag, and Harper had eaten one by the time we'd realized. I'd never been as scared as I had been then, watching the panic sweep over her eyes as her throat closed up. The same panic I saw reflected there now.

"How long?" I asked, already tearing through her things, knowing what we were looking for. I opened drawers, rummaged through them without delicacy or care, looking for her life-saving device. I didn't know if I was asking how long it had been since she ingested them, how long since her throat had started closing up, or how much longer she thought she had before she couldn't breathe at all.

In the end, it didn't matter because all she responded with was a slight shake of her head, her movements turning clumsy as she continued her search. My heart thundered in my ears, my hands frantic as I tore apart her room, searching everywhere. The space looked like a tornado had decimated it, exactly how I'd expected it to look when I'd come upon her the other night —when our tit for tat had all started.

Something clicked in my mind at the memory. The EpiPen could have fallen out of her bag that night, maybe rolled under something so she hadn't even realized it was out of place. The dresser, the nightstands, the bed...

Dropping to my knees, I peered under the dresser, shining my phone flashlight into the small sliver of space between it and the floor, but coming up empty. I did the same to both night-stands, shooting a glance toward Harper when my search was fruitless. Her wild eyes were locked on me, fear and panic written across every inch of her.

As soon as I had that fucking pen in my hands, I knew what to do—after that first time, I'd practiced over and over in case it ever happened again. But I truly didn't know if I was going to find it in time.

Not giving up but not willing to risk her life, I pulled out my phone and dialed 9-1-1. As soon as the operator picked up, I barked the necessary information at Delores, who confirmed a unit—my brother included—was on the way.

I glanced at Harper again, doing a quick sweep over her, noticing the rapid decline. "Two minutes, sparrow. Ford'll be here in two minutes. Just stay with me."

With a nod, she braced herself against the wall and slid to the floor, gripping the front of her shirt. The sound of her labored breathing echoed in the space as panic clawed at my throat, the thought of losing her front and center—another death on my conscience.

I couldn't—*wouldn't*—allow that to happen. Never again, and definitely not to her.

"Mother*fucker*!" I yelled, unable to keep my emotions in check. "Where is it?"

As a last hope, I dove to the floor and rummaged around under her bed, desperately hoping I'd find what I was looking for. The sound of sirens broke through at the same moment my fingers brushed over something cool and cylindrical. I grabbed it, yanking the EpiPen out from under her bed, and rushed to her. I didn't even have time for relief to slam into me. Not when she was still gasping for every single breath.

All the steps I'd learned so many years ago came back to me all at once, just like riding a bike. Crouching at her side, I pulled off the safety cap, shoving her skirt up while I did so. No time for delicacy because every second counted. Time slowed, centered on this moment as she stared up at me, her eyes wide with panic. Without hesitation and with as much force as needed, I jabbed the pen into her thigh muscle and injected the medicine into her body.

Once the pen was depleted, I carefully pulled it out before tossing it aside. The next ten seconds were the longest of my life as I massaged her thigh to help the absorption of medicine into her body, all the while studying her face and hoping like hell she felt the relief she urgently needed.

I gripped Harper's face, brushing my thumbs along her cheeks. "Come on, sparrow. Eyes on me."

She did as I demanded, lifting her gaze to mine, pure terror written in her eyes. Gripping her hand, I placed it on my chest, putting my other on hers. I took an exaggerated breath in through my nose before blowing it out in a slow, controlled exhale.

"Breathe with me, baby. Just breathe." I stared, helpless, as she struggled for breath, feeling like my heart was being torn straight out of my chest with each gasp from her throat. "Don't you dare fucking leave me. Not now. Not when I finally got you back."

CHAPTER THIRTY-THREE

LEVI

FORD WAS the first one in, my brother by my side in mere seconds as he quickly assessed the situation. Harper's labored breathing had lessened in severity, her breaths coming easier now, if not effortless. But still, she kept her hand on my chest, my shirt clutched in her fist.

And I'd be damned if I was going to move an inch.

Ford seemed to realize that, dropping his bag on Harper's other side and crouching down so he was eye level with her. "If you wanted to see me again, you could've just let me know, Harper. This seems a bit excessive." Though his tone was teasing, his gaze was focused and assessing, his movements quick and efficient but sure and steady.

Harper rasped out a short laugh but otherwise didn't speak, still focusing on taking measured breaths that matched in time with mine.

"You feel comfortable talking with this guy around?" he asked, tipping his head in my direction as he pulled something from his bag.

Without hesitation, she nodded, and relief immediately

swept over me. I didn't deserve her loyalty, but fuck if I wasn't going to take it.

"All right. Can you tell me what happened, then?"

"Walnuts," she managed, her voice raspy and weak. "I'm guessing cross-contamination on my salad."

I swore under my breath, wanting nothing more than to hunt down whoever had been so fucking careless with her life and make them regret that they'd even woken up that morning.

Ford nodded, ignoring me completely as he took Harper's pulse, and tipped his head toward the discarded epinephrine shot. "How long ago did you administer the EpiPen?"

The questions went on like that as he checked Harper's vitals, and she answered everything as best she could, looking to me when she wasn't sure of the answer. I was on autopilot, making sure she had exactly what she needed, all while barely keeping it together on the inside, my fears staring me straight in the eyes.

I was terrified of losing someone at my hand, of having that on my conscience again when my mom's death already ate at me day in and day out. But I wasn't terrified of losing just *someone* else, but of losing *her*. I could no longer lie to myself and pretend she didn't mean every-fucking-thing to me. And quite frankly, it was laughable I'd even tried.

Those minutes as she and I had sat waiting for my brother and the rest of his crew to show up were some of the longest of my life. Counting the seconds in my mind and urging Harper to match my breathing, even as I watched her struggle with every inhalation.

She'd clutched the front of my shirt, resting her hand above my heart, and focused solely on me. Even after Ford had rushed in, Harper's eyes never left mine, gratitude and something else I couldn't focus on shining in their depths.

A while later, after Ford and his crew had done whatever the hell they'd done to check Harper out while I'd spent the entire time studying her face, my brother had not so gently suggested she head to the ER. And she'd not so gently passed and then outright refused to go.

I shouldn't have been surprised. She *hated* hospitals and spent her measured breaths assuring me, as well as everyone else, she was totally fine. Even as her skin flushed from the straight shot of adrenaline and I could nearly *see* her nerves vibrating beneath her skin. Both of which she'd reminded me were totally normal, because, yeah, she'd done this before. And that, as soon as the shot wore off, she was going to crash, and she wanted to be home when she did. But even her casual use of *home* couldn't distract me from worrying about her.

Finally, when it was clear she wasn't budging after her twentieth refusal to be transported, the firefighters—save for Ford—admitted defeat and headed out, but I called bullshit on the whole thing. And then I called my sister-in-law.

Quinn was at Harper's and my apartment ten minutes later, and I'd never been more grateful than I was in that moment that my brother had married up.

After a quick knock on the front door, she strode into the apartment with a medical bag, her gaze darting around and assessing everything in seconds flat. "Tell me what's going on."

Ford's brows hit his hairline when he registered his wife was here, then he turned to me with narrowed eyes. "You don't trust my vast knowledge? I'm wounded—not to mention qualified!"

"You are, sweetie. But the MD behind my name says I'm *more* qualified." Quinn patted her husband's chest as she brushed past him. "Now, shush and let me talk with my patient."

All three of their voices blended together, blurring into background noise as I stood off to the side, nearly fucking beside myself. My brain refused to focus on anything but every alternative possibility that could have played out... If I hadn't texted Harper that morning. If I hadn't gotten pissed enough to go looking for her. If I hadn't found her up in the apartment.

If I hadn't found her pen in time.

And then I thought about what would've happened if I hadn't run scared this morning... If I hadn't bailed before she'd woken up. If I'd just stayed in that bed, we might not have even left it at all. And maybe she wouldn't have had to face any of this in the first place.

But because I'd tucked tail and run, she'd come far too fucking close to death for me to do anything but hate myself for it.

Once Quinn had monitored Harper long enough and was satisfied with her progress, my sister-in-law gave us an oximeter, an auto blood pressure cuff, and a log for any medications or symptoms—as well as strict orders to use each and every one and call her with hourly updates or she'd be camping on the couch tonight. She also called in a prescription to the pharmacy to replace Harper's EpiPen as soon as possible.

As Ford and Quinn said their goodbyes to Harper, I stood by the apartment door, waiting and ready for them to leave. Ready to forget this whole fucking day.

"Still think I could've handled everything fine on my own," Ford said as he and Quinn strolled toward me.

My sister-in-law rolled her eyes. "But then I wouldn't get to hear you complain about it all night, and where would the fun be in that?"

"I'll give you something else to listen to all ni—" Ford's words cut off on an *oomph* when Quinn jabbed an elbow into his stomach.

"I'm glad you called me," she said, squeezing my forearm. "Despite how much my husband is whining about it."

"I'm not *whining*," he mumbled before turning his attention to me. "But I'm glad you called her, too. And that you called 9-1-1 and didn't wait until..." He trailed off, but he didn't need to say the words. Not when they were already burned into my brain.

Until it was too late.

Ford cleared his throat. "You did good, man."

But I didn't deserve his praise. Not when things might've been—probably would have been—different if I'd made different choices.

Story of my fucking life.

"Thanks for sticking around," I said to my brother before turning my attention on my sister-in-law. "And thanks for making a house call. I owe you one."

She scoffed and squeezed my arm twice before letting go. "You absolutely do not. And you never have to thank me for something like that. You're family. And by extension, so is she."

An ache bloomed in my chest and spread, Quinn's simple words lighting up something inside me I hadn't allowed myself to even consider for more than a decade.

Quinn glanced back at my brother, a silent exchange passing between them before she headed out of the apartment and down the stairs. Over her shoulder, she called, "And I mean it! Every hour, or I'm showing up with an overnight bag and my jammies."

"Every hour, Doc. Promise." That was one thing I absolutely would not be fucking up.

Before Ford followed his wife down the stairs, he stood on the threshold and pinned me in place with his all-knowing gaze. Having death so close dredged up memories I'd have liked nothing more than to keep buried. I dwelled on them often enough that I didn't need an outside reminder. And from the look in Ford's eyes as he clapped a hand on my shoulder, he saw every bit of that struggle in my expression.

"Give me a call if you want to talk about this"—he tipped his head toward the living room where Harper was curled on the couch, fully in her crash portion of the night—"or about Mom..." He cleared his throat. "Or Dad. Any of it. I mean it, all right? Any time."

Without waiting for me to respond, he squeezed my shoulder and headed down the stairs, offering me one last glance before he slipped outside to where Quinn waited for him. He said something to her, and though she tried to scowl, a smile curved her lips when he bent to kiss her. Her laugh floated up the stairs to me as my brother linked their fingers together and tugged her along beside him, as natural as if they'd been doing it their whole lives. Giving me a glimpse of the happiness I would never deserve.

And then it was just Harper and me and all those regrets I couldn't seem to shake.

After shutting the door, I strode into the living room and studied Harper. Her eyes were closed, her expression serene as she lay curled up in the corner of the couch. As if none of this had happened.

Except it had. And it had changed...everything.

I sank down on the other end of the couch, bracing my elbows on my knees as I stared at her. The woman I'd loved even before I knew what love was. The one who'd been one of my very best friends before shifting to more. Who'd taken all my firsts, just as I'd done for her. The one who'd haunted my dreams for half a lifetime.

And I'd almost lost her.

Worse, it hadn't happened by pushing her away in some

misguided attempt to ensure she lived a life she deserved. But for real. For good.

Because I'd shoved her away. *Again.*

The reminder that I'd given her up once—on fucking purpose—nearly choked me. I'd spent years convincing myself it'd been the right thing to do, that by ending things between us, I was sparing her from the wreckage of my life. But after everything that had happened—then and now—it made me realize just how hollow those justifications had been. Especially when my shoving her away today had nearly cost her *everything*.

The truth was, I was terrified of loving too deeply, only to lose it all again. But that fear had nothing on the terror I'd felt today watching Harper struggle for every single breath.

I couldn't afford to fool myself anymore, not when every day that ticked by was one less day in a finite number that I'd have the privilege of calling her mine.

CHAPTER THIRTY-FOUR

HARPER

I'D SPENT years fantasizing about the day I could make Levi fall to his knees. I'd obsessed over it, wanting him to feel just a tiny bit of the pain he'd caused me.

But this wasn't what I had in mind at all.

Levi sat at the other end of the couch, head bowed, his shoulders stiff as tension cloaked every inch of him. He looked wrecked. Ravaged. Completely wrung out. And that didn't make sense with the story I'd been told, nor the one I'd been telling myself for years.

If this was nothing to him—if *I* was nothing to him—as he'd made me feel this morning when he'd bailed, then why would he look so fucking destroyed? Especially when he thought no one was watching. That, paired with everything else that had happened between us since I'd arrived, and things weren't adding up. But none of it was more confusing than the single word that had shocked me just as much now as it had when I'd remembered it from last night.

None.

I had to be recalling it wrong. He hadn't meant it like that, or

I'd heard incorrectly. Because there was simply no way Levi hadn't been with anyone else since me. Sure, he seemed to get off on deprivation, denying himself his release as long as possible, but *twelve years*? That was going a little far, even for him.

"I figured you'd be happy about this, considering how much you hate me," I said, my voice still a little scratchy from all the swelling.

Levi snapped his head in my direction, and the devastation written across his face nearly took my breath away. "Happy? Jesus Christ, that's what you think of me?"

I shrugged, shifting myself back into a sitting position. "What am I supposed to think when the hate you feel toward me has never been a secret?"

He was quiet for long moments, and when he finally spoke, his voice was ragged. "I've never hated you, sparrow. Not for a single second. But I did everything in my power to make sure you hated me."

I didn't know if it was the aftereffects of the epinephrine or something else, but none of this made any sense. Not his reaction when he'd found me, already in the throes of anaphylaxis. Not his admission to me the night I'd been drunk. Not last night when, even during the times he'd said the filthiest things—*done* the filthiest things—I'd felt...cherished.

And definitely not when held up against the fact that he'd thrown me away in the first place.

"Maybe not hate," I conceded. "But it had to be something close. You couldn't even be around me anymore. One day, we were in love, and the next, we were nothing. Instead of breaking up with me and going back to the friends we'd always been, you just cut me out. Blocked me everywhere you could. Erased me like I never existed."

"You and I both know we could never be friends." His gaze

pinned me in place, so many emotions swirling in his ice-blue eyes. "I've loved you since I was ten fucking years old, sparrow. There was no way I could go back to being friends after I had you."

I sucked in a shocked breath, stunned as his words settled in, so different from what I'd thought for nearly half my life. "So, what? It was better to go no-contact? Act like I'd *died*?"

He flinched at that but didn't back down, his determination seeming to grow more resolved as he squared his shoulders. "When it was that or you lose out on the life you'd worked so hard for? Yeah, that's what I chose. I chose *you*. I'll always choose you. Even at the expense of myself."

I shook my head, my brow pinched as I tried to process what he was saying, everything I'd believed for the past twelve years slowly falling away to reveal the truth. "Levi, this doesn't make any sense. What do you mean, lose out on the life I'd worked hard for?"

"I heard your dad the night we got caught." He cleared his throat, staring down at his hands loosely clasped between his knees. "I heard him. The whole fucking station heard him."

Levi saying the words shoved me straight back to that night, after we'd gotten caught in the back seat of my dad's car. I'd never seen my father so angry. Angry enough that he'd slipped that night, showing a crack in the facade he'd perfected for years as I'd cried and he'd yelled at me, not caring who heard.

"He was going to cut you off if I was still in your life," Levi continued. "For good reason, too. He might've been an asshole, but he was right about that. I would've been nothing but a stain on your future. You were meant for so much more than me."

Tears filled my eyes as he spoke, partially because of the words he was saying, but more so because I could see exactly how much he believed them.

He *believed* them.

"I knew you'd never do it...would never end things," he said. "So I did it for you."

For several moments, I sat there, stunned into silence. I huffed out a disbelieving laugh, though this situation was anything but funny. Thinking about all the years wasted—more than a decade—made me equal parts furious and distraught.

And what cut the most was the fact that what he'd been trying so hard to save me from, I'd chosen anyway.

"You didn't choose me. You chose *for* me," I said, my voice as firm as I could make it. "And regardless of whatever white knight bullshit reasoning you had for doing so, it's no different from what my parents put me through for years."

Realization swept over him, regret and guilt swimming in his eyes before he seemed to shove it all away with a shake of his head. "I'm not good enough for you, Harper. Never was, never will be."

"That's not for you to decide!" I snapped. "*I* get to decide that. It's my life, and it's my choice who I do and don't want in it. Which is exactly why I cut out my parents."

He snapped his head toward me. "You what?"

"Cut them out. The day I turned eighteen, I left and never once looked back."

It hadn't been a difficult choice. I didn't grow up in a loving home. It may have looked that way from the outside, but in reality, I was raised by nannies and cooks because my parents couldn't be bothered to deal with any of the messiness that came with having a child. The only time they concerned themselves with me was when I could do something for them—namely, pretend for all the world that I was a perfect little girl and we were the perfect little family.

All the while, outsiders were none the wiser that my nanny

signed my school papers and showed up for parent-teacher conferences. That the only birthday celebration I'd had when I was seven had been at school because my parents had forgotten. Or that I'd never been allowed to select my own interests or extracurriculars...those had all been chosen for me.

Everything had been chosen for me.

And Levi had done the same damn thing.

While I knew, logically, that Levi's choice for me had come from a place of love, while my parents' decisions had come from a place of control, the end result was the same. A life I didn't have autonomy over.

And I wasn't going to go back to that. Not even for him.

It hadn't hurt when my parents cut me off and willingly removed themselves from my life because they couldn't respect the boundaries I'd set. Losing Levi, though? Not just the Levi who'd been my boyfriend for three years, but the Levi who'd been my best friend for eight... Losing him along with Chase— both of them the only two souls in the world who knew me— had hurt more than anything I'd ever faced.

"You were supposed to go to Harvard," he finally said, his voice unsure. "You were set to leave in ten days. Ten fucking days. That's not something you just turn your back on."

That was what my parents had thought, too. When I'd told my dad I had no plans to keep living under his thumb, he'd laughed, assuming I was lying. That because I'd grown up with a silver spoon in my mouth, I wouldn't be able to survive without it.

And then I'd walked out of their house forever.

I turned eighteen the day before the semester started, withdrew my admission, and left the prison my parents called a home with a single bag. I went to the college I'd wanted to go to as long as I could remember. The one my parents had said wasn't good enough, that what I wanted to study wasn't realistic. They'd said I'd never find a job or make a living with a journalism degree. I'd worked my ass off, holding down three jobs to be able to cover rent until the spring semester, when I enrolled with a full scholarship. And that was it.

My life truly started the day I walked out of my parents' house. A life that wasn't perfect, but it was *mine*.

I'd been so tied up in thinking that Levi and I could've been together back then if he hadn't taken that choice away from me. But maybe, if he hadn't taken that choice away from me, my life wouldn't look anything like it did now. Maybe I wouldn't have attended my dream college or studied journalism or traveled the world. Maybe I wouldn't have gotten that first gig with *Weekend Wanderlust*...maybe I wouldn't have gotten *this* one.

Maybe everything would've been different...and in the end, I still might have been without him.

While I didn't appreciate his methods and I wouldn't stand for it going forward, I could admit that his doing what he'd done had allowed my life to turn out exactly as it had. Exactly how I'd designed it to.

"Well, I did turn my back on it," I said, my tone softer than it had been. I could see from the gutted look in his eyes that he was coming to the realization I'd already faced—that if he hadn't done what I'd done, we might've been together this whole time. "I'm a big girl, Levi. And I can do hard things. With or without you. But it's *my* choice. What I do with my life, who I want in it, and who I want to be with."

I sat up and crawled to him before settling astride his lap. Gripping his jaw in my hands, I stared into his eyes, so full of love for me, it took my breath away. I had no idea how I'd never seen it. "And right now, despite you being a complete dumbass, I choose you."

CHAPTER THIRTY-FIVE

LEVI

WITH EACH DETAIL that Harper shared, I realized just how little I knew about the life she'd led since she'd been gone. And *none* of it had turned out how I thought...how I'd expected it to. But that was because I'd willingly been kept in the dark.

While curiosity frequently ate away at me, I knew if I'd gone digging for information about Harvard or Harper's job or any of a thousand other details... If I'd known anything at all about her life besides the tiny glimpses I'd gotten the few times she'd been in Starlight Cove, I wouldn't have been strong enough to stay away.

We'd spent the summers of our childhood saying goodbye at the end of every single one of them. Our entire relationship had been prepping me for the inevitable final goodbye. Because I'd known from the first moment I'd laid my eyes on her that she was never meant to be mine. Was meant for far more than I could ever give her.

She was meant for greatness, and I was doomed to a life of shackles and chains, haunted by memories I couldn't escape. Didn't *deserve* to escape.

"What's going through your head right now?" she asked, tipping my face back so I didn't have a choice but to look at her.

I blew out a breath, resting my hands on her hips as she straddled me because I couldn't stop myself from touching her. Just to remind myself she was here and she was safe. "You don't want to know."

"If that were true, I wouldn't have asked."

I studied her expression...the open curiosity written on her face, the concern swimming in her eyes. This woman had just nearly *died*, and she was concerned about *me*? I didn't deserve her, and this only emphasized that.

"I'm so fucking sorry, sparrow," I finally said, my voice thick with emotion. "For everything. For not trusting you to make your own choices and for thinking I somehow knew better." I shook my head, ashamed that my idiotic decisions and nothing else had ultimately been our downfall. "I was an arrogant little shit, and I fucked up."

Just one more to add to my list.

Harper was quiet for long moments. So long, the only thing that reassured me she wasn't going to tell me to fuck off was the gentle brush of her thumbs over my jaw, her soft body against mine. Finally, she said, "Thank you for saying that."

"I wasn't just saying it." I squeezed her hips, needing her to understand my sincerity. "I meant it."

"I know." She nodded, her gaze darting across my face. "And I know you did it because you loved me, not because you wanted to control me. But your intention doesn't erase the impact."

"You're right. Chase tried to talk me out of it, but I ignored him and swore him to secrecy. I should've just talked to you about it."

"Ya think?"

I huffed out a laugh at her dry tone, tucking my thumb

under the hem of her shirt to rub soft circles against her skin. "I'm not sure if you know this, but talking isn't exactly my strong suit."

"I *may* have realized that over the years." She finally cracked a smile, and the sight would've sent me to my knees if I hadn't already been sitting.

Knowing just how close I'd come to seeing that smile snuffed out forever was a wrecking ball to my chest. If one tiny thing had gone differently today, I could've lost her forever without ever being able to tell her what she meant to me—what she'd *always* meant to me. Without confessing the past. Without voicing things that had been left unsaid between us. And without getting a second chance to love her exactly how she deserved.

A second chance I hadn't earned, but fuck if I wasn't going to take it anyway. For as long as I had her here.

"*Christ*, I almost lost you today." Emotion bled into my voice, my throat thick and rough.

"But you didn't. I'm still here." She grabbed my hand and placed it on her chest, just over her heart, and I reveled in every thump-thump. "I'm still here," she said again, softer this time, her tone shifting and allowing a different meaning to seep into my mind. Settle into my heart.

I pressed my lips against her forehead and inhaled deeply, her sweet scent filling my lungs. And I couldn't help myself any longer. I needed to hold her, to wrap my arms around her and remind myself she was here and she was okay. I hadn't lost her.

Sliding my hands up her back, I tugged her close. She came easily, settling against me as if it were the most natural thing in the world. She tucked her head beneath my chin, her ear pressed to my chest, and I'd never felt more content than I did right now, in this moment, with her.

Never in a million years had I thought we'd be here again...

that I'd have the privilege of being with her like this. And while nothing in this world could convince me she was meant for me, I was going to be a selfish bastard and hold on with both hands anyway. For as long as we had left.

Harper

BETWEEN THE SHOT of epinephrine and the talk with Levi, I was exhausted. I'd taken some ibuprofen to get ahead of my inevitable headache that always came after anaphylaxis for me, and it was just a dull, manageable ache now.

I'd been dozing on and off as Levi moved around the apartment, snippets of sounds sneaking into my subconscious. At one point, I thought I heard Beck's and Mabel's voices, but I was out again before I could confirm.

I shifted, blinking open my eyes to a now-darkened apartment. Levi sat on the other end of the couch, slumped down in what looked like an incredibly uncomfortable position, his eyes closed. My feet were resting in his lap, his hand cupped possessively around my ankle. And for once, I didn't try to ignore the butterflies that took flight in my stomach at the sight, at the feel of him. Finally allowing myself to enjoy it.

I had no idea what time it was or how long I'd been out. All I knew was I was starving. With the kitchen in mind as my destination, I tried to slip my feet out of Levi's lap, but he tightened his grip on me immediately.

Rolling his head toward me, he opened his eyes and allowed his gaze to sweep over me in a way that made me feel looked after...cared for. "What do you need?"

I blinked, frozen for a moment and taken aback. I'd spent

most of my life on my own because relying on people who were paid to take care of me didn't count. Which meant I'd gotten really damn good at providing exactly what I needed. So, allowing someone else to take care of me was altogether new. And something I didn't easily succumb to.

"I can get it."

"I never said you couldn't." He squeezed my ankle, his thumb brushing soft circles against my skin and sending a shiver rolling through my body. "But I watched you nearly suffocate a few hours ago, so let me do it. Now, tell me. What do you need?"

"I'm just a little hungry."

He nodded, as if he'd been expecting that. "What sounds good? We've got sushi, pizza, fruit, cheese and crackers... I can make you some cinnamon toast or oatmeal if you want something a little more bland. Beck also dropped off some of his homemade mac and cheese."

"Oh, is that all?"

Levi's lips quirked up in a grin, a sight I hadn't seen in far too long. One that shot straight to my heart. "No...I also had Addison grab some of those banana pudding cups you loved."

Memories swarmed me, and emotion welled in my throat. He remembered. Even after all these years, after being apart for so long, after a decade of life between us, he remembered the exact food I ate after an allergic reaction. He recalled just what I needed, as if he'd been providing it for me this whole time.

And it was then that it became clear he *had* been, at least while I'd been in Starlight Cove. With the spaghetti the night of the thunderstorm and picking me up from One Night Stan's after too many drinks and grabbing my coffee just how I liked it more days than not.

Levi had never stopped, even when he'd pretended otherwise.

He squeezed my ankle, his touch reassuring in a way I hadn't realized I needed. "If none of that sounds good, we've got cookies, too. But they came from Mabel, and I'm pretty sure there's weed in them. She dropped them off after she heard about the scare and told me if anyone deserved a little manufactured mellowing, it was you."

I cleared my throat, filing away my realization for later. "I'll maybe save the pot cookies for tomorrow. But I'll take some of that banana pudding."

The smile he shot me reminded me of everything I used to love about him. Made me realize exactly how much of that had hung on over the years, clinging to me even when I'd tried to run from it. And just how far I'd already fallen.

CHAPTER THIRTY-SIX

HARPER

Text thread with Mabel, Levi, and Harper:

8:53 a.m.

MABEL:

Sorry, kids, but I need to cancel today's little excursion. Gladys pulled a muscle trying out her new swing.

LEVI:

I already set everything up, which means I'm still charging you for this.

MABEL:

I'll bake the cookies in the morning and drop them off so your payment is fresh.

LEVI:

Hey, we can reschedule for a different day so you actually have something to write about.

IF I KNEW one thing for certain, it was that if the day ended in Y, Mabel would be meddling. The woman loved sticking her nose into business she shouldn't be concerning herself with, and I didn't see that changing anytime soon. It was probably the journalist ingrained in her.

But there was no way this was anything but nefarious. Okay, so nefarious was probably being slightly dramatic, but the timing and circumstances were far too suspicious to suspect anything else. Besides that, Mabel had been trying to shove Levi and me together at every turn from the moment I'd arrived—*hello*, surprise roommate situation. And I didn't believe she'd suddenly stop after three weeks.

As for rescheduling as Levi suggested in his text, there was no way I was passing up an afternoon alone on a boat with him. I hadn't been sailing in far too long, and I fully intended to rectify that today.

I strolled down the dock toward *Endless Summer*, the same boat I'd learned to sail on when we were kids. At the sight of it, a photo book of memories flipped through my mind—from that very first sail when I met Levi for the first time, to the last outing he'd taken me on a week before things had gone to shit, and everything in between.

A pang settled in my chest at the thought of all the opportunities we'd missed in the time since. While I'd accepted the years lost between as payment for the life I was currently living —a life I was proud of because I'd created it myself—that didn't mean the subtle stings of regret didn't crop up once in a while.

Though I'd seen Levi completely naked, had tasted every inch of him, unapologetically ogled him while he showered, there was something absolutely delicious about seeing him here, in his element. So sure and confident.

He stood on the boat, wearing nothing but a backward baseball hat and a pair of board shorts that hung indecently low on his hips. The cut V of his abdomen and his happy trail drew my gaze straight down to where I definitely shouldn't be looking. At least not while we were in public. That scowl he was famous for was firmly in place as he secured the lines, and it didn't take a genius to figure out he was probably pissed that he'd spent his morning prepping the boat for a group tour that was no longer happening.

My *God*, this man was hot. And I was woman enough to admit the sight of him like this—all scowly and competent—did something to me. Made me so stupid, it was honestly embarrassing.

The muscles in his back, shoulders, and arms bunched and flexed with every movement, drawing my eyes to the tattoos inked across his skin. Tattoos I was still yearning to know more about, to learn the meanings of. I wanted to ask him details about each and every one... Especially the sparrow over his heart. But I'd been too chicken to bring it up.

Once I was close enough, I called out, "Got room for one more?"

He snapped his head up, his eyes connecting with mine immediately and sending a shiver racing down my spine. I had no idea how this man always seemed to find me right away, no matter what. Like there was an invisible string connecting us at all times.

Without hesitation, he dragged his gaze over me from head to toe, his eyes heating as he took in my pink sundress, the red ties to my bikini top visible around my neck. "Couldn't stay away, sparrow?"

"Something like that." I climbed aboard, accepting Levi's hand as he helped me.

"Didn't you get my text?"

"I did. But I figured there was no reason for this afternoon to go to waste. I'm sure the two of us can figure out something to do."

"You really couldn't stay away, huh?"

Rather than answering, I said, "Are you up for it, or what?"

Levi stared at me for long moments, his gaze darting over my face as if in search of something.

Finally, I reached up and swiped a hand over my mouth. "Do I have something on my face?" When he still didn't respond, I huffed and rolled my eyes. "Fine. You're right. I wanted to spend the day with you. Is that a crime? Should we call Brady?"

Levi cleared his throat and shook his head, glancing down at my hand still clasped in his. "My afternoon is all yours," he said, his voice low. "But do you mind if we swap this boat for something smaller?"

I glanced around at this one, so familiar it made my chest ache. But maybe it would be better to try something new with him. "That depends. Is this smaller boat one of your projects?"

His stare felt weighted as he watched me for a beat before squeezing my hand, his thumb brushing over my knuckles. "As a matter of fact, it is."

"Then lead the way. I can't wait to see it."

Without a word, he took my laptop bag from me, then shouldered it along with a backpack he grabbed from the cockpit locker. He stepped off the boat and immediately turned back to help me. Reaching out, he gripped me around the waist, holding me steady as I climbed down.

And then I was standing in front of him, and he was kissing me. He wrapped his hand around my neck, sliding his fingers into my hair, and pressed his lips against mine. It was soft and sweet, something we hadn't experienced all that much now as adults, and I melted into him before my eyelids had even fluttered shut.

I rested my hand on his bare chest, allowing him to guide my mouth exactly how he wanted it. And soon enough, it wasn't so soft or sweet anymore. I moaned when he slid his tongue against mine and kissed me deep before finally pulling back, a smirk on his lips.

"Gotta save a little something for later..." he said, linking our fingers and tugging me along beside him.

"You planning to have your wicked way with me on this boat you're taking me to?"

"Thought about it once or twice."

And I absolutely wouldn't say no.

We strolled down the docks toward where Levi kept his personal boat. Being down here brought back so many memories from the summers I'd spent in Starlight Cove...summers I'd spent with Levi.

It was easy to get overwhelmed by the melancholy of it all— of lost time and what was or what could've been—but I didn't want to do that anymore. I didn't want to spend what little time I had left in Starlight Cove dwelling on the past.

While Levi and I could never truly start over because of the magnitude of our history, we could start fresh.

"Should I guess which one is yours?" I asked, swinging our clasped hands between us.

Levi glanced over, a slight smirk playing on his lips, and raised a brow. "You think you can?"

"I guess we'll find out." I scanned the boats in the marina, cataloguing the features of each and discarding them just as quickly. "Well, it's not Moby's Dick with the giant whale painted on the side. Too gaudy. And it's not Mr. Overcompensator. Too ostentatious."

With each one we passed, I discarded them all until my gaze snagged on one toward the end of the line. The hull was hidden by the boat next to it, so I couldn't see the name yet, but it just felt right. "That one has promise. Looks well-kept. Pretty but not too flashy. If it's named something like *Ship Happens*, I'll have my answer."

"You think I'd give my boat a ridiculous name?" he asked, something I couldn't quite identify threaded through his voice.

"Not unless you lost a bet with one of your brothers. I think you'd give it a name that meant something. A name that was important to you."

He cleared his throat. "You're right."

"I knew it. Maybe something with your mom or your siblings or maybe—" I glanced back at the boat I'd pinpointed as his, stopping dead in my tracks when the letters written in black script came into view.

The Sparrow.

Emotion clogged my throat as I stood stock-still, unable to do anything but gape at the two little words branded there. Something he'd just told me meant something to him...was important to him.

I could feel Levi's stare on me, his gaze heavy and weighted, as if he was gauging my reaction. The trouble was, I didn't know how to act casual. Didn't know how to pretend that it was no big deal he'd done this... Named his boat the same thing he'd been calling me since we were thirteen.

"How long ago did you restore it?" I finally asked, attempting to make my voice even. Maybe it was a coincidence. Maybe it didn't have anything to do with me.

He swallowed, breaking eye contact and glancing over at it. "It's been a while."

I squeezed his hand, needing to know the answer. "How long, Levi?"

"Eleven years."

Back when I'd thought he hated me.

"What does it mean?"

"You know what it means, sparrow," he said, his voice gruff but sure and steady.

My breath caught in my throat, and I bit my lower lip to keep from crying because the truth was so beautiful and heartbreaking, it made my chest ache. When I'd been spending my nights crying and cursing Levi's name, he'd spent his restoring a boat, only to name it after me.

I turned toward him and traced my fingertips over the delicate lines of the sparrow tattooed above his heart, in its mouth a rope attached to the anchor below. "And this?"

"That, too." He reached up and brushed a flyaway strand of hair back from my face before trailing his fingers down the curve of my jaw. "And all the rest of them."

"All the rest—" My words cut off as his meaning registered. I darted my gaze over every inch of his exposed skin, my fingers following suit. First to the script arcing over his shoulder, then to the compass rose on his side. Then to the peach tree and the Ferris wheel and the sailboat on ocean waves, every single one of them a call back to us, now that I knew what I was looking at...what I was looking *for*.

They were all reminders of what we'd been. What he'd hoped we could be.

As tears filled my eyes, I swallowed repeatedly, attempting to shove down the sob that was working its way up my throat. I was overcome with emotion, finally aware of just how much this man had devoted himself to me, even in the years we were apart.

"I think you might be a little obsessed with me," I finally said, my voice thick and wobbly. "You should maybe see someone about that."

"You're such a shit," he grumbled, but I could hear the underlying affection in his tone.

Honestly, how had I ever missed it?

Then he smacked my ass hard enough to pull a yelp from me before linking his fingers with mine and tugging me, breathless and laughing, behind him.

Straight toward *The Sparrow*.

CHAPTER THIRTY-SEVEN

LEVI

IT'D BEEN a long damn time since I'd been out on the ocean when my thoughts weren't an echo chamber of grief and regret and self-blame. Being on the water—whether in my boat or the boat my mom taught me to sail on—always brought up too many memories to be anything but bittersweet.

While I loved sailing, loved the ocean, I loved those things *because* of my mom. And anytime I thought about her, it wasn't the sound of her laughter or the feeling of one of her hugs or the sight of her smile when we caught the wind just right. It was the crushing guilt I carried for being the reason she was gone from this world, forever stuck in a loop on the night when everything changed. When I fucked up so many lives because I was callous and careless and fucking selfish.

Something I reminded myself of daily. For years, it had been my constant soundtrack as I sank deep into it, held it inside, and let it eat away at me. Never sharing it with a soul because I was the one responsible, and I deserved to feel every bit of this pain.

It was only now, as the salty ocean air blew against my face and the waves lapped at *The Sparrow*, that I realized those usual roars in the back of my mind had been quieted to a murmur lately. I knew it was more than likely just the temporary distraction provided by Harper's presence back in my life.

And I also knew I didn't deserve the reprieve. This was my cross to bear. The weight of carrying these thoughts the absolute least I could sacrifice in comparison to what my mom had given up.

"So...exactly how many awards *have* you won?" Harper's question tugged me back to the present, and I forced my dark thoughts away to focus on her. Her eyes were full of mischief, a smirk on those gorgeous lips, and I loved that we were finally back to this place. Where we could laugh and tease and have fun with each other despite our history.

"You been Googling me now, sparrow?" I asked, a throwback to our first conversation in the apartment.

She lifted a single shoulder, bare except for the strap of her dress and that little tie at the base of her neck from her swimsuit. "Part of the job. Gotta do my research on a subject."

"And what did your research tell you?"

"That you're the youngest master craftsman ever inducted into the American Boatbuilders and Restorers Guild, you've designed and built over thirty-five custom boats, and you won Boatbuilder of the Year three times before you were thirty. How'd I do?"

I tipped my lips up, regarding her with amusement. I'd never once questioned whether she was good at her job. Of course she was. She was Harper Davidson, and I wasn't sure she'd ever found anything she didn't succeed at. But knowing it on a base level was entirely different from witnessing it.

"I think you pretty much hit all the highlights, so we're probably done."

She laughed, the sound bouncing off the water around us,

and I smiled right along with her. "Nice try, but you're not getting out of this."

For the next thirty minutes, she peppered me with questions, each one thoughtful and insightful, pushing just enough to get what she needed without being intrusive. And the entire time, I had to sit here watching her and answering as intelligently as possible, all the while pretending I wasn't hard as a fucking rock.

Watching her doing something she obviously loved only amped up my reaction to her. Of course, it didn't help with how hot she looked, sitting across from me in full work mode. Her hair was pulled into a messy bun on top of her head, and she bounced the end of her pen against her bottom lip as she read over her notes. Add in that fucking swimsuit, the straps taunting me, and I was a goner. Every time I glanced at that bow at the back of her neck, I was reminded exactly how little effort it would take to have her tits in my face.

I shifted in my seat, attempting to get myself under control, but it was a losing battle. "Watching you work is sexy as hell."

She tugged the pen from between her teeth and snapped her gaze to mine, a slow smile spreading across her mouth. "Your little distraction isn't going to work. At least not until I get this idea down..."

Focusing on her notepad, she scribbled notes faster than the ideas would've even come to me. And all the while, I sat quietly, studying every inch of her and loving how I could practically see the ideas lighting up in her eyes. It was clear this was exactly what she was meant to be doing. Not being a lawyer like her father wanted. This, right here, talking with people, learning about their lives, and crafting their stories.

"You really love this, don't you?" I asked.

"My job?" she clarified, not lifting her eyes from the notepad on her lap. "Yeah, I do."

The sincerity in her answer left no doubt as to just how true it was, and it had me wondering what came next. I had no illusions that Starlight Cove could be what she needed—not with her career. The *Gazette* wasn't exactly a shining example of international accreditation, which was exactly what she deserved.

"So...what are your plans after this assignment?" I asked as casually as I could, hoping to hide my selfish wants.

Because what I wanted didn't matter.

I'd shoved her away twelve years ago so she could live the life she deserved. While it hadn't been the life I'd thought she wanted, she'd done exactly what my hope had been. And though I'd learned my lesson and had no intention of doing something like that again, I also couldn't live with myself if I held her back.

My sparrow had always been meant to fly, and I wasn't going to clip her wings now.

So, I'd take whatever she was willing to give. If she wanted to do this long-distance, I would in a heartbeat. If she only wanted a hookup when she happened to come back into town, I'd handle it. If she wanted to go our separate ways, I'd find a way to deal.

Though I knew, on my end, it didn't matter what she chose. There was no one else in the world for me, and I would always and forever be completely devoted to her and only her.

She shot me a smile, though it seemed a bit forced. "If I nail this article, hopefully there's a permanent position waiting for me at *Weekend Wanderlust*."

"Where will that take you?"

Clearing her throat, she averted her gaze, tapping her pen on the notepad. "Their office is in New York."

Fuck me. Though I'd known her being here in Starlight Cove was temporary, it still cut deep to hear her confirm it. Especially knowing how little time we had left.

"New York, huh? Love that city life?"

"I thought I was the one asking questions."

I raised a brow at her obvious avoidance of the question. "You just got me to talk for longer in a single sitting than I usually do in three days. I think you succeeded."

She lifted a shoulder. "What can I say? I'm good at my job."

"That you are." I reached over and pressed the red button on her phone screen to stop the recording. "But I think we've done enough work for today."

"Oh, you do, do you?" She relaxed back in her seat, a soft smile on her lips, this one genuine. "And what do you suggest we do for the rest of our time?"

I stood and grabbed the pen and notepad from her hand before tucking them and her phone back into her bag. Then I braced my hands on the table and leaned toward her. "It's well past time we got you wet."

CHAPTER THIRTY-EIGHT

LEVI

WITH HER BROWS RAISED, Harper stared at me, an indulgent smirk curving her lips, and I wanted to kiss it right off her face. "Is that your way of telling me you're about to toss me overboard? Wouldn't be the first time."

I grinned, thrown back in time but unable to pinpoint any single memory because it'd happened so often. Especially in those early teen years before I'd admitted how much I liked her...*loved* her. Without warning, I'd wrap my arms around her and send us both overboard, clinging to any little touch I could get.

"Actually..." I pulled off my hat and set it on the table before lying down on the padded bench seat, tapping my chest. "That's my way of telling you to get over here and sit on my face."

She breathed out a shocked laugh, a flush working its way up her cheeks as she glanced around, no doubt for any nosy onlookers. As if I hadn't planned for this when we'd dropped anchor, and as if I'd allow anyone else the privilege of seeing her naked.

"You looking for someone to save you, sparrow? I'm afraid

you're going to be searching for a while. There's no one around for miles. So how about you finally put me out of my misery and show me what's under that little pink dress?"

She bit her bottom lip, indecision written across her face as she scanned me from head to toe. I didn't know if it was the pure hunger written on my face or the very obvious bulge in my shorts, but she eventually stood and walked to my side. Then, with her eyes locked on mine, she slowly slid her fingers up the outsides of her thighs as if for the sole purpose of tormenting me before slipping them under her dress.

Gathering the material in her hands, she pulled it up her body, each inch of skin revealed torment and ecstasy wrapped up in one. I watched with rapt attention, my mouth going dry as she finally tugged the dress over her head and tossed it to the side. Beneath, she wore a red bikini. The top tied around her neck and barely held in her tits, the bottoms just a scrap of fabric that hugged her full hips, and I wanted to rip every stitch of it off her.

"That was quite the tease."

"You did say you wanted to see what was under my dress…"

"I believe I also told you to sit on my face." I licked my lips. "Get up here. I'm starving."

Still, she hesitated.

I couldn't stop myself from reaching for her, sliding my hand up the outside of her thigh. "I promise you I'm gonna love it."

She breathed out a laugh. "I already know that. I lived it the first time around, remember? You begged for it every chance you got."

"Then what's the holdup?"

"It's just been a long time since I've done this. And I weigh a hell of a lot more now than I did back then."

I tugged her closer, running my hands along every inch of

her I could reach. "Your body's fucking perfect. I love every single inch of you."

And though I wanted those inches settled on my face, my mind had a tendency to fixate on things. Once it latched on, it was hard as hell to shake it off. That was the only excuse I had for why I thought it was a good idea to dig into the other half of her statement.

"How long?" As soon as the words were out of my mouth, I wanted to take them back. I didn't want to know a single detail about any of the men Harper had been with in the years we'd been apart, or I'd lose my fucking mind.

She shrugged, interlocking our fingers when I reached for her hand. "As long as it's been for you."

Her answer slammed into me so hard, it took me a moment to acclimate myself to this sudden new reality. I'd been preparing myself for a bit of torture in her answer and instead found nothing but relief and satisfaction. The summer before we'd finally had sex, we'd done everything but, and I'd spent a hell of a lot of those three months with my face buried between her thighs. Some of which with her perched on my mouth.

The first time I'd asked her to do it, she'd been so tentative, so unsure. And I'd done everything in my power to make her feel comfortable because it had been heaven on earth for me. I *wanted* her weight pressing down on me. Wanted nothing more than to drown in her pussy.

"I'm fucking dying for it, baby," I rasped, not bothering to hide just how badly I wanted her. "Take those bottoms off and give me my lunch."

After shimmying her bottoms off, she climbed on top of me and straddled my lap, grinding against where I was already so fucking hard for her. Her pussy was so hot I could feel it through my shorts, the heat of her damn near dragging a groan from my throat. I slid my hands up her legs, digging my fingers into the soft flesh of her thighs and hips, needing to have her closer. To sink inside her and fuck her until she screamed.

But it wasn't even close to time for me to get mine.

She rested her hands on my chest as she stared down at me, her lip caught between her teeth. Pressing harder against my cock, she rotated her hips, dragging a moan from us both.

Jesus Christ, I fucking loved this woman. And I didn't deserve any of the pleasure she made me feel—in my body, mind, or soul—but I was going to take every ounce of it while I had the chance.

With every rock of her hips, every brush of my cock against her clit, she was driving me wild. All while bringing herself closer and closer to the edge and making a mess of my shorts while she was at it.

"You trying to mark me, sparrow?" I asked, gripping her hips and guiding her movements as I held her firmer against me. "Want to drench my shorts with your needy little cunt? I can feel you soaking through the front, so goddamn desperate for it. Time for you to stop fucking around, climb up here, and sit on my face."

"Stop bossing me around. You know I don't like it."

"You keep saying that, but your pussy tells a different story. Now, untie that little bow at the back of your neck and show me your gorgeous tits. I want you playing with them while I fuck you with my tongue."

She glanced around one more time as if to reassure herself we were the only two souls around. When I dipped my chin in a nod to confirm no one could see us, she reached up and did as I said before repeating the action with the bow at her back. And then my gorgeous girl was straddling my lap, wearing absolutely nothing at all, her body on full display.

Her tits were heavy and full, her nipples hard little pebbles I wanted to suck deep into my mouth. Her stomach was soft and round, her hips and thighs full and lush. The kind of body I could lose myself in for hours, could drown in and never come up for air. And then there was her perfect little pussy, grinding down on me, no doubt aching for release.

"Good girl," I said, my voice low and rough, all decorum gone. "Now, climb up."

She scooted forward and braced her knees on either side of my head, her cunt pink and swollen and so fucking wet it made my mouth water.

I couldn't hope to hold in my groan and didn't bother trying, allowing the sound to tear straight from my throat. "Oh, fuck me."

"Later. I did what you said." She hovered above me before slowly sinking down, her fingers delving into my hair and drawing my gaze to hers. "Now it's your turn. Make me come."

A slow smile spread across my mouth as I gripped her ass in both hands. I tugged her down until my lips brushed against her, a tentative touch at first, though it didn't last long. Her taste was fucking addictive, and I wanted it on my tongue, wanted to swallow every ounce of her pleasure over and over again until she begged me to stop.

I licked through her seam, swirling my tongue around her clit before affixing my mouth to her and devouring her whole. I groaned at the taste of her—sweet and musky and *mine*. For now, at least, she was mine. And I was going to soak up every second.

She rode my face tentatively at first, the subtlest shifting of her hips as she rocked over me. Never giving in. Never surrendering. Never completely letting go.

Until finally, after I'd made enough gruff noises in my throat, digging my fingers into the soft flesh of her hips to keep her affixed to my mouth, she finally rode my tongue with abandon. Tipping her head back on a moan, she cupped her tits in both hands, her thumbs and forefingers tugging her pebbled nipples. I wanted nothing more than to focus solely on them for hours just to see how sensitive I could make her.

But right now, my only job was to stay alive long enough to satisfy her, all while she tried to suffocate me with her pussy. A death I would gladly surrender to.

"Oh fuck..." She choked out a gasp and fell forward, bracing her hands on either side of my head as she rolled her hips against me. "God, Levi, you're making me come."

I groaned into her flesh, holding her tighter to me as I worked my tongue against her. The possessive part inside me lit up at the fact that she'd designated this orgasm as mine. *I* was the one making her come, and I had no intention of stopping anytime soon. I kept at it, working my tongue against her and pushing her through the first one and straight into another.

Drawing out orgasm after orgasm, I pushed her as much as she could take, until her arousal covered my mouth...dripped from my chin down my neck. I fucking loved that I was covered in her. Loved that she was all over me...her taste and her scent and everything I was wringing from her body.

"*Levi.*" Her voice was raspy, a pleading edge to it as tremors racked her body while she tried climbing off my face for a reprieve.

Instead, I flipped us around so she was lying on her back, her legs over my shoulders, and my face level with the most gorgeous pussy in the world. "You trying to get away from me?"

"Yes." She reached down, feebly shoving my head away. "I can't take any more."

"You can't, huh? You remember your word?"

Another shudder worked its way through her as I softly circled her clit with my tongue. Pulling back, I slid my middle two fingers inside her, curling them up and seeking the spot that made her jerk against me. She gasped when I found it, but she rolled her hips in time with every stroke.

"Sparrow. Do you remember your word?" When she still hadn't answered, I slipped my fingers from her, brushing them softly against her clit before bringing them down in a sharp smack.

She yelped before letting out a low moan, her wild eyes tracking my every movement, my desperate, greedy girl.

"Answer me. Do you remember?"

"Yes."

"And do you want to use it?"

Rather than answering, she spread her legs wider, sliding her fingers into my hair, and tugged my face until it was directly against her pussy.

"There's my dirty girl," I said, slipping my fingers back inside her before licking up her slit.

And then I made it my mission to see just how many times I could make her come undone.

By the time she'd shuddered through two more, I had precome leaking from my cock in a damn near steady stream. She was shaking, her entire body quivering as tears leaked from the corners of her eyes and rolled down her temples.

"Levi," she said, her voice hoarse. "I need you. *Please*. I want to feel you inside me."

As a rule, Harper didn't beg. She said exactly what she wanted and went after it until it was hers. So when my gorgeous girl was desperate enough to do it, I was damn well going to give her whatever she wanted.

After swiping my tongue through her pussy one last time, I

climbed up, shucked off my shorts, and settled between her thighs. "How do you want it, baby?"

"Like this," she said, reaching for me. "Just like this."

She wrapped her hand around my neck and tugged me down until our foreheads were pressed together as I settled between her thighs, my favorite place in the world. My cock jerked at the first brush against her cunt—hot and so fucking wet—and we both groaned as I swiped my head through her slit, flicking my piercings against her clit.

With a whimper, she dug her nails into the back of my neck. "Need you," she said, the words little more than a breath.

I didn't know if she meant it in the same way I needed her, like the earth needed the sun. Or if she just meant this, our bodies rocking together and my ability to give her pleasure until she cried. But it didn't matter, because I was hers to command. Would give her absolutely anything she needed for as long as I had the privilege.

I sank into her, groaning as she took me deep. Then Harper lifted her legs, wrapped them around my hips, and allowed me to settle inside her those last couple of inches. Until our bodies were flush, her cunt taking me all the way in as if she were made for me.

She let out a breathy sigh as I fucked into her, steady and deep, trying to keep myself under control because there was no fucking way I was going to last otherwise. Not after feasting on her pussy for over an hour and edging myself that entire time. Not when my cock was so primed for her I could barely see straight. Not when she took me so well, her little cunt spread wide around my girth. And sure as fuck not when she breathed those little fuck-me moans straight into my mouth, her eyes glazed with pleasure.

"Fuck," I gritted out between clenched teeth, trying to hold out until she got another one. "I'm so fucking close."

She hooked her ankles at the base of my spine, lifting her hips up to meet my every thrust. "Good. I want you to come."

"You first." I slipped a hand between us, thumbing her clit, but she reached down and shoved my hand away before pulling me so tight against her, there was no space between us.

"You've given me plenty. Now it's your turn." She threaded her fingers through the hair at my nape, holding me as close as she could. "I want to feel you come inside me."

At her words, my cock jerked before I even knew what was happening, the orgasm slamming into me without warning.

I couldn't do anything but surrender.

Harper tipped her face up, capturing my mouth with hers as I lost myself in her body. Forever grateful we'd found our way back to each other, while at the same time mourning how little time we had left.

CHAPTER THIRTY-NINE

HARPER

AFTER SPENDING all afternoon on *The Sparrow*, part of it doing what I needed to do, and the other part enjoying myself far more than I thought possible, Levi and I docked the boat and walked up the hill toward Chase's parents' home.

"You guys got here just in time," Chase said, jogging down the deck stairs to greet us. "Dinner's just about—" He cut off, his gaze snagging on something behind me, and I turned around to see what he was looking at, but *The Sparrow* was the only thing in his line of sight.

"That's how you both got here?" he asked Levi, brows raised damn near to his hairline.

"Looks like," Levi said.

"It's about damn time." He grinned, hooking his arms around both our shoulders and leading us toward the house.

I narrowed my gaze at him, realizing the little shit had known this whole time—whenever we'd grabbed lunch or dinner or drinks anytime we happened to be in the same place. And not *once* had he mentioned it. "Exactly how long have you known Levi's boat was named after me?"

He wiped his expression clean and shook his head. "Sorry, what?"

"Exactly how long—"

"Oh, I think I hear my mom calling for us." He turned toward the house, yelling, "What's that, Mom?"

I rolled my eyes and elbowed him in the gut, basking in his sharp oomph. "You're such an ass."

"You gonna let her talk to me like that?" Chase asked, glancing at Levi.

"Why wouldn't I? It's the truth."

"Great, so this is what it's gonna be like with the trio back together," Chase said. "Both of you ganging up on me, as usual."

"Do you want me to call your wife and have her swing by?" I asked. "Protect you from us?"

"I hate you both."

"You love us both," I tossed back.

He dropped his arms from our shoulders and turned around, walking backward as he split his gaze between Levi and me. "That I do. And I'm happy as fuck I don't have to keep secrets anymore. That calls for a celebration. Did you bring something to toast with?"

Levi snorted. "Maybe if you'd given us a bit of notice. We came straight from the cove, man."

"Damn. Well, I'm sure Mom's got something," Chase said as he opened the sliders to the house and strode inside.

"What does Mom have?" Marianne called from somewhere in the house.

The Lockharts' home had been such a staple in my childhood that a pang of nostalgia settled over me as soon as I stepped inside. Levi reached down, linking our fingers together and squeezing as if he understood exactly what I was feeling. Though he probably would since this place was just as much a second home for him as it had been for me. More so. Especially after his mom passed away.

It must've been hard for him, coming here with so many memories seeped into these walls. A constant reminder of what used to be. Of what would never be again.

"Harper!" Marianne said, scooting around her son to engulf me in a hug. A *mom* hug.

Her familiar scent washed over me as I melted into her embrace. I wasn't expecting tears to prick my eyes at that first squeeze, but a wave of emotion crashed into me as she held me tight. As if I were her own. It was a hug I hadn't had in years. Not since her. Not since Grace.

After several long moments, Marianne finally pulled back to hold me at arm's length. Thankfully, she'd hugged me so long I had enough time to get my shit together, so I hoped my eyes were no longer shiny.

"I'm so happy you're here," she said. "We have a lot of catching up to do. Tell me, do you have any babies yet?"

"Jesus Christ, Mom," Chase said, scrubbing a hand down his face. "She's been here for ninety seconds. And you can't say shit like that anyway."

"Why not?" she asked, sounding affronted.

"Because it's A) rude as hell, and B) none of your business."

"Well, I was just curious." Marianne sniffed. "Wondering if I had a place to put all this grandmotherly love."

"You *do* have a place for it." Chase rolled his eyes. "Or did you forget my wife is pregnant with our baby, aka your first grandchild?"

"No, I didn't *forget*. But do you see any babies lying around here?" She held out her arms and looked pointedly around the great room and the decidedly baby-free space. "I want to love on a baby *now*, and I've gotta wait until March. Unless..." She looked back at me with raised brows.

I laughed and shook my head. "Sorry, Marianne. I'm afraid you're going to have to wait for your son and daughter-in-law's little bundle."

She blew out a long-suffering sigh and hooked her arm through mine, tugging me toward the dining room. "But some-day, yes?"

"*Mom*," Chase said, sounding so much like the aggrieved thirteen-year-old I'd once known and loved that I couldn't help but laugh.

"Hush now. Harper and I are having girl talk, and it doesn't concern you."

Chase grumbled under his breath as Marianne looked at me with an expectant expression, and I didn't know what to tell her.

Kids had never been part of my plan. Not with the childhood I'd had and growing up as I did. Not considering the nonexistent relationship I had with my parents and the damage they'd done. And not considering my lack of any serious romantic relation-ships in the past...ever. Truthfully, I still wasn't sure if kids were in my plan.

So then, why the hell did my stomach flip as I imagined a life like that with Levi, him and me with a little kid, each of us holding on to one of their hands and swinging them between us as the three of us strolled along the beach?

And why the hell did it flip even more when I slid my gaze to Levi, only to find his attention already on me?

CHAPTER FORTY

HARPER

LUNA:

We've got another girls' night coming up, and we want you there. *I* want you there. I need you to save me from my obsessive soon-to-be sister-in-law.

HARPER:

What's Addison done now?

LUNA:

She's got a binder for the wedding. A freaking BINDER.

HARPER:

Organization isn't a bad thing when it comes to wedding planning, or so I've heard.

LUNA:

Maybe not. Except I'd be perfectly happy eloping on the beach.

HARPER:

I'm starting to see the issue…

LUNA:

> Tomorrow night at Stan's. Mark it on your
> calendar. I'm not taking no for an answer!

A FEW DAYS after dinner at the Lockharts', I was keeping an eye out the windows of the *Gazette,* just as I'd been doing all morning like a creeper. But tough times called for tough measures, and I'd do whatever needed to get the job done. Thus far, I'd been unsuccessful in nailing down either of the last two Steele brothers, and I wanted to try my luck at all four guys before I gave up on this avenue.

So as soon as I saw one of them roll up on a motorcycle in front of the bar, I was out of my seat before the door to One Night Stan's swung shut behind him. With no time to waste, I grabbed my phone and my notepad full of the questions I'd been jotting down and strode out the front door of the *Gazette* and straight across the street.

In the time that had taken me, Brother #3 was already on his way out of the bar and headed for his bike once again, straddling it just as I got to him.

"Hey there." I lifted my hand in greeting. "I was hoping to catch you before you left."

He planted both feet on the ground, eyeing me up and down with a raised brow. "Do I know you?"

"We haven't officially met. I'm Harper Davidson."

With suspicion cloaking every inch of him, he shook the hand I offered. And dammit, these Steele boys were hard nuts to crack. "What can I do for you, Harper?"

The request was kind enough, but from the way he asked the

question, he wasn't much—or at all—interested in accommo-
dating the answer.

"I'm in town working on an article about the secret of
Starlight Cove and why so many high-profile people decide to
make this their forever home. I was hoping to ask you a few
questions about your da—"

I didn't even get the last word out before he turned on his
motorcycle, the engine rumbling to life beneath him.

"I've got somewhere to be. But maybe you'll have better luck
with one of my brothers." With a lift of his chin, he revved the
engine, waited until I stepped back, and tore off down the street
without a backward glance, taking shot three out of four
with him.

My shoulders slumped as I watched him tear out of here and
away from me, blowing out a frustrated breath as he went. "If
only those brothers of yours were any help," I mumbled to no
one but myself.

While I'd managed to unearth quite a few details about Stan
in my internet sleuthing, I much preferred to have the personal
touch that came from firsthand accounts. It was just too bad
Brick Wall wasn't alone in shutting down this line of questioning. All three of them had done the same thing, albeit in
different manners—Brick Wall being blunt, Charmer being,
well, charming, and Mr. Avoidance blowing me off entirely. God
only knew what I'd be in for with Brother #4.

Fortunately, I'd anticipated this outcome, covering my ass and
moving in a slightly different direction just in case this path didn't
lead anywhere. In doing so, I'd talked to some truly remarkable
people who either currently or had in the past called Starlight
Cove home. I knew the article, with or without the inclusion of
the elusive Stan, was going to knock my editor's socks off.

Which meant my ticket to permanence...to roots...was around the corner.

I'd just made it back across the street and opened the door to the *Gazette* when my phone rang in my hand. Speak of the devil—Naomi's name flashed on my screen.

I exhaled a deep breath and shook off the rejection from Mr. Avoidance, not wanting whatever feelings I had about my interaction with him to bleed into my conversation with her.

When I was sure I'd stripped everything away, I answered. "Hello?"

"Harper, hi. Just checking in. How's the article coming?"

"Great," I said, allowing every ounce of excitement I could manage to reflect in my tone. "I've uncovered a lot of surprising and interesting sources, and I'm happy with how it's developing."

"That's what I love to hear. Really looking forward to seeing the finished piece. As well as what the future holds."

Her words were innocuous enough and could've meant a dozen different things. But I knew they didn't. I knew they were in reference to the exact reason I'd taken this assignment in the first place, and they sent me into a tailspin. Nerves and excitement and...trepidation overwhelming me.

After confirming my deadline in two weeks and saying our goodbyes, I ended the call, exhaling a deep breath as I placed my phone on my desk.

Except it wasn't really mine because Starlight Cove wasn't really mine.

From the beginning, this had only been a stopping-off point. Just a detour on the way to my next adventure. Namely, a permanent position at *Weekend Wanderlust* and a permanent home in New York City, a place where I could finally put down roots.

I hadn't had a permanent home in close to a decade, hadn't

had roots in longer than that. My apartment in Boston was a pre-furnished placeholder that had never felt like anything but.

I'd traveled around the world, gone to so many different places, had lived in Chicago and Philly and even a brief stint in DC, but I'd never felt *permanence*. Never felt like if I put down roots, they would sink into the soil and ground me. Hold me safe and secure.

Not like I did now, here, with him.

———

THE FOLLOWING DAY, I walked into One Night Stan's, knowing the rest of the girls were already here by the sheer volume inside the space. A few other patrons were scattered along the bar and in a couple booths against the wall, but the vast majority of the noise came from the table directly in the middle of the establishment and the lovely group of women I was meeting.

A group of women I could actually call friends.

Every single one of them had reached out to me at one point or another since our first night out all those weeks ago, whether via text or stopping me to chat if they saw me around town or popping into the *Gazette* just to say hi. And I was sort of... loving it?

For as much as this was uncharted territory for me, I couldn't deny how much I'd begun to look forward to those interactions and how touched I'd been when Luna had invited me along tonight. It felt a little like I was becoming a part of this group. Like, maybe, I had a place here.

As soon as I walked up to the table, all attention swiveled to me, and a chorus of "Harper!" went up from everyone.

"Hey," I said with a smile, hanging my purse over the back of my chair before sinking into it.

"Just in time." Luna shot me a forced grin. "Addison was about to pull out the wedding binder."

I rolled my lips in, barely withholding a laugh. "Sorry I'm late."

"No worries." Everly waved a hand through the air. "The pitcher of margaritas just arrived."

"Busy at work?" Addison asked, clutching the binder to her chest like a prized possession.

"Yeah, actually. I was working on an interview, and she was *real* chatty."

"Ooh!" Avery said, her eyes sparkling as she rested her elbows on the table and leaned toward me. "Tell us more!"

"Definitely fill us in." Quinn poured me a margarita. "How's the article coming?"

"Really great. I just got done interviewing Betty Baker. She's led a pretty amazing life."

"Isn't she that famous pinup model?" Avery asked.

"That's the one. She's celebrating her hundredth birthday next week."

"A legend." Avery held her glass in the air, toasting to my source. "Truly."

"Can't wait to read the article when it's all done," Quinn said.

"That reminds me." Everly reached toward me, tapping her hand on the table between us. "I've been loving your weekly column in the *Gazette*. I wish I'd had something like that when I first moved here."

"If you'd had that, maybe you wouldn't have pestered my brother, and then where would we be?" Addison asked.

Everly laughed, elbowing Addison in the side before returning her attention to me. "No, but seriously. I felt like such an outsider. Starlight Cove was such a well-oiled machine, and I couldn't see where I fit in. Having this would've really helped. And I think it's going to be great for new residents we have coming into town."

"Well, don't get too attached," Addison said, eyeing me in a way that left me feeling open and vulnerable. "There's only going to be, what, two more?"

While I'd been doing my best to compartmentalize the timeline I had to work on this article and the time I had left in Starlight Cove, allowing myself to focus on one and not the other, I had no way of dodging this reminder. It slammed into me, the reality that I had mere days left in town sinking like a brick in my stomach.

I didn't know if this was the nervous jitters that always bubbled under my skin before diving into my next project or if this was something more. Something telling me that maybe New York wasn't the right place for me. Or maybe it was just the part of me that was already feeling the loss of these connections I'd made in the one place I wasn't meant to stay.

CHAPTER FORTY-ONE

LEVI

I WAS NEVER MORE of a coward than I was on this day, and no matter how many years had gone by, that never changed. But instead of facing it head on, instead of telling my siblings why this date hit me the hardest, instead of admitting I was the reason Mom was dead, I slunk away. Always hiding away in my workshop until they dragged me from it.

And this year was no better.

I'd slipped out of bed this morning, leaving a sleepy Harper looking like a fucking angel lying there nestled in my sheets. I'd left her without a word, without even a fucking note, and headed straight to my workshop because I'd been unable to do anything else.

It was the one and only place I could hope to get an ounce of reprieve from the overwhelming weight of grief that rested on my shoulders today. Though, it hadn't been just the workshop that had quieted my thoughts lately. Harper and the distraction she provided had been an unexpected respite.

But it didn't matter where I went or who I was with because nothing could silence them today.

My phone buzzed with an incoming text, and I glanced over at it, already knowing who it was.

ADDISON:

Beach at 5

Rather than the usual stream of absolute bullshit that followed any single text, my brothers were silent, our mom's death weighing heavily on each one of us.

For years now, we'd done our own thing during the day before meeting up at our mom's favorite spot on the beach in the evening. Those first couple years, facing the reminder of what I'd done and what I'd taken from my family ate me alive. Especially when the six of us would sit in the sand, nothing but silent tears in the space between us.

As the years had gone by, things had changed, shifted. Where once we'd been silent, in the past few years, we'd begun to talk, to share, reminiscing about our favorite memories of Mom.

And that was just as painful as the silence.

Because while I wanted nothing more than to remember her, I knew that remembering her meant acknowledging what we'd lost. What I'd stolen from everyone.

SEVERAL HOURS LATER, after I'd sanded boards until my hands were raw and blistered, the door to my workshop opened, the sound of heels clicking on the concrete floor filling the space. I knew Addison wouldn't come out here—not today. So that left only one person, and my heart both sank and soared at that realization.

I glanced up as Harper came into view, her eyes brightening

and a smile sweeping over her mouth when her gaze landed on me. It was a sucker punch to the chest—this beautiful woman I was lucky enough to call mine. For as long as she'd allow.

"What are you doing here?" I asked.

She tipped her head to the side as she regarded me, a furrow between her brows, no doubt from my lack of greeting. But that didn't stop her from walking right up to me, slipping her hand around the back of my neck and tugging my face down to hers.

"Hi," she said against my lips before brushing hers over mine. The kiss was slow and sweet and so tender, it made my fucking heart ache.

I hadn't said a word about what today was, and yet somehow she knew something was off.

"Hey," I said when she finally pulled back, wanting with everything I had to both draw her close and shove her as far away as possible.

"I thought I'd get some pictures like we talked about." She ran her gaze over me, snagging on the rough state of my hands. "But I'm sensing maybe today isn't the best day to do that. What's going on?"

I shook my head and avoided her eyes, unable to get the words out. "I'm not really in the mood to talk about it."

As if I was *ever* in the mood to talk about it.

Harper studied me for long moments, her gaze scrutinizing but concerned. And I was the last person who deserved her concern. "All right. No pictures. So, what are we doing today?"

Relief swept over me as I exhaled a heavy sigh, unsure how I got lucky enough to have her, not once, but twice in my life. This amazing woman who accepted me, all the rough, jagged, and wrecked pieces of me. And instead of trying to find a solution, instead of telling me what to fix, she just settled in and sat down beside me, weathering the storm by my side.

"There's some place I have to go," I said, my voice low and rough. "And I'd love if you came with me."

She darted her gaze all over my face, no doubt reading the emotion in my voice and wondering what the hell was going on. Finally, she nodded once and slipped her arms around my waist, hugging me tight. "Then that's where I'll be."

EVERY STEP I took closer to where I knew my family would be felt like walking to the gallows. Harper held my hand, squeezing twice when my siblings and their significant others came into view, the ten of them sitting in a group along the shore.

Luna sat between Brady's thighs, her back against his chest, as he buried his face into her neck. Avery was perched sideways on Aiden's lap, whispered words shared between them. Beck and Ford were clustered together with Everly and Quinn, respectively, nestled against their sides. And Addison sat tucked in the protective cocoon of her husband, Chase's legs drawn up and his arms wrapped around his knees with her in the middle.

This was the first year it was all of us, the family ours had grown into spanning more than just my brothers and sister. It now encompassed not only the people I loved more than anything, but those they loved, too.

I lifted my chin in greeting to everyone, unable to say a word, and dropped down onto the sand, tugging Harper along with me. She came willingly, leaning into my side as she wrapped her arm around me, her hand a comforting presence against my back.

Having her here felt like cracking my chest open and laying it at her feet. I'd never had someone else share this with me. Hell, none of us had. And though it was scary to know she was going to witness my pain, I couldn't deny how relieved I was to have her here with me by my side. Her presence alone was a support I hadn't known I'd needed.

"Remember how Mom used to wake us up on school mornings?" Ford asked, amusement in his tone. "If we didn't get our asses up when she said, she came barging in, flipped on the lights, and had a dance party in the doorway. She blasted that fucking music as loud as possible, so not even Levi could sleep through it."

As chuckles sounded from everyone else, a memory slammed into me. Mom bursting into my room while "Livin' on a Prayer" played at a volume the guests staying in cottages could have heard.

"And when dancing around didn't work, she'd jump on the bed until you had no peace left," Beck said.

"She never did that with me," Aiden said.

Brady lifted a brow in Aiden's direction. "Probably because you've been running your own schedule since you were six."

"What about when she let me play hooky so I could help her plant flowers in all the cottage planters? Did that really happen, or did I make that up?" Addison asked, her voice quivering.

Sometimes I forgot how young Addison had been when we'd lost Mom. She might've only been two years younger than me, but she'd been just a baby then. Hadn't even graduated high school yet. So many of her memories with Mom had been lost with time.

"Yeah, little D," Ford said. "That happened."

The five of them continued sharing memories, most of them happy, but with every word out of their mouths, the knife plunged further into my chest, the evidence of the life I'd taken from them too blatant to ignore.

I wanted to speak up, to ask them if they remembered how

Mom used to sing along, loudly and off-key, to every song that came on the radio, or how she'd always make whatever we wanted on our birthdays, no questions asked. But the words got stuck in my throat.

I couldn't shake the feeling that I didn't deserve to participate in her remembrance. Didn't deserve to recall the happy times when I was the reason they were gone.

I was the reason my siblings no longer had a mom.

I was the reason my future niece or nephew wouldn't get to experience her as a grandma.

I was the reason we gathered here every fucking year to remember the most amazing mom in the world.

Harper's hand was a steady presence on my back, grounding me when it felt like the grief was trying to pull me under. Those constant thoughts of, "Why couldn't it have been me? It should've been me," a never-ending vortex in my mind.

During the time my siblings had been recalling memories, their voices an uninterrupted cadence interspersed with the crashing waves, something shifted. Their happy tones turned into low murmurs, and unease swept through the group.

I glanced over to find them all staring off to my right, their mouths agape. For half a second, I had a fleeting, ridiculous thought that it was our mom. That somehow, even though we'd buried her, she was here. Had decided to show up after eleven years without her.

But I knew that was just my mind trying to protect me from the reality. It was why it took me so long to turn my head and glance to where they were looking. And it was why the man standing there didn't immediately register.

At least not until Brady said, "Now's really not the time, Dad."

CHAPTER FORTY-TWO

HARPER

FROM THE SECOND I'd woken up alone, I'd known something was off. I could feel it. And not only because it was so different from how Levi and I had been spending our mornings —waking up together, sipping our coffee in between stolen kisses before heading off for the day. So ridiculously domestic, it was achingly sweet.

Finding his side of the bed empty hadn't immediately sent me into worst-case scenarios like it had that first morning after we'd slept together. I'd figured he'd left a note somewhere, maybe a text. But when I didn't find either, I shrugged it off and figured he'd get in touch at some point.

When late afternoon had rolled around and I still hadn't heard from him, I'd decided to take matters into my own hands. Levi didn't like to talk about things, and it was clear from his silence that something was bothering him. I wanted to do what I could to help.

I'd been able to feel the change in the air when I'd walked into his workshop. Could practically see the sadness and grief hanging on his shoulders like shackles chaining him down. My first instinct had been to comfort him. Let him know that whatever he was going through, I was here to go through it with him.

And now, seeing Patrick McKenzie standing at what I'd deduced was the yearly memorial Levi and his siblings held for their mom, I knew I'd made the right choice.

Levi's body stiffened under my hand as soon as his gaze landed on his father. "What the fuck are you doing here?"

"You should go, Dad," Brady tried again, his tone firmer than it had been before. "Come back another time."

"Listen to Brady," Levi said, nothing but ice in his tone. "Run away and hide. We all know how fucking good you are at that."

Patrick fidgeted where he stood, his fingers tugging on the hem of his shirt, but his voice was strong when he said, "I know you might find it hard to believe, but I loved your mom, too. I deserve to remember her."

Levi was on his feet before I even knew what was happening, stabbing a finger in Patrick's direction. "You don't deserve shit, and you and I both know exactly why."

Patrick cleared his throat. "I wanted to talk to you. Talk to everyone."

"And you chose today of all days to corner us?" Levi yelled.

"I've been trying to—"

"What, make this better? Came to try to make amends?" Levi scoffed. "Or were you hoping to somehow make me forget I'm the reason Mom's dead?"

At Levi's words, my mouth dropped open in disbelief as gasps sounded around me, my shock mirrored in everyone else.

"What?" Addison stood and took a step toward Levi. "That's not—"

"True? No, it is. Isn't that right, Dad? It's true all because I trusted my drunk, worthless father to deliver a message." Levi huffed out a laugh. "Do you want to tell them what happened instead, or should I?"

Patrick cleared his throat, his face flushed a deep red, though not from anger. "I passed out."

"Like usual," Levi agreed. "And I went off and did whatever the fuck I wanted while trusting you to do what I'd asked, and now Mom's dead. You and I both know exactly why she was out in a storm. Because she was looking for me...for us." He tossed a hand in Addison's direction, but I couldn't look away from Levi to see her reaction.

I was transfixed by him, by the pain and agony etched across every inch of his body, stitched into every single word he spoke. I wanted to go to him more than anything, wanted to comfort him as he so very clearly needed. Especially if he believed what he was saying...

My God, had he been carrying this around with him for eleven years?

"Levi," Addison said, her voice strained. "That's not true. You aren't to blame for Mom's death."

"I was the one who left, Addison," he shot back. "I was the one who put all my faith in a father who's done nothing but let us down. And because of it, she's not here anymore."

"But *I* was the one who wanted to leave that night. I asked you to take me. Do you blame me, too?" Addison asked, her voice challenging and firm even through her tears.

"*What?*" Levi asked as he snapped his gaze toward his sister, pure devastation written on his face. "God, no. *Never.*"

"Then why do you blame yourself?"

"Because it's the truth! It's my fucking fault. I should have known better than to give Dad a message for her when he was already halfway drunk. I should have waited around. I shouldn't have gone in the first place. She'd already told me not to go out, and I was so sure I knew better that I ignored her and I left anyway."

"You didn't ignore her, man," Chase said, his voice soft but sure as he held Addison against him. "We didn't go to that party."

"That didn't matter. That was exactly why she was out on that boat, trying to get to us before the storm did."

"Son, if you just—"

Levi spun on his dad, the level of his restraint showing in every inch of his coiled body. "Don't you dare fucking call me that. I'm not your son. My dad left all of us during the hardest years of our lives. We buried him the same day we buried Mom. So you don't get to come back here now, clean-shaven and with your gold chip from AA, and slide in like you never left. Because *you fucking left*. Long before Mom did. And then I took her from us all."

With every tortured word that fell from his lips, my heart broke a little more for him, my tears a near-constant stream now. Levi had always been stoic, more so now as an adult, but I was watching him shatter right in front of me. Laying bare all the burdens and guilt and self-blame he'd carried on his shoulders for so long.

It was something he shouldn't have had to carry at all, let alone by himself.

Brady stood and strode toward Levi with intention, his voice low and firm. "Mom's death wasn't your fault."

"It was *my* choice to leave that night. My choice to storm off like a fucking child because I couldn't get my way."

"You *were* a child. A punk kid no different from any of the rest of them. You were *nineteen* years old, Levi. That's when you're supposed to make mistakes and figure shit out. That's when you're supposed to fuck up."

"My fuckup cost our mom her life!" Levi yelled. "My choice means she's dead. She's not here to wake us up by dancing. She's never going to bake chocolate chip cookies again or plant flowers or walk along the beach. And her grandchild is never going to know her. Because of *my* choice."

"No, because of *her* choice. She chose to go out that night, even knowing it was a bad idea. Stop blaming yourself for something Mom chose to do. It wasn't your fault." Brady cupped Levi by the back of his neck and tugged him close, their foreheads nearly touching. *"It wasn't your fault."*

Levi fisted the front of Brady's shirt, his tone steeped in anguish. "Why wasn't it me? It *should've* been me."

A sob slipped free at Levi's words, and I held a hand over my mouth, trying in vain to hold back my tears as I watched the man I loved break down in the arms of the only father figure he'd ever had. Levi collapsed into Brady, gripping him tightly and burying his face in his shoulder as sobs racked his body, all while Brady murmured something too low to hear.

Almost as one, his siblings strode toward them, each of them gathering around Brady and Levi and holding them in a tight embrace. This moment was so private, so raw, I felt like an interloper for witnessing it. But the knowledge that Levi wanted me here kept me rooted in the spot.

At least until several moments later when Patrick took a step toward his children, and now was not the time for him to be here.

Without hesitation, I walked toward him, placing myself between Levi and the man who'd made so many mistakes in his life. The one who probably had no idea who I was, despite how often I'd been at the resort when I was younger. Whether he was trying to make amends now didn't matter. Not right now.

Even through my tears, I held up my hand to stop him in his

tracks, making my voice as firm as I could. "You need to leave. Now isn't the time for you to do this."

"But I—"

"No," I cut in, my tone harder this time. "This isn't about you. This is about them and what they need to work through together. They've been doing it their whole lives. They don't suddenly need you added into the mix."

For several moments, he absorbed my words before pressing his lips together and nodding. After swallowing several times and glancing out at the ocean, he croaked, "Yeah, you're right. You're right."

"Find another way to tell him what you need to, but don't ambush him. He deserves better than that. And his father should have known it."

Patrick gave another nod, glancing once more at his children before walking away, and I breathed a sigh of relief, grateful I'd been able to protect Levi from this, at least.

I turned around to find my friends standing together, watching their persons hold one another up while breaking down. I made my way over and stood next to Chase, who immediately wrapped an arm around my shoulders and tugged me into his side.

"I knew it was bad, but I didn't know it was this bad." His voice broke on the last word, and he cleared his throat. "I didn't know he's been carrying this on his shoulders for years."

I shook my head, unable to speak but wanting him to know it was the same for me. And I had no idea how to help Levi navigate this. But I knew, without a doubt, I was going to do everything in my power to try.

CHAPTER FORTY-THREE

LEVI

AFTER EVERYTHING HARPER had seen on the beach, I knew she had questions. And I knew it was far past time for me to open up about the demons that had been plaguing me for years. But I was too raw right now, too exposed. The truths that had been buried inside me for so long were now dislodged, jagged and sharp, but still present. Still there.

And right now, after everything that had happened, all I wanted was her and the reminder that she was mine.

For now, she was mine.

More than anything, I wanted—*needed*—the comfort of her arms tonight. The comfort only she could provide.

Harper seemed to sense that I didn't want to talk, being silently supportive as we made our way back home. The thought jolted me. I hadn't thought of a place as home in so long. The house I'd grown up in, had made so many memories in, had been haunted by ghosts that plagued me whether I was there or not.

But this space, with her? Felt like home.

I shut the apartment door behind us, but Harper didn't let me step another foot into the space before she turned on me.

She pressed her hand against my chest, directly over my heart, directly over her sparrow, and looked up at me. Really *looked*, her eyes searching for something I wasn't sure I could give her. Finally, she whispered, "What do you need from me?"

No hesitation, no judgment. Just the unequivocal promise in her voice that no matter what it was, no matter what I asked for, she would give it to me.

The problem was, I needed *everything* from her. I needed to be her first hello in the morning and her last kiss goodnight. Needed that bright smile she shot my way every time her eyes landed on me. Needed her laughter and her hugs and her whispered words. The cuddles on the couch I didn't ever want with anyone else.

I needed her everything.

But I couldn't tell her that. Not with words. I couldn't lay everything out for her and let her see into the darkest crevices of my mind. Not after everything that had happened tonight. Not when she was leaving next week. So instead, I laid myself bare as best I could...let her think I meant only the physical.

"You," I said. "I just need you right now."

She wrapped her arms around my neck and tugged me into a hug, embracing me with her entire being. It was one of the things I loved most about her. She put her whole body into it, made me feel like I was the only person in the world.

I buried my face in her neck, breathing her in as I held her to me. So grateful we had this time, no matter how fleeting it was. Lifting her feet off the floor, I tapped her ass so she'd wrap her legs around my waist. And then I strode us both toward the bedroom, her lips already on mine.

We stripped each other slowly, the usual frenzy between us

absent. In its place was something softer. Something sweeter... something more intimate. And I sank into it. I *felt* it. Felt her and allowed myself to be vulnerable enough so she could feel me, too.

We didn't speak as I sank inside her, nothing more than soft gasps and groans as we linked our fingers and moved together. But I allowed my body to say what I couldn't yet voice.

I was in love with this woman, had been my entire life. So fucking devoted to her. And it no longer mattered if I thought I wasn't good enough, because she deserved someone who strived to be. She deserved someone who worked through their issues, exorcized their demons, and became better. *For* her.

And I was sure as hell going to try.

THE ROOM WAS bright when I finally stirred the next morning. I woke slowly, my body heavy and my mind an unfocused mess of thoughts, except the one that never failed to greet me with complete clarity, day in and day out.

It should have been me.

I reached for Harper, finding her side of the bed not only empty but cold. In the time she'd been staying here, especially since she'd begun sleeping in my bed, she'd never once woken up before me. Usually, I'd slip out of bed after brushing a kiss on her shoulder and head into the main room to read or screw around until I heard her shuffling in here. Then I'd prep her morning coffee, just how she liked it, and set it out for her. She'd come out, bleary-eyed and beautiful, and shoot me a soft, sleepy smile the second her gaze landed on me.

Seriously, what the fuck did I ever do to deserve this woman, and why wasn't she lying here with me?

Then, all at once, yesterday came back to me in a rush. Taking Harper with me to the beach. My family reminiscing about Mom. Our father showing up and demanding things he had no right to. Me confessing the secret I'd kept locked up tight for more than a decade, that guilt I'd carried with me like an albatross around my neck.

For so long, I'd hoarded the pain, clinging to the blame I'd placed on myself because I deserved it. I'd tucked it deep inside where no one could see. But yesterday, it had all come out. Every awful, painful secret. Every whispered thought I had—shame and regret pouring out of me once the dam had broken, all for my siblings to witness.

But they hadn't turned away. They hadn't yelled or screamed at me for what I'd done. They hadn't cut me out of their lives. Hadn't thrown me away like I'd been secretly fearing for years.

Instead, they'd embraced me. Held me as I'd broken down, right there in front of them. And then, they'd tried to take some of the burden I'd been carrying for years. Over and over again, they'd told me it wasn't my fault. That I shouldn't blame myself. And that they didn't—would never—want it to be me.

And Harper had seen it all. She'd *heard* it all. Every painful word torn from my throat.

Which meant I had nowhere left to hide.

I scrubbed a hand over my face, shame and unease churning in my gut. Yesterday, after she'd witnessed me baring my soul, she hadn't judged me for it. She'd held me close, had let me inside her. We'd fallen asleep curled around each other, no words spoken, but I didn't think we'd needed them.

Now, though, in the light of day, I couldn't help but wonder if she'd see things differently since she knew at least part of the truth. Would she still see me as the man she'd once loved, or had I become a stranger to her overnight?

For too long, I lay there, staring at the ceiling and trying to figure out how to share this gaping, festering wound with her. But the truth was, there was no easy way. No polish I could put on this stain inside me, nothing to make it shine. These thoughts were the most difficult parts of me, like tar coating my insides, and there was no way to make them anything but ugly.

When I could no longer make excuses for why I hadn't gotten up, I finally rolled out of bed, pulled on a pair of sweatpants, and strode out into the kitchen. Prepared to handle whatever questions Harper threw at me, because she deserved the truth.

But instead of badgering inquiries or cool detachment, she greeted me with troubled eyes and a tentative smile. My beautiful girl worrying about me.

I walked over to where she sat at the breakfast bar, cupped my hand around her neck, and pressed my thumb under her chin to tip her face up to me. Though it was clear she tried, she couldn't hide the concern etched across her features, that divot between her brows, or the worry in her eyes.

She rested her hands on my hips, her thumbs brushing lightly back and forth against my skin just above my waistband. "Morning."

I leaned down, pressing my lips to hers and pouring as much love into the kiss as possible. Because I'd been right last night. Now was not the time to tell her how I felt. Actually, *never* was the time to tell her how I felt, despite it thrumming like its own heartbeat inside me.

She was set to leave in just days, and it wasn't fair of me to pile that on her before she went. Not when this was the life *she'd* chosen. Not one that had been chosen for her.

Finally, I pulled back even though it was the last thing I wanted to do. "Morning, sparrow."

After dropping one more soft kiss on her lips, I sat on the stool perpendicular to her and raised a brow at the steaming cup of coffee in front of me. "Isn't this my job?"

She smiled at me. "You're not the only one who's been paying attention to coffee orders."

I lifted the cup to my mouth, hiding a grin behind it, and took a sip. One sugar and more than a splash of cream, exactly how I liked it. "Thank you. I'm not used to sleeping this late, but I guess I needed it."

And now that I'd acknowledged it, the pink elephant was front and center in the room. No more avoiding.

Clearing my throat, I set the mug on the counter and wrapped my hands around it before forcing myself to meet her eyes, afraid of what I'd find. But all that greeted me was worry. "I'm sure you want answers after yesterday."

She shook her head and reached out, curling her fingers around my forearm. "You don't owe me anything."

I huffed out a laugh and shook my head. "Next to my family, I owe it to you the most."

She darted her gaze over my face, though I wasn't sure what she was looking for. Finally, she said, "Then talk to me. Tell me as much or as little as you want."

"I don't even know where to start."

"How about at the beginning?"

That made the most sense, but it also meant telling her about that night—the night I simultaneously tried never to think about and yet couldn't ever shove out of my mind. The one that filled my nightmares, a never-ending loop of not being able to get to Mom in time, her not hearing me scream for her from the shore, her not seeing me when I was standing right next to her. In my nightmares, it didn't matter what I did. She still ended up dead.

"I was so fucked up that night. Pissed at the world and taking it out on everyone," I finally said, shaking my head. "I wanted to go to some stupid party on one of the islands because I wanted to get wasted and block out everything."

She furrowed her brow. "What was going on? What happened that day that you needed to avoid?"

I thought back to it, before the worst had happened. Could recall the exact emotions swimming in my gut. Relief and regret and complete hopelessness, because I'd known it was over. For real and for good.

"It was the day the sold sign went up in your yard." I braced my forearms on the counter and glanced over to her. "I'd been the one to push you away, but part of me hoped you'd come back. That day, I knew you were never going to. And even though it was exactly what I wanted for you, it still hurt like hell."

I cleared my throat, staring into my coffee mug as I relived the worst twenty-four hours of my life. "Mom and I got in a fight about it. I wanted to pick up Chase and head over on the boat, but a big storm was coming. She told me I knew the rules, and what made me think she was going to allow me to break them? And I..." I shook my head, recalling every cruel word I'd said to her. Each one like a knife in my heart. "I was a complete asshole. I told her it was stupid that I was nineteen years old and still living by Mommy's rules. That I was a fucking adult and should be treated like one. That I should be able to do whatever I wanted." I huffed out a humorless laugh. "I actually said that to her. Just before I told her it was all bullshit and stalked off. I didn't know that'd be the last time I'd ever see her."

Tears filled my eyes, and I didn't even bother trying to hold them back. It was no use, not when I was talking about this. Harper kept her hand on my forearm, the soft brush of her thumb against my skin soothing in a way that allowed me to continue.

"She left to run an errand in town, and I ignored her when she knocked on my door to tell me. While she was gone, Addison asked me to take her to Morgan's—you remember she and Chase's sister were close back then? Anyway, since I couldn't go to the party on the island, Chase's was the next best place. So I agreed. I told Dad to let Mom know where we were. I'd never trusted him with anything in my life, but I was still so fucking mad at her and too goddamn stubborn for my own good. The next morning, I got a wake-up call from Brady at the Lockharts', and he told me to come home immediately."

I swallowed several times, attempting to force back the emotions clawing their way up my throat, but there was no escaping them. Nowhere left to run. "The second I walked into the house, I knew something was wrong. For one thing, all my brothers were there. They'd all moved out by then, and not even Mom's blueberry muffins could get them there before 8. And then I spotted my dad on the couch. His arm was hanging over the side, mouth wide open, completely dead to the world. And I knew. I just knew Mom had never gotten my message."

"But you have to know that wasn't your fault," Harper said, her voice rough. "Your dad didn't deliver it. But you tried, Levi."

"What I did was pawn it off on the man I'd always known I couldn't count on. And I was right. The one time I tried, we paid the biggest price."

Harper made a gruff sound in her throat, and she squeezed my arm. "I'm so sorry you've been carrying this, but it's not your burden to bear."

"If not mine, then whose? For years, I've asked myself so many questions, trying to figure out why it happened the way it did. Why did she have to run into town? If she'd been home, I could've told her myself. And why didn't she call the Lockharts to see if Addison and I were there before she took off on the water? Why was her first instinct that I'd fucked up? That I'd done exactly what she'd specifically told me not to?"

But I already knew the answer to that, because I'd been fucking up for years by then. Ever since I'd pushed Harper away, I'd been drunk or high or both, doing what I wanted whenever I pleased with little regard for the rules my mom had set out. With little regard for anything at all.

"Levi..." Harper said, the heartbreak clear in her voice. No doubt because she realized exactly how fucked up I was. After everything I'd shared, finally believing I was the one to blame. "I don't know why your mom did what she did that night, and we never will. You and I both know I did not grow up with a shining example of loving parents. But I did feel that here, with her. That was why I was drawn to you and your family in the first place. Even when I was ten years old, I could see how much she loved you. She would've done absolutely anything for you."

She reached for my hand and held it between hers, squeezing gently until I met her eyes. "So there's not a doubt in my mind that when she came home and found you and Addison missing while a storm was raging, her first thought wasn't rational. Her first and only thought was getting you home safely because she loved you both beyond reason."

Her words sank in, an avenue I'd never allowed myself to venture down. Because if that was true, that meant my mom died because she'd loved me too much. And the last words I'd ever said to her were *This is bullshit*.

"Why does that make it so much worse?" I asked, voice breaking. "That night at Chase's was the last time I got blackout drunk. Because I don't deserve to dull this pain. Not after what I did. And I've sat with it every moment of every day since.

Wondering the entire time why my mom's dead and not me. *Wanting* it to be me."

With tears brimming in her eyes, Harper stood and cupped my jaw in her hands, tipping my face back to hers. "Oh, Levi."

Then, without a word, she wrapped her arms around me and held me tight while I fell apart for the second time in as many days.

WHEN I WAS WRUNG OUT, feeling like little more than a husk of a human being, Harper and I lay on our sides on the couch, our legs entwined. One of her hands resting on my chest, the other on the small of my back as I held her close. I pressed my nose to the crown of her head and breathed her in, taking her scent deep into my lungs. So grateful she hadn't bailed when everything had come tumbling out of me. So grateful she was still here with me.

"How're you feeling?" she asked, her breath soft against my chest, her fingers tickling lightly on my back.

"Like I've been run over a couple times." I reached up and brushed her hair back, tipping her head so I could look into her eyes. "How're *you* feeling? I dumped a lot on you."

Tears filled her eyes, and she bit her bottom lip as it started to wobble.

"Sparrow..." I kissed her trembling lip, searching her eyes. "What is it?"

"I'm scared. For you. Scared of what the future might bring. Scared you've been struggling with this for so long. Struggling *alone.* I know our traumas are vastly different, and the grief of losing a mother you loved versus losing the life I never wanted to have are two very different things. But therapy helped me come to terms with it. And I think it'd help you, too. Not just to deal with the grief of losing your mom but to get a handle on these intrusive thoughts. Because as much as I want to take them from you or magically wipe them away, I know I can't. But I also don't want to lose you." Her voice broke on the last word, the tears finally spilling over, and my heart cracked in two. Just split straight down the middle.

"You're not going to lose me, sparrow. I promise. I'm going to be here as long as you want me." I caught her tears with my lips, pressing a kiss to both her cheeks, her eyes, then her forehead. "It's hard to explain, but my thoughts have never been active. I've never planned anything out, never taken it past contemplations. I swear I haven't." I cleared my throat, readying myself to say aloud what I never had before. "But you're right. I do need help. These thoughts have run my life for so long, I don't remember what it was like before them."

I pulled my phone out of my pocket and navigated to an email I'd had saved for years. One I pulled up a couple times a month but never went any further with. I handed my phone to Harper and watched her scan the contents, realization lighting in her eyes. "Marianne sent me a list of therapists a few years ago. Back before I was in a place to listen."

Back before I thought I deserved any kind of help.

But between my siblings and Harper, I now wondered if that had only been a lie I told myself. And while I couldn't yet shake the feeling that I still deserved to carry this burden, I was at least now open to the possibility of someone changing my mind.

And at this point, that was as good as I could do.

With a soft smile, Harper wrapped her arms around me and squeezed tight. "I think that's a great first step."

CHAPTER FORTY-FOUR

HARPER

SPENDING six weeks working on a single article was a luxury I'd never been afforded in my career. At least, not until this assignment. While I tended to skew investigational with my work, which generally meant it took a bit more time, I still had to turn things around fairly quickly. Because of that, I didn't necessarily connect deeply with every subject I had written about. There were people who stood out, of course. Their stories branded on my heart in a way I knew would never go away.

Kind of like Starlight Cove.

I'd felt a kinship with the people I'd interviewed, every single one of them. But it had been more than that. I felt a kinship with Starlight Cove itself.

I knew at least part of that was nostalgia. This had been the home of so many childhood memories, so many happy times, when my life had held so few. And now, it held even more, the memories I'd collected over the past several weeks enough to fill me up for a lifetime.

But somehow, I was supposed to leave it all behind in forty-eight hours.

Today had started like every other day for the past several weeks. I woke to find Levi already in the kitchen, a cup of coffee waiting for me. After we had a quiet conversation, he snuck into the shower behind me, kissed me within an inch of my life before slipping inside me and kicking the day off with a bang. And then we went on our separate ways, each of us heading off to do our own things.

All while I tried to figure out how I was supposed to live without him.

We'd only grown closer since everything had come out that night on the beach and the morning after. I knew he'd been broken and raw, feeling exposed and more vulnerable than anyone would be comfortable with. And for him to confide in me after that was something I would never take for granted. Especially when I knew his opening up meant he was getting the help he needed. The help he deserved.

My phone rang, and I glanced away from a draft of my last editorial column for the *Gazette* to see who was calling. Naomi's name lit up the screen, and my stomach swooped, a vortex of nervous butterflies spinning wildly out of control. I had no idea what I wanted the outcome of this call to be, and that was a predicament I hadn't foreseen.

If she offered me the permanent position at *Weekend Wanderlust*, it would be everything I'd been working for these past six weeks. Everything I'd been working for the past eight years. Permanence. Roots.

But taking it would mean leaving all this behind. Leaving *Levi* behind.

I swallowed down my nerves and answered. "Hi, Naomi."

"Harper, I'm glad I caught you. I got your article this morning. Apologies for not getting back to you sooner, but I had to put out a few fires over here."

"It's no problem at all."

"I read it right away when I got it, and I have to say, I was quite surprised. Seemed like you went in a slightly different direction from what we talked about." The tone of her voice gave away nothing, and that only made me more anxious.

"I did," I said tentatively, my nerves getting the better of me. I'd known I was taking a chance by doing that, but it was what my gut had told me to do. And thus far in my life, my gut had never let me astray. "Since I had more than enough sources, I thought it would be better to focus on the current residents of Starlight Cove choosing to make it their home now, rather than anyone who'd done so over the past fifty years. That angle removed Duke Nova from the article completely."

Naomi hummed thoughtfully, and I held my breath, waiting for her response. "Well, I think your gut led you in the right direction. It was a great choice."

I held the phone away from my mouth and breathed out a sigh of relief. "Thank you."

"I've got a few suggestions for you that I'll send over, but overall, I'm thrilled with the piece. It's exactly what I hoped it would be. Exactly the kind of work I've come to count on from you."

Pride bloomed in my chest, that feeling of a job well done settling over me. I worked hard, and I was damn good at my job. I knew that. But it was reaffirming when another industry professional not only noticed but acknowledged as much.

"That's why I'd love to offer you the permanent position of senior travel writer."

As she rattled off the details and what the job would entail, I could barely hear her through my heartbeat thrumming like a drum in my ears, the whoosh-whoosh-whoosh too damn loud.

This was everything I'd ever wanted. Everything I'd worked for.
It was exactly what I'd blown up my entire life for.

It was here, within my grasp.

All I had to do was say yes.

CHAPTER FORTY-FIVE

LEVI

I'D SPENT the entirety of my adult life trapped in the shadows of my own making. For years, my siblings—minus Addison— had allowed me to keep myself removed from the group, to do my own thing without being bothered. But ever since that day on the beach, that way of living was ancient history.

I didn't know if the five of them had a schedule or what, but not a single day went by when one of them didn't reach out to me in the *Trivial Bullshit* text thread. And though it had taken some getting used to because my knee-jerk reaction was irritation, I finally allowed myself to see it for what it was—my family caring about me. Wanting me to be safe and healthy. Supporting that as best they could.

I'd had my first appointment with a therapist earlier in the week, and it'd left me unsettled in a way I hadn't been expecting. My hour with her had felt less like a conversation and more like a battle—something I was going to have to prepare for every single week.

As I'd sat across from her, excavating all the shit I'd spent years burying, my initial gut reaction had been to walk out and never return. Just keep on living this half-life. But I shoved those feelings down and reminded myself *why* I was going. And even though my therapist's questions grated like sandpaper across my skin, I promised myself—as well as my family and Harper—I'd give it a few sessions before making a judgment.

I knew years of deep-seated beliefs were going to take a while to unpack, and my therapist had told me as much. Suicidal ideation wasn't something that just went away overnight. It didn't suddenly pack its bags and leave. This unwanted visitor would be sticking around for the foreseeable future. Maybe forever. Now, all I could do was manage it. Find the tools that helped me shift my thoughts away from the pitch black of my mind so I didn't dwell on them.

Fortunately, my family understood it wouldn't be a sudden shift. That it would take time. Understood but still didn't shy away from checking in daily, each of them doing it in their own way.

Addison demanded TV-bingeing time without an ounce of subtlety.

ADDISON:

Fucking hell, Levi

Damon is going to be another century older if you don't get your ass over here soon

Like tonight

And bring me a pint of chunky monkey while you're at it

Ford framed it as hanging out.

FORD:

> Quinn challenged me again, so I need to sharpen my axe throwing skills. Levi, you up for Kick Some Axe tonight?

Beck went straight to food.

BECK:

> I've got extra blueberry scones. Anyone want any? And by anyone, I mean Levi.

Aiden camouflaged it with resort shit, even though he already knew the answers to ninety-nine percent of the questions he asked.

AIDEN:

> Levi, how many boat tours did you run last month?

And Brady was always straight to the point and just asked.

BRADY:

> Levi, you good?

Even my best friend got in on the party, except Chase didn't do texts to check in. He just showed up at my workshop whenever the hell he felt like it. Because I guessed that was what former pro hockey players could do with their time—whatever the fuck they wanted.

This morning, Harper had sent off the finished article about Starlight Cove to her editor, and she expected to hear back sometime today. After, I'd dropped her off at the *Gazette* with a deep kiss and a smack on her ass before heading to my workshop. While there, I spent the entire day working my way through every possible scenario, every possible outcome, and exactly what my response to each would be.

I'd considered asking her to stay a thousand times. Had whispered it to her after she'd fallen asleep for the past five nights, but I knew that was as far as I could take it. She'd been working toward this her entire adult life. The very thing I'd sacrificed us for was what she'd fought for for herself. On her own terms. And if—*when*—she was offered this position that she'd busted her ass for, it would be well deserved, and I was damn well going to celebrate her for it.

When Harper walked through the front door later that night, I stood in front of the stove, stirring the spaghetti sauce I'd made for dinner. My gaze snapped to her immediately, trying to read something in her expression that would give me a clue what had happened, but she was locked down tight.

"Smells good," she said, coming up behind me and wrapping her arms around my waist. She laid her cheek between my shoulder blades and breathed in deeply before letting it out in a slow exhalation.

"I figured spaghetti was a safe bet."

"You figured right."

"I also figured you probably didn't eat much today while you waited for Naomi to call."

"Right again."

I put a lid on the sauce, turned the burner down, and twisted around to face her. She kept her arms around me—something I sure as hell didn't mind—and tipped her head back to meet my eyes. Christ, I loved this woman so much it made my chest ache. Made me wish for things I'd never before allowed myself to. But more than anything, I wished for her happiness.

I brushed her hair back from her face, tucking it behind her ear. "When should we crack open the champagne?"

Her brows flew up. "*When?* You're so sure she offered me the job?"

I gripped her face in my palms, running my thumbs along her cheeks, and leaned down until we were mere inches apart. "Never a doubt in my mind."

She rolled her lips in, her gaze never leaving mine as a sheen of tears filled her eyes.

"Hey. What's this? We're supposed to be celebrating, not crying." I brushed a kiss over her lips, felt them quivering under mine. And I couldn't keep my mouth shut anymore.

While I wasn't going to ask her to stay and put her in that position of choosing me or the job she loved so fucking much, I was damn well going to make sure she knew I was willing to do *anything* to be with her.

"We can make this work, okay? Just because you don't live in Starlight Cove doesn't have to mean anything when it comes to us. Because we're *us*, and if anyone can do it, we can. I'll fly out to you. Hell, maybe I'll go on some assignments with you. Take this boatbuilding gig to the masses." I bent my knees so I was eye level with her, needing her to see my sincerity. "I love you so fucking much. I've lived without you for so long, and I don't want to do it again. So I'm ready and willing to do whatever it takes, sparrow. Whatever it takes. All right?"

I swiped away at the tears that overflowed her eyes, rolling in fat droplets down her cheeks. She gripped my forearms tightly as if to anchor herself. Clearing her throat, she shook her head as she stared up at me with what looked an awful lot like love.

"That's not why I'm crying," she said, her voice tight with tears. "I'm not crying because we're going to be apart. I'm crying because no one has ever believed in me like you do. No one has ever been so certain of my abilities that they already bought champagne to celebrate something that would, theoretically, take me away from them."

I dropped a kiss on her lips. Because I could. And because I had no idea for how much longer I'd have the chance. "I've always believed in you. From day fucking one, when you set your mouth in a stubborn line, asking my mom to teach you how to tie a bowline knot when you'd never even tied a figure eight. And that's never once waned. It's only—" I froze when her words finally caught up to me. "Wait. What do you mean, *theoretically*?"

She breathed out a watery laugh. "Took you long enough to latch on to that."

"Sparrow…"

"Naomi offered me the job. And when I turned her down—"

"You *what*?"

She bit her bottom lip, lifting a single shoulder in a shrug. "I turned her down. Because what I thought was going to be the worst six weeks of my life turned out to be the best." She squeezed me tighter, pressing a kiss on my chest, directly over her sparrow. "But when I told Naomi I couldn't take the job because I wanted to stay, she laughed. I've never heard that woman laugh a day in my life, and she thought it was the most hilarious thing. When she got herself together, she asked me why the hell I would think I'd have to move to New York for this position that would take me all over the world anyway."

"What does that mean?"

"It means I can work out of the *Gazette* if I want."

"The *Gazette* office is in Starlight Cove…"

"Is it really?"

"Stop playing with me, sparrow. Are you saying you got the job *and* you're staying?"

"Yes. But just so there's no confusion or misunderstandings, I'm not staying because of you."

"No? Why, then?"

"Well, there's Mabel's cookies, for one. The *Gazette* office is a pretty sweet setup, and I bet I could talk Mabel into letting me use it permanently. There's girls' night out with your sister and the rest of my girlfriends. There's the beach, of course. Nothing beats the Starlight Cove beach. They've got this carnival that comes to town once a year with the best lobster corn dogs I've ever had, and the Ferris wheel's not bad, either. And I don't know if you know this, but one of my two childhood best friends lives here. He's a pretty big deal in the hockey world, so I'll get to spend more time with him."

"Right, of course." I gripped her hips and walked her backward until she bumped into the countertop, then I lifted her up so she was eye level with me. Bracing my hands on either side of her hips, I leaned toward her. "And how about that other childhood best friend? Whatever happened with him?"

She tucked her fingers into the waistband of my jeans and tugged me closer, a soft smile lighting up her face. "It's kind of a funny story, actually. I sort of fell in love with him. Twice."

CHAPTER FORTY-SIX

HARPER

FOR YEARS, the end of summer had punctuated the best part of my life. As August gave way to September, I'd always been long gone, back to reality, my time in this little slice of heaven over.

This year, however, September felt like just the beginning because there was no end in sight. No period on my time in Starlight Cove, only continuations that I hoped never ended.

Levi had taken his first steps on what I knew would be a grueling path to traverse, probably for the rest of his life. And today was just another of the many steps he'd be taking in the coming weeks, months, and even years. He'd already come so far in such a short amount of time. Whereas once, his first instinct had been to flee, to escape and avoid, he now at least recognized he was doing it and adjusted.

So, this morning, instead of waking up to cold sheets and an empty bed, I awoke to Levi's lips on my forehead, his gentle fingers brushing the hair away from my face, his soft words letting me know he needed some time before our plans this afternoon.

And then he'd been gone.

But I didn't begrudge him that time. Levi had spent so much of his life alone, it was only natural for him to retreat. And I could see just how hard he was trying. It was in the brief wake-up call this morning. In the prepared coffee in my travel mug. In the note telling me to meet him at the marina at noon. And it most definitely was in the scrawled "I love you" above his name.

Eventually, I hoped he would heal enough to where he felt comfortable experiencing these lows with me rather than retreating into himself. But until that time came, I had no problem meeting him exactly where he was. Exactly where he needed me to be.

And that was what I planned to do today. I'd known him long enough to know he needed a little distraction—one I was all too willing to provide.

The ocean lapped at the shore as I strolled down the path toward the marina, my sundress fluttering in the breeze and my secret tucked safely in my purse. It was mid-September, and though the weather was absolutely gorgeous, I knew this would be one of the last beautiful weekends before fall settled in.

Just like that day all those weeks ago, Levi was standing on *Endless Summer*. Shirt off, shorts slung low on his hips, backward baseball cap topping off the whole hot-as-fuck thing he had going on. This time, though, neither frustration nor irritation cloaked his features. All I saw now was how unsettled he looked, no doubt thinking about our afternoon plans. But that was exactly why I was here.

"Hey, sailor."

Levi's gaze snapped to mine, his brow furrowing when he glanced down at his watch. "Hey, I wasn't expecting you yet."

"You busy?"

He immediately abandoned what he'd been doing and strode toward me, holding out his hand for me. "Not for you."

He helped me aboard, tugging hard enough that I stumbled into him with a laugh before he guided me into the companionway. Bracing my hand on his chest, I pressed up on my tiptoes and brushed my lips over his. Levi hummed against my mouth, the kiss quickly deepening into something more.

His groan filled the space between us as he slid his tongue against mine, slipping a hand down my back to palm my ass. He gave it a squeeze, and I knew the moment he realized what I'd done because he stilled beneath me. When I opened my eyes, I found his already on me.

"What are you doing, sparrow?"

"What?" I asked, all faux innocence. "Did I forget something?"

He raised a brow and slid his fingers along the outside of my thigh, trailing them beneath the hem of my sundress. His brows inched up the farther he went without meeting resistance. "Did you walk all the way over here without any fucking panties?"

I attempted to bite back a smile, but it was no use. "Seems as if that's the case."

"Did my dirty girl come to play?"

"Yes. And I even brought a toy."

I knew the second my meaning landed because Levi froze, his gaze dropping to the small purse I clutched in my hand.

"A toy, huh?" He leaned close, his whiskers brushing against my jaw as he pressed his lips to my ear. "Are you trying to get fucked on this boat, sparrow?"

"I was sort of hoping, yeah."

He pulled back and studied me for long moments, the corner of his mouth ticking up the slightest bit. "Is this a distraction from what's coming this afternoon?"

"I guess that depends on if it's working or not."

Rather than answering, he spun me around so I was facing the dock, pressed me against the side, and pushed his very hard cock against my ass. He braced his hands on the lifelines on either side of mine, his body flush against me, effectively trapping me in. But I had never felt more safe.

He dropped his face into the crook of my neck, brushing his nose up along the column. "Does that feel like you've provided an adequate distraction?"

I breathed out a laugh, my body already tingling in anticipation of what was coming. "I think you and I both know it's way more than adequate."

He huffed out a laugh and glided his palm up the inside of my thigh until he reached my bare pussy. With a groan, he cupped it, sliding his fingers through the wetness he was quickly coaxing out of me. "Looks like somebody got started without me."

"Do you blame me? You know how much I love my toys."

His chuckle turned into a groan when he slipped one thick finger inside me. "Well, what are you waiting for? Pull out your toy, and let's play together."

My gaze darted around, cataloging all the people strolling down the promenade, walking along the beach, hanging out on their boats, their laughter and conversations floating to us on the water. And if *I* could see *them*, they could sure as hell see—not to mention hear—us. "Let's go below deck."

Levi hummed and sank another finger inside me, fucking me with them in slow, measured strokes. "Let's stay right here."

"Here?" I asked, breathless. A flush was already working its way up my neck and pooling in my cheeks, embarrassment flooding me at the thought of getting caught. Embarrassment *and* exhilaration.

"Don't pretend like you don't love the thought of me fucking you out here in front of all these people. You forget I've got my fingers buried in your cunt, so I can feel exactly what the idea does to you?"

I shuddered at his words, at the knowledge of what he wanted to do. At the knowledge of what he was *already* doing. To all the passersby, we just looked like a couple in love. If anyone glanced our way, none of them would guess that Levi's fingers were inside me, pumping deep, his palm grinding against my clit in an effort to make me come. And they sure as hell wouldn't guess I was fumbling with my purse to pull out a small bullet vibrator to use on myself right out here in the open.

I gripped the toy in my hand as I clutched the lifelines, biting my lip to hold back a moan when Levi curled his fingers inside me.

"There's my good girl," he murmured, his voice just a low rumble against my ear. "Such a contradiction, aren't you? So sweet and yet so fucking dirty. Tell me what you wanted when you showed up early. Did you want me to finger you until you came? Force you to whimper through your release so no one watching knew exactly what we were doing?" He scraped his teeth along my earlobe, sending a shudder through my body. "Or did you want me to stuff you full of my cock while I press this little toy against your clit until you didn't know one orgasm from the next? Until your legs were shaking and I had to wrap an arm around you just to hold you up?"

I barely bit back a moan, my pussy fluttering around his fingers while the situation he described played like a movie in my mind. And I wanted it. Desperately.

"I think we have a winner," he said with a self-satisfied hum. "Now, reach back here, pull out my cock, and lean forward. I'm gonna flip up this little skirt and sink so deep you won't be able to breathe."

He slipped his fingers from me and grabbed my hand, tugging it between my legs. "While I'm doing that, I want you to put your toy on this perfect little clit. And then you're going to try not to scream when you come."

A soft buzz split the air as he turned on the bullet vibe and passed it to me. The first press of the toy to my skin nearly buckled my knees. But Levi was there, his arm wrapped around my waist, holding me against him. He hummed low in his throat when he swiped the head of his cock through my slit, his piercings rubbing maddeningly against my clit.

He notched his cock at my entrance before sinking inside me in a slow, steady glide, the soft rumble of his groan lighting me up from the inside out. "Christ, you feel so fucking good. Always *So. Fucking. Good.*"

I could only nod my agreement, all my thoughts centered on where he sank inside me and the incessant throb of my clit. Unable to wait any longer, I did as he'd told me to and circled the vibrator around it, my body already climbing toward my peak.

Levi groaned, and though I'd figured he was going to fuck me right away, I should've known better. This was Levi, after all, and restraint might as well have been his middle name. So rather than slide in and out as he worked us both toward our peaks, he settled deep, his hips flush against my ass.

And then he didn't move.

With my thighs together, my body pitched forward toward the lifelines as Levi held me to him with an arm braced around my waist, I'd never felt so full. I attempted to shift in an effort to encourage him to move, but he just tightened his arm around me, not allowing me an inch of space.

"Uh-uh, sparrow," he said, a low taunt in his voice. "You wanted to play with your toy, so play."

His cock was so deep inside me, I could barely breathe. Could barely think.

"Wh— I—" My body was already strung so tight with need, I couldn't even make sense of what he was saying. Couldn't find the words to tell him as much, either.

He reached between my legs, slipping his hand over mine, and tutted. "You don't even have the toy pressed to your clit. Where's the fun in that?"

Without waiting for me to respond, he shifted our hands until the vibrator was pressed right where he wanted it. My entire body jolted with the shock, a soft moan I couldn't hope to hold back slipping out.

A low, satisfied groan rumbled up from his chest. "There we go. That's what you needed."

At the incessant vibrations against my clit, my pussy went into overdrive. My walls pulsed around every inch of his cock as he stuffed me as full as possible, still seated completely inside me.

"You feel that, sparrow?" he asked against my ear. "You feel that greedy little cunt, desperate to come? Don't worry, baby. We're gonna make her. You just better hope you can muffle those screams, or everyone is going to know exactly how fucking dirty you are."

I cast my gaze around at all the people, the knowledge of them there only cranking me higher. I bit my bottom lip, but I was in trouble. When I used a bullet vibrator on myself, I never made direct contact with my clit. It was too overpowering. Instead I circled it, the vibrations giving me the exact amount of stimulation I needed.

But Levi was on a mission, and there was no stopping him now.

Without mercy, he pressed the toy against me, the harsh buzz throwing me headfirst into an orgasm. I exploded like a firework in the night sky, my body shattering around him while he groaned but stayed completely still, his cock buried to the hilt.

"There it is. *Fuck*, your pussy feels so good around me."

He continued murmuring words of praise in my ear as I came and came and came again. So many times, I didn't know up from down or left from right. Had no idea where I ended and he began. Even as I tried to pull the toy away from myself, he held it steadfast against me, the vibrations permeating my very bones. Making my teeth chatter, my nipples tighten into painfully stiff peaks beneath my sundress, my entire body humming like a live wire of sensation.

We hadn't moved, but somehow it felt like the earth had shifted beneath my feet, my entire world tipping on its axis while Levi was a steady, unwavering presence against my back. I had no idea how many times he'd made me come out here in the open, but there was no way I looked like anything but a girl being fucked over the side of a boat. And that shouldn't have made me as wet as I was, shouldn't have had me arching my back in an effort to get closer to him, to get him to shift inside me.

"*Levi*. Please. Please-please-*please*..." At this point, I had no idea what I was begging for—relief or mercy, I wasn't sure, but I trusted him to provide me what I needed.

"You know I'll always give my girl whatever she begs for."

And then, *finally*, he started to move.

He pulled his hips back just enough to push forward again

in quick, shallow thrusts. His piercings rubbed against my G-spot, and I gasped, my knees nearly giving out.

"I know how hungry this greedy little cunt is for my come, but I know you've got one more for me. I want to feel you squeezing me one more time, sparrow. And I want you to look out at all these people around us while you do it." He tightened his grip on my hips, his fingers digging deliciously into my flesh as he fucked me. "They don't have any idea, do they? They don't know you're stuffed full of my cock. That you've got a toy pressed on your clit or that you've come so hard, so many times, you've soaked the front of my shorts. They have no idea how sweet this pussy is or how fucking badly I want to fill you up. Come on, baby. Come one more time, and I'll let go. I'll finally give us what we both want."

Levi pressed the toy harder against me and increased the speed. Then he snaked his other hand up between my breasts until he wrapped his hand around my throat from the front. He brushed his thumb achingly sweetly down the column as he tugged my head back to rest against his shoulder.

And then he squeezed.

Not hard. Not enough to cut off my air supply. But enough to narrow my attention on that. On *him*. Separating myself from the overstimulation against my clit and focusing only on Levi.

That and his low murmured plea of, "Let me feel you, sparrow," was all it took.

I came apart in his arms, biting my lip to stifle a scream, and Levi did as he'd promised. He fucked into me in quick, shallow strokes until his cock jerked and warmth filled me as he groaned through his own release. All the while, he murmured how much he loved me over and over until that was all I could hear.

At some point, the world came back into focus. The sound of the waves lapping against the boat, the wind through the trees, the people walking past *Endless Summer* while having no idea what we'd just done. What we were *still* doing, as Levi's cock softened inside me.

All at once, the mood shifted, Levi's fierce, teasing touch turning gentle, reverent as he brushed his lips over my bare shoulder. He wrapped me in his arms from behind and pressed a kiss to the underside of my jaw, the corner of my mouth, my temple.

Then, against my ear, he murmured, "Thank you."

CHAPTER FORTY-SEVEN

LEVI

FOR ELEVEN YEARS, I hadn't allowed myself to visit this place that had once held so many memories. Telling myself the lie that I didn't deserve to be here. And I sure as hell didn't deserve the solace or comfort it provided. I still felt that way, deep down.

That was a daily struggle that wasn't suddenly going to disappear. But I was working on it, slowly trying to rewrite the narrative I'd been spinning to myself for so long. Slowly trying to forgive myself. It wasn't going to happen today or tomorrow or next week. Probably not even next year. But sometime, I hoped. There were no quick fixes for wounds that ran this deep. I knew that. But having Harper by my side—having my family's support —while I did so made it feel like I'd be able to get there. One day.

The waves lapped at the shore, a soft breeze blowing across our skin as Harper and I sat on a soft, worn blanket, spread out beneath an old oak tree on the resort property. The same tree my mom used to read under on sunny summer days or crisp fall afternoons. The same one she'd taken me and my siblings to hundreds of times in our lives.

My head was in Harper's lap as she gently ran her fingers through my hair, the two of us talking about everything and nothing at once because I didn't know what else to do.

She hummed, her gaze set on the beach and the crashing waves before she looked down at me with nothing but love shining in her eyes. "Do you think we hit all the highlights?"

We'd given an abbreviated version of why she was back in town and why she'd left in the first place. Talked about my business expansion plans and that I was considering taking on an apprentice in the spring. Addison and Chase's baby, Brady and Luna's upcoming wedding, Harper's job offer, Chase's new hockey multiplex, the resort renovations, and about a hundred other things that had slipped in.

But even factoring in all that, did I think we'd been able to touch on every aspect of our lives over the past eleven years in the short while we'd been sitting here? Not even close. It would take months...*years*...to share it all.

But it didn't matter.

It didn't matter if we'd forgotten something or if it was another eleven years before I settled in this spot.

Because this wasn't where my mom lived.

As soon as Harper and I had walked up to this tree, standing tall and sturdy and so much larger than I remembered, and the grave marker below it, I'd known Mom wasn't here. Her name might've been on the gravestone below *beloved wife, mother, and friend*, and this might've been her final resting place, but she wasn't *here*.

Which meant this wasn't the place I needed to be in order to connect with her spirit or feel her presence in my life.

I'd tried my hardest to deny myself of her over the years— deny myself of anything good at all. But I knew now just how impossible that had been. Realized now that she never would've left my side, regardless of if I thought I deserved her there or not.

She'd been with me during every trip out to sea, through every lonely day spent in my workshop. She was there in every crack of thunder, every wave against the shore, every whistle of wind through my hair. She was there in Brady's unwavering protection, in Aiden's eye for detail, in every scone Beck made, in each new planter Ford built, in every flower Addison planted. She was in the eyes of my siblings, in their laughter and their tears. In their quiet resolve and steadfast support.

She'd been with me even when I'd felt as if I was all alone... as if I'd *deserved* to be alone.

And nothing I could do would ever change that. She'd continue to be with me. Regardless of where I went or how far I roamed. Even if the resort was no more...even if I no longer lived in Starlight Cove. She'd be with me—with all six of us—no matter what happened in this life.

"I think we probably missed a few things," I finally said, brushing my thumb against Harper's leg. "But that's okay. She already knows."

Harper smiled down at me, the late-afternoon sun casting a halo around her golden hair, the wind blowing a strand across her face. My beautiful angel. An angel I had never thought I would deserve. But it didn't matter because I wouldn't let it.

I vowed to spend every day of the rest of my life trying to be the kind of man worthy of Harper's love. The kind of man I knew my mom would be proud of.

I'd get there. One day at a time. And each one of those would be spent with Harper by my side.

EPILOGUE
LEVI

Two months later

HAND IN HAND, Harper and I ran across Main Street, dashing toward the entrance to the apartment while rain drenched us. Brady and Luna's rehearsal dinner had ended just before the sky had opened up, soaking all twelve of us as we scattered, heading out in different directions.

Harper's laughter chimed like bells in my ears as she leaped over puddles and dashed inside our building, the sound a balm to my soul. All I'd ever wanted was her happiness. And some-how, she was happiest here. With me.

"Oh my God, I'm soaked," she said, pulling her shirt away from where it clung to her skin.

I swatted her ass as she ran up the stairs in front of me. "Not the first time I've heard that. Maybe not even the last time tonight, if you're lucky."

"If *I'm* lucky? So it'd all be for me, huh?"

"Mostly. You know the rule is fifteen to one."

She laughed as she unlocked the front door and strode inside our apartment. "You overexaggerated just a little."

I hummed, making a mental note of that challenge. "We'll see."

Harper's eyes heated as she stared at me, catching her bottom lip with her teeth. Her hair was plastered to the sides of her face, her clothes saturated and dripping on the floor. And I wanted nothing more than to give her everything those eyes were begging for. But we'd have plenty of time for that later tonight.

So instead, I swatted her on the ass again and tipped my chin toward our bedroom. "Change first. I want you to be soaked from me, not the rain."

She sauntered away, tossing me a smirk over her shoulder. "Too bad all five of the T-shirts you own are in the dryer and not hanging in our closet like they're supposed to be. You could've watched me strip."

I started after her, determination in my stride, but she squealed and ran into our bedroom, slamming the door behind her.

"Little shit," I muttered and turned around, tugging my wet T-shirt off on my way to the laundry room. "Like I can't strip her out here whenever I want…"

After grabbing a dry but wrinkled shirt, I pulled it on and made my way to the still-open front door. Shaking my head, I started to close it when a note taped to the front caught my eye. Mabel, probably, though I was surprised at her restraint in not just using her key and leaving the note inside instead.

Walking into the kitchen, I lifted the flap on the envelope and pulled out a folded piece of paper. Something slipped out and drifted to the counter as I did so, but before I could glance down at it, the handwriting on the note caught my attention. Handwriting I recognized.

My entire body stilled, parts inside me warring with one another, wanting to toss this outside into the wind, while at the same time desperate to read what was written. In the end, the latter won out, and I couldn't stop myself from scanning the words on the page.

LEVI,

I'M SORRY.

THOSE TWO WORDS AREN'T NEARLY ENOUGH. I KNOW THAT. EVEN IF I LIVED A THOUSAND YEARS AND TOLD YOU EVERY DAY, IT STILL WOULDN'T BE ENOUGH FOR WHAT YOU'VE GONE THROUGH. WHAT I'VE PUT YOU THROUGH.

I'M NOT ASKING FOR ANYTHING FROM YOU, LEAST OF ALL YOUR FORGIVENESS. I KNOW I DON'T HAVE THAT RIGHT. I WASTED THE YEARS AWAY, GETTING LOST IN A BOTTLE RATHER THAN STRIVING TO BE THE BEST MAN I COULD BE FOR THIS FAMILY I LOVE.

AND I DO... I LOVE YOU ALL SO MUCH. YOU PROBABLY DON'T BELIEVE ME, AND THAT'S FAIR. I CAN'T BLAME YOU FOR IT BECAUSE I HAVEN'T ALWAYS SHOWN YOU. WORSE, I SHOWED YOU THE EXACT OPPOSITE. BUT I HOPE ONE DAY I'LL EARN YOUR TRUST ENOUGH TO BE ABLE TO DO JUST THAT.

EVEN IF I DON'T, I NEED YOU TO KNOW ONE THING. YOUR MOM'S DEATH WAS NEVER YOUR FAULT. NEVER. I CAN'T TELL YOU HOW MUCH IT GUTS ME KNOWING YOU'VE HARBORED GUILT THAT DIDN'T BELONG TO YOU. GUILT I THOUGHT I'D BEEN CARRYING ALONE.

I KNOW MY WORD DOESN'T MEAN ANYTHING—NOT YET

—BUT I HOPE THIS NOTE I ENCLOSED WILL. I'VE HAD A LOT OF REGRETS, BUT THIS IS MY GREATEST. AS A REMINDER OF MY FAILURE, I'VE CARRIED THIS NOTE WITH ME EVERY DAY SINCE I FOUND IT UNDER THE COUCH THE MORNING AFTER.

EVERYTHING WAS MY FAULT. I'VE KNOWN IT EVERY DAY FOR THE PAST ELEVEN YEARS THAT YOUR MOM HAS BEEN GONE. AND I'VE TRIED TO ESCAPE IT EVERY SINGLE ONE. TRIED TO KILL MYSELF IN THE ONLY WAY I KNEW HOW. I WAS A COWARD. AND EACH TIME I TRIED AND FAILED TO GET SOBER WAS JUST ANOTHER REMINDER OF HOW UNWORTHY I AM TO CALL MYSELF YOUR FATHER. TO HAVE THE PRIVILEGE OF BEING IN YOUR LIVES.

BUT I'M TRYING. I WANT YOU TO KNOW THAT. EVERY DAY, I'M TRYING. I'VE BEEN SOBER FOR 312 DAYS, AND I PLAN TO BE SOBER FOR 312 MORE, AND 312 MORE AFTER THAT. I'LL BE HERE WHEN OR IF YOU'RE EVER READY TO TALK.

DAD

I glanced down at the counter to the scrap of paper that had fallen out of the envelope. It was yellowed with time, the lines across the page faded, the edges worn. Trepidation kept me rooted in place, but curiosity had my hand moving of its own accord.

With unsteady fingers, I picked up the note, the paper soft as silk under my touch. I had no doubt this was exactly as old as he'd claimed, and I gently unfolded the note to read what was inside.

GRACIE,

LEVI AND ADDISON WENT TO THE LOCKHARTS'. I KNOW THIS WEEK HAS BEEN ROUGH, AND I'M SORRY. BREAKFAST TOMORROW MORNING LIKE USUAL?

P.S. I LOVE YOU MORE TODAY...

The rest of the words came to me as easily as if I were reading them. As easily as if I'd heard it just yesterday rather than eleven years ago.

I love you more today than I did yesterday, and I'll love you more tomorrow than I do today.

That, paired with seeing my mom's nickname, was like an ice pick to my chest, stabbing deep. A wound I couldn't hope to escape. The sudden, sharp pain as much for the memory of her and what we'd lost and also the fact that I hadn't heard it in so long. It was one of those things that had been forgotten with time. Something I hadn't even realized was missing until now.

My usual barrage of thoughts came at me, swift and unrelenting.

It was my fault. No matter what he said, it was still my fault.

Why hadn't it been me?

Why couldn't it have been me?

It should have *been me.*

I dropped the note, allowing it to flutter to the counter as I braced my hands along the edge. Hanging my head, I closed my eyes and worked hard to push those thoughts away and ground myself in the present. Attempting to course correct and not allow myself to go any further down the familiar path I'd walked so many times before. The path of solitude and loneliness, the destination nothing more than drowning in regrets.

But I was trying not to be that man anymore. *By choice.*

It was a struggle—some days harder than others—but I

chose to be here. Chose to engage rather than retreat. Chose to love the people in my life how they deserved to be loved.

Chose to allow myself to receive the same.

Harper's sweet scent washed over me as she walked to me and stood by my side, her warmth a welcome presence as she settled a hand low on my back. Thunder reverberated in the sky, a slow, rolling rumble, and she stiffened next to me, her fist tightening in my shirt.

And suddenly, everything else faded into the background while I focused on my girl.

I wrapped an arm around her, tugging her into my side, and pressed a kiss against her forehead. So fucking grateful to have her here with me, no matter the path we'd taken to get to this moment.

She pressed a hand to my chest and stared up at me, her eyes darting back and forth between my own, a furrow between her brows. "You okay?"

I didn't know if she'd read the letters sitting on the counter, or if she was just so in tune with me that she knew when something was off. But it didn't matter because the answer was the same, regardless. "I will be."

She studied me for long moments, her gaze scrutinizing. Then a soft smile curved up the corner of her mouth, and she tipped her head to the side. "Because it's time for a laced Mabel cookie and some *One Tree Hill*?"

I placed my hand on her lower back, allowing my fingers to dip below the hem and humming when I met only bare skin. "Yeah, it's definitely that and not the fact that my girlfriend is wearing one of my old holey T-shirts from high school and nothing else."

"My panties got wet too. And we both know they're going to

be pointless anyway. Besides, you know how much I love this shirt."

"How you managed to hide that you had this for so long while living here is still a fucking mystery. I looked for that for years, I hope you know."

She shrugged, completely unrepentant. "And I hope you know I'm not sorry. I'd do the same thing if I had to do it all over again."

I leaned down until her breath ghosted over my lips. "I bet you would, you little thief."

Thunder rumbled again, a crack of lightning illuminating the sky as rain battered the windows. Harper jumped, her grip on me tightening and her unease apparent. And that wouldn't do. We'd gone through enough thunderstorms that we had a routine—pot cookies if we happened to have any on hand and cuddles on the couch as we binged *One Tree Hill*. And, if the storm was bad enough, as many orgasms as it took to get her mind off it.

I tugged her into my side and guided her toward the couch, pulling my phone out with the other hand to type out a text.

Group text titled: Trivial Bullshit
with Brady, Aiden, Beck, Ford, Levi, and Addison
9:22 p.m.

LEVI:

Everyone get home okay?

AIDEN:

Back at the inn and finally dry. Avery's just upset the lighthouse reno hasn't started yet because she wants to be out there in this shit. So I'm obviously looking up how much it would cost to rebuild the whole damn thing with reinforced steel.

BECK:

Everly and I are home. Chuck was going nuts and is currently burrowed under the blanket between us. Goddamn cockblocker.

ADDISON:

I felt the baby kick for the first time

So Chase broke about twelve laws driving us home

Nothing to see here, Sheriff Grumpypants!

Now my husband is laying with his head in my lap and talking to the peanut

BRADY:

Tell Chase there's no brother-in-law exemption. If I catch him speeding, I'm giving him a ticket.

FORD:

Pretty sure we all knew that was coming.

BRADY:

As you should. I'm the sheriff. Family doesn't get preferential treatment.

Luna and I are finally home. Had to clear a couple downed tree branches on the way. And damn near had to handcuff her to me again just to get her ass inside. That woman's gonna be the death of me.

FORD:

That woman's gonna be your WIFE! Breakfast at
the diner in the morning before the big day?
Quinn's been craving Beck's goodies.

ADDISON:

Beck!

Make me some blueberry scones

BECK:

Blueberry scones for everyone but Addison,
got it.

ADDISON:

What????

RUDE

BRADY:

Maybe you'd get somewhere if you said please.
Luna's requesting her usual toilet water for
breakfast, Beck. Please. See how easy that is?

ADDISON:

PLEASE!

PLEASEPLEASEPLEASEPLEASE

AIDEN:

Everyone realizes that's Chase using Addison's
phone, right?

LEVI:

Obviously. Addison doesn't say please.

Harper and I will be there, with or without the
blueberry scones.

Harper and I settled on the couch, and I lifted my arm for
her to snuggle in. She burrowed between me and the back of the
couch, her hand on my stomach and a look of pure mischief on
her face.

"What?" I asked, brow raised.

"Nothing. I just remember a time not too long ago when you hated that text thread. You even named it *Trivial Bullshit*, if I remember right."

"Yeah, well. You used to think I hated you too." I turned on *One Tree Hill* and grabbed a cookie from the batch Mabel had dropped off yesterday, offering half to Harper. "And we both know how that worked out."

"And how's that? You trying to say we're in love or something?"

"Something like that," I murmured, pressing a kiss to her forehead.

Harper shifted, settling against me, her body soft and pliant even as the thunderstorm lit up the night sky outside our home.

Some days, it felt like nothing had changed. Like I was still stuck on the hamster wheel in my mind, my intrusive thoughts too much to escape. But it was times like this when I was reminded just how far I'd come in only a few months.

I was Harper's safe space. And instead of running from it, instead of hiding or turning my back on it, I embraced it. Diving headlong into this life I wanted. With her.

As our second pass through season three of *One Tree Hill* played in the background, I pulled out my phone and navigated to the family text thread, quickly making a change. Then I tossed the phone on the coffee table and wrapped my arms around the woman who'd always been and would always be my whole fucking world. The woman I strived every day to be worthy of...the man my mom had raised me to be.

Levi renamed this conversation Gracie's Legacy.

THANK YOU FOR READING REBEL HEART! Want to see if that future Harper envisioned came true for her and Levi? For many glimpses into their HEA, scan the QR code below to receive their bonus epilogues spanning ten years delivered straight to your inbox!

ACKNOWLEDGMENTS

Endings are always bittersweet, and this one is no different. While I'm so very sad to say goodbye to the McKenzies (or, at the very least, ta ta for now), it's only because I love these characters immensely. After two and a half years, they've become a part of me. Fortunately, they will forever continue to be. And I hope they will for you too.

This book, more than all the others, was a labor of love. I'd known from the beginning—before I'd even written one single word in *Defiant Heart*—that Levi was going to be my sad panda book. But even I didn't realize just how broken he was. I hope I was able to portray his struggles and his triumphs with authenticity, care, and sensitivity.

Thank you to Alexandra W, Heather P, Stacey, Jen D, Hannah H, Emily C, Libby R, and Heather F for your early eyes on this and sharing your insights, struggles, and lived experiences with me in order to better enrich Levi's character. Special thanks to Hannah, Emily, and Heather for doing a full sensitivity read and ensuring there were no harmful portrayals. I'm so very grateful for each and every one of you, for being brave enough to share your experiences with me and for helping me make this book what it is today.

Thank you to the Emerald Elite—Zoe, Selena, Annika, Molly, and Ellis—for our weekly chats and our daily Zoom rooms. And to Molly for her early eyeballs on this baby. This book—this series—would not be what it is without your guidance, advice, and ideating. I'm forever grateful the pandemic brought me this group.

Thank you a million to Christina, my bestie, unwavering cheerleader, and fiercest supporter all rolled up into one sweet southern package. Every neck graze, bite, or hand necklace I write is all for you.

Thank you to Lisa for always pulling through in the clutch, for flagging my crutch word du jour, and for catching the dictation homophones that always slip through. You are the bestest (even though you suggest I cut down on my beloved em-dashes).

Thank you to all the gorgeous souls in the Queen B's. I love you all so much for loving my books enough to bring them into your worlds and share them with Romancelandia. I can't wait to see what we do together next.

Thank you to the Brigaders, who laugh and cry and swoon and pant right along with me. I'm so lucky to have your support. With every release, I can feel your excitement grow more and more, and I'm so very lucky to have you.

Thank you to *you*. My readers. Those who've just hopped on this train and those who've been with me for eleven years. I wouldn't be able to do this amazing job if it weren't for you. This series has been a wild and amazing ride because of you. Thank you for supporting me, cheerleading me, and loving these books that live in my brain until I purge them from my system for you to glom. I'm beyond grateful for you.

Last but never least, thank you to my guys, who understand when I'm on a tight deadline (yes, again) and support me in all the ways I need. You are my everything.

OTHER TITLES BY BRIGHTON WALSH

Our Love Unhinged

———

Stand-Alone Titles

Dirty Little Secret

Plus One

ABOUT THE AUTHOR

Award-winning *USA Today* and *Wall Street Journal* bestselling author Brighton Walsh spent a decade as a professional photographer before taking her storytelling in a different direction and reconnecting with her first love—writing. She likes her books how she likes her tea—steamy and satisfying—and adores strong-willed heroines and the protective heroes who fall head over heels for them. Brighton lives in the Midwest with her real life hero of a husband, her two kids—both taller than her—and her dog who thinks she's a queen. Her boy-filled house is the setting for dirty socks galore, frequent dance parties (okay, so it's mostly her, by herself, while her children look on in horror), and more laughter than she thought possible.

www.brightonwalsh.com

tiktok.com/@brightonwalshbooks

instagram.com/brighton_walsh

facebook.com/brightonwalshwrites

9 781685 180416